Nick & Slim

The Legend of the Falcon Mine

Pamela L.V. Henn

White Wolf Studio

www.nickandslim.com

Main character designs and art direction by Pamela L.V. Henn
Villain character design and chapter illustrations by Simon P. Cox
Cover painting by Tom Lange
Edited by Lari Bishop
Interior design and composition by Greenleaf Book Group

Published by White Wolf Studio Inc.

Library of Congress Cataloging-in-Publication Data
2004096782

Henn, P.L.V.
Nick & Slim, the Legend of the Falcon Mine / by P.L.V. Henn

Summary: Estranged from his father after his mother's death, Nick finds himself confronted by Slim Marano's spirit, a notorious murderer from the 1860s. Stepping back in time with Slim, Nick begins a journey to find the real killer.

ISBN 10: 0-9760654-0-1
ISBN 13: 978-0-9760654-0-1

1. Fantasy – Fiction. 2. Ghosts, Spirits – Fiction. 3. Imps – Fiction.
4. Schools – Fiction. 5. Colorado – Fiction. 1. Title
2006

Printed in the United States of America

10 9 8 7 6 5 4 3 2 1   08 07 06 05

First edition

To the great Almighty—for the "Breath of Life" and for planting this idea and these characters in my imagination.

To Colin Mariano—for believing in this artist and for always getting behind me and pushing me to continue.

To Jim Keller—for keeping me sane throughout this long journey of building my life.

I love you all. P.H.

CONTENTS

Prologue
A GLIMPSE OF HEAVEN

Heaven's golden, sparkling streets bustled with activity. Laughter, chatter, and children's voices filled the air. Boys playing ball ran and jostled as music from an open-air concert drifted in the breeze. Painters captured scenes on canvases as admiring observers marveled at the wonder of life becoming art before their eyes. All were bathed in the radiant light of a tranquil blue sky.

Keenan, Christopher, Michael, and their horses were a strange sight in this heavenly vision—three rough and rowdy cowboys in a bright and peaceful world.

"How long 'til he's back?" Michael drawled, hunching over his saddle horn to give his horse an affectionate pat.

"Depends on how long the Almighty wants to talk to him," Christopher replied.

"He had enough papers and books to pack a mule."

"That's Slim for you—he's thorough," Keenan said.

"Yeah. Think he'll get permission?" asked Michael with a worried crease in his brow.

Keenan laughed. "Even the Almighty would be hard-pressed to turn Slim down. Nobody researches a case like him. And he's had plenty of time to prepare."

"Time to prepare!" howled Christopher, "I'd say so—only the last hundred and forty years." His face suddenly became serious. "This frustration needs to be settled one way or another."

The three cowboys fell silent with nods of agreement. Keenan dismounted and plucked a long blade of grass from the ground, sticking the sweet end between his teeth. Detaching his bullwhip from his belt, he cracked it lightly in the air, creating elaborate designs with a flick of his wrist.

A tall, slightly bowlegged cowboy sauntered down the street toward them. Beside him strolled a lovely blond woman in a light blue dress. Christopher was the first to spot him.

"There's Slim!"

"He must be done pleading his case. Hey! Who's the gal with him?" asked Michael.

"Don't know," Keenan said, "but she sure is purdy!"

They watched as the pair drew nearer. They could hear the woman talking to Slim. "He's a good boy, Slim. You two will get along well."

"I sure hope so, ma'am," said Slim. "We just have one shot at this."

Stopping in front of the three cowboys, he reached out his right hand to introduce his friends. "Here we are. These are my best friends, Mrs. Stewart. Men, this is Mrs. Laura Stewart." They removed their cowboy hats, bowed quickly in polite acknowledgment, and chorused, "Glad to meet you, ma'am!"

Mrs. Stewart acknowledged the men with a smile. "Please call me Laura. My friends do, and I consider you my friends."

"Laura, I'm pleased to introduce you to my partners on this assignment," said Slim. "This here is Keenan, Michael, and Christopher. We've worked together many times before, and these gentlemen are the best. They have big hearts and good instincts. If anyone can figure out how to get the most out of a situation, or just plain get out of it, it's these guys." Laura shook each man's hand.

"So, Slim, did the Almighty give you His permission to complete this assignment?" asked Michael.

"Yeah," replied Slim. "And thanks to Laura here, we'll have some extra help. Her son, Nick, is going to work with us."

"Well, I should be going," Laura said. "I know you probably have lots to do before you go. Slim, here's something to give you a better idea of Nick's circumstances." She removed a piece of paper from the pocket of her dress. "He's a wonderful boy, but I should warn you that Nick and his father are having problems and don't get along."

"That's okay. We'll manage just fine, Laura," replied Slim. Taking the paper, he grasped her hand firmly.

Looking gratefully into his eyes, she smiled and said, "Take care of him, Slim. He's my only child."

"I will, Laura . . . I will. I promise."

With a respectful tip of her head, she turned and walked away. Just before disappearing around a corner, Laura stopped and glanced back for a moment to wave to the four cowboys.

Christopher responded first. "Whew! Very pretty lady."

"What was that all about?" asked Michael.

"Yeah, we've saved plenty of kids before, but we never had to work with one on an assignment. What's going on?" asked Keenan.

"The Almighty would only approve this case if I was willing to work with someone on Earth. Seemed he already had someone in mind. So he called for Laura to join our meeting."

"What's on the paper she gave you, Slim?" asked Keenan.

"Let's take a look," replied Slim.

Unfolding the paper, he scanned the contents as the guys peered over his shoulder.

"It's a newspaper article about a car accident and the ongoing investigation surrounding Laura's death. According to witnesses and police reports, a drunk driver in a stolen car caused the accident. He left the scene on foot and disappeared into the crowd," said Slim. "He's never been found."

Pointing to a grainy newspaper photo, Christopher added, "That must be Nick."

"Yep, you're right: that's Nick and his dad," said Michael. "Nice-looking kid."

"How are we going to explain everything to Nick and convince him to help us?" Christopher asked.

"The Almighty promised that an opportunity would present itself. We need to be patient and wait for the right moment," replied Slim.

"I don't know about this, y'all," said Keenan uneasily.

"I know, I know," Slim sighed. "But the way I see it, we're on assignment. We'll just have to handle problems as they come up. Let's get out to the ranch and make our preparations before we head out." Slim reached for his horse. The four cowboys climbed onto their mounts and rode toward the distant hills.

"You know," said Michael, "I have to admit . . . I sure do like getting sent out on these assignments."

Coaxing his horse to a gallop, Slim turned to answer. "Yeah. Me too!"

Chapter One

THE FIELD TRIP

The bus rolled out of the school parking lot with a loud groan. It was full of animated sixth-graders; some were jumping around and trading seats, while others were diving for cover from spitballs.

Eleven-year-old Nick Stewart dodged a spitball as it flew toward his head. Groaning, he thought, *It's only my second week at this school, and I'm already stuck on a bus full of rowdy kids on a history class field trip.* They were on their way to an Old West ghost town named Silverado.

Lost in thought, Nick stared out the window. A new school, a new house, and a new life. He and his father had moved to Beavercreek, Colorado, in August after his dad accepted a full-time job to head the anthropology department at the local university. Nick's father was a well-known archaeologist who specialized in bones. In the past, Nick had traveled all over the world with his family while his dad supervised digs in different countries.

This year, though, something terrible and unexpected had happened. One day, while they were vacationing back in the States, Nick's mom was struck by a car as she crossed the street. The driver, who appeared to be drunk, fled the scene, disappearing into the crowd without a trace. The police discovered that the car had been stolen. The fingerprints found on the steering wheel revealed that the driver was an escaped convict who the police had already been tracking for several days. He was still on the run.

The funeral was a blur of relatives, friends, and his father's colleagues. After several weeks of family and friends offering condolences and help, life went back to normal—for everyone except Nick and his father. The overwhelming loss haunted both father and son and drove a deep wedge in their relationship.

Nick's mom, Laura, had been the keeper of the weekly schedule, and she had made sure that Nick's dad, Lee, came out of his work shell to spend time with the family. As they traveled around the world, his mom had become Nick's best friend. The days following her death were dreary and empty. Lee did not know how to talk to his grieving son, and Nick was too lost in his pain to respond to his dad's feeble efforts. So, weeks went by as they whittled away the hours in their own separate worlds.

Two months after the funeral, Nick's father received an invitation from a colleague to join a dig out West. Nick did not want to go, so he was sent to live with friends, the Thomases, for the summer while his father checked on the assignment. Nick's time at the Thomases' house was the best he could remember. He was treated like one of the family. Brett, the oldest son, became his best friend and more—a brother and, at times, even a father. Nick was dreading the day when Brett would leave for college.

The same day that Brett received his college schedule for the fall, Nick received an e-mail from his father. It was short and direct. Nick's dad had accepted a full-time position at a university in Colorado to head the anthropology department. Their belongings were going to be completely packed and moved for them, and their family house in Washington, D.C.—the only real home Nick had ever known—was going to be sold. The sudden move angered Nick. He had been hoping that he and his dad would move back to D.C. and start a real life, not keep moving from place to place. He didn't need any more changes right now, let alone surprise changes.

The screeching voice of Mrs. Glen, Nick's history teacher, jolted him back to the present. She struggled to be heard over his classmates' shouts. "Silverado was built in the 1860s. It's still intact, with all of the original buildings in the main part of town. During the day, families and tour groups spend hours walking through its streets to experience the past, listen to the local legends, and check out the museum. After sunset, Silverado is transformed into a profitable and very lively casino town. From a historical perspective, the main interest in this particular ghost town is the legend of the Walkins's Falcon Mine Company," she shouted over the kids' chatter.

"The owner, Mr. Walkins, was murdered in his office one evening in 1866, and his foreman's journal was found near the body. The presence of the journal seemed to place the foreman, Slim Marano, at the crime scene. It was flimsy evidence, but panic set in and the townspeople pressured the local sheriff to arrest Slim. One week after his arrest, Slim was brought to trial, convicted, and hanged.

"Several weeks later, evidence was found pointing to the possibility that someone else had committed the crime. The thought that they had hanged an innocent man horrified the townspeople. The evidence was given to the sheriff's department and later transported to a bank safe until more research could be done. Unfortunately, the bank was robbed and, along with some gold, the evidence was stolen and never recovered."

Mrs. Glen surveyed her class sharply. "Why was the evidence stolen? Could the culprit have been a Silverado resident trying to save the town from an embarrassing situation? Or was the real murderer covering his tracks? Was justice really served here? Or was an innocent man hanged for a crime he did not commit? According to legend, this tragic incident led to the demise of the town of Silverado. And every generation of the Marano family since has suffered the embarrassment of being linked to this murder.

"Now, for your assignment," Mrs. Glen continued. "Go through the museum; read and take notes on every artifact and exhibit. Walk through the town. Explore every building you can and get a feel for the time period. You will be required to write a paper discussing the crime and, based on the evidence you uncover today, you will decide whether or not Slim Marano was guilty. Use any information that you discover to help you argue your case. Who are your suspects? What kind of motives did they have? As you step off the bus, I'll hand you a fact sheet with additional book and video references concerning this legend that are available in the school library."

Nick glanced around as some of the students groaned and rolled their eyes. Others had listened and were writing everything down. A few students remained deeply asleep in their seats. Nick sat back with a blank look on his face. *This paper is going to take a lot of work,* he thought. *More work than I've ever had to do for a class before.*

As the bus approached the town of Silverado, Nick was amazed at how much it still looked like a town in the Old West. There was one main street, and all of the buildings were wedged together on either side, facing each other as if preparing for a gunfight. The bus turned before entering the town, heading down a dirt path that lead to parking lots behind the buildings on one side.

The bus came to a halt behind the museum, and Mrs. Glen counted the students as they stepped off. Nick watched as his classmates gathered into small groups, discussing the assignment and where they would go first, or chattering about something else entirely. Nick had not tried to make friends yet, and was beginning to feel lonely. Being the new kid was bad enough, but being stuck working on this project alone was a real bummer.

Once off the bus, the students walked to the door in the rear of the museum, which was a modern, state-of-the-art facility. A long metal box ran the length of the back wall. The words FARGO ALARM SYSTEM were stamped in big red letters on the box.

"Well," whispered Nick, "they must be protecting a lot of valuable artifacts." Nick glanced at his watch: 10:00 a.m. Mrs. Glen instructed the students to return to the bus at 3:30 p.m., then turned and entered the museum, leaving them on their own.

Nick watched as some of the more serious students filed one by one into the museum, following Mrs. Glen. Another group of students struck out on their own, slipping into an alley next to the museum to get to the main street. The four rowdy kids who had started the spitball fight in the back of the bus began to walk along behind the buildings, heading to the end of town. They regularly peered over their shoulders, checking to see if they were being watched. Nick suddenly realized he was alone. Hoping he could make it to the main road without running into anyone, he cut through the same alley that the other group had used.

As he emerged onto Silverado's Main Street, he felt like he had taken a trip back in time. If he ignored the tourists wandering around, he could really imagine that he was visiting a small town in the Old West.

Several feet away, a dust devil swirled around and danced down the street until it surrounded a hitching post and disintegrated. As Nick started to walk along the street, a tumbleweed with scrawny, bony branches greeted him. It rolled past him and continued its path down the dusty road.

"Wow, this is cool," he whispered to himself as he pictured cowboys strutting down the street, leading their horses to watering troughs.

Approaching the main entrance of the town, Nick noticed a small line of people at one of the buildings. A few of the girls from his class were waiting there. A sign in front of the building read:

WALKING TOURS AVAILABLE
$5.00 PER PERSON
LEARN ABOUT THE LEGEND OF SILVERADO'S NOTORIOUS SLIM MARANO,
THE FALCON MINE MURDERER

Deciding that this was the best place to start his investigation, Nick bought a ticket and stepped to the back of the line.

The ticket holders were divided into two groups of fifteen and told to wait in front of the building. Nick was placed in the second group, along with two girls from his history class. A female tour guide took the first group and disappeared down the street. Fifteen minutes later, a male tour guide appeared from inside the building and began the tour for Nick's group.

"Good morning, everyone. My name is Freas, and I'm your tour guide. If everyone is ready, we'll get started. Follow me, please."

Freas was a tall, thin, middle-aged man dressed in button-fly jeans and tan leather chaps. A black belt with a big silver-and-gold belt buckle held everything together. He also wore dark brown leather boots with silver spurs, a blue long-sleeved cotton shirt with pearl and silver buttons, and a tan leather cowboy hat.

Walking down the street backward, Freas began talking. "The original town of Silverado was built in the early 1860s. The town grew to its present size before the end of 1865. Silverado consisted of one general store, two saloons, a brothel, a feed store, and other establishments you'd expect to find in a thriving town of that era."

Pointing to the distant mountains at the end of the town, Freas continued his speech. "The reason for the town's tremendous growth was the discovery of gold ore in one of the nearby streams. Later, a cave that led deep into the mountain was discovered. A man named Otis Walkins purchased it. Using the cave as a natural corridor for the equipment, Walkins's Falcon Mine Company successfully drilled several tunnels deep into the mountain. Mr. Walkins discovered many rich veins of gold ore and large deposits of pure silver in these mountains. Falcon Mine was one of the most productive mines of that time."

Freas turned and began walking toward a building, then stepped onto the porch. "Mr. Pernell Billings, who was the owner of the nearby Black Stallion Mine Company, purchased the Falcon Mine soon after Otis Walkins's death in 1866. The Black Stallion Mine Company was the original rival to the Falcon Mine Company. Mr. Billings—unlike Otis Walkins—was well-known for his lack of concern regarding mine safety. Soon after Billings took control of the Falcon Mine, there was a major flooding accident at the Black Stallion Mine in which many men were killed. Things settled down for a few years. But eventually, Billings's lack of concern for safety led to several fatal cave-ins at the Falcon Mine, and the U.S. government decided to shut down both companies."

Turning toward the building, Freas reached forward and opened the front door. "This first building is the Land Claims and Patent Office. If you were staking a claim for land to build a house on, or if you discovered a deposit of gold, silver, or minerals that you wished to lay claim to, this is where you would go. Please follow me." He led the group through the open door and let them file into the dusty little lobby.

It took several minutes for Nick's eyes to adjust to the dim light. Nick noticed a small caged office with waist-high walls. Metal bars continued from the walls to the ceiling. Openings were cut into the bars so that papers and money or gold could pass between customers and employees. *This reminds me of a bank,* thought Nick. Beyond the bars, wooden desks and chairs were arranged throughout the office. The only entrance was a door with a large, old-fashioned lock.

A series of glass-framed maps hung on the walls. Some outlined the town and the surrounding areas. Others charted the mountains, with spidery black lines that seemed to represent a network of tunnels.

"The maps on the walls are the original maps that were used back then," said Freas. "The scale that you see on the back table was used to weigh gold nuggets. They were weighed, certified, and then placed in a leather pouch with the emblem of the mine stamped on it. The pouches were later moved to the bank vault for safekeeping.

"Many people thought they were rich in gold nuggets only to find out that what they had discovered were iron or copper pyrites. Another well-known name for pyrite is fool's gold—hence the name of our saloon, the Fool's Gold Saloon. As you can imagine, there were some heated debates in here."

Freas unlocked the door and allowed one person at a time to walk around in the small caged office. The desks were constructed of a dark wood. The scales Freas had pointed out were made of black iron and had several small, flat, circular weights. Nick picked one up and weighed it in his hand. Since he'd brought his digital pocket camera, he took pictures of everything, including the different maps. *Pictures and maps will be good visuals,* he thought. *If nothing else, they'll take up some room in my paper.*

As the tour group exited the building, Nick was the last person in line. Just as he was getting ready to step out of the front door, he turned to take a quick picture of the lobby. The flash went off and bathed the room with its bright light, momentarily blinding Nick. Through a white haze, he saw a man standing at the counter with his back to him. The man turned his head toward Nick and looked at him. Nick blinked to clear his eyes—and the man was gone. The lobby was empty. *That was weird,* thought Nick. Shutting the door behind him, he ran to catch up with the rest of the group.

Freas was addressing the group outside the general store when Nick caught up with them. "The general store was the largest building in town," he said as Nick joined the group. "It carried everything a person might need, from food products to hardware, even fabric for the young ladies' fashions. If you requested something that they didn't have, the general store put in an order to one of the larger towns."

Freas opened the door. "Ladies first, please," he said, smiling brightly at the women in the group.

They filed into a large open room that had a long wooden countertop along the back wall. The shelves in the store displayed a variety of items. On the counter, large glass jars were lined up in order of size next to an old-fashioned brass register. *The jars were probably filled with rock candy to sell to the kids,* Nick thought.

Crates filled with nails, big wooden barrels overflowing with thimbles, and large spools of thread were arranged near the door. A spinning wheel sat in a corner with a spindle full of cotton thread that looked like it had just been spun. Even the walls were used to display items for sale—a carpenter's ax, a long saw, a leather bullwhip.

Despite the musty smell, the store was full of bright light shining in from the large front windows. The tour group slowly roamed the room, examining all of the different wares. There was a flight of stairs in one corner, and

Nick followed several others up the steps to look around. The second floor was crammed with wares and contained the owner's office.

It was darker and damper upstairs because there were no windows. Nick was slightly unnerved. He couldn't help but pick up an eerie feeling in the air that made the hairs on his arms and neck stand up. The warm light from several small lamps was a welcome sight.

In the owner's office, there were bookshelves above the main desk and a chair was placed in front of it. An old-fashioned oil lamp stood on the desk. There were pictures on the walls and several flintlock rifles propped up in the corner.

The small group that Nick had followed finished poking around and started back down the stairs. Nick decided to stay a moment longer and take a few photos of the office. When he snapped the last shot, he put his camera away and headed for the stairs.

Thump!

Nick's head turned sharply at the sound of an object hitting the floor. Afraid that he might have knocked something over, he retraced his steps back into the office to look around. Seeing nothing amiss, he turned around to leave again. As he passed the desk, Nick glanced down and saw a book lying on the floor.

It must have just fallen off the edge of the desk, he thought, relieved that he hadn't broken something. Stooping down, Nick picked it up and turned it over to look at the front cover. The book was labeled *Inventory Lists.* It had fallen partially open, so Nick took a peek inside. A loose page fell out into his hand. Handling it gently, Nick realized the piece of paper was an actual order form from the Falcon Mine Company. He placed the book carefully back on the desk, and then raised the paper closer to the lamp so he could read it.

Nick heard Freas's raised voice echo through the store. "Let's go, everyone. There's more to see." He sighed as he looked at the order, wishing he had more time to read it. Nick reached down to replace the list in the book, but the book wasn't there! Nick looked under the desk and around the chair thinking that he might have accidentally knocked it off the desk again and kicked it. After a moment, he realized that the book wasn't anywhere in the room.

"I know it was here. Where did it go?" he whispered.

Nick heard the front door open downstairs and the shuffle of shoes as his group departed. His heart beat faster as he glanced around one more time. He reached into his backpack and grabbed his notebook, slipping the form inside. Then he bolted down the stairs and made it to the door just as it was closing.

Inside the general store, invisible eyes watched the tour group cross the street and enter the saloon. A chuckle echoed in the now-empty store as the inventory book floated gently back up the stairs to settle in its rightful place on the small bookshelf above the office desk.

Inside the saloon, Nick unsuccessfully tried to figure out what had happened back at the general store. Where had the book gone? Finally, he gave up and focused on his surroundings. The saloon had swinging doors that led into a huge room with a long bar along the opposite wall. Round tables were randomly scattered around the room.

"These tables were for gentlemen who enjoyed a casual game of cards," Freas explained.

In the back area, a stairway led from the first floor to a second-floor balcony. The wall behind the banister on the upper floor was lined with doors.

"The rooms upstairs were used by gentlemen who were into more serious card games, or were rented out to boarders when the hotel was full," Freas continued. "Now if you'll please step up to the bar, Marcy will bring out some sodas. We'll stop here and sit a spell, and I'll tell you our most famous story."

As if on cue, Marcy burst through the swinging door behind the bar with a large tray of glasses filled with ice. She had big blue eyes and brown hair that was pulled back in a rubber band. One strand of hair kept falling across her eyes. She placed the tray down on the counter with a big smile and disappeared through the swinging doors again. When she returned, she was carrying a second tray with a variety of sodas, which she set next to the glasses of ice.

It was a warm and dusty day, so the refreshments were a welcome sight. Nick dropped his backpack on a table, went up to the bar, and grabbed a glass of ice and a can of Coke. He headed back to his table, which had filled up mostly with adults from the tour group. He noticed that the two girls from his class were sitting at the table to his left—and they were watching him.

Somewhat unnerved by this sudden attention, Nick tried to look busy by opening his notebook to take notes. His gaze fell upon the order form that had fallen out of the strange disappearing book. Handling the old paper, he could see that the order was written by hand in bold, black ink. He wasn't sure of the significance of the form, but it was interesting work trying to decipher the list. He couldn't understand most of it, but the one word that jumped out at him was *dynamite*. *Wow,* thought Nick, *that's a lot of dynamite.* He knew a bit about dynamite because he used to listen to his father talk about using it on his archaeological digs. Sometimes Nick's dad would even bring him to a site to watch the explosions that would reveal ancient buried cities. He knew it didn't take much to create a pretty big explosion. *Well, maybe dynamite back then wasn't as strong,* he concluded.

Seeing that everyone had settled down, Freas straddled a stool and gathered everyone's attention. Nick quickly returned the order form to the back of his notebook and picked up his pen to take notes as Freas began:

"I've heard about the paper you youngsters are working on. You'll find this part of the tour very interesting. The story I'm about to tell has been passed down from generation to generation. Some of the details have either been lost or embellished over the years, but the main story is true."

Chapter Two

THE LEGEND
OF THE FALCON MINE

"This valley is an ideal place for a town," explained Freas. "Shortly after the area was settled, gold was discovered in a nearby stream. It didn't take long for businessmen to establish their claims. The two men with the most claims were Otis Walkins, owner of the Falcon Mine Company, and Mr. Pernell Billings, owner of the Black Stallion Mine Company. Once both mines were operational, a fierce competition began between the two owners to see who would bring up the most ore.

"Both mines were producing about the same amount of gold and silver ore. The incredible riches coming out of the mines drew wealthy people here. As a result, Silverado expanded rapidly.

"Then there was an unexpected catastrophe. According to the mining logs and incident reports, a major cave-in occurred at the Black Stallion Mine. A torch was accidentally left burning in one of the tunnels after the last shift.

When it burned down, it caught a rag on fire, which sparked a stick of dynamite that had been dropped by one of the workers. There was a huge explosion. Fortunately, it happened late at night, so no one was killed. However, this event was a major setback for the Black Stallion Mine Company and frustrated many of the investors. The situation got worse several weeks later when another main tunnel collapsed, making it difficult to get to the other tunnels. After these incidents, the Black Stallion Mine was not able to keep up with its production schedule. This put a major strain on the owner, Mr. Billings, especially when the bank was pressuring him for payments on his new equipment.

"Then, to make matters worse for the company, the Falcon Mine hit a major gold vein. The Black Stallion Mine was losing money daily and its investors began to get restless. As the success of the Falcon Mine continued, investors pulled out of the Black Stallion Mine and transferred their money to its rival."

Nick wrote furiously, focusing on Freas's words.

"It was rumored that the success of the Falcon Mine was largely due to foreman, C. G. "Slim" Marano. He was born with the name Colin Gerard Marano. Even as a child, Colin was very tall and thin. Friends and family began to call him Slim, and the name stuck.

"Slim had always been fascinated by the mountains and explored their caves extensively as a young boy. His knowledge of the caves made him extremely valuable later in life. When Slim grew up, Otis Walkins hired him to research rock formations in the Falcon Mine caves and tunnels. One of his responsibilities was to maintain safety in the mine. Slim kept extensive notes and drawings of the tunnels. Mr. Walkins supported him fully, insisting that his men follow Slim's orders. Slim was always right and, thanks to him, the Falcon Mine was very successful.

"The evidence we have of Slim Marano's professionalism and knowledge," Freas continued, "is his journal, which was found at the scene of a brutal crime. The journal documents safe excavation methods and contains coded notes, which to this day have still not been deciphered. They may refer to potential gold and mineral deposits.

"Due to Slim's success at the Falcon Mine, Pernell Billings tried to recruit Slim to work for him instead. However, Slim wrote in his journal that he declined Mr. Billings's generous offer and stayed with the Falcon Mine, remaining loyal to Mr. Walkins.

"Rumors suggest that a frustrated Mr. Billings also talked to Otis Walkins about the possibility of the two companies merging, the Falcon Mine taking on the Black Stallion Mine's increasing debt. Mr. Walkins declined the partnership with the crippled mining operation. Several miners near the office that day claimed an argument broke out, and Mr. Billings stormed out of the Falcon Mine office.

"Several weeks after this incident, things seemed to be back to normal. It was a known fact that Slim assisted Mr. Walkins with all of the paperwork concerning the weekly payroll. The payroll was issued by the bank every Wednesday morning, and it was Slim's job to pick it up and bring it to the mine's office on his way to work. After the day shift ended, Slim and Mr. Walkins met at the office in the evening to prepare the payroll for distribution the next day.

"It was just another typical evening. Slim left the office at 9:00 p.m. Mr. Walkins finished putting everything into the safe and got ready to lock up the office. Slim was on his horse and about to leave when he saw Mr. Walkins turn out the light and step outside the door. Slim said he saw nothing else after he turned his horse and headed toward town.

"Early the next morning, one of the miners stopped by the office to see Mr. Walkins. The office door was slightly ajar. He pushed it open and found the office ransacked. Papers and books were scattered everywhere. The desk was turned on its side. Behind the desk was a terrible sight. Mr. Walkins was lying on his back in a pool of blood, his body marked by vicious wounds. Otis Walkins had been murdered.

"The miner ran out, calling for help. Another miner rode back into town to notify the sheriff. Unfortunately, the crime scene was compromised by the time the sheriff got there. Curious workers had already tramped back and forth through the office to view the body."

In the margin of his paper, Nick wrote, *One of the workers who walked through the crime scene could have planted Slim's journal. But who, and why?*

Freas continued. "Slim came in to work that day and learned that his boss had been murdered. The payroll that had been locked up in the safe was stolen. Slim got the miners back to work as quickly as possible so that the sheriff could take control of the crime scene.

"The sheriff discovered that Slim was the last person known to have seen Mr. Walkins alive. And, unbeknownst to most of the people in Silverado, upon Otis's death Slim became the new owner of the Falcon Mine, as he had been named Otis's beneficiary many years before. The sheriff questioned Slim intensely, but the crime remained a mystery. So the investigation continued.

"Back in that time, most news was spread by word of mouth. Before going home, most miners would stop by the saloon for a spell. In no time, the whole town knew of Mr. Walkins's murder and the mystery surrounding it. Gossip led to the troubling rumor that there was a dangerous murderer among them. Mr. Walkins might be just the first victim.

"Panic set in and many children were kept home from school because parents feared that a killer was loose in Silverado. Wives begged their husbands not to go back to work in the mines the next morning. As the days went by, things got progressively worse. By the end of the following week, you could walk down the main street of town and not see a soul. Everyone was holed up at home."

Nick drew a breath. The story brought up a very sudden memory of his mother. Whenever they would travel to a new country and he would get nervous about getting lost in the new streets full of strange faces and languages, his mom would tell him never to panic, no matter what the situation. "There's always a way to find the truth of things, Nick," she would say, "and sometimes all you need is a map."

"The Falcon Mine had no choice but to shut down," Freas was saying. "By the end of the week, money was tight for mining families and people were getting angry with the sheriff because he had not arrested anyone.

"But the sheriff was having problems with his investigation. He had found a number of potential suspects who were connected to the Black Stallion Mine. But he could not tie any of the evidence to them.

"In his search of Walkins's office, the sheriff's deputy found Slim's journal underneath a pile of papers near the body. The sheriff was stunned when he learned of this discovery, because he knew that Slim kept that journal with him at all times. Slim was the sheriff's best friend, and he knew that Slim wouldn't hurt a fly, let alone take a human life. Nevertheless, anything and everything found at the crime site was evidence. The sheriff hoped that as they continued their search through Otis Walkins's office that something else would surface, pointing in another direction."

Nick wanted to ask Freas the sheriff's name, but Freas continued the story without a pause. He started scribbling notes again. Suddenly a whispering voice echoed in his ear. "His name was Artemus." The voice was so clear that Nick whipped his head around to see who had spoken. But everyone appeared to be completely engrossed in the story that Freas was telling.

Baffled, Nick turned his attention back to Freas.

"When Otis's body was first examined, his right hand was clenched around a gold watch fob. The sheriff reasoned that Otis must have grabbed it off the killer just before he died. Although this fob was not identified as one of Slim's possessions, he remained the prime suspect in the eyes of the town, particularly because he was Otis's beneficiary.

"The story goes that the mayor of Silverado was feeling the heat from the townspeople and shopkeepers. They told him that business had all but dried up. Just barely into the second week of the investigation, the mayor paid the sheriff a visit. Feeling pressured, the mayor ordered the sheriff to arrest Slim. That evening, the sheriff went to Slim's ranch and took him into custody. Slim was not officially charged with the crime, but once the townspeople heard what had happened, they quickly labeled him as guilty.

"A local lawyer took Slim's case. Now that the 'murderer' had been caught, the town quickly came back to life and the miners of the Falcon Mine went back to work under the temporary supervision of Mr. Billings of the Black Stallion Mine. Mr. Billings immediately filed all of the necessary paperwork to begin proceedings to officially buy the Falcon Mine. It seems he had received an inflow of cash from an investor.

"Two days after Slim's arrest, restless townspeople began to question why Slim wasn't being brought to trial. Despite the sheriff's protest that this was an incomplete investigation without concrete evidence, the mayor pushed for a trial to begin.

"The trial took just two days. A most troubling question remained unanswered: What was Slim's motive? His only link to the murder was circumstantial. However, there were no other witnesses who came forward to testify that Otis was seen alive after Slim left the office. Slim's journal at the crime scene made Slim the one and only identifiable suspect. The jury, facing tremendous pressure, decided to convict Slim Marano for the murder of Otis Walkins. By the end of the week, Slim Marano was hanged from a large oak tree on the edge of town. That tree is still alive today and can be seen in the distance from that window," said Freas pointing to the window just behind Nick.

Freas paused to take a drink of water. There was dead quiet in the room. Taking advantage of the silence, Nick raised his hand.

"What was the sheriff's name?"

"His name was Artemus Chamberlain. Only his closest friends called him by his first name, though."

The hairs on the back of Nick's neck stood up and a chill coursed through his body. *How did I know that?* But he only had a moment to dwell on the strangeness before Freas resumed the story.

"Two weeks later, the sheriff found the body of Stanley Watts, a Falcon Mine worker who had disappeared a few days before Otis Walkins's murder. Stanley had drowned in a natural spring in Eagle Cliff Mountain and appeared to have been dead for only a few days. Foul play was suspected.

"Chills of panic and horror ran through the townspeople as they realized that perhaps Slim had not been the real murderer.

"The sheriff continued to search for the owner of the broken watch fob. He considered this a solid lead. It was too late to save his friend Slim, but the least he could do was catch the real killer and clear Slim's name.

"But as he showed the chain to different townsfolk, the sheriff must have inadvertently tipped off the killer. Well into his investigation of the second death, the bank where the sheriff had placed the chain for safekeeping was robbed. The sheriff's deposit box was broken into, and the chain was stolen. Some gold was also taken, but the money in the bank remained untouched. The sheriff continued to investigate the murder until the day he retired, but without the key piece of evidence that could lead him to the real killer, he never solved the case. And there you have it. That is the legend of Slim Marano and the Falcon Mine."

Nick tapped his pen on the table as he glanced at his notes. *Something is not right about this whole thing,* he thought. *It feels like something bigger was going on, but what?*

"But there was one more sad and strange twist to the story. Three of Slim's closest friends had come to Silverado during the trial to support him. After he was hanged, they stayed in Silverado and got jobs as miners at the Black Stallion Mine. But shortly after Slim's death, a major catastrophe hit the Black Stallion Mine. It seems that they were tunneling too close to an underground spring and an explosion broke through a retaining wall and flooded many of the tunnels. A number of men were killed, including Slim's three friends.

"Now, as I mentioned before, Mr. Billings and the local investors had begun proceedings to purchase the Falcon Mine soon after Otis Walkins's death. After the flood at the Black Stallion Mine, they pursued ownership of the Falcon Mine even more vigorously. They were shocked when they received notification from Washington that Slim had sent transfer of ownership papers to Washington the day before he was arrested. The rightful owners of the mine were his three friends—the men who had just been killed in the flood at Black Stallion Mine.

"There were a number of suspicions about the flood: Was it an accident? Was somebody trying to get rid of the owners of the Falcon Mine? But in a flood, most of the evidence is obliterated. The questions were never answered, and Mr. Billings and his investors purchased the Falcon Mine and incorporated it into the Black Stallion Mine holdings. They quickly went to work to quell any rumors, and an investigation never revealed anything.

"The Black Stallion Mine was able to climb out of debt with the profits made from the Falcon Mine, which really skyrocketed in the following years. There were rumors that maybe something more than gold and silver was coming out of the mine. However, three years later, Mr. Billings made some very bad business decisions. After several more terrible accidents at the Falcon Mine Company and the Black Stallion Mine Company, the United States government stepped in and uncovered major safety violations and illegal accounting practices. Officials confiscated both mines from Mr. Billings and his investors. The mines became the property of the U.S. government, but they seemed to be dry at that point, and they were ultimately closed for good."

Freas stopped talking to take another long drink from his water bottle and then glanced around the room at his group. He still had everyone's full attention.

"Rumor has it," he continued, "that Slim's ghost still wanders the streets of this town looking for the truth, as well as justice. Several of our own staff members have heard doors opening and closing, as well as whispers when no one else was around. Occasionally items have been moved from one location to another without any explanation.

"Personally, I don't believe in ghosts, and I have never had any similar experiences, even though I've worked here for the past twenty years. However, being constantly surrounded by the legend can give you a colorful imagination or play tricks on your mind. You can decide for yourselves."

Chapter Three
STRANGE MOMENTS

"Okay," said Freas. He stood up and pushed back the stool he had been sitting on. "I'm going to give you fifteen minutes to look around the saloon. Restrooms are behind me, and please help Marcy out by taking your glasses and empty bottles or cans over to the bar."

The sound of chairs scraping the wooden floor echoed through the room as people got up to explore. Nick remained in his seat writing in his notebook. The possibility of Slim's ghost haunting the town had captured his interest.

He tapped the top of his pen upon the last line he'd written. *Something sure is going on here,* he thought. Twice now, something inexplicable had happened to him—and only him, it seemed. *It has to be one of the staff members playing the legend up by rigging things to spook people. That's the only thing that makes any sense.* Nick rubbed his aching hand, feeling quite satisfied with all of his notes. He'd gathered more information than he thought possible, and he was feeling better about his history paper.

Rising from his chair, he put his notebook in his backpack and picked up his glass and soda can. Placing them on the counter, he noticed that a small line had formed outside of the women's bathroom. There were a couple of people standing around talking to Freas, and a few others wandered around upstairs.

Grabbing his camera, Nick headed up the stairs to the landing. He surveyed the saloon below, shooting several pictures. He then turned his attention to the doors lined up behind him, most of which were at least partially open.

Nick entered several different rooms. Each had a window directly across from the door. The bedrooms accommodated large beds and dressers. On the nightstand next to each bed was a large ceramic basin with a ceramic pitcher sitting inside of it. The card rooms simply contained large, round wooden tables surrounded by plain wooden chairs.

As he proceeded down the hall, Nick came to a door that at first seemed to be locked. But when he rattled the knob a second time, the door swung open easily. An intense, musty smell overwhelmed him. As his eyes adjusted to the low light, Nick saw a room of the same dimensions as the other rooms. However, this one was clearly used for storage. Frames leaned against a wall, and stuffed buffalo heads hung above them. Several tables were stacked on top of each other in the middle of the room. Flintlock rifles and several swords stood upright in a corner. A box holding some old-fashioned handguns sat on the floor next to the door. Antiquated clothing hung on hooks on another wall. There were barrels filled with bullwhips, and large glass bottles stood near stacks of old flyers and newspapers.

In the dimness, Nick could barely make out the headline of the newspaper on the top of the stack. It looked like it had Slim Marano's name on it. Cautiously walking over to the pile, Nick picked it up and scanned it quickly. It was an issue from 1866 and the lead story was an article on Slim's arrest. Nick didn't want to steal anything, but he knew this would be an excellent addition to his history paper. He wondered if there was a photocopier any-where in the town. Rolling up the newspaper and tucking it under his arm, he exited the room, quietly closing the door behind him.

There were several people still milling around upstairs as Nick walked away. Nick couldn't help wondering why none of them had followed him into the room. Just as he started to head down the stairs, he heard the jiggle of someone trying to open a door. He turned his head and saw a man at-tempting to open the storage room. The door remained stubbornly closed. Nick's forehead wrinkled in confusion as he continued downstairs.

Just then, Freas called to the man upstairs: "Sir, you won't be able to open that door. It's been busted for years. Management keeps meaning to get it fixed, but it's just not a priority."

Puzzled, Nick approached Freas.

"Yes, buckaroo," Freas said as he turned to Nick.

"That door opened for me," said Nick.

Freas looked at him with an odd expression. "Kiddo, that lock is broken and the door is swollen into the frame. Believe me, until they bust that door in, no one will get in there. Maybe you walked into the closet right next to that room."

Nick just stood there with a blank look on his face, not sure if he should argue the point. He decided to agree, and changed the subject. "You're prob-ably right. Hey, is there a copier anywhere around here?"

"Yep, there's one in the museum. Ask the woman at the front desk when you enter. Tell her you're with the school group. She'll point you in the right direction. Oh yeah, there's also a copier in the ticket office. Just tell Gladys that you're part of my tour group. She'll let you use it."

"Great. Thanks, Freas," said Nick.

"No problem."

Nick headed over to his table. He glanced again at the newspaper and put it in his backpack. *I don't know what's going on here, but I was in that room.* As he finished zipping up his bag, Freas's voice boomed throughout the saloon. "Time to go!"

The group filed through the swinging doors and back out onto the dusty street. It was about noon and the sun was high in the sky, beating down on them.

Freas was the last one out of the saloon. "Lunchtime!" he announced. "Let's break for an hour and meet back up at the sheriff's office. The bakery is on the right. They fix great sandwiches. If you don't mind the hike, there's also a cafeteria in the museum." Freas waved and smiled, then turned and walked in the direction of the museum.

Most of the group headed toward the bakery. Figuring that the line was going to be long for a little while, Nick decided to walk over to the small ticket office to copy the newspaper.

As he stepped up to the ticket window, an older woman with white hair and glasses looked up from the book she was reading. "Can I help you?" she asked.

"Yes, I'm looking for a copier. I'm part of Freas's tour group, and he told me to come here."

"Step up to the side door and I'll buzz you in. The copier is in the office behind me. It should be on already," she told him.

Nick went to the side door and heard the buzz. He swung the door open and stepped inside. Gladys had already returned to her book.

Nick walked into the cramped office just behind Gladys's ticket room. There was a desk on one side and a copier on the far wall. Across from the desk was a large bookcase that occupied most of the room. He pulled the Falcon Mine order form from his notebook to copy first. Then he dug the rolled-up newspaper out of his backpack and copied the front page. There were only four sheets to the paper, so he was hoping that it wouldn't take too long to copy the whole thing. He felt nervous about having the paper to begin with.

After he finished copying the first page, he heard the door buzz and open.

"Gladys, how is the belle of Silverado doing this fine day?" bellowed Freas.

"Just fine, you old geezer. How's your tour group going?"

"Got 'em eating out of my hand," Freas replied.

Nick hurriedly copied the second page, hoping and praying that Freas would not see him with the newspaper. He didn't want Freas to think he was stealing an important artifact.

Nick had just pushed the button to copy the third page when he heard Freas's heavy footsteps heading toward the small office.

Nick's heart was racing and his breathing quickened. "Come on, come on . . . almost there," he whispered. Suddenly a crash came from the front office.

"Confound it!" Gladys yelled.

"Well, that's strange," said Freas.

"I'm telling you, this town is haunted," exclaimed Gladys.

"And I'm telling you that this town is just old," said Freas. "The way the wind keeps whistling through these buildings, it's a wonder stranger things don't happen."

Whatever had happened bought Nick time to finish copying all four pages. He quickly tucked his copies into the back panel of his notebook, and then put the notebook into his backpack. Walking over to a pile of unkempt papers on the desk, he slipped the original inventory order form and the newspaper under the stack and breathed a sigh of relief.

He was just picking up his backpack when Freas stepped through the door into the office.

"Whoa, buckaroo!" exclaimed Freas, "I didn't know you were back here!"

"Sorry, Freas, I didn't mean to startle you," Nick apologized. "I was using the copier."

"Wow, you don't waste any time do you?" asked Freas.

"Well, there was such a long line at the bakery that it made more sense to come and make copies first," Nick replied. "What was the crash I heard?"

Freas sighed deeply and rolled his eyes. "Oh, a shelf fell from the wall next to Gladys. Be careful, or Gladys will have you convinced that Slim's ghost was just here. She'll say he knocked that shelf off the wall just to scare her.

The reality is that this is an old building and that wall is probably somewhat rotten or just weak, so it couldn't hold the weight of the shelf. See, a totally logical explanation," said Freas.

"You weren't kidding when you said that people really believe this town is haunted."

"Yep," replied Freas. "Strange things are bound to happen in an old ghost town. Even though it has been refurbished, the walls groan and creak when the wind passes through them. Some employees love a good practical joke, and take it upon themselves to scare the tourists."

"How do they do that?" asked Nick.

"Oh," laughed Freas, "last year a couple of guys got fired for dressing in western garb, dusting themselves with flour, and scaring the wits out of a couple staying at the hotel. They hid a small tape recorder underneath the bed in the couple's room. The recording was full of moaning, chains rattling, and the sound of clicking boot spurs. It was on a timer. When it went off, they appeared on cue in the second floor window, strapped in stilts.

"I heard that the guests flew out of their room, bolted down the stairs, and shot out the hotel's front door. By the time the desk manager caught up with them, they were halfway down the street. It took several hours to calm them down. We had to reimburse them for food and lodging, and give them some money to gamble in the casino."

Nick felt a sense of relief. His strange encounters probably had simple explanations as well.

Freas turned to look at the clock. "It's half past noon. Betcha everyone has gotten through the bakery line by now. How about you and I go and grab some lunch?"

"Sounds good," Nick said as he shrugged his backpack onto his shoulders.

"By the way, kiddo, what's your name?" Freas asked.

"It's Nick."

"Let's go, Nick. Hey, Gladys, Nick and I are going to get lunch. I'll talk to you later," called Freas.

Nick heard Gladys mumble some response as he followed Freas out the side door. They headed down the dusty street toward the bakery.

When they entered, the smell and warmth of fresh-baked bread surrounded them. Nick and Freas inhaled the tantalizing aroma. Half of Freas's tour group was still there finishing their lunch and talking. Nick hadn't realized how hungry he was. As he ate, Freas entertained the group that soon gathered around the two of them with funny stories about his childhood in the Silverado area.

The big clock hanging over the cash register chimed one o'clock.

"Time to get going," said Freas as he gulped the last of his tea. Nick and Freas cleared their table and followed the others out of the bakery into the street. The rest of Freas's group milled about nearby. Freas's loud whistle caught their attention.

In a few minutes, everyone had gathered together for the next part of the tour. After a quick head count, Freas turned and headed down the street. They walked to a stone building with iron bars on the windows.

"Now that you know the full story, I want to show you the jail Slim was locked up in. If you go to the back cell and look through the side window, you will see the large oak tree where Slim was hanged. Slim could see the tree from his cell while he waited for the trial to end.

"The small building next to the jail is the sheriff's office. Right across the street is the courthouse where Slim was tried. Take forty-five minutes or so to look around, then let's meet back here and I'll show you the church and the graveyard where Slim is buried. After that, I highly recommend that you visit our museum. We have artifacts from that time and old photos of some of our more famous characters.

"For those of you who are planning to stay with us for some gambling later on, the casino is located in the modern saloon at the entrance of town. Okay, those are all of the announcements. I'll see you in forty-five minutes."

Freas turned and headed down the street to the ticket office, and the group dispersed. Some went to the courthouse, others to the sheriff's office. Nick headed over to the jail.

Pushing open the heavy wooden door, Nick entered the small lobby, which contained only a wooden desk and a chair. On the wall, several large iron keys dangled from a metal ring. Another wooden door opened onto a hallway. Nick could see the thick, black iron bars of three cells. Each cell housed a cot, blanket, and pillow. All of the windows had bars. A chill ran down Nick's spine. *It feels so hopeless,* he thought.

The door to Slim's former cell was wide open, so he hesitantly walked in. Because it was in the back of the building, this cell seemed larger and had two windows. Nick stood on the cot so he could peer out of the windows. From one, he could see the stone wall of the building next door. From the other window, he could see the large oak tree clearly in the distance. Nick stared at the tree for several minutes as thoughts of Slim's death filled his head. He shuddered again. *Knowing you only had a day or two to live would probably drive you insane,* he thought.

Nick was still gazing out the window at the distant tree when he heard a deep sigh behind him. Thinking someone else had come in, he didn't pay much attention.

"It's a hard thing," a voice said, "to pay such a horrible price for a crime you did not commit."

"I wonder if he was scared," said Nick.

"More scared for his family and the price they would end up paying than anything else."

Continuing to stare at the oak tree, Nick asked, "What kind of price?"

"They would carry the shame of my crime from generation to generation, as the truth got buried deeper and deeper in legend."

Nick's heart began to pound hard in his chest. *"My" crime?*

He gulped and tried to keep the conversation going. "Generation to generation? C'mon, that's a strange thing to say, isn't it?" Nick asked.

This time there was no response.

Nick turned around very slowly. No one was behind him. Swallowing nervously, he zipped over to the other window and searched for anybody who might be playing a joke on him. He saw no one.

"I know I talked to someone," he whispered. Nick climbed off the cot and checked the other cells. Finding them empty, he ran to the lobby. The front door opened and others from his group walked in. He tried not to let his panic show as he scanned the lobby.

Chapter Four

THE SCAPEGOAT

One of the men from the tour group looked at Nick a little strangely. "Are you all right, kid? You look like you just saw a ghost."

Nick stuffed his hands in his pockets. "Um, I'm fine, sir. I think I just saw a rat in the back cell," he lied.

Nick made a hasty exit from the jail. Remembering that some employees liked playing jokes on guests, Nick walked around the building several times looking for footprints. The only ones he found were his own. The warmth of the sun and a soft breeze seemed to clear his head. He breathed in a few large gulps of air and let them out slowly. *Man, I am overreacting. My imagination is working overtime,* reasoned Nick.

Nick walked next door to the sheriff's office still shaking his head, wondering if he had completely lost it. In the lobby was a desk with a chair up against the wall. As he walked down a narrow hallway, Nick passed a small kitchen on the right with barely enough room for a small table and a few chairs. Just past the kitchen was a larger office. On the door, SHERIFF was painted in bold black letters.

Nick entered the sheriff's private office. There was a large wooden desk and a chair. A small bookcase against the wall was full of old books. A large window looked out toward the mountains. A stack of paper on the sheriff's desk gave the impression that the sheriff had just stepped out for a moment, but would be back soon.

On the walls were framed portraits—WANTED posters. Nick counted fourteen men and two women. Some were wanted for bank robbery, others for cattle rustling and for train robberies. Only three were wanted for murder.

Nick took a closer look at the sheriff's desk. Lying on the desk, protected by a pane of glass, were newspaper clippings. Looking closer, Nick discovered that they were accounts from the week before Slim's hanging.

Looking past the papers on the desk, Nick noticed a framed black-and-white photograph of two smiling men standing together. The one with the star pinned to his shirt was definitely the sheriff. The other man wore traditional cowboy duds, including chaps and a cowboy hat with an arrow piercing one side.

"That's Slim and the sheriff," someone behind him said. Nick was too startled to move. The voice continued. "They were best friends. The sheriff did everything he could to clear Slim. It's even rumored that he tried to help Slim escape."

Nick was afraid to turn around for fear that he would see an empty room again. Cautiously he raised his head and turned to see Freas standing behind him. He let out a big sigh and smiled in relief.

"How did the sheriff handle the hanging of his best friend?" asked Nick.

"If I understand correctly, the night before the hanging, Sheriff Chamberlain slipped Slim from the jail and brought him here to his office. Then he sent for his wife, and she fixed them dinner. They spent the entire night sharing memories of old times. Before dawn, Slim was taken back to his cell.

The sheriff refused to take his best friend to be hanged. He made one of his deputies do it.

"The sheriff was so distraught that morning that he went to the small white church at the edge of town. One of his sons was to let him know when it was over.

"Normally outlaws did not get funerals; they were buried outside of town. But the sheriff made sure that Slim got the best coffin and a small, private funeral. He had Slim buried in his own family's plot. Sheriff Chamberlain paid for it out of his own pocket to honor his friend and to show everyone that he still believed that Slim was innocent."

"Wow, that's some friendship," Nick said.

"Yep," said Freas. "The sheriff and his wife are buried right next to Slim."

Man, I wish I had a friend like that, thought Nick. Looking around the room, his heart suddenly felt heavy. It was a familiar sensation these days. Nick could relate to the pain haunting the sheriff's office. He couldn't help but think about his mom, buried thousands of miles away in Washington, D.C.

Freas walked away to speak with someone else. Nick pulled out his camera and took some pictures. He wanted to remember this room. Carefully framing a picture of the desk in his viewfinder, Nick made sure that the picture of Slim and the sheriff was in the shot. Retracing his steps through the building to the front door, he stepped onto the dusty street again.

Glancing at his watch, he realized he had spent too much time in the jail and sheriff's office. Only ten minutes remained to check out the courthouse where the trial took place. He rushed across the street and entered the front door.

The courthouse felt big and empty. On either side of the lobby, a staircase led to a second-floor landing, which opened onto a balcony. Deciding that he should check out the ground floor first, he walked through one of the open double doors into the courtroom. An aisle, flanked by rows and rows of chairs, led up to a wooden gate. Beyond the gate were the judge's bench and the witness stand. The jury box took up most of the wall next to the witness stand.

Walking to the gate, Nick turned and checked out the balcony. *It would have been used for the overflow of people who wanted to come and watch the trial,* Nick thought.

Nick wanted to spend more time in here, but he knew he had to work quickly. He shot a couple of photos on the first floor, and then decided that his best vantage point would probably be from upstairs.

Nick took the steps to the gallery two at a time. Moving up and down the length of the banister, he took photos of everything. The last two pictures he took were of the witness stand, and as the flash from the first picture dissipated, he could have sworn he saw someone sitting there.

As the flash receded the second time, Nick saw it again. This time his eyes didn't clear so quickly, and he could clearly make out the ghostlike image of Slim Marano watching him from the witness stand.

Nick closed his eyes, shook his head, and leaned over the banister. He opened his eyes again . . . and saw nothing except the empty stand. This time Nick believed it was quite possible that the town of Silverado could be haunted, despite Freas's protests. He could not shake the feeling that he was being watched.

Either I'm getting paranoid or I'm losing my mind, reasoned Nick as he hurtled down the stairs. *All this talk about ghosts is getting to me.* He smiled when he walked out of the main door and spied Freas across the street with people gathered around him. *Wonder what he would say if I told him I saw Slim.*

The last stop on the tour was the small white church at the edge of town. Freas pointed out the cemetery next to the church where most of the townspeople rested.

They entered the vestibule of the church and proceeded through the large doors into the sanctuary. The group was respectfully quiet as they walked down the aisle and found places to sit. There was a large wooden cross hanging from the ceiling just behind the pulpit.

"Most of the buildings you saw today are currently in some form of use," said Freas. "Especially this church. Services are held here on Sunday morning at nine o' clock and Sunday evening at six o' clock. Many a loser at the casino has come here seeking comfort." Freas chuckled.

"Well, it's two o'clock, and this concludes our tour. You are welcome to stay here and have a look around. Make sure you see the museum. I hope everyone has enjoyed learning about the legend of the Falcon Mine. It has been my pleasure to be your tour guide. I'll be in the church lobby to answer your questions. Thanks again for joining me today," said Freas.

A few people got up and walked to the lobby with Freas. Nick lingered for a few minutes with his head bowed in remembrance of his mom, Slim, and the sheriff. Then he headed to the lobby. When Freas spotted Nick, he paused for a moment in his conversation and reached out his hand to him.

"It was nice to meet you, Nick. I hope you get an A on that history paper. Come back and let me see it when you finish it, if you don't mind. Something tells me it's going to be great," he predicted.

"Thanks, Freas. You gave me a lot to think about. I'll let you know how it turns out," replied Nick. He turned and left the church, heading for the museum and wondering what strange occurrences would happen there.

The glass door slid open automatically and Nick felt a welcome blast of cool air. The museum attendant checked his name against the school list and pointed him in the direction of the lockers, where Nick secured his backpack. He held on to his camera so he could take more pictures for his paper. He planned to see as many of the important exhibits as he could in the limited time left.

Rounding a corner into the first large room, he saw some other students. The museum displays were life-size scenes, complete with props and wax figures of townspeople. A blacksmith was frozen in the act of nailing a horseshoe onto a horse's hoof, and women motionlessly churned butter on the front porch of a house.

Nick finally stopped in front of a cave entrance scene. A wax figure stood next to a mining cart full of rocks, looking closely at a stone in his hand.

A description on a small podium beside the display read, *Slim Marano, the foreman of the Falcon Mine, examines a piece of rock for traces of gold or silver.* Down at the bottom, it continued in fine print: *These wax figures are based on some of the actual black-and-white photos of the townspeople of Silverado.*

So this is Slim, thought Nick. He walked around the wax figure. Slim looked exactly like he did in the photo on the sheriff's desk. He was tall and thin, dressed in a light blue shirt, button-fly jeans with leather chaps, brown leather boots with spurs, and a black cowboy hat with an arrow coming out the right side of the hat.

Slim's features were striking: a strong jaw, high cheekbones, and a big nose, with small spectacles perched on the tip. He had piercing blue eyes and bushy eyebrows. The hair sticking out from under his hat was blond with some white strands peppered throughout, and a few scraggly hairs grew below the cleft in his chin.

Nick stared at him for several minutes. He looked like someone's favorite uncle, not like a cold-blooded murderer. Glancing around the room, Nick saw that he was alone. He slipped under the ropes surrounding the scene so that he could take a better picture. As the flash fired, he quickly shifted his position. He knew he shouldn't be standing inside the display.

He took two more shots, and then sudden laughter erupted on the other side of the room. Nick glanced around again. Still not seeing anyone, he aimed his camera and looked through the viewfinder to get a full-length shot of Slim. Slim's glass eyes looked directly at the rock he was holding. A second before Nick pushed the button down and the flash went off, he could have sworn the eyes moved to look directly at him.

The flash momentarily blinded him. As soon as his eyes adjusted, he quickly looked at the wax figure's eyes. *They really had changed position.* Nick shivered and slipped out of the scene, hurrying to leave the room. As he rounded the corner, he accidentally ran into a group of students. Nick and several of the other boys ended up sprawled out on the floor.

"Hey, man, whaddaya think you're doing?" a voice sneered.

Nick struggled to his feet. "Sorry. I wasn't watching where I was going," he said. He extended his hand to help one of the guys get up.

The kid knocked Nick's hand away. Nick realized these were the rowdy boys from the back of the bus, and he was hit with a sense of dread. Several of them were now climbing around in the scenes, grabbing artifacts.

"Well, I'd better get going," Nick said. "Sorry about running into you."

The boys continued to stare at him with silent dislike as he quickly retreated to the next room. Nick kept moving and hoped he was putting enough distance between those guys and himself.

After a few minutes Nick began to relax. As he wandered into the document room, he wondered whether he should report what he had seen to his teacher or one of the museum staff members.

Several glass cases displayed newspapers and photos of the townspeople. There were also maps, books, and many other interesting artifacts. Checking his watch, Nick realized that he only had half an hour to return to the bus. Deciding that he had seen enough, he turned to head into the next room.

The sudden glitter of something on the floor caught his eye. Curiosity got the better of Nick, so he walked toward it. When he picked it up, he realized it was a piece of glass.

Why would there be glass here? he thought. Glancing at the display case, he noticed that the side panel was shattered and that something was missing from the case. The description card in front of the empty space read, *Slim Marano's personal journal.*

Slim's journal had been stolen.

Nick realized he was going to have to tell someone. He had just turned around when a voice behind him said, "So, new kid, think you can keep your mouth shut, or are we going to have to shut it for you?" It was the leader of the rowdy group he'd just escaped.

"Put the journal back, and I won't say anything," replied Nick.

"No deal. This belongs to someone else. They want it back, and they don't mind paying for it."

Nick had no time to react to the punch in the eye, let alone to the second one aimed at his stomach. He crumpled against the display case, and as his head hit the floor, everything went black.

The boys just stood there staring at him.

"Is he dead?" one large boy whispered.

Another boy leaned down close to Nick, then answered, "No, but he's out cold."

"Why did you have to hit him so hard?" the stocky kid asked.

"It just happened," said the leader, aggravated. "I just wanted to scare him. But this might work out all right for us. Let's go! After Mrs. Glen does the head count on the bus, she'll come looking for him."

They started to leave when they heard voices coming in their direction. Thinking quickly, the leader pulled Slim's journal out of his pocket, and slipped it into Nick's front pocket.

"What are you doing? That guy said he wanted it tonight," complained one of the boys.

"I know, I know, we'll have to get it later," he replied. "Right now we have a bigger problem. We need this kid to take the rap for us."

Just then, Mrs. Glen and one of the museum supervisors turned the corner and entered the room. Mrs. Glen was talking when she looked up. "Boys, you should be heading to the bus!"

The boys parted, exposing Nick's unconscious form on the ground.

"My goodness," exclaimed Mrs. Glen. She rushed forward and gently touched Nick's neck to check for a pulse, then glared up at the boys, demanding, "I want to know what happened here!"

The museum supervisor called for help on the portable radio.

"We caught him stealing Slim's journal. We got in a fight trying to take it away from him. He fell and knocked himself out," said the group's leader.

Mrs. Glen eyed him incredulously. The boy quickly pointed back at Nick. "I'm telling you the truth. If you don't believe me check his front pocket," he exclaimed.

While they waited for medical assistance to arrive, Mrs. Glen and the supervisor gently checked Nick's head for wounds. A deep bruise was developing over Nick's left eye and his lower lip was split. Mrs. Glen found a knot on the side of his head. The paramedics arrived moments later and began checking his vital signs.

"He might have a concussion," said one of the paramedics. "We need to take him to the hospital and have him checked out right away." Mrs. Glen nodded in agreement.

"Do you know how to contact his parents?" asked the museum worker.

"No. He's one of my new students. I haven't received his paperwork yet," Mrs. Glen replied.

"Does he have any personal belongings?" the first paramedic asked.

"I think he has a backpack," replied Mrs. Glen.

"I'll check with the front desk to see if he checked one in," said the museum supervisor.

"I'll check his pockets, too," said Mrs. Glen.

She checked the right pocket first and found Nick's receipt for lunch and his camera. Then she checked his left pocket and pulled out Slim's journal. Mrs. Glen looked up and saw the smug looks on the rowdy boys' faces.

"Told you he was trying to steal it," said the leader.

"Enough!" she snapped. "Now back to the bus. I will deal with you later."

The museum supervisor gently took the journal out of Mrs. Glen's hand. "I'm sorry," she said. "I have to report this."

Glancing up, Mrs. Glen watched the group of boys head out of the room. "I know, I know, but I don't believe he did it," she replied.

"Well, either way, I have to report it to the administration. I'll also have to call the police. So regardless of what happened, everyone will have to be interviewed," said the museum supervisor. "I'm going up front to find his backpack. Maybe I can locate his home phone number. I'll call you at the school later. But right now, I believe you have a bus full of students to take care of."

Mrs. Glen checked her watch. "I'll get one of the other chaperones to handle the kids on the bus. I'm going to go with Nick to the hospital. I'll call the school to check the file for his permission slip; the information we need should be on it."

As Nick was being loaded onto a gurney, Mrs. Glen lightly ruffled his hair. "Don't worry, we'll get to the bottom of this," she whispered to his limp body.

Chapter Five

THE CAVE

Nick woke up in the emergency room with a pounding headache. Through half-closed eyes, he saw nurses and doctors attending to other patients as worried family members huddled together. Nick saw a police officer, his father, and Mrs. Glen hovering nearby. The stern looks on everyone's faces warned Nick that whatever had happened wasn't good.

The police officer noticed that Nick was awake. He strode over to him with his clipboard.

"How are you feeling, Nick?" the police officer asked.

"Got a whopping headache right now," Nick murmured.

"Don't doubt that at all. Nick, I have some questions for you," the police officer said.

Nick's father joined the officer. "I don't think my son should be answering any questions right now. He's had more than enough to deal with for one day."

"You're probably right. I'll return in the morning to get his statement." Flicking his notebook closed, the officer walked out.

Lee let out a huge sigh. Nick saw the strained, tired look on his father's face.

"Nick, they're going to keep you here overnight for observation. In the morning I'll come back to be here when the policeman takes your statement."

"Dad, I didn't start the fight. Honest!" Nick burst out, causing sharp pain to shoot through his head.

"Nick, it's not the fight you should be worried about. They think you stole a journal from one of the display cases in the museum. They found it in your pocket."

"I didn't steal anything, Dad. The journal was already gone when I looked in the case. Those other kids stole it."

"Well, it's going to be your word against theirs. They're all saying the same thing: that you were in the process of stealing it, and they tried to stop you."

"Dad, please believe me! I didn't even touch it. You've got to believe me!" pleaded Nick.

"I really don't want to discuss this right now," said his father. "The nurse is here to take you to your room. I have to get back to the university for my last class. In the meantime, I'll call a lawyer. This doesn't look good. Now get some sleep. I'll see you in the morning."

A young aide began pushing Nick's gurney toward the hallway doors. Nick's father reached up, squeezed Nick's shoulder, and gave a half smile. Turning away, he walked out the emergency room doors.

Nick's heart sunk. He could tell his father didn't believe him. What had started as a relatively decent day in this new town had turned bad quickly. *Tomorrow doesn't look much better either,* he thought. He felt more alone than he ever had before, and he missed his mother as much as he had just after her funeral.

Nick tossed and turned all night. His headache was a constant dull throb against his temple. When the pain finally melted away, all he could think about was talking to his father and the police the next day. He must have finally slept, because when the nurse came in to give him his breakfast and check his vitals, he could barely open his eyes.

The nurse's chatter was a welcome distraction for Nick as he began to eat—until the door opened. In strode the police officer with a clipboard and pen.

"Good morning, Nick. Sorry for catching you during breakfast, but I have some questions to ask you. I need to get your statement about what happened at the museum yesterday."

In between bites, Nick told his side of the story. He recounted everything that he did during the visit to Silverado, particularly while he was in the museum.

The officer wrote everything down. At one point, he stopped writing and just stared at the page he had finished. He tapped his pen on the paper.

Nick had some questions of his own. He wanted to try to understand what the police were thinking.

"Officer, I noticed a large unit attached to the museum with *Fargo Alarm System* printed on it. With all of those valuable artifacts, wouldn't the alarm be on all the time?"

The officer looked at Nick and nodded.

Nick continued, "How was the journal removed from the display case without the alarm going off? The side panel was broken. Doesn't that set off the alarm?"

The officer began writing again. "If this was preplanned, then the thief would have had someone working inside the museum to disarm the alarm."

"I just moved here from Washington, D.C. I've been in this state for three weeks. This is only my second week in school. How could I even begin to try to pull something like that off when this is the first time I've ever been to Silverado?"

The officer paused in his note taking. "Nick, the journal was found on you. I also have statements from several other students saying they saw you take it from the display case."

"But isn't that just circumstantial evidence?" asked Nick. He remembered the term from Freas's telling of Slim Marano's trial.

"True, but I'll have to investigate further. At this point, things don't look good," he said frankly. "The doctor is going to release you this morning. I recommend that you remain under the full supervision of your father. As of yesterday, you have been temporarily suspended from school, along with the other boys, until we get to the bottom of this. If the evidence points to you, then you may have to stand trial for attempted robbery. If convicted, you could be placed in a juvenile home for a few months," the officer said.

"But I didn't do it!" protested Nick.

"Now, Nick, calm down. You haven't been arrested or charged yet," said the officer. "Trust me, you made some good points. I'll find out the truth one way or another."

At that moment, the door opened and Nick's father and the doctor stepped into the room. A deep frown crossed Lee's face when he saw the officer.

"I wanted to be here when you questioned my son!" exclaimed Nick's father.

Glancing up, the officer responded, "I just took Nick's statement, which is standard operating procedure for witnesses. But if you'll have your lawyer contact me directly, I'll make sure he receives a copy of the statement." Reaching out, he handed his business card to Nick's father.

The officer turned to look at Nick. "Thanks, Nick. You've been a big help. I promise I'll get to the bottom of this." He nodded his head toward everyone. "Good day, gentlemen." Turning, he left the hospital room.

The doctor turned his attention toward Nick. "Well, my boy, you are free to go. You did fine last night. You might have recurring headaches over the next couple of days, but that should be all. If you experience any dizziness or nausea, contact me right away."

"Get dressed! We're leaving," Nick's father said brusquely.

"Mr. Stewart," the doctor said. "I need you to come to my office while Nick gets dressed. You'll need to sign his release paperwork before he can leave the hospital."

Nick's father nodded curtly and then turned and walked quickly out of Nick's room with the doctor on his heels.

"Don't worry, Nick," the doctor said as he closed the door behind him.

Nick slowly got out of bed and began to put on his clothes. This was not going to be a good day at all.

The nurse came in a few minutes later to find Nick sitting on the bed, ready to go.

"Come with me," she said. "Your father is still in conference with the doctor. You can wait for him in the lobby."

Nick waited in the lobby for another half an hour. He surveyed the gift shop window and watched as people came to visit sick family members.

Nick's doctor came around the corner and walked over to him.

"Nick, call me if you need anything. Your father and I had a talk about your family situation. He's worried about you, so take it easy, okay?"

Nick dug the toe of his tennis shoe into the floor and averted his eyes.

"Listen, Nick. I just want you to stay quiet for the next couple of days. Think you can do that for me?" asked the doctor.

"Yes, sir." Nick sighed.

Mr. Stewart rounded the corner holding a Styrofoam cup full of hot coffee. He stopped in front of them and extended his right hand to the doctor. "Thanks for everything, Doctor."

"No problem. Check on him from time to time while he's sleeping. And if it takes him longer than usual to wake up in the morning, then you need to call me." The doctor looked back down at Nick. "It was great to meet you. Hang in there and everything will work out." He shook Nick's hand and departed for the main corridor of the hospital.

Nick glanced up at his dad, who was taking a sip of coffee.

"Let's go, Nick," his father said.

The drive home was quiet. Nick hated this silence. It told him just how much trouble he was in. At the house, Nick walked into the kitchen to get something to drink. His father followed him and threw away his coffee cup.

"I need to get back to work. Take it easy today and rest. Whatever you do, don't leave the house. You cannot go out without my supervision," he warned.

"Okay," Nick replied unhappily.

His dad pointed at the still-unpacked boxes stacked against the living room wall. "If you're feeling ambitious, you can tackle some of those boxes. Call my office if you have any problems and my assistant will get me. The number is on the counter. I'll let you know if I end up having to work late. You and I will talk about everything later."

Nick's father headed out the front door. Nick locked the door behind him, and leaned his back against it. A wave of weariness washed over him. Staring at the wall of boxes, he shook his head in disgust. Then he headed up the stairs and down the hallway to his room. Right now, all he could think about was how tired he was.

Nick slept the rest of the afternoon and straight through the night until the next morning. He awoke to his father's voice calling him.

"Nick, get up!"

Groaning, Nick rolled over. "But I thought I was suspended from school."

"There's a problem at my dig site. I need to be there with my students to supervise it. So, get up and get ready. You're coming with me," said his father, walking into Nick's bedroom.

"Ugh! But Dad, I don't want to go. Can't I just stay here?"

"No, Nick! I am on the verge of losing my job because my colleagues think I can't handle my own son. I want you in my presence until this thing with the police is cleared up. So you don't have a choice. You're coming with me. That's the only way I'm going to keep everyone happy." He turned to leave.

"Everyone except me," muttered Nick.

Nick's father turned back in anger. "I heard that! Now who got himself into this situation in the first place? Good grief, Nick, we've only been here three weeks, and you managed to get yourself suspended. And to top it off, you're involved in a theft that could land you in juvenile detention."

"I didn't do it!" yelled Nick. "Why won't you believe me?"

"It's hard to ignore the fact that the journal was in your pocket. Your mom would be so disappointed in you, Nick," said his dad.

"Leave Mom out of this. She's dead!" Nick shouted.

Father and son glared at each other, with memories of Laura hanging heavily in the air between them.

Nick's dad finally broke the silence. "It's too late for me to send you to your aunt's to live. So we're going to have to make the best of this situation, whether we like it or not. Get ready to go. Bring your backpack, books, and homework." Turning briskly, he left Nick's room, slamming the door behind him.

An hour later, Nick and his dad headed to the university.

Nick waited for his father to gather permits for the dig from the faculty office. Once his father's students were accounted for, they all left the building and climbed onto a bus.

The dig site was only about a mile and a half away from the Silverado ghost town, at the base of one of the nearby mountains. As they approached the site, white tents were visible through the bus windows. Nick could only stare blindly at the looming mountains. Nothing here would lift his spirits.

Once off the bus, the university students got their first look at the partially exposed pit they would be working in. There was a murmur of excitement as Nick's father stepped up beside them and began to give instructions about what the students were going to be doing.

The entire morning, Nick's father seemed distant from him. That was normal when he was preoccupied with a dig, but he spent almost the entire time doting on his students. Nick noticed how his dad beamed proudly when he looked at his students, how he spoke kindly and supportively to them. He couldn't recall one time in his own life when his father had looked at him with such pride.

Nick was growing increasingly bored and sullen watching the students make their way inch by inch with brushes and picks over the excavation site, and watching his dad praise and support them. *He doesn't even know I'm here,* he thought, as he ate his lunch alone.

Nick decided to go exploring. There was a huge outcropping of rock low on the side of the mountain that looked interesting. Maybe he'd discover gold. He borrowed some of his dad's tools and a flashlight from his bag, and stuffed them into his backpack. He realized that if he disappeared for a while, his dad might realize he was gone and get pretty angry. *But only because he's worried about his job and what his criminal son is getting into now.* And then he stalked away.

Halfway up to the outcropping, Nick spotted the mouth of a cave. Unable to resist its mysterious appeal, he quickly made his way to the cave's entrance. Standing there, he looked back down the mountain to see if his father or anyone else had noticed that he was gone. He could just make out his father bent over the ground as he explained something to one of the students. No, he hadn't noticed.

Nick turned and shook his head. Maybe it would be a better to go into the cave and get lost. Probably after a couple of weeks, they would give up the search. Somehow, he would find another exit from the cave. He would find a way to begin his life all over again. Bending down, Nick picked up a small stone and threw it into the distance in frustration. His mom had always accused him of having an overactive imagination. *I wish she were still here. Things would sure be a lot different.*

Shaking himself, he climbed into the cave. Pulling out his flashlight, he played the light over the walls to look at the different rock formations. There appeared to be drawings on the wall farther down the shaft of the cave. He covered the distance swiftly and climbed onto several large rocks that lay on the ground in front of the wall. Nick balanced himself carefully to get at eye-level with the drawings. They looked like crude images of buffalo and deer. There were also several stick-like people wielding spears against the animals.

Nick had seen drawings like this before in his father's books. These were Native American drawings from centuries ago. He grabbed his camera from his pocket and repositioned himself to take some pictures. He framed the drawings in his viewfinder and shot a photograph.

As the flash went off, Nick thought he heard a rumbling sound in the distance. The ground trembled, and suddenly rocks came crashing and thundering through the cavern. Nick was propelled into the air and thrown deeper into the cave.

He came down hard, and his last thought before he lapsed into unconsciousness for the second time in two days was, *Something is wrong.*

Chapter Six
A GHOST

As the dust and the cascade of small stones settled, Nick lay on his side, unconscious and dirty. His backpack was near his feet, covered with rubble, his flashlight was still in his hand, and his camera was still attached to his wrist by the strap. From deeper in the cavern, a strange greenish glow floated toward Nick. When the light washed over him, the faint outline of a man could be detected. Nick groaned, opened his eyes, and slowly rolled onto his back. He tried to focus on the person standing above him, but the pain was too great and he slipped back into unconsciousness.

The specter bent and checked Nick's pulse. Then he gently touched the abrasion on Nick's forehead. He uncovered Nick's backpack and slung it over his shoulder, then stooped down and picked up the unconscious boy. With a brief backward glance at the blocked entrance of the cave, the ghostly figure turned and walked deeper into the mountain.

Some time later, Nick slowly awoke to another throbbing headache. He was lying on a cot in small cavern. A brown wool blanket covered him. Opening his eyes slowly, he saw that a fire crackled in a small potbellied stove, warming the room. Turning his head slightly, he caught movement on the other side of the room.

Nick closed his eyes and waited a minute, then gingerly opened them again. But the picture before him did not change. Nick could see an eerie greenish aura of light surrounding an older man wearing cowboy clothing. And Nick could see right through him. Thinking he must be hallucinating, Nick closed his eyes again. When he opened them, the smiling face of the strange man was just inches away.

"Hi there. Glad to see you've come around. That was a nasty bump you took on your head."

Feeling distinctly surreal, Nick struggled up to a sitting position and took a good look at the ghostly man. "Where am I? Am I dead? Who—or what—are you? You look kind of familiar."

"Whoa there, boy. First off, you're not dead. You're in a cave, and you're very much alive. But, we need to get your strength up a bit. Hold off on all the questions until after you eat something. Then I'll explain everything."

Nick's head spun slightly, so he lay back down on the cot. He squinted suspiciously at the apparition in front of him. The fact was, he *was* exhausted, so he decided to figure out who his host was later.

The cowboy retrieved a tray with sandwiches and a pewter mug on it for Nick. The mug held a brown liquid that the cowboy told him was ale. Despite his discomfort, Nick was quite hungry. He propped himself up and ate and drank everything that was placed before him. When he finished, he felt much better and considered the strange man—or being—again.

Nick's memory went into search mode. *I know I've seen his face before, but where?* Glancing around the room, his eyes fell on a table. On it sat a cowboy hat with an arrow piercing one side.

Memories of the day he had spent at the Silverado ghost town flooded his mind. He remembered the old black-and-white photo on the sheriff's desk, and the wax figure in the museum. He recalled all of the strange events that day. He remembered how Freas kept denying the existence of ghosts in Silverado.

"Hey, wait . . . I know who you are! You're Slim Marano!" he blurted out. "I went to Silverado ghost town Thursday for a history class field trip. I learned all about the legend of the Falcon Mine. Freas, my tour guide, kept saying over and over again that there was no such thing as ghosts. But you look an awful lot like the man I saw in a picture in the sheriff's office . . . and the figure in the museum. You're the ghost of Slim Marano, aren't you?"

The cowboy grinned. After pulling a short barrel closer to Nick's cot, he sat down. "Nick, the most important thing you need to know is that this is not a dream or a hallucination or your imagination working overtime. I am Slim Marano. Folks like me are called spirits, ghosts, and apparitions, but the truth is that we are the imaginations, thoughts, personalities, and spirits of former living beings. I'm a living spirit.

"You see, most people think death is an end to life. But truthfully, it is the beginning of a new life. In the spirit world, those like me are not confined by the same rules of time and space that limit you on this earth."

Nick sat there in stunned silence, trying to pay attention.

Slim went on. "I am governed by the laws of Heaven. If I am sent to Earth, it's for a reason; when I get an assignment, it's usually to help someone. Each situation is different.

"In the spiritual world good and evil are very real. Evil wants to govern the world by its own rules. It destroys children, adults, and civilizations without a second thought. It ran rampant in my time. Evil destroyed my life and devastated my family. It lives in your world, too."

Nick was mesmerized by Slim's words. Yet the warmth of the room made him sleepy. He struggled to stay awake and hear the rest of Slim's story.

"Both worlds are a fact of life. All of the decisions you make will affect your life not only on earth, but also in my world."

Lying back on the cot, Nick closed his eyes, unable to keep them open any longer. Whatever Slim was didn't really matter to him at this moment.

Although he still had many questions, Nick could no longer resist the allure of sleep.

Slim chuckled. "Go to sleep, Nick. I'll be here when you wake up. There will be more time tomorrow for questions."

Nick yawned deeply as he fought one last time to keep his eyes open. "Slim, how do you know my name?"

"Your mother told me, Nick. She told me quite a bit about you."

"Really?" Nick whispered as he finally drifted off.

Slim stood and looked at Nick for several minutes. He reached forward and rustled his brown hair gently, then turned and walked over to the old stove and stoked the fire. He added a few more logs and looked back at Nick.

"Till tomorrow, my boy. Till tomorrow." With a yawn and a stretch, Slim slowly faded from sight.

Eight hours later, Nick stirred. He absentmindedly reached up to rub his temple only to discover a large and painful knot there. Yawning, he stretched, opened his eyes, and slowly sat up. A candle on a barrel spread a flickering golden glow around the room. Nick felt panic beginning to rise in his gut. *I thought I was dreaming!* But his surroundings matched those in his dream. It was cold, and Nick pulled the blanket closer around him, trying to stifle the panic.

The man in his dream had been tall, and looked older because of some of the lines on his face. Nick remembered that his chin had been covered with scraggly stubble, as if he hadn't shaved for a long time. He'd worn western clothing, complete with chaps, boots, and a cowboy hat with an arrow in it. The strangest thing was that he had been nothing more than the transparent image of a man with an unearthly glow surrounding him.

Nick rubbed his head again. "Was he really Slim Marano? That must have been some blow I took, to come up with a dream like that," he whispered to himself.

Then he heard the distinct sound of somebody whistling in the distance. The noise grew louder. Suddenly, the green apparition of Slim rounded the corner with an armful of firewood. "Morning, Nick. Hope you slept well. Give me a few minutes, and I'll have this room warmed up real quick."

Nick blinked hard and sat motionless as Slim stoked the remains of the fire in the potbellied stove. Before long, the cold stone cavern began to warm up and the chill Nick felt started to fade away.

"Are you hungry, Nick?"

Nick still sat there, dazed by Slim's reappearance. Finally he asked, "Am I hallucinating?"

Slim looked at Nick and chuckled. He went to a barrel that served as a table, picked up a couple of eggs, and cracked them on an iron pan. He set the pan on the top of the potbellied stove.

"No, Nick, of course not. Do you remember anything from our conversation last night?"

Nick looked at him wide-eyed. "I thought that was just a dream."

"No, my boy, everything we talked about is very real. I was once a man, just as human as you, but I was framed for Otis Walkins's murder, rushed to trial, and hanged for a crime I didn't commit. From Heaven I've watched every generation of my family suffer because of my notoriety. To this day, I still don't know who actually killed Otis Walkins. Several weeks ago, the Almighty finally granted my request to try to clear my family's name, with one stipulation: I have to work with a person here on Earth. He brought your mom into our meeting, and she recommended you."

Nick stared at him in disbelief. "But my mom . . ." he began, trailing off. He tried again. "My mom is dead," he whispered. "A drunk driver killed her."

"I know, Nick. I also know that she wrote you a special note in a card for your eleventh birthday, and that you keep the card in a wooden box you carved that is in the back of your closet by your old baseball bat."

Nick looked at him incredulously and finally said, "How could you know that?"

"I've been with you for the last several weeks, Nick," Slim replied. "I know that you didn't break into that museum display case. I know that you didn't take my journal."

The statement had Nick's full attention. "How would you know that?"

"I was there," said Slim.

"Were you at the general store, too? Did you have anything to do with the inventory book there? What about the voice at the jail and the moving eyes of the wax figure?" asked Nick, realizing that his imagination wasn't so overactive after all.

"That was all me. Sorry, I got a little carried away. I wanted to see if you could hear and see me." Slim chuckled. More soberly, he added, "By the way, my journal has been stolen again since the cave-in."

Nick's jaw dropped open.

"I discovered that it was removed from the police officer's evidence locker sometime this morning," he continued.

"Wow! This proves that I'm not the one after your journal. But I have no idea why those boys were stealing it."

"Hmm, something strange is going on here. Why *would* anybody want my journal now? Unless someone is planning to enter the old Falcon Mine. Maybe it's someone from my past," Slim said.

"Someone from your past? Do you mean that a spirit could come from your time looking for something in this time? To take it back to the past?" Nick asked.

"Yes, Nick. Like I told you last night, we're in a continuous battle with the dark spirits. They constantly try to block any and all of our efforts to help people. There has to be a specific reason that my journal was taken. I wouldn't be surprised if imps were at the root of this."

"What are imps?"

"Exactly what you would imagine. They are the evil spirits."

"Would I be able to see them, just like I see you?" Nick asked.

"Yes, but only in my time. You'll be able to see more than other human beings see."

"Do you appear to very many people?"

"We mostly help children who are in trouble. They can see us more easily than adults can. Some of us have been assigned to grown-ups whose situations were so traumatic that we could appear to them. These adults see us as normal human strangers who suddenly show up and help them through their crises."

Nick sat in thoughtful silence. Who would ever believe that he had been talking to a spirit? He wasn't even sure he believed it. But no matter how many times he closed his eyes and reopened them, Slim was still there.

"Nick, I need to ask you for a very big favor. Would you be willing to help me?" asked Slim.

"How?"

"I have been granted this one opportunity to solve the mystery of Otis Walkins's murder. Are you willing to come back to my time to help with this assignment? Maybe we can also find out why anyone would want my journal. We could clear your name, too."

"Can I really do that? Go back in time?" asked Nick

"Yes," Slim replied. "You are here for a reason. As long as you are with me, you can go anywhere I go."

"What if I don't believe any of what you have told me, or even want to help you?" Nick asked defiantly, suddenly feeling a bit scared.

"Well, Nick, look at your situation. At the moment, you're stuck in a cave with no way out. I'm not sure how long it will take them to dig through to find you. That is, if they even know you're in here."

"You mean, I could be in here for a long time?"

"It's quite possible. I would have gotten you out of here a lot sooner than this if I'd been allowed to, but for some reason, you have been chosen to take this journey. To be honest, this is the first time I have ever heard of a human being chosen for an assignment. This is an honor, believe me. But the final choice is still up to you."

Slim stood up and stretched. He left Nick alone in the cavern to think. Nick felt excited, but also frightened. He certainly didn't want to stay in the cavern waiting for somebody to find him, but he wasn't sure he wanted to go back in time with a ghost, either. Slim returned after a bit and sat down beside him.

Nick hesitated as he took a good, hard look at Slim's earnest face. Finally, he made a decision, "There's not much for me back at home, anyway. So sure, I'll help you if I can."

Slim jumped up, shaking Nick's hand vigorously. "Thanks, Nick. I hoped I could count on you."

Startled by Slim's enthusiasm, Nick could only smile weakly. "When do we get started?"

"How about after breakfast? Are you hungry? The eggs are ready and I've got some bread and cheese," said Slim.

"How did you find eggs, bread, and cheese in a cave?" asked Nick.

Slim smiled. "I'll tell you later. I've already given you lots more than breakfast to digest. One thing at a time."

Nick stood up from the cot. "That's fine with me. I still have to get used to the idea that I'm talking to a spirit." He yawned and stretched. "I really am hungry. Let's eat!"

Over their feast of eggs and toast, Nick asked, "What's the deal with the arrow in your hat?"

"Oh that," replied Slim. "That's been there since I was young. A couple of us were planning to steal a horse from an Indian tribe. We almost had it untied from the pack when we suddenly heard this swishing sound. Before I could even look up, the arrow had pierced my hat and it flew off my head. I tell you, we were good and scared. I grabbed my hat and we took off running. When we looked back, there was no one there. I've kept the hat ever since. It sure made for some great stories for my family."

"You had kids?" asked Nick.

"Two boys, Peter and Brent, and a girl, Leeann," replied Slim. "Of course, they're already grown in 1865, so you probably won't be meeting them." Nick noticed that Slim's expression had changed and his face had become rigid. The older man quickly switched subjects.

"Are you done with breakfast? We have a bit of a walk ahead of us."

"I'm ready," said Nick.

Slim handed Nick his backpack. Nick slung it over his shoulder and followed Slim out of the entrance to the small cavern and into a huge open area, where the ceilings were supported by massive square wooden pillars.

"Welcome to Eagle Cliff Mountain. It's part of the Falcon Mine holdings. This is the main shaft, where the miners could move equipment back and forth to the smaller shafts." Slim pointed to several small darker openings along the walls. "There's a major network of tunnels down those smaller shafts; it's easy to get lost down there if you don't know where you're going."

"Have a lot of people gotten lost in here?" asked Nick, thinking about meeting up with more ghosts in the dark tunnels.

"Not in my day," said Slim. Turning to the left, he began to walk farther down the corridor. "The mine was very active during that time, and since it was producing a lot of gold ore, my boss, Otis, had guards at all of the entrances twenty-four hours a day. No one could go in or come out without someone knowing about it. But since the mine closed down, there have been people rooting around in here, seduced by the thought that they would find an undiscovered vein of gold. It's like a fever when that idea gets stuck in someone's head. I've been called on several times to come back here and help people find their way out."

Taking in the darkness in front of him, Nick asked, "How did you help them?"

Slim stroked his chin. "I've learned to be creative, using sounds and glimpses of light to guide people to the tunnels that will eventually lead them to safety."

Nick and Slim walked deeper and deeper into the cavern. Nick could not help but feel a little nervous. But Slim's green aura was strangely comforting as it lit their path.

To cover his jitters, Nick made conversation. "So the payroll that went missing the day Mr. Walkins died was never recovered?"

"No," replied Slim. "To this day, it has never been found. The last time I saw it, the payroll was in Otis's office. I helped him count it, and put it in the safe. The next day, they found his office in shambles and Otis dead behind his desk. The safe was open and empty."

Nick thought for a moment. "So how did you get blamed for the crime if the last time you saw your boss, he was alive and had the payroll with him?"

Slim looked down at Nick and smiled ruefully. "Some of the miners that were guarding the mine that night told the jury that I was the only one they saw coming and going from his office that evening. Besides that, they found my journal on the floor not too far from his body. My journal had been missing for several days before that night. I figured it was probably at home in my tool bag. Anyway, that was enough for the jury to convict me. I was hanged one week later. Redefines a speedy trial, huh?"

Eventually they came to a fork in the main tunnel. Slim came to a stop and started tapping his right boot and scratching the stubble on his chin.

"Is something wrong?" asked Nick.

"Nothing, really. I just need to make sure that we enter the correct tunnel. For me, each tunnel represents a different time period. If we enter the wrong shaft, we could end up in the middle of one of the Chinese dynasties."

"You mean that if I took off down any one of these shafts, I could end up in a completely different time and place?"

"Nick, if *you* entered, you'd just be lost. But if we enter it together, then yes, we could end up anywhere, in any time. The rules of time and space no longer apply to me. If I were traveling alone, I wouldn't have to use the portal we're heading to at all. I can picture a place at a particular point in time in my mind, and then I just appear there—gradually. It's called transmigration. For you, it's not quite as simple. But as long as I go first, you can travel with me through any portal."

Nick stared at the mineshafts before him in wonder. "Wow! You're like H. G. Wells's time machine."

"Who's H. G. Wells? And what's a time machine?"

"*The Time Machine* is a book that I read for school. It's about a professor who goes backward in time and forward to the future using a machine he builds," said Nick.

"Well, it sounds like I have an easier time of it than he did," replied Slim, and headed down the right fork in the path.

Chapter Seven
THE TIME PORTAL

After they had walked for some time, Slim frowned and stopped in front of an opening that was covered by rocks.

"It's been a while since I've been here. It looks like things have changed."

Kicking a small stone down the corridor, Nick glanced up at Slim. "Slim, when I was on the tour, the guide talked about some major cave-ins that happened after your death. He said the owner who took over both mines had a reputation for not caring much about the safety of the miners," said Nick.

"That would be Pernell Billings, who bought the Falcon Mine after Otis's death. He managed to get himself and the Black Stallion Mine Company out of debt with the earnings from the Falcon Mine. He never cared about anything or anyone but himself. So it's no big surprise that he ended up losing both mines," Slim said. After another good look at the blocked entrance in front of them, he changed subjects. "This is the spot, all right."

"Can we get through?" asked Nick.

"Oh, sure . . . but not without a bit of work. Roll up your sleeves, Nick. It shouldn't take too long, but we need to dig a hole big enough for us to pass through."

An hour later, Nick sat back on his heels and wiped the sweat from his forehead. "This is tough work!"

Slim straightened up as he stretched his lower back. "You're getting first-hand experience of what life was really like for us miners." He rubbed the back of his neck and glanced down at Nick with a grin.

Nick got up and grabbed the next rock in front of him. He pulled, but it didn't budge. He pulled harder, but still nothing happened. Finally, he gave it everything he had. The stone popped out, sending Nick sprawling backward onto the ground.

Slim had just turned to grab another rock when he heard Nick fall. He turned to see Nick picking himself up off the ground.

Slim chuckled. "Lost control of that one!" he exclaimed. "Are you okay, Nick?"

"I'm fine. It just got away from me, that's all." As he finished dusting himself off, he looked up and noticed a glimmer of light coming through the spot where the rock had once been.

"Slim, come and check this out. I think I see something!"

"Way to go, Nick!" cried Slim, peering at the tiny beam of light. "I believe you found a way in." He gave Nick a hearty slap on the back. Nick grinned. For the first time in a long time, he felt like he had actually accomplished something, instead of just getting in the way.

"Come on, boy," said Slim. "We need to make this hole bigger so we can get through. We're almost there."

Slim started to move more rocks. Nick watched him as he worked. It sure looked like he knew what he was doing. Slim's transparent appearance didn't seem to hinder him. Nick admired his determination. He was feeling a lot more at ease with the cowboy. He liked being treated like an adult rather than like a difficult kid.

After about fifteen minutes, they had created a hole big enough to expose a long, narrow tunnel. Slim checked the edge of the tunnel for stability until he was satisfied the passage was safe.

"Well, it's going to be a little tight," he said. "The tunnel looks to be about twenty feet long. Keep your head down and scoot on your stomach. I'll go first, so if there are any surprises, I can talk you through them."

Nick gazed unhappily at the small opening. Slim touched his shoulder. "Nick, are you all right? You don't look so good."

"I'll be okay. It's just that small, tight, and twenty feet don't thrill me," he explained.

"Do you want to dig some more to make the opening bigger?" Slim asked.

"No! No more digging," said Nick, rubbing his scraped knuckles. "I can handle this."

"Attaboy. If anyone can do it, it's you. Let's go now. The sooner we get this over with, the better."

"Okay, let's do it."

Slim walked over to the tunnel's entrance and crouched down. He squeezed into the opening and slowly disappeared.

Darkness surrounded Nick now that Slim was in the tunnel. He moved closer to the entrance and bent down so that he could keep his eyes fixed on Slim's body as he shimmied through the tunnel. Once Slim popped through on the other side, Nick could see the bright light again, as well as the cool green glow that surrounded Slim.

"It's not too bad," Slim called through the tunnel. "There are some little loose rocks, but it's safe. Are you ready?"

Nick let out a huge sigh. Glancing behind him, all he saw was darkness, but in front of him lay a tight, suffocating journey. He tied his backpack to his ankle, took a deep breath of air, and slid into the opening on his stomach with his arms extended. *Better to brave this little tunnel than to spend the rest of my life back there in the dark,* he reasoned.

"Come on," Slim encouraged him. "You can do it. Just focus on the light."

Nick's hands were clammy, and his heart was pounding. Taking a big gulp of air, he began to shimmy through the tunnel, never taking his eyes off the light at the other end.

The tunnel floor was mostly smooth, with the occasional rock that jabbed Nick's ribs. But what really unnerved him were the loose pebbles that kept cascading down on him as he moved. He could feel a layer of gravel building on his head and back.

Slim talked Nick through the process as he scooted forward inch by inch. After what seemed like an eternity to Nick, he was finally close enough for Slim to reach in and grab his hand.

"Come on, Nick. You're almost through. It's just a few more feet."

Nick put his head down on his arm and closed his eyes. Just a couple more feet and he would finally be out. Taking in a deep breath of air, he opened his eyes and pushed with all his strength.

"I got you," said Slim. "Keep your head low and I'll pull you out the rest of the way."

Once he was free, Nick rolled over onto his back and began to breathe deeply. Slim sat down beside him and patiently waited for him to regain his composure.

"You did good." He patted Nick's shoulder. "Just rest a minute and get your wind back. When we get to the water, you can take a swim."

Nick opened his eyes and glanced around at the cavern. Darkness still surrounded them. He then raised himself to a sitting position. "Aren't we in your time period yet?" he asked.

Slim looked at Nick and smiled. "Almost, just a little farther. We still have to pass through a waterfall."

Nick slowly got to his feet, still feeling somewhat unstable. "Well, I'm just glad it's not another small tunnel," he said.

Slim stood up and stretched. "So am I," he said. "Wow, you're white as a ghost there."

Nick chuckled, starting to feel more clear-headed. "Very funny."

Slim walked over and threw his arm around Nick's shoulder. "Come on, let's go. Soon you'll see that my humor is one of my better traits."

Nick could tell as they walked that this tunnel was leading them even deeper into the mountain. Ten minutes later, Nick heard a faint, steady roar.

"What is that?" he asked.

"That's the waterfall. It should be just down around the bend," Slim answered.

As they got closer, the sound grew louder and louder. When they rounded the bend, they walked into a much larger cavern that spread out before them. There were several lit torches attached to the wall. Opposite the wall was a huge waterfall of sparkling, gleaming water cascading into a large, clear pool.

When Nick glanced back at Slim, he was startled to find that Slim's appearance had changed. He was no longer the greenish, glowing, ghostly image of a man. Now he stood there, his arms folded across his chest, just as solid and real as Nick himself.

"Slim! What happened?"

"As a spirit I can do a lot of things. For example, I can be invisible, transparent, or solid. I can even appear as somebody else if I have to. I thought that in the beginning, it would be best to appear as you would expect a ghost to appear to help you believe that what I was telling you was true. I think you believe me now," Slim said with a chuckle. "Besides, I'll need to be solid when we go through the portal so that you can hold on to me." Switching topics, he asked, "What do you think of the waterfall?"

"It's amazing. I've never seen anything like it before!"

"It is pretty darn impressive. You are in one of the mountains that used to be a part of the Falcon Mine holdings. This tunnel was mined out long ago and abandoned. We used to sneak over here on breaks and take a swim. This area is sitting on a natural underwater spring. It's about fifteen to twenty feet deep. Now over there," he pointed, "is a smaller spring if you're thirsty. The water tastes great!"

Nick took note of the spring that was pouring out of a small opening on the rough rock wall. Closing his eyes, he listened to the roaring of the water. A deep calm came over him. It was something that he had not experienced since his mom had died. It was as if he felt his mother's presence, and it comforted him. He let out a huge sigh, opened his eyes, and smiled.

Slim had been watching Nick. "You okay?" asked Slim.

"Yeah," replied Nick. The thought that Slim knew and spoke to his mom overwhelmed him. But many unexplainable and strange things had happened. Nick now knew that anything was possible.

Nick was nudged from his thoughts when Slim laid his hand on his shoulder.

"We have a little time now. Why don't you take a swim?" said Slim.

Nick turned and looked at the water. It was crystal clear and looked inviting. "Sure," he replied. He kicked off his shoes and took off his socks and T-shirt. Stripping down to his boxer shorts, he walked to the pool's edge and tentatively dipped his toe in the water. The temperature was perfect. Swinging his arms behind him, Nick jumped into the pool.

Slim smiled, stripped down to his long underwear, and joined Nick in the pool. As the two floated lazily, they swapped stories of the places they'd been and the exciting things they'd done. They both had some good stories: Slim's were mostly about cave exploration, and Nick's were mostly about foreign countries.

After a while, Nick noticed that the waterfall had begun to change colors very subtly and was glowing with a pale light that was growing brighter. He pointed it out to Slim.

"Not much longer, Nick," Slim said. "I'm going to get out and check on a few things. You may want to give your clothes a dunk in the water to freshen them up a bit."

"Okay." Nick watched Slim climb out of the pool with one eye open while he floated on his back. Before retrieving his clothes, he decided to dive to the bottom of the pool to have a look around.

The basin of the pool was lit by the waterfall, so Nick could see the different shapes and sizes of rough rocks and polished stones that were resting down below. Fine white sand covered the entire bottom of the pool. Nick explored a little bit and worked his way around the basin, carefully avoiding the turbulent waterfall.

Nick came up for air and dove again, collecting several small, multicolored stones. It was on his third dive that he caught the twinkle of something under a large rock. He swam closer to it and realized that it was a gold chain. He quickly kicked back to the surface and placed his stones along the edge of the pool. Taking another gulp of air, he dove back down. When he reached the chain, he touched it just to confirm that it was real. His heart raced as he grabbed the rock on top of it. He moved it slowly. It was heavy and Nick had to return to the surface for air several more times.

Finally, Nick had moved the rock enough to pull the chain free. A small leather pouch fell out of a crack in the rock as it tumbled over. Grabbing the chain and the pouch, he quickly scanned the area looking for other artifacts. He saw nothing else, so he kicked to the surface.

Breaking the surface of the water, Nick took in several huge gulps of air. He could see Slim in the distance; he seemed to be talking to someone. Nick swam to the edge, deposited his findings, and heaved himself out of the pool.

He examined the gold chain first. It was about five to six inches long and had a small square with a raised carving on one end. Nick could feel the raised shape when he ran his finger over it, but it had eroded too much to be recognizable.

He turned his attention to the pouch. After untying the knot in the drawstring keeping the pouch closed, Nick emptied the contents into his hand. Several gold coins fell out, as well as a gold nugget and a large crystal.

"Nick?"

Nick looked up to see Slim walking toward him. "Did you rinse off your clothes yet?"

"No, not yet. But come look at what I found."

Slim squatted down beside him. Nick held out his hands to display the items. Slim picked up each one and looked at it carefully.

Nick handed him the faded leather pouch. "Nick, where did you find these?" Slim asked.

"On the bottom of the pool," said Nick. "The chain was caught under the rock and the bag was stuck in a crack."

Slim's eyebrows knitted together. "Well, this chain looks like an old gold watch fob. Only the wealthy townspeople could afford the gold ones. Most of us had either silver or leather.

"The coins are from my time. The gold rock is actually a real gold nugget—looks like a nice, pure piece, too. This other rock I'm not sure about. By the way it twinkles, I believe you might have found a crystal of sorts. It could be a diamond in the rough. It's a good-size one, too," said Slim.

"The bag seems to have had a stamp on it, but it's too worn to make out," he added. "This is similar to the bags we used to send out rock samples to be tested and evaluated. But without seeing what the original stamp was, I can't tell you which mine it came from," Slim said. Glancing at Nick, Slim came back to the present. He handed everything back to Nick and he ruffled his hair. "Here you go, buckaroo. As far as I'm concerned, this belongs to you now.

"Now go ahead and rinse out your clothes and get dressed. The wind blowing through that corridor over there should dry you off quickly."

Nick laid the pouch down and then rinsed out his clothes in the pool. He walked over to the windy corridor. Putting on wet clothes was challenging, but Slim was right: In just a few minutes, his clothes were dry.

Nick walked back to where he had left the pouch and picked it up. He put it in the front pocket of his jeans. He ran his fingers through his hair to get it under control as he headed over to Slim.

Slim was hunched over a small fire. He had cooked two pieces of fish. There were also several pieces of bread and cheese off to the side.

"I've been trying to figure out who might have owned what you found," said Slim, looking up as Nick approached.

Sitting down, Nick asked, "Any ideas?"

"Some, but we won't know for sure until we get over there and can poke around a bit," said Slim.

"When will we be heading over?" asked Nick.

Slim turned his gaze toward the waterfall. "As soon as you eat," said Slim. "It shouldn't be much longer now."

Nick had just picked up a piece of fish and some bread, wondering again where the food had come from. He was just about to ask when he noticed that the waterfall was glowing and sparkling more brightly than before. The color of the cascading water was faintly changing from white to green, to pale blue, and back again.

"Wow!" he exclaimed.

"Quite a sight, eh?" asked Slim. "This is the portal. When it turns solid white, then we'll pass through it and be back in my time."

With his mouth full, Nick asked, "How does it work?"

"I'm afraid it's too hard to explain," Slim said. "I'm just going to have to ask you to trust me."

"Well, can you at least tell me where the food comes from?"

"Sure. A friend of mine drops it off for me. His name is Keenan—it means wise warrior. You'll meet him later."

Nick finished eating and went to the spring to drink some of its cool, sweet water. He glanced up and saw that the waterfall had turned white. It was growing more intensely bright with each passing moment. The water shimmered with clear sparkles of light, as if small diamonds were cascading into the pool.

"Are you ready?" Slim asked

Nick took a big breath. He knew there was no turning back now. He cleared his throat and nodded. He followed Slim around the edge of the pool to stand directly across from the waterfall. The water was now brighter than a lighthouse beacon.

Slim stepped off the edge and stood calmly on the surface of the water.

"But the pool is deep," Nick whispered. The water shimmered and continued to move under Slim's boots.

"Just follow my lead," Slim said.

Without looking down, Nick placed his right foot on the surface of the water. It didn't sink. He leaned forward a bit, shifting his weight to his right leg, but the surface of the water supported him.

When he stood directly behind Slim, his friend said, "Good. Let's go!"

Slim walked slowly toward the roaring waterfall. He turned to Nick and said, "Nick, take my hand, and whatever you do, don't let go until we get through."

Nick nodded and grabbed Slim's outstretched hand. Slim slowly disappeared into the waterfall, gently pulling Nick in with him.

The sound was deafening, and Nick could feel the force of the water even before it came down on him. Though he could no longer see Slim, he could still feel the pressure of his hand. When the water hit his head and shoulders, he was surprised at the tingling, cooling sensation. He had expected the force of gallons of falling water, but instead it was the whisper of butterflies touching down and taking off again. Savoring the moment, Nick reached out with his free hand and let the jewel-like water run through his fingers. After several moments, the roaring sound began to lessen as he continued forward. Then sunlight fluttered ahead, and he could make out Slim's back in front of him. Looking past Slim, he could see another cavern ahead of them.

In just a few more steps, Nick and Slim passed through the wall of water completely and were standing on solid ground. Nick gazed in wide-eyed curiosity at the cavern they had entered. On one side of the cave was an opening in the rock wall that led outside. Sunlight streamed in a bright beam into the cavern.

Slim leaned against the wall watching him. "Well, Nick, welcome to the past. You are in Silverado—in 1866."

"I can't believe it," said Nick.

"Believe it," said Slim. "We're over on the other side of Eagle Cliff Mountain. We'll need to head down the mountain before it gets dark. Then we'll have to cut through the back side of town to get to my ranch; I don't want anyone to see you yet."

Nick and Slim crawled out of the cave opening just as the sun was beginning to set. They were standing on a hard-packed dirt trail. Nick glimpsed the town below, nestled in the valley. It looked like the same old Silverado—except now the town looked fresh and very much alive with people.

By the time they followed the path to the bottom of the mountain, it was dark. As they entered the town, Slim kept Nick in the shadows behind the buildings. Slowly, they moved toward the town's main entrance.

"My ranch isn't far from the entrance, but we'll still need to go on horseback. The guys should already be here waiting for us behind the saloon," said Slim.

"Your friends?" asked Nick.

"That's right. Keenan delivered all the food while we were in the cave. Michael and Christopher are the other two," Slim explained. "I think that's them up ahead. Stay here and wait for me until I make sure."

Nick crouched down behind a barrel next to the saloon. He heard loud music, women laughing, an occasional argument, and the sounds of someone being thrown out onto the street.

Slim walked out into the dark and approached the three cowboys, who stood by five horses. Two of the men were tall, while one was slightly shorter and stocky. He looked like someone you didn't want to mess with. There was a lot of shoulder slapping as Slim greeted them. After talking for a few minutes, they glanced around carefully. Slim looked Nick's way and motioned for him to come over.

Nick stood up and ran over. The guys quickly surrounded him so no one would see him.

"Nick, I'd like you to meet Keenan, Michael, and Christopher," said Slim. Each cowboy reached forward and shook Nick's hand. Keenan was the tallest, followed by Michael, and Christopher was the stocky, muscular cowboy.

"Nice to have you as a part of our team," said Christopher.

"Slim has said some great things about you. You'll fit right in," said Michael.

Keenan smiled. "I've been keeping an eye on you lately, Nick. You're just what we need."

"Well, boys, let's get to the ranch. We have a lot of planning to do. We need to get out of here before anyone recognizes us," said Slim.

Michael pulled something from one of the saddlebags. "Here, Nick, put this on," he said, tossing the bundle to Nick.

Nick quickly donned a poncho and cowboy hat as each of the guys climbed on their horses. Slim helped Nick onto a horse before hoisting himself onto his own.

"It's a short ride, Nick, so just hang on," said Slim. "Let's ride, guys." Slim flicked the reins and took off. The horse's hooves created a cloud of dust as they took off into the darkness. At that same moment, a man swaggered unnoticed out of the back of the saloon for a smoke. He was a big, burly man and kept to the shadows. He reached to light his cigar off a hanging lantern and noticed the five horses riding out of town at a gallop. He inhaled deeply and slowly blew out a long, thin line of smoke. He reached down and pulled his pocket watch from his vest to check the time. A gold chain from his watch swung gently back and forth. "More visitors!" he mumbled in disgust. He watched as the last horse disappeared from sight, taking another drag on his cigar. Blowing out a last line of smoke, he snuffed out his cigar on the ground with his boot and turned back to the saloon.

Chapter Eight

THE PLAN

The ride out to Slim's ranch took about fifteen minutes.

The modest ranch consisted of a main house, a stable for the horses, two barns, and another small building. They rode right up to the front porch. Slim dismounted, and then turned to help Nick down as the others hopped off their horses.

Keenan spoke first. "It's really dark in there, Slim. Where's the real you right now?"

"My real self is in Cartersville rustling up some supplies and doing some research," replied Slim.

"So how long do we have in the house before you return?" asked Christopher.

"I've got about one more week in Cartersville. When I get back, we'll have to move out of the house and into the workshop. I never got a chance to work on my projects after I got back from Cartersville anyway, and we've got permission to set up some protection so that we won't be noticed," said Slim.

Michael stepped forward and grabbed all the horses' reins. "Go on in and get everyone settled, Slim. Christopher and I will put the horses in the stable."

"Where'd you get the horses, anyway?" asked Slim.

"Borrowed 'em from Black Feather, an old friend of mine from the local tribe," replied Christopher over his shoulder as he headed toward the stables.

"Well, they sure are nice specimens," replied Slim. "Keenan, let's go in and fix some dinner."

Slim opened the door and stepped inside the dark ranch house with Keenan and Nick.

"Stay there, guys. I don't want you to trip over anything," said Slim as he walked farther into the room. He struck a match and lifted the glass globe of an oil lamp. He lit the wick and a warm, friendly light illuminated the room.

"Come on in, fellas," Slim said. He then turned his attention to the fireplace and set to work building a cozy blaze.

The main house was a large log cabin. The wooden furniture was simple and sturdy. A thick wool rug covered most of the floor in the spacious main room. A big ten-point buck's head hung above the mantel, looking down on the room. To the right of the fireplace was a hallway. To the left of the fireplace was a door that led to the kitchen and the dining room. Once he had the fire going, Slim retreated in that direction.

Keenan followed Slim into the kitchen to help him with dinner. Nick walked over to a rocker next to the fireplace and sat down. Comforted by the warmth, he let himself relax and enjoy the flames as they danced on the logs.

Keenan came out of the kitchen and walked down the right-hand corridor. By the light of the fireplace, Nick got his first good look at him.

Keenan was thin and muscular. He was a tall man, just a few inches shorter than Slim. He had unruly, reddish-brown hair, and his green eyes and mischievous grin made Nick think he must be the jokester of the group.

The front door opened as Michael and Christopher entered, carrying their gear. Michael settled everything on the floor in the corner, and then sauntered into the kitchen. He was almost the same height as Keenan and the best-looking guy among Slim's friends. He had a neatly trimmed mustache and goatee, and his light brown hair was immaculately groomed.

Christopher followed Michael, turning before he went through the door to wink at Nick. His friendly blue eyes belied his stocky, muscular frame, which made him seem all business.

Nick continued to watch the jumping flames in the fireplace. He felt the exhaustion of the day slip over him. He knew he could fall asleep at any moment, but the sound of Slim's voice jolted him just as he was nodding off.

"Nick! Dinner's on," Slim called.

Nick got up, rubbed his eyes, stretched, and then entered the kitchen. He walked over to where the guys were finishing setting up a small kitchen table.

Everyone sat down at the table. Slim offered a prayer of thanks for a safe journey and the food. Nick inhaled the aromas of roasted chicken, potatoes, and rolls. The spirit cowboys ate like any normal person and drank black coffee—a lot of it. When dinner was done, Keenan cleared away the dishes. Slim refilled coffee mugs, then poured Nick a cup of the best hot chocolate he had ever tasted.

"Slim, how long do we have at this point?" asked Michael.

"We're several weeks away from the murder," replied Slim.

Talking a long gulp of coffee first, Keenan asked, "So what's the plan?"

"A lot is going to depend on what we can discover at this point. I can't be seen in town at all because the real me is in Cartersville. So the first thing we need to do is get Nick placed in a job in town. That way he can meet all the townspeople," said Slim.

"Hey, do you think Otis Walkins would take him on as an errand boy at the Falcon Mine?" asked Keenan.

"I already have a plan. Let's set Nick up in a job as an errand boy with Mr. Guillot at the general store. Nick will have access to almost all of the key people through the general store—everyone has to go there at some point. And the best part is that he'll get to make deliveries to both mine companies, too."

"But doesn't Mr. Guillot already have a delivery boy?" asked Keenan.

"Yeah. What are you planning to do with Ben?" asked Christopher in a concerned tone.

"Oh, nothing bad," Slim reassured them. "We're going to make Ben an offer that will allow him to take a vacation for a couple of weeks. Then he'll train Nick as his replacement at the general store."

"That's a great idea," said Keenan.

"I happen to know that Ben has been saving for a horse," explained Slim. "I think he would go for our idea if we offered to help him buy it. That would give him the transportation he needs to take a vacation."

The cowboys considered this plan for several moments. Then Slim spoke. "I think we have a place to start. Are we all in agreement?"

"Yes," the cowboys answered in unison.

Keenan spoke up. "I'll head into town first thing tomorrow morning and have a chat with Ben to see if I can get him interested. I'll take Nick with me, because Ben will probably want to talk to him, too."

"Okay, let's start there and see how far we get with this idea," responded Slim. "We're going to have to keep a close eye on Nick, so try to keep a low profile."

"How come?" Nick asked.

"Nick, although we're spirits, you can see us as real men. That means that everyone else can see us, too. This wouldn't necessarily be a big problem, because Michael, Christopher, and Keenan actually live in Cartersville. They could be seen in town without alarming anyone. But there are also evil spirits running all over town. We don't want them to know that we're here. If they find out we're up to something, they could cause us a lot of problems.

"Also, when my real self returns to town, I'll have to be very careful not to come face to face with myself. That's the sort of experience that could drive a person insane. Right now, we have more than enough problems to contend with without me driving myself—my real self—insane.

"So to be safe, we'll only appear at night. During the day, most of the time, we'll have to stay invisible to hide from the imps. You'll be able to hear us, Nick, but you won't be able to see us unless it's safe and we want you to," Michael added.

"Invisible, huh?" said Nick. "But what about Keenan and me going into town to talk to Ben tomorrow?" asked Nick.

"Keenan should be okay for the next couple of days because there won't be much activity yet. But the closer we come to Otis's murder, the more imps will appear," Michael said.

"Say, what if Nick is questioned about where he is staying? What do you what him to say?" asked Michael.

"Already thought of that. If anyone asks you, Nick, just say that you have a room at the hotel. I registered you there before I came to get you. If they ask if you have a guardian, tell them yes. Don't get specific; just tell them a couple of your mother's friends are checking on you," explained Slim.

Nick found himself stifling a yawn. A wave of weariness and fatigue, held at bay by the excitement of developing a plan of action, flooded over him. "Okay, guys, let's wrap this up for the evening," Slim said. "There's more we have to brief you on later, Nick, but by the look of you, it's time for you to get some sleep."

"Slim's right, the last couple of days have been quite an adventure." Keenan chuckled.

"How long was I in that cave, Slim?" asked Nick.

"Two days. The first day you were out cold—you took quite a nasty bump on the head during that cave-in," Slim said.

"I wonder if my dad has even noticed I'm gone." Nick hoped he didn't sound like he was sulking.

"I'm sure he has," Slim assured him. "But if you really want to know, we can find that out for you. Christopher, why don't you show Nick where his room is, and you take the spare bedroom."

"Sure thing, Slim. Come on, Nick, let's go," said Christopher.

"The sheets are clean, and I threw a nightshirt out for you," said Keenan.

Nick pushed back his chair, stood, and stretched. "Thanks for dinner and . . . for everything. See you in the morning."

"Good night," Slim, Michael, and Keenan said in unison.

Nick left the kitchen following Christopher.

"I like him," said Keenan decisively. "I think he's going to be more help than any of us could have hoped for."

"Laura was right; he is a great kid. An extraordinary kid," said Slim. "Michael, do me a favor; go back and see where Nick's dad is right now. Unless they have discovered the cave-in, they may think Nick has run away. We may need to help change his ideas a little. Take this hat—Nick was wearing it when I found him. Put it at the entrance of the cave-in, and then find a way to encourage one of Mr. Stewart's students to walk up that way and find it."

"They sure do wear some strange hats a hundred-odd years from now," mused Michael. Turning Nick's hat around in his hands several times, he shook his head, then stood and stuffed Nick's baseball cap into his jeans' pocket. "I'll be back soon," he said, then slowly began to fade away, disappearing into thin air.

Slim rose and walked to the sink to wash the dishes, while Keenan cleaned up the kitchen.

"I'm done, Slim, so I'm off to bed, too." Keenan yawned, after scrubbing the table and stove. "See you in the morning."

Slim stopped to stoke the fire in the main room, while Keenan headed down the corridor to bed. Then Slim quietly slipped into Nick's bedroom and stood watching over him for a moment as he slept. His hair had fallen back from his forehead, exposing a large black-and-blue bruise on his forehead.

Slim reached out and touched it lightly. Nick's face flinched slightly in his sleep, and Slim withdrew his hand.

"I'll do everything I can to help him," Slim whispered to the darkness. "Sleep real well, Nick. You're going to need it."

He turned and left the room, closing the door gently behind him. Back in the family room, he sat down in the rocking chair and stared at the flames as the logs crackled and popped.

Slim took a deep breath and blew it out slowly. "A lot is riding on our success with this one," he sighed.

Chapter Nine

NICK THE COWBOY

Many hours later, Michael reappeared in Slim's kitchen. It was dark and very quiet. He walked to the icebox to pour himself a glass of milk. Feeling tired and disturbed, he leaned against the icebox. He sighed deeply as he threw his head back and gulped down the milk.

As he wandered into the living room, Michael took off his cowboy hat and ran his fingers through his hair. The fire had almost gone out in the big fireplace. All that remained were a few red, glowing embers. Slim was sound asleep in the rocking chair. Michael stifled a yawn and walked over to him, giving his shoulder a gentle shake.

"What? . . . Huh?" sputtered Slim. "Oh, Michael, you're back. I must have dozed off."

"I'll say you did. You were snoring real loud." Michael sat down on the hearth, across from Slim.

"How was your trip? Any problems?" asked Slim.

"Well, it's just like you thought. Mr. Stewart has assumed that Nick ran away. He didn't even know he was gone until the police showed up to ask Nick a few more questions about the journal incident. Mr. Stewart and his students were just closing up the dig site in the late afternoon when they finally noticed Nick was missing."

"So how do things stand now?" asked Slim.

"Mr. Stewart is angry. The police have listed Nick as a runaway. They're putting up flyers with his picture on them—posting them on poles throughout town," Michael replied.

"What did you do with the hat?" asked Slim.

"Nothing yet. I decided that it wasn't necessarily a bad idea for Nick to be listed as a runaway right now. This situation might buy us some time while Nick is here with us. If they think he ran away and then later find out he was trapped in the cave-in, maybe they won't be so hard on Nick when he goes home. And with the fancy equipment they have, it will take them very little time to get through the rubble from the cave-in."

"I think you're right. We don't want them to focus on the cave just yet."

"How about this, then," Michael suggested. "When we get closer to your hanging, I can set the wheels in motion for them to refocus their search on the cave."

"Sounds good to me. But I'm still not sure what to do about Nick's dad right now. To be honest, I'm not too happy with him at the moment."

"Maybe you need to think about things a little differently. Grief affects people in many different ways. Mr. Stewart finds relief in his work. He doesn't know how to handle Nick's feelings of grief, let alone his current problems. So he's been shutting down, with the hope that Nick will somehow figure it out on his own. Both of them are hurting, so why don't we just keep an eye on them for the moment? Give them a little time and space."

Looking over his spectacles at Michael, Slim nodded. "It's late and you look tired, Michael. Why don't you hit the sack? All the beds are full, do you mind bunking in with Keenan? There is a bedroll below the window. There should be enough room on the floor to roll it out."

"That's fine, just as long as Keenan doesn't step on me when he gets up," said Michael.

Slim chuckled softly. "I can't think any more tonight. I'm going to bed too. By the way, don't tell Nick about any of this. He has enough to deal with right now. He doesn't need this distraction."

"My lips are sealed. See you in the morning, Slim."

"Good night, Michael. Thanks again."

"No problem." Michael yawned and strolled down the hallway, disappearing into his room.

Slim rose and checked the fire to make sure it was out before he headed off to bed. Shutting the bedroom door behind him, he walked over to his bed and pulled back the covers. He threw his cowboy hat on the chair, pulled off his boots, and removed his clothes all the way down to his long red underwear. Then he climbed into bed, pulling the blankets up to his chin. It was dark and quiet only for a moment. Then Slim began to snore softly.

The warm sun climbed slowly in the eastern sky, over the mountain. Christopher and Keenan were the first to stir. They both dragged themselves into the kitchen at exactly the same time.

"Ouch! That was my foot you just stepped on," Keenan howled.

"Sorry, buddy," said Christopher.

Keenan jumped around like a jackrabbit, holding his foot. Through clenched teeth, he asked, "Why in the world do you have your boots on this early in the morning?"

Christopher shrugged. "I didn't even think about it. I'm just so used to wearing them."

Keenan sat down on a nearby chair to rub his foot. "Do you wear them to bed, too?"

"Sometimes," said Christopher, grinning. "Hey, I'll make it up to you and get the coffee started."

"Now, wait a minute. The last time you made the coffee I had to remake it," Keenan said. He limped over to the stove. "It was so thick, my spoon could stand up on its own in the middle of my mug."

Neither of them noticed that Nick stood in the doorway listening to their banter.

Christopher looked over and saw him first. "Morning, Nick. How did you sleep?"

Touching the bruise on his forehead gingerly, Nick said, "Pretty good. My head's a little sore, but I can think straight again." He looked at them in amusement. "Why are you limping, Keenan?"

Keenan sighed. "Just look at my poor feet. Now take a good look at Christopher's. Boots!" he complained. "One of those big booted feet stomped on my poor socked foot."

Christopher started to laugh. "You'd think someone took his foot off, the way he was jumping around here and hollering. It was quite a sight."

Nick laughed at both of them.

"Well, what can I say?" said Keenan. "I'm graceful on my feet. I used to be one of the best dancers in town."

"Yeah, if someone else was doing the leading," Christopher taunted him.

"Now, that was only because Annabelle didn't know how to follow. She spent so much time having to lead when she was teaching dance classes that it was hard for her to remember," Keenan argued.

"Sure was funny though."

"Okay, okay, enough, big boy. Here's your coffee. Now, Nick, can I fix you a mug of my famous hot chocolate?" Keenan asked.

Nick nodded decisively. "Yes, sir. Please! Where did you learn to make hot chocolate?"

"You can buy chocolate by the pound at the general store in town. I learned the recipe for hot chocolate from a little Chinese man I met when I lived in Cartersville. Chocolate is expensive, so it's a treat when we can get it," said

Keenan as he headed to the stove. "Do you guys feel like some muffins for breakfast?"

"Sounds good to me," said Christopher.

"Yum," said Nick.

"Say, where are Slim and Michael?" asked Christopher. "Slim is always up before us."

"I bet Slim was working late. You know how he gets when he's on an assignment," said Keenan.

"Is Slim afraid we won't solve the mystery?" Nick asked.

"He's mostly worried about his family," Christopher said. "The stigma of having a notorious murderer as a family member led others to assume that they were all bad seeds. Townspeople mistrusted and ostracized the entire family.

"Some of Slim's kin couldn't get work, let alone receive fair treatment. So they had to steal just to survive. Other Maranos went bad because they chose to embrace their false heritage. It became a vicious cycle, and it never should have happened that way."

Keenan turned from putting the muffins in the oven and gave Nick a serious look. "Listen, you're going out on a limb for us, Nick. This is very dangerous work, and rest assured one of us will always try to be with you to watch your back. But I need to emphasize to you that this is a dangerous and possibly deadly assignment, so do keep your eyes open. The one good thing is that you're just a boy. That is your best cover. Most of the adults won't pay you any mind, and we're counting on the real culprit to do the same."

Keenan brought Nick's hot chocolate to the table and sat down beside him. "It's important to remember," he said, "that this is a very real world. Please be careful. We are dealing with unscrupulous people who have no sense of right and wrong."

Nick sipped his hot chocolate slowly, trying to absorb everything Keenan and Christopher were saying. Part of him wanted to panic and run. But the more he listened and thought about it, the more curious he was. He felt just like he was in an action movie, and his assignment was to infiltrate the bad guy's camp and collect intelligence. It felt pretty good to be needed, he decided.

Setting down his empty mug, Nick looked back at the two cowboys. "I can do this. I'm not afraid. I promise to be careful and do my best."

Keenan smiled broadly. "I think we got blessed with the right kid," he said, standing up. He reached over to tousle Nick's hair before heading back to the stove to check on the muffins.

Christopher sighed deeply. "We thought you might decide not to help us. We're awful glad you're on our team."

"I'm glad to be part of your team, too," said Nick. "Say, Keenan, could I have another cup of hot chocolate?"

"You betcha, kiddo."

Keenan popped open the door of the cast-iron stove. The strong aroma of fresh-baked corn muffins saturated the air in the kitchen and then traveled through the house.

"If this doesn't wake up those guys, nothing will," Keenan said, setting the tray down in front of Nick and Christopher. "Here you go, guys. Get 'em while they're hot. That's when they're the best."

They had just dug into their muffins when Slim's tall, sleepy figure appeared in the doorway.

"Okay, Keenan. You have my full attention. With the amount of noise you guys are making, you'd wake the neighbors—if I had any." Slim chuckled. "But first things first. I need a cup of fresh coffee."

"Coming right up." Keenan got up from the table and headed over to the stove to grab the coffee and a mug. Slim made his way to the kitchen table and sat down beside Nick.

"What time did you end up going to bed last night?" asked Christopher.

"It was sometime this morning, actually," said Slim as Keenan set a mug of hot coffee and a couple of muffins in front of him.

"Michael was up most of the night running an errand for me. I waited for his return. But let him sleep a little longer. He only got back a few hours ago," Slim explained.

"So what are we doing this morning?" asked Nick.

"You and I are heading to town to see if we can talk Ben into taking a vacation," Keenan answered. "He can use you as his replacement at the general store, if we help him get the horse he wants. As soon as you're done eating, go get cleaned up and we'll take off."

Slim looked at Nick. "There are some clothes in the chest in your room. You can't go around in your own clothes—you'd draw too much attention. This way you'll look like all of the other boys."

"Okay," replied Nick, feeling his excitement growing. Getting up from the table, he dashed out of the kitchen and through the living room back to his room.

Nick entered the bedroom and threw open the chest. There were several shirts, button-fly jeans, two sets of cowboy boots, and a dark brown cowboy hat. Nick threw off the nightshirt he had worn, picked out several items from the chest, and got dressed. He found putting on the cowboy boots a little more difficult than he'd expected. It took some muscle getting his foot to slide down the shaft of the boot and then into the pointed toe. Once he got them on, he walked around the room getting a feel for them. They were much heavier than his tennis shoes, but they also made him look taller. Nick didn't mind that at all.

He pulled a belt on, then grabbed the cowboy hat and closed the chest. He glanced at his reflection in the window and placed the cowboy hat on his head, turning from side to side to get a good look at himself. He hardly recognized the image in the glass. He looked like an ordinary ranch kid from 1866.

Nick placed his tennis shoes and the clothes he had worn, along with his camera and flashlight, in his backpack. After slipping the backpack under his bed for safekeeping, he headed back to the kitchen, where he could hear Keenan, Christopher, and Slim chatting. When Nick stepped through the doorway, everyone stopped talking.

"Wow!" said Keenan.

"Say there, Nick, you look like a real cowboy!" Christopher exclaimed. "Well, Slim, what do you think?"

"You'll blend in with the townspeople real well, Nick," said Slim in a subdued tone.

"Well, guys," said Keenan, "Nick and I need to be heading into town. We'll take Ben to lunch and have a talk with him. Nick, if you're ready, why don't you head out to the barn. Take some sugar cubes with you. I just have to get my boots on, and then we'll be off."

A huge smile came over Nick's face. He loved horses. Slim pushed a small container toward him. Nick lifted the lid and pulled out several sugar cubes.

"Head through that door," Slim said, pointing to a small door on the back wall of the kitchen. "The stable's the first building across the yard."

"Okay," Nick replied, "I'll see you guys later."

"Have fun, but keep your eyes open," Christopher reminded him.

"I won't forget," Nick answered. He bounded out the back door to the barn.

"Well, guys, I have to get my stuff together. I'll see you later," said Keenan.

"Be careful. We don't want to draw any attention to ourselves at this point," warned Slim.

"Hey, Slim, what were you thinking when you saw Nick dressed in the clothes we got for him? You were real quiet," Christopher said.

Slim sighed deeply. "It was like I was here for real, back when my children were young. Nick looked so much like my own sons did when they were that age."

Chapter Ten

THE TOWN OF SILVERADO

Silverado Town

Est. 1830

Out in the barn, Keenan and Nick saddled up two horses and rode toward town. Nick's horse was named Rusty. He was a beautiful brown stallion with black spots on his hindquarters. Thanks to the Thomas family, Nick had learned to ride over the summer. It was a bright and cool morning. The sun was still rising slowly in the soft blue sky, but it promised to be a hot day later on.

Slim's ranch was hidden among the trees at the base of a large mountain. The ride to the main road was short once they made it over a small hill. Keenan and Nick stopped at the crest of the hill for a moment so Nick could get a better idea of the lay of the land. Nick could see the town in the distance. The road was full of coaches, wagons, and riders making their way in and out of Silverado.

"See, Nick," said Keenan, "Silverado is situated in a valley. Over there," he pointed to the left, "just past the town is the mountain you and Slim traveled down. The mountain to the far right of the town is where the Falcon Mine is, and that rise just beyond Falcon Mountain is the site of the Black Stallion Mine. There are roads branching out in every direction. But stay on the main roads and it will be easier to get around."

Nick's eyes followed Keenan's finger as he pointed out all the different places he was referring to. He wanted to make sure he didn't get lost.

"Wow," whispered Nick. "The town is much busier now than in my time."

Keenan chuckled. "You're seeing it in its early days, Nick. There's a lot of money in the town now, but the construction is slow because most of the men are in the mines digging for gold and silver. That'll change soon, because a wealthy construction company will move in and build Silverado up even more."

Nick heard Keenan's voice change slightly. He shifted in his saddle to look directly at him as he spoke.

"Word sometime travels slowly here. We didn't find out about Slim being arrested until the trial was already under way. We made it to town just in time to watch him get sentenced and then hanged. The sheriff, who is a friend of ours, filled us in on everything that had happened. We knew Slim was innocent, so we stayed in Silverado at Slim's ranch and began our own little investigation into Walkins's death. We were unaware at that time that Slim had transferred the Falcon Mine to us prior to his arrest. If we had known, we wouldn't have gone to work for Billings. I often wonder if the reason he hired us was because he had found out that we were the new owners of the Falcon Mine. He was overseeing the operations of both mines by then. We ended up working in both mines at different times, as needed."

"Were you able to find out anything while you were working?" asked Nick.

"Yes . . . a few tidbits. There was a lot going on inside and outside both mines. It was hard to keep track of it all, though. Some of the miners talked and they said that Slim's hanging was a setup. They also told us that a few groups of miners had been reassigned to a deeper section of the Falcon Mine. That particular section was guarded, and the only men who were allowed in the area were those who had been handpicked by Mr. Billings. Believe me, those guys were not talking. Rumor had it that Mr. Billings had found a large gold or silver deposit and didn't want to share the find with his shareholders. That way he could bypass the books and keep the profits for himself."

Nick's thoughts went back to the waterfall and the small leather pouch he'd put in his pocket. *Could it be that they found something other than gold or silver?* he wondered. *The strange rock in the pouch—Slim said it could be a diamond. If it was a diamond, they'd really want to keep it quiet.*

Nick looked into Keenan's eyes. "Keenan, I don't think it was gold or silver that they were trying to hide. I think it might have been something else."

"Like what?" asked Keenan.

"I'm not too sure. But while I was in the cave, I found this small pouch in the pool by the waterfall. Slim said that the pouch came from one of the mines, but the stamp was worn off. It held some coins, a gold nugget, and a clear, sparkling crystal. Slim wasn't sure, but he thought that the crystal could be a diamond."

Keenan whistled softly through his teeth. "If Slim is right, and that stone is a diamond, that might be what Billings was guarding so carefully. We'll talk to Slim about this later, but we are going to have to have the stone checked out by our friend Lucas Marley. He would know what it is. If it really is a diamond, Billings might have killed to keep things quiet. Don't let anyone here know that we even have an idea about this."

He urged his horse forward and Nick followed suit. They started down the crest of the hill toward the bustling road. "It will be lunchtime soon and we need to try and find Ben before he takes off."

Nick pushed his horse forward to keep up with Keenan. He was excited. He was back in the real 1866, stepping into a real mystery. He couldn't help but ponder all the clues they had collected so far.

Keenan's voice broke into Nick's whirling thoughts. "Goodness, Nick, you sure know a lot more about this case than we expected," he said.

Nick felt himself sit up a little straighter in his saddle with a swell of pride.

They rode down the main road into town among the traffic of people and horses. Nick glanced around and recognized the main buildings of the town from his recent field trip.

"The town doesn't look too much different than it did when I was on the tour. Only it's nicer and there are a lot more people," Nick said.

"Yes, it should be just about the same. There are a few differences, but you'll pick up on those. Let's head over to the store and see if we can find Ben."

They stopped at the hitching post in front of the general store, dismounted, and tied up their horses. They had just stepped up on the boardwalk when a dark-haired young man exited the store and began to make his way down the street.

"That's Ben," whispered Keenan. "He must be heading out for lunch." Keenan cupped his hands around his mouth and hollered, "Hey, Ben!"

The boy stopped and turned around. He scanned the crowd until he saw Keenan waving at him.

"Do I know you, sir?" asked Ben as Keenan and Nick approached.

"Yes and no, Ben. I'm a friend of Slim Marano. This is Nick Stewart, a friend of ours. Slim mentioned that you were interested in buying a horse," Keenan said.

"Ah, Slim is checking up on me. By the way, where is he?" asked Ben.

"He's in Cartersville picking up some supplies and doing some research for the Falcon Mine," replied Keenan.

"Well, you can tell Slim I'm closer than the last time I talked to him. I'm about a month away from buying my horse. That is, if the owner doesn't decide to sell him before then. I stop and talk to him every day before work to remind him I'm close, but I don't think he cares either way," Ben said with a sigh.

"I'll tell you what, Ben, I think I might be able to help you. How would you like to buy that horse today? Are you available for lunch? We can't discuss this on an empty stomach."

"That's one way of getting my full attention. I was just heading to the bakery. Let's all grab a bite there," Ben replied eagerly.

Keenan, Nick, and Ben found a private table at the bakery and sat down. Nick listened quietly while he ate. He was highly entertained by Keenan's skillful salesmanship.

"So let me make sure that I understand this," said Ben finally. "You and Slim are willing to buy Mr. Green's horse for me. In exchange, I'm going to take a vacation for a couple of weeks and introduce Nick to Mr. Guillot as my replacement?"

"That's right," said Keenan.

"Sounds like something funny might be going on around here," said Ben, with a skeptical look at Keenan and Nick.

"Nothing that you would find very interesting," said Keenan. "We just need to keep Nick here busy for the next several weeks. Something happened in Nick's hometown, so things need to settle down a bit before he returns."

Ben glanced over at Nick and winked. Nodding his head knowingly, he said, "Oh, I understand."

By the time lunch was over, Ben had agreed to let Nick have his job at the general store for several weeks in exchange for the purchase of the horse. Ben assured Nick that he would work with him for a couple of days before he left, to make sure that he had the entire delivery route down.

Ben asked Keenan to bring Nick by the store an hour before closing so he could meet the owner, Mr. Guillot. After closing time, Ben would take Nick and Keenan to the stable so that they could keep their end of the bargain and buy the horse for him.

Keenan and Ben shook hands and sealed the deal. Ben left to return to work, and Keenan decided to give Nick a tour of the town.

They started down the street and came to the Land Claims and Patent Office. Nick could tell by the voices he heard that there was a lot of activity

inside. Keenan stopped and glanced through the window. He smiled broadly. "I thought this would be interesting for you," he said. "Mr. Billings, the
owner of the Black Stallion Mine, is in there with Mr. Jenkins, his biggest
investor. Want to get a look?"

Nick nodded. He quietly opened the door and stepped inside. There were
two arguments going on in the lobby. A tall, lanky man with his back toward
Nick was yelling at the teller behind the protective bars. His fist slammed
repeatedly down on the counter.

"I'm telling you that I got that piece from the main river bed in the same
place where the man ahead of me got his. Now you're telling me that his is
real and mine is fake?" the prospector fumed.

"I'm sorry, sir, but what you have here is not gold. It's pyrite, commonly
known as fool's gold, sir."

The prospector threw the piece of pyrite across the room and strode out
of the office angrily, slamming the door behind him.

The second argument was not as dramatic or as loud. It involved two
gentlemen standing apart from the crowd in the far corner of the lobby.
One was a large, burly man who stood with his back toward Nick, partially
blocking a smaller man dressed in a gentleman's suit. Nick moved quietly to
a table against the wall so he would be closer to the two men.

The larger man spoke in low, harsh tones. "I'm asking you one more time,
Angus, don't do this, please. The Black Stallion Mine will turn a profit, I can
assure you. This is just a small setback."

"Pernell," replied Angus Jenkins, "although I appreciate your positive
thinking and enthusiasm concerning the Black Stallion Mine, I'm still not
happy with the weekly numbers. Frankly, I'm not happy with your management, either. The reckless way you continue to forge ahead, digging
more and more tunnels with no concern for the safety of your men, is
hardly comforting.

"These little accidents that have been happening are warnings, Pernell.
More will follow if you don't change your ways. You have been lucky so far,

but we all fear that one of these days your men will not be so fortunate and someone will be killed," said Mr. Jenkins.

Mr. Billings did not respond.

Nick noticed a short shadow dancing along the wall nearby. It moved constantly in no apparent pattern. Nick looked around the room but couldn't figure out whose shadow it was. It almost seemed to have a mind of its own. Suddenly, the shadow pulled away from the wall and began to circle Mr. Billings and Mr. Jenkins, but neither man seemed to notice. Nick tried to hide his shock. The shadow was vaguely human in shape, with arms and legs, but it was small, almost child-sized, and it seemed to have pointed ears. Except for white empty slits where Nick expected eyes to be, it had no distinguishable facial features. He kept one eye on the shadow's movements as he tried to concentrate on the conversation. Nick started to write on a piece of paper that was lying on the table. *Something really strange is going on here,* he thought.

"Call me a weak man if you wish, Pernell," continued Mr. Jenkins, "but I will not change my mind. I am going to move the majority of my investments over to the Falcon Mine Company. Now if you will excuse me, I have some paperwork to complete." With a brief touch of his finger to his hat, Mr. Jenkins turned and walked to the teller's window.

Mr. Billings was standing very still, but the strange shadow was circling him repeatedly. Suddenly, it stopped directly behind Mr. Billings and assumed his stance. Then, with a simple step forward, it disappeared into Mr. Billings's body. Mr. Billings shuddered, then turned to watch Mr. Jenkins's retreating figure.

Mr. Billings's face was red and his brows were knitted together in fury. He towered high above Nick. Nick got a good look at his face, then turned and resumed writing, hoping not to be noticed. Billings's eyes were fixed vacantly on Mr. Jenkins's back.

Finally, Billings began to move forward. Reaching the front door with just a few long strides, he grabbed the handle and turned his head back toward Mr. Jenkins one more time. Through gritted teeth, he growled, "Mark my words, Angus, you will regret this decision. I guarantee it!" He sneered as he walked out, slamming the door behind him.

Mr. Jenkins turned and stared at the closed door. He shook his head, then turned back to the teller to complete his business.

Nick took a deep breath and let it out slowly. Glancing around the room, he noticed that other people had also witnessed this dramatic scene. They quickly resumed their business.

Nick tapped his pencil on the piece of paper. He had written down almost everything that he had heard.

It's a beginning at least, he thought, remembering Freas's story about how the investors of the Black Stallion Mine had switched their allegiances to the Falcon Mine.

Heading outside, he looked around, searching for Keenan.

But Keenan was nowhere to be found. *He must have headed over to the general store,* thought Nick. He started to walk back toward the store and then paused when he heard music. Looking across the street, he saw one of the saloons. It took a minute for Nick to realize it was the Fool's Gold Saloon, the same saloon Freas had taken his group into during his tour.

I wonder how it looks now. I bet it's okay if I take a quick peek, he thought.

Nick dashed across the street, dodging horses and carriages. Stepping up to the swinging saloon doors, he tried to catch glimpses of the interior each time a cowboy went in or came out. He heard loud music and the clinking of glasses. There were so many voices talking at once that it sounded like a low roar just beneath the sound of the music. Every few minutes, the piercing sound of a woman's high-pitched laugh rose above all the hubbub.

Suddenly a coach pulled up in front of the saloon. Nick coughed as the dust the carriage stirred up billowed around him. He wiped his eyes and looked up as the door of the coach opened.

At first, all Nick saw was a fancy shoe on the end of a shapely leg stepping down onto the carriage step. Raising his eyes upward, Nick gazed in fascination at the beautiful blond woman in a shimmering green silk dress stepping out of the coach. She was very curvaceous and the dress she wore only emphasized her figure. Her hair was swept up and pinned in place by a small green hat decked with several large feathers. She stood on the boardwalk and shook her skirts lightly. Then she looked at Nick and smiled.

"Hello. My name is Teresa Treadway. And who might you be?" she asked.

"Nick, ma'am. I'm pleased to meet you," he said. He quickly removed his hat and gave a short bow.

"Nick, you're more of a gentleman than most of the men I know," she replied, laughing softly. "Could I trouble you to help me move some things into my shop just across the street?" she asked.

"I would be happy to, Miss Treadway," said Nick.

"Thank you so much. And please, call me Terri," she added. "I just need to step in to the saloon for a moment and speak to a friend of mine."

The coachman stepped up beside her. "Ma'am," he said. "I would not recommend you go into the saloon unescorted." Taking a slight bow, he smiled and stuck out his arm to escort her.

Ignoring his outstretched arm, she said, "You're very kind, but I have an escort already." Turning to Nick, she rested her hand on his arm. "Why don't we unload my supplies first? There is my shop," she said, waving her hand toward an ornate glass and wood door across the street. "After we're done here, could I also trouble you to escort me into the saloon?" she asked Nick.

Nick could feel his cheeks grow warm. "Yes, ma'am," he answered enthusiastically. He went to the back of the coach and Miss Terri followed. He lifted two boxes that had been unloaded, she picked up a bag, and they crossed the street. Miss Terri unlocked the door to her shop, allowing Nick to enter first. Nick set the boxes down on one of the countertops. Miss Terri laid down her bag and took off her hat. Nick glanced around and realized that the shop was empty.

"Uhm . . . Miss Terri, is this a new shop, or have you been robbed?"

Miss Terri laughed a sweet, tinkling laugh. "Yes, it's new. I've just arrived in town to open the business. My friend, Mrs. Corrine Hall, has been helping me get established. She is the friend I need to see in the saloon."

Hearing a noise, Nick turned around to see the coachman, as well as several other cowboys, entering the shop laden with additional boxes. They approached the counter and placed their boxes beside Nick's.

"I believe that's all, ma'am," said the coachman.

Miss Terri reached for her handbag, removing several coins and handing them out to the coachman and the three men who had helped. "Thank you, gentlemen," she said.

"You're very welcome, ma'am," they responded, tipping their hats and bowing slightly.

The coachman again walked toward her, wringing his hat in front of him. "Ma'am, if you're planning on going back over to the saloon," he said, "I would feel much better if you would allow me to escort you."

"Thank you for your offer. I do appreciate it. But as I said before, I already have an escort," she replied, smiling at Nick.

Nick glanced up and could tell by the glare he got from the coachman that he was not very popular right about now. Nevertheless, the man bowed politely.

"Very well, ma'am," he said stiffly. He raised his right hand to touch his forehead in a salute, then turned on his heel and followed the others out of the shop.

Miss Terri sighed as she watched him leave. "He has been showing inappropriate interest in me since we left Boston." Looking at Nick she said, "You were a welcome sight when we pulled up outside of the saloon. Come, let's head back over to the saloon. I need to find my friend, and the least I can do is buy you a lemonade."

"You really don't have to, Miss Terri," said Nick.

"Nonsense, I insist," she said. She took his arm and walked him out of the shop.

Chapter Eleven

THE FOOL'S GOLD SALOON

"Miss Terri, what type of store is your shop?" asked Nick.

"It's a women's boutique. I sell ladies' undergarments from Boston," she replied.

They pushed through the swinging doors of the saloon, and a sudden silence fell over the room. The music still played, but Nick noticed that all eyes were turned to the beautiful, well-dressed woman on Nick's arm. He felt uncomfortable having so many eyes on them as he walked Miss Terri to the bar. He wasn't sure that this was what the guys meant by being careful. He could feel his cheeks turning red.

"Ma'am, can I help you?" asked the bartender as they approached.

"Yes, please," Miss Terri said. "I'm looking for the owner, Mrs. Corrine Hall."

"She's in the office at the moment. If you'd like to follow me, I can take you to her," the bartender said.

He came out from behind the bar and led them to a separate room across the saloon. The saloon's office had a large glass window that looked out into the main room, but the thick, red curtain was pulled closed. The bartender knocked and waited, and then he opened the door slowly. He ushered Miss Terri and Nick into the room, and quietly closed the door behind them.

Nick could hear the silence break in the saloon. First, there was a low whistle, and then the sounds of conversation started back up again. Nick looked around the office. At the large desk across the room, an older brunette woman studied paperwork.

Then she looked up and cried out, "Terri, you're here!" Jumping up, she rushed around the big desk to embrace Miss Terri.

"It's so good to see you," she said. "How was your trip?"

"Fine," Miss Terri said, "Just a little bumpy and hot."

The owner noticed Nick and asked, "And who is this young man?"

"Corrine, this is Nick. He rescued me from the coach driver," she said with a merry twinkle in her eyes.

Corrine walked over to Nick and extended her hand. "Nice to meet you, Nick," she said.

"Nice to meet you, ma'am," Nick replied, shaking her hand.

"Corrine, could I trouble you for some lemonade?" Miss Terri asked.

"By all means, yes!" Corrine returned to her desk and wrote something on a small piece of paper. "Terri, you go ahead and make yourself comfortable. Nick, could I ask you to take this note to the bartender for me?"

"Sure," he replied, taking the note and heading back out of the office to the bar. After a few minutes, the bartender emerged from a back room.

"Excuse me, sir," Nick said. "Mrs. Corrine asked me to give this to you."

The bartender took the note from Nick and read it. "Okay, son, why don't you come back here while I get this ready. I could use some help carrying all this."

Nick nodded politely and followed the bartender around the end of the bar.

"So what's your name, son? I'm Ike."

"Nick."

"Well, Nick, while you're behind the bar, I'd recommend that you stand over by those boxes so that you don't get yourself trampled. This will take me a few minutes," said Ike. Then he disappeared into the back room once more.

Nick settled into his partially concealed position beside the boxes. From this vantage point, he could see most of the activity in the saloon. At the far end of the bar sat the man who had angrily thrown the fool's gold onto the floor at the patent office. There was a half-empty bottle of whiskey sitting by his elbow. His face was flushed, and his eyes were glassed over and vacant. It was obvious he was drunk.

Nick continued to study the room until his eyes rested on another familiar figure sitting by himself at a table—Mr. Billings from the Black Stallion Mine. As Nick continued to watch, Mr. Billings left his table and walked up to the bar, sitting down right next to the prospector. Nick observed the two men with interest from his concealed position.

At first, they just sat silently, staring into their glasses. Then Mr. Billings turned and spoke to the prospector, who seemed to be ignoring him as he continued to gaze into his glass. But Mr. Billings must have finally said something of interest, because the prospector's head snapped to attention. The Black Stallion owner continued to talk, moving closer to the other man and reaching into his coat pocket to pull out what looked to be a good-size gold nugget. The prospector's eyes focused narrowly on the rock as it glittered before him. Then he nodded his head. He took the rock from Mr. Billings's hand and rolled it gently around on his palm before he finally closed his fist around it and then placed it in his own pocket.

Mr. Billings smiled, reached again into his jacket pocket, and pulled out a leather pouch. It jingled slightly as he handed it to the prospector. Turning his attention back to his glass, Mr. Billings finished his drink. The prospector opened the pouch and several gold coins fell out. He quickly slid them back inside the bag and tucked the pouch into his pocket. Mr. Billings pushed his glass away and rose from his stool, exiting the saloon. A few minutes later, the prospector left, too.

Nick realized that he had witnessed something significant, and his first thought was to follow them. But as soon as he decided to leave the saloon, Ike appeared with a pitcher of lemonade and handed it to him. Then Ike gathered a tray of glasses and a plate of small sandwiches and cookies. "Let's go," he said. "The ladies are waiting."

Frustrated, Nick cast a last glance toward the swinging doors of the saloon. With a sigh, he followed Ike toward the office. *Well, I've only been here less than twenty-four hours, and I'm sure I'll cross paths with those two again,* he thought.

Ike knocked on the office door.

Corrine opened it up and ushered them in. "Thank you, Ike. Would you please place the tray on the desk?"

Nick followed Ike, placing the pitcher on the desk beside the tray.

"If that will be all, ma'am, I'll just be heading back to the bar," said Ike.

"Yes, of course." Corrine walked over to Ike and handed him a small tip.

"Thank you, ma'am. Nice to meet you, Nick," said Ike as he departed.

"Well, Nick, I haven't seen you around town before. Did you and your family just move here?" Mrs. Corrine asked as she poured lemonade into the glasses and handed them out.

Nick accepted the glass of lemonade and took a long drink. He decided to try to keep his story simple and stick to the truth as much as possible. "I'm originally from Washington, D.C. and I'm here visiting some of my mother's friends. But there is talk that my father and I might be moving to this area permanently. So in the meantime, I have a room at the hotel and a possible job at the general store until my father comes."

"What does your father do?" asked Miss Terri.

"Uhh . . . he's a teacher. His specialty is science."

"Oh, how interesting," said Mrs. Corrine. "And will your mother be coming west with your father?"

Taking a big breath, he said, "My mother was killed by a drunken man." He lowered his eyes and stared at his half-empty glass, embarrassed to feel tears prickling his eyes. "Sorry," he said with difficulty. "It's hard to talk about." Nick glanced up to see that both women were teary-eyed.

Uncomfortable, he cleared his throat. "I'm sorry," he said. "I should be going. I have a meeting at the general store for a job."

As Nick prepared to leave, both women stood up and gave him a hug.

"If you need anything, Nick, anything at all, just let me know," said Mrs. Corrine.

"The same goes for me," added Miss Terri. "You know where my shop is, and I'll be staying at the hotel until I find a place to live. Just ask for me at the front desk." She gave Nick another hug.

Nick hugged her back. *Wow! She smells good,* he thought giddily.

"Thanks for the cookies, Mrs. Corrine. I'll be seeing you," he said.

Nick raised his hand and waved at Ike as he made his way across the floor to the saloon's swinging doors. The bartender smiled and waved back.

Nick stepped out of the saloon and headed down the street toward the general store. The street was full of hustle and bustle. Cowboys rode their horses slowly through the busy streets as children played games and women gathered outside the shops to talk.

Nick breathed in the warm air. *I feel at home here,* he thought. *I've made more friends here in one day than I did in the last couple of years traveling with my family.*

When Nick arrived at the general store, he stepped inside and looked around. It looked just as he remembered—full of merchandise. Barrels lined the wall, and the shelves were filled with wares.

Ben came around a corner carrying a load of blankets. "Hey there. How are you?" he greeted Nick. "Let me put these away, and I'll be right with you."

Nick heard a small bell ring above the door and turned to see Keenan enter the store.

"Nick!" Keenan said. "It's been hard to keep up with you."

"What do you mean, keep up with me? When I came out of the patent office you were nowhere to be found!" Nick replied indignantly.

"Shhh . . . I'll explain later. Ben, how are you?" exclaimed Keenan loudly.

"Hello, Keenan!" Ben said, rounding the counter to shake his hand.

"Is everything set up on your end of things?" asked Keenan.

"Uh-huh. Mr. Guillot has approved my vacation, and he's happy that I found my own replacement. Nick can start tomorrow. I'll work with him for a couple of days before I take off to go visit my sister and her family."

"Ben!" a booming voice called out. "Are you still here?"

"Yes, Mr. Guillot! I'm back from my delivery. Could you spare a minute, sir? There are some people I'd like you to meet."

"I'll be right down!" Mr. Guillot called back.

"That's the owner," whispered Ben. "He's in the office working on the inventory books."

The mention of the books reminded Nick of the page he had copied during his field trip. It was still in his backpack at Slim's ranch. Showing genuine interest, he asked, "What is the inventory book, exactly?"

"Well, actually, there are several of them," said Ben. "There are a couple of books to keep track of store-to-store transfers. There are two that are used strictly for the two mining companies' transactions. We order lots of specialized supplies for them. But you don't have to worry about the books, Nick. Mr. Guillot handles them. We just deal with the deliveries to the mines and anywhere else in town."

The sound of footsteps on the stairs drew their attention; a tall, broad, middle-aged man with graying temples was descending from the second floor.

"Good afternoon," he said pleasantly. "What can I do for you?"

"Mr. Guillot, let me introduce you to Keenan and Nick. Nick has agreed to cover for me while I'm on vacation," explained Ben.

"Oh, yes. Nick, I'm glad to meet you." Mr. Guillot turned to his employee. "Ben, your horse bridle and saddle came in while you were gone. It's in the back. Why don't you go get it and give me a few minutes to show Nick around?"

"It's here!" exclaimed Ben. "Keenan, come back with me. I'd like for you to see it."

"Let's head to my office, Nick," Mr. Guillot said.

Nick followed Mr. Guillot up the stairs. He wondered what the man would think if he told him that he had been here before, but in another time. How would he feel if he knew his store was now a part of a tourist attraction? Nick chuckled softly, but figured it was best to keep his mouth shut.

"Well, Nick, Ben has told me that you are a good, responsible young man. That's important in a job like this. What we do here is to try to provide speedy delivery service and good merchandise to the shops and offices around town. When we don't have a particular type of merchandise available, we order it from one of the larger towns. Depending on what it is and how far the order has to travel, sometimes the merchandise takes a few weeks to arrive here. All the orders arrive on either the morning or afternoon coach."

Mr. Guillot walked over to the shelf above his desk and pulled down an inventory book to show Nick.

"We also have contracts with the two mines here in town. You'll spend part of your week delivering orders to the mining sites. Their goods have to be delivered the same day they arrive. I do not want to be responsible for any supply losses, especially since they order large quantities of gunpowder, dynamite, and fuses. We don't keep their explosives in the store overnight for safety reasons. You may have to work late now and then to make a delivery to them."

Mr. Guillot showed Nick his office and the upstairs storage area. After they finished, they headed back downstairs to view the other storage areas.

"Well, Nick, you seem like a smart boy, and I think you'll fit in just fine. Why don't you plan to be here around 9:00 a.m. tomorrow? Ben will be here a couple more days before he takes off. He can show you the entire delivery route. It's pretty simple, so you shouldn't have any problems."

Mr. Guillot and Nick rounded the corner to the back storage area and bumped into Keenan and Ben. Ben was carrying his new saddle and bridle, and had a satisfied grin on his face.

"Well, Ben, shouldn't you be heading out to go pick up your horse? I think you have everything you need," said Mr. Guillot.

"Yes, sir!" Ben replied.

"I have some work to do now," groaned the store owner. "I'll see both of you tomorrow morning. Keenan, it was nice to meet you."

"Well, we'd better get going," Ben said. Hefting his saddle onto his shoulder, he grabbed his bridle and headed out the door with Keenan and Nick.

They walked down the street to the blacksmith shop at the end of town. As they approached, the sound of clinking metal got louder and louder. When they entered the side door of the shop, Nick was hit by an overpowering wall of heat coming from the red-hot furnace.

Standing at the iron anvil, a large man pounded away on a horseshoe.

"Mr. Green!" yelled Ben. The man was in mid-swing when he heard his name. He brought the hammer down for a final blow, then picked up the horseshoe with tongs and placed it into a barrel of water.

"Ah, Ben," said Mr. Green. "Here to pick up your horse, eh?"

Ben smiled. "Yes, sir. I brought a bit, saddle, and reins."

"I see that. Well, your horse is shod and ready to go."

The four of them walked through a back door leading to the stables and a corral surrounded by a split-rail fence. Nick followed Ben to the fence, and stood on the first rung to get a good look at the horses.

"Which one is yours?" asked Nick.

"The black one with the white mark on his forehead. Isn't he beautiful?" sighed Ben.

"Wow, he's amazing," said Nick.

Nick glanced around and saw Mr. Green and Keenan sealing the deal. After pocketing his payment, Mr. Green grabbed a rope and reached for a bucket that sat on the ground. He opened the gate to the corral and stepped in.

Several of the horses ambled over to him and he gave them each a carrot from the bucket. Then Ben's horse slowly came forward to receive his treat. While the horse ate, Mr. Green slipped a rope over his head. Gently, he led the horse out of the corral and handed the rope to Ben.

"He's all yours, son. Take good care of him. If you have any questions, let me know," said Mr. Green.

Ben stroked the horse's nose, grinning from ear to ear.

"Are you going to saddle him up or just walk him home?" asked Keenan.

"I'm going to put the saddle on him. Would you mind giving me a hand?"

Nick watched as Keenan and Ben saddled up the horse and walked him around.

"He's been eying that horse since it came in here as a colt," laughed Mr. Green. "It was a really nice thing you guys did, helping him get it. I was afraid that I was going to have to sell him before Ben could come up with the money."

Nick just nodded, not sure what to say. Life seemed so much simpler in this time. The kids in his world wanted cars to get around, not horses. Keenan helped Ben mount up. At first the horse was restless and pranced a bit from side to side; but after a few moments, he got used to Ben's weight and settled down.

"Well, Ben, you should be getting home, shouldn't you?" asked Keenan.

"Yeah, my mother will be holding supper for me. Thank you, Keenan, and you too, Nick. This means a lot to me. I feel like I'm getting the better end of this deal, though. Are you sure there's nothing else I can do for you?" Ben asked.

"What you're doing is already a big help to us, more than you can imagine. Just enjoy your new horse. You've earned it," said Keenan.

"Okay, good night, then. Nick, I'll see you in the morning," said Ben.

"Okay," said Nick. "Have a good ride."

Mr. Green grabbed the reins and led Ben and his new horse around the building to the main road. Nick and Keenan followed them. The three of them watched as Ben and his horse trotted down the town's main road.

"He's so proud of that horse," said Mr. Green.

"Your first horse will do that for you, every time," said Keenan. "Well, Nick, I think we need to get going. I am guessing that dinner is almost ready. Mr. Green, it was nice doing business with you. Thanks for all your help."

"Anytime, Keenan. You boys have a good night."

As the sun slowly sank in the sky, casting a warm glow over the town, Keenan and Nick headed back to the general store to retrieve their horses. They mounted and made their way through town toward Slim's ranch.

"So, what do you think after your first full day here in Silverado?" asked Keenan.

"I love it here," replied Nick. "But there seems to be a lot going on under the surface. Something tells me that it won't be easy to figure out who's involved in the crime."

Keenan chuckled softly. "Well, remember, Nick, this is only day one, so don't be too hard on yourself. We'll just piece it together one clue at a time."

Chapter Twelve

THE IMPS

They arrived at Slim's ranch just as the sun sank behind the mountain. Its glowing orange rays lit the western sky. Keenan and Nick passed the house and rode toward the stables. The barn smelled heavily of fresh-cut hay and feed. The straw beneath their boots crunched softly as they walked the horses into their stalls and untacked them. Keenan handed Nick a brush. As they were brushing the horses down, Christopher suddenly appeared in the open doorway.

"Hey, guys. How was your day?" he asked.

"Good, good. I believe we were more successful than we expected to be. Nick met a lot of people," answered Keenan.

"That's great, Nick. The more people you meet, the better," said Christopher.

"What's Slim been doing today?" Keenan asked.

"He's trying to fix dinner right now. He spent most of the day getting the workshop ready for us. We'll have to move into it by the end of the week. That's when the real Slim will be back from Cartersville. We're going to have to be extremely careful not to run into him. Are you guys about done?"

"Just need to feed and water the horses," replied Keenan. "Say, why don't you help me with the horses, Christopher, and let Nick get a head start on getting cleaned up."

Nick had been half-listening to the guys talk while he was brushing Rusty. As soon as he stopped brushing, Rusty turned his head and looked at Nick accusingly, then nudged Nick in the back with his nose.

"What the . . . ?" Nick grunted.

Christopher laughed. "Rusty is letting you know that you're not done yet. He wants his mane brushed out."

"Oh, yeah? How do you know what he's thinking?" asked Nick.

"I can read Rusty's body language. See how he's rolling his head around?"

"Oh, so sorry," Nick told the horse as he reached up and petted its nose. Nick picked up the brush again and began to brush out Rusty's mane.

"Say, don't worry about it," Keenan said. "Christopher will finish him up. Why don't you go on into the house and get cleaned up for dinner? Slim has a surprise for you tonight."

"Okay," said Nick. He handed the brush to Christopher and headed toward the door.

Keenan placed his hand on Nick's shoulder when he passed. "You did good today," Keenan said in a lower voice.

Nick grinned and bounded across the yard toward the house.

"Hmm, sounds like dinner is going to be very interesting tonight," observed Christopher.

"We'll see. I think the conversation will be interesting. I *am* concerned about Slim cooking dinner. My hope is that he cooks the meat long enough without burning it. We all know he's not at his best in the kitchen."

Nick had taken a short walk around to the front of the ranch to gaze out toward the distant town. He stood on the porch for a few moments thinking about his father. *Maybe it would be better for both of us if I just stayed here,* he thought. Heaving a big sigh, he turned and walked into the ranch house.

Michael came around the corner carrying wood for the fireplace. "Well, hello, Nick," he said. "How was your first day in town?"

"It was definitely interesting," said Nick.

"Sounds like you're going to be the storyteller tonight," said Michael, chuckling. "You'd better hurry and get washed up for dinner. I just filled the tub with hot water."

Nick nodded, then hastened to his room. He opened up the chest, grabbed a set of clean clothes, and then headed to the washroom.

The water in the tin tub was warm and welcoming when Nick climbed in. He was amazed at how filthy he was, as days of caked-on dirt and grime drifted to the surface. Once he was clean and dressed, he headed back down the hallway into the main room, where Michael had built a roaring fire. Nick heard voices coming from the kitchen, so he pushed open the door to see what was going on.

Judging from the puzzled look on everyone's faces, he didn't think the cowboys staring at the stove knew what they were doing.

"How do you know they're done?" asked Christopher.

"Well, they're supposed to be golden and crisp on the outside and soft on the inside," Slim said.

"They look strange," said Keenan.

"Maybe we should get started on the salad," Michael suggested. He grabbed a large wooden bowl and turned around, spying Nick in the doorway.

"Hey, how long have you been standing there?" he asked.

The rest of the cowboys' heads came up like a shot. They quickly turned around, gathering together to block Nick's view of the stove.

"It was supposed to be a surprise," said Slim.

"Well, if we don't get some help, we'll end up making him sick. That won't be a very good surprise," said Christopher.

Nick walked toward them, afraid of what he might see. "What are you trying to cook, Slim?" he asked.

"Well, okay," Slim said reluctantly.

The cowboys parted slowly so Nick could step up to the stove and see what they had been working on.

There were French fries sitting in a pan, hamburger patties in a wooden bowl, and uncut tomatoes sitting on the counter.

Nick laughed. "You guys are a trip. I can definitely help with this."

Nick organized the items on the counter. Then he sent Keenan over to the kitchen table to cut tomatoes and onions into slices. Michael was given the responsibility of cooking the fries in a pan over the top of the potbellied stove. Nick explained that he had to be careful to turn them over to brown them evenly on all sides. He gave a large wooden bowl full of lettuce to Christopher, who joined Keenan at the kitchen table to cut up mushrooms, cucumbers, and carrots. Nick showed Slim how to cook the hamburger patties and brown the buns.

It took about half an hour to prepare dinner. Nick glanced around the kitchen and had to smile. Everyone was having a great time, talking and laughing as they worked. When everything was done, they moved the food to the dining table. Slim brought out small dishes of mustard and ketchup, and then he produced pickles and cans of soda. Michael said a blessing, and they began to pass food around the table. Nick started building his burger and realized that everyone had stopped to watch him.

"This," he said "is how you put it together. You stack the things you like on the burger, and then you use both hands to eat it." Then he showed them how to dip their fries in the ketchup.

Nick was amused by the cowboys' reactions. For the first time they were tasting food that Nick had grown up on. He could tell they were delighted with dinner. Watching them tackle the canned soda and the carbonation that tickled their noses brought Nick to the point of hysterical laughter. As they finished eating, Keenan let out a deep satisfied sigh, leaned back in his chair, and rubbed his stomach.

"Boy, oh, boy," he said. "I could get used to eating like this every day. That was the best meal I can remember."

"You're sure lucky, Nick. You're not stuck with beans all the time," said Christopher.

Slim cleared his throat. "Well, we want to hear all about your day in town, Nick, but before we get started, why don't we have dessert and coffee?"

Keenan and Michael stood and picked up the dirty plates. Michael returned with wooden bowls and spoons. After a few moments, Keenan came out, grinning from ear to ear. He carried a large carton of chocolate-chip-cookie-dough ice cream.

Nick's mouth fell open. "How did you guys get this stuff?" he wondered out loud.

Slim just smiled and scooped generous portions of ice cream into each bowl. Keenan poured coffee, then handed a mug of hot chocolate to Nick. They all settled down again to enjoy.

"Boy, if I had a choice, I would have asked to live in your time," said Keenan to Nick.

"Just for the food?" asked Slim.

"Well, maybe not just for the food. You do have some really beautiful gals there, too," replied Keenan.

The guys exchanged knowing glances as Slim changed the subject. "Nick, tonight's dinner came from your time. Michael went back and picked up the items we needed."

"Let me get this straight. You're saying that he traveled back to my time, went to a grocery store, and picked up tonight's dinner?" asked Nick. "But how did he pay for everything?"

"When we're on assignment, our resources are almost unlimited. The gold coins we use here turn into whatever coin we need in whatever time we are in," Slim said.

"And like we mentioned last night," added Michael, "we can also become invisible when we need to."

"That was how I was able to keep my eye on you today," explained Keenan. "And why you couldn't find me right away."

"I still can't believe it—it just sounds so sci-fi. How do you do that? Become invisible?" Nick asked.

"Sci-fi?" Keenan repeated curiously. Then he shrugged. "Like this."

One minute Keenan was there, and the next he was slowly fading away, until he disappeared like a wisp of smoke. Nick was dumbfounded. Then the spoon that was still sitting in his empty bowl slowly rose up as if it were floating on its own.

"See," said Keenan's voice, "I'm still here."

"Wow," whispered Nick. "I wish I could do that."

Suddenly, Keenan reappeared. "There is a way that you can experience invisibility," he said. "By—"

Slim cut him off. "Keenan's right, but that comes with some important restrictions. If you're in danger, or if you're in the wrong place at the wrong time and need to disappear, all one of us has to do is wrap our arms around you. When we disappear, so will you. Now enough about us. Tell us what happened today."

Nick pushed his empty bowl away so that he could lean forward on the table. He told them about everything that happened to him during the day, starting with the two separate arguments at the land claims office and describing the interaction between the prospector and Mr. Billings in the saloon.

"Oh, there was one especially strange thing that happened," Nick blurted out suddenly.

"What was that?" asked Slim.

"Well, while I was at the land claims office I saw a shadow circling around Mr. Jenkins and Mr. Billings. It was moving all on its own."

"A shadow?" asked Christopher.

"A shadow?" Michael echoed.

"Uh-oh," said Keenan.

"What did the shadow actually do?" Slim asked him.

"At first it circled around both men. Then it stopped and seemed to concentrate on Mr. Billings. At the end of the argument, the shadow stepped right behind Mr. Billings and disappeared into him."

"Did Mr. Billings become especially angry at that point?" asked Slim.

"Yeah. When he turned around, his face was so red I thought he was going to explode. Then he stormed out of the office, yelling at Mr. Jenkins before he left."

"Imps," whispered Keenan.

"Oh, no. They're here," Christopher let out a low whistle.

"Nick, did the shadow notice or focus on you at any point?" asked Slim.

"No," said Nick. "So that was an imp? Like the ones you were telling me about in the cave, Slim?"

Michael, Keenan, and Christopher turned to look at Slim.

Slim shifted his position in his chair. Clearing his throat, he began to explain. "Yes, Nick. Imps are a nickname we have given to evil spirits."

Nick looked puzzled. "Why was the imp so interested in Jenkins and Billings? And what did it do to Mr. Billings?"

"You see," explained Slim, "everyone has the capacity to do good or evil. It's a choice we all make on a daily basis. Those who choose to embrace the evil nature within them are not necessarily bad people. They're just ordinary folks who keep making bad decisions over and over again. But these mistakes open the door for imps. The imps show up one at a time at first, but then they start moving in groups. Each one that gains access to you is a little stronger than the next. Once they start affecting the way you think, there's no hope. Little by little, you find that you have given up all control. Your life continues on a self-destructive course.

"Nick," Slim continued, "anger is the main weapon that imps use. It is a powerful, controlling, destructive force, and everyone feels angry sometimes. Learning how to manage it can be tricky. The best thing is just to be aware of it. When you do get angry, do not let it consume you—otherwise, you might open the door to imps."

Christopher spoke up. "I'm surprised Nick can see them. They're invisible to most humans. Spirits are usually the only ones who can see them."

"He's not in his time, and he is working with us," said Slim. "He should be able to see most of what we see."

"Is it dangerous for me to see them?" asked Nick, feeling a stab of fear.

"It's not a bad thing," said Michael. "It's good for you to be aware of them. But be very careful. We don't want them to know that you can see them, and we absolutely can't alert them to our presence here—otherwise we couldn't move around as freely."

"It's like another world; I can really see what's going on all around me," said Nick.

"You're right!" said Slim. "There's a war being waged between good and evil in the spirit world. This has been going on since soon after the beginning of time. Now that you have been given this glimpse into our world, please be careful. The imps are strong and very persistent. They have successfully destroyed the lives of many powerful people."

"What should I do if they notice me looking at them?" asked Nick.

"If you notice one circling a person, always focus on the person's face, and not on the shadow," advised Christopher. "If one takes an interest in you and starts circling, beware; it's looking for an entrance. Ignore the bad thoughts that will be flooding your mind. Try to distract yourself for as long as you can. Imps get bored easily, and if they can't find a way into you, they'll leave you and look for another victim."

"This is a lot to think about," said Nick, shaking his head.

"Say," Slim said, "I think I have a blank journal. Why don't I give it to you; then you can write down things you want to remember. You could also note the people you meet in town and anything you happen to overhear."

"I like that idea," said Nick. "I've almost run out of space on the piece of paper that I picked up from the claims office."

"Oh, and you probably need a pocket watch, too. You can't use the watch from your time," said Slim. "I've got an extra that you can use."

"Great, I'll put my wrist watch in my backpack," said Nick.

The conversation continued while they drank more coffee and cocoa. They talked about the different townspeople, describing some of their more embarrassing exploits. Laughter filled the air as stories of some of their crazier antics from their past were shared. Finally, Slim noticed Nick stifling a yawn.

"You know, guys," he said. "It's getting late. We have a big day tomorrow, and we all need to be in town early. Time to hit the sack."

They all nodded in agreement and pushed back their chairs. Christopher and Michael collected all the bowls and spoons and followed Keenan into the kitchen.

"Go ahead and get ready for bed, Nick," said Slim.

Nick got up from his chair and walked to the kitchen. All three of the cowboys were elbow-deep in water and bubbles.

"Good night, guys," Nick said.

"Good night, Nick."

He turned and headed toward his room. Getting undressed, he slipped into his nightshirt and crawled into the bed. The evening was cool and he welcomed the thick, warm blanket, snuggling deep beneath it. Before he could begin to dwell on the day's events, he slipped off to sleep.

Slim stepped into the room later to check on him and listened for a few minutes to Nick's deep breathing. He placed a small, blank leather journal on the table by Nick's washstand, then turned and headed to his own room.

Climbing into bed, Slim whispered a prayer into the cool air. "Whatever we do, help us to protect Nick." Moments later, he drifted off to sleep.

Chapter Thirteen
THE NEW JOB

"Time to get up, Nick," echoed a faint, distant voice. "You have to meet Ben this morning for your first day of work."

"Ugh!" Nick groaned, burying his head under his pillow.

"Come on, Nick. Breakfast is almost ready!" said Keenan.

Nick rolled over again and rubbed his eyes, staring at the edge of sun that was just beginning to climb over the horizon. "Okay, I'm up."

Keenan left the room, closing the door behind him. Nick climbed out of bed, dressed, and opened his door, letting in the smell of homemade biscuits wafting from the kitchen. He heard the cowboys' voices as he slowly shuffled to the swinging door and walked through, yawning. He sat down at the kitchen table. Keenan brought him a mug of hot chocolate and some hot, fresh biscuits.

"It's hard adjusting to a new schedule," Michael said sympathetically. "But it'll get much easier soon."

"I hope so," replied Nick. "I don't want to ride into the wrong town because I fell asleep on my horse."

Slim started chuckling. "Not to worry, one of us will always ride in with you."

"What are you all doing today?" asked Nick.

"Well," said Slim. "We'll be either in town or out at the mines looking for clues. Then, we'll be watching certain people, looking for some sort of pattern. I'm guessing that one person committed the murder—although it's still possible many people were involved. The most important thing, at this point, is to make a list of anybody who could have been involved. Did you see the journal that I put on your nightstand, Nick?"

"Yes, it's in my pocket. I need to transfer what I wrote down yesterday into the journal, then I can make some notes about the things you told me last night. I'll keep a list of all the people I meet, too."

"Good. Tonight we'll go over whatever we find out today."

"More biscuits are ready!" Keenan declared. "Come and get 'em!"

Nick had taken the journal out of his pocket and was writing in it when he heard Christopher's heavy footsteps approach the kitchen.

"Morning, all!" Christopher said. "Is the coffee ready yet, Keenan?"

"Coming right up," said Keenan.

"Sure smells good in here," Christopher said appreciatively.

"Come on, guys, let's sit down and make some plans for today," said Slim.

With the coffee poured and everyone eating biscuits and jam, Slim mapped out a plan of action. "Christopher, you keep an eye on Nick in town today. Keenan, you take the Falcon Mine operation and see what you can find out. Michael, you can head over to the Black Stallion Mine and see what's going on there," said Slim.

"Where are you going, Slim?" Christopher asked.

"I'm following Mr. Billings around today to see what he's up to," Slim responded. "He's up to his neck in debt and motive. But it still feels like something's missing from the picture."

Slim lapsed into silence, sipping his coffee. Michael got up and touched him lightly on the shoulder.

"You still with us?"

"Yeah, sorry; there's just so much we don't know yet," he said.

"Slim, we will find all the answers," Christopher promised.

"You're right. Of course we will," Slim replied, smiling slightly. "Well, we'd better get going."

"Hey, Nick, here's some pocket money to use for lunch or whatever you want," said Christopher. He threw Nick a small leather pouch that jingled when he caught it. "Come on, it's time for us to head out if we want to get to the general store before it opens."

Nick got up and followed Christopher to the stables. "See you later, guys!" he yelled.

A moment later, Slim opened the kitchen door a crack. He and Michael watched Nick's retreating figure.

"I'm worried about Nick. We're asking a lot of him," Slim said.

"Maybe—but look how much happier he is since you first met him. And we can all tell that he's one smart kid," said Michael.

"You're right. You're right, my friend. I need to relax and remember the bigger picture. We'll just have to do what we can and see what unfolds."

"All will be revealed when the time is right. Till then, we still have a lot of work to do," Keenan chimed in. "I'm done with the dishes. Are we ready to go yet, guys?"

Slim shut the back door and secured it. "Let's get moving."

"We're ready, Slim," Keenan said as they walked into the main room.

"Okay, you know your assignments. Try to stay invisible. We can't afford for any imps or miners to see us."

"Hey, Slim, how about letting me get dinner tonight for everyone?" asked Keenan, before they dispersed.

"What do you have in mind?" asked Slim suspiciously.

"Have I ever failed you before?" Keenan asked, with a twinkle in his eye.

"Okay, just make sure it's edible," Slim said.

Keenan slowly faded from sight. "Bye, guys," his voice called.

"Remember, Slim, no worries. Everything will be fine," said Michael. Then he, too, began to fade.

Slim sighed deeply and slowly disappeared.

★ ★ ★

Christopher and Nick rode into town and arrived at the general store five minutes before it opened. Christopher dismounted first and held the horse still for Nick while he dismounted.

"Nick, I'm going to leave you right now and take the horses over to Mr. Green's stable. When I return, you won't be able to see me. But I'll let you know that I am back by flicking your earlobe. If you need to talk to me about anything, just head to a quiet place and call out my name," said Christopher.

"Okay," Nick told him.

"I better get going; Ben is heading this way. I'll see you later." Christopher grabbed the reins of both horses, turned them around, and headed toward Mr. Green's blacksmith shop and stable.

Nick stood on the boardwalk and waited until Ben walked up to him.

"Morning, Nick," Ben said as he slipped the key into the front door of the shop.

"Hey, Ben! Where's your new horse?"

"Oh, I left him at home today. I am trying to give him a day or two to get used to his new surroundings. But I have to say, he sure is a beauty. Are you ready for your first day at work?" he asked.

"Yep. As ready as I'll ever be," Nick said a little nervously.

"Let's head in and take a look at the delivery schedule for today, first," said Ben.

Ben opened the door and he and Nick walked in. They moved through the main room toward the back where, among the shelves, a single desk sat.

"Welcome to my office. It's a little cramped back here, but it works."

He rustled through a pile of loose papers. "Here it is," Ben exclaimed. "I usually get the next day's schedule at the end of each day. It is easier to find it when you hang it on that wall. Yesterday I was so excited about the horse I just threw it on my desk. So let's have a look to see what we have to do today."

Ben tapped his finger on the paper as he read. After several moments, he looked up at Nick and smiled broadly.

"Well, you're in luck. We have a lot to do. We'll be heading out to the Black Stallion Mine early this afternoon, since it's the furthest away. Then we'll stop by the Falcon Mine on our way back toward town. But this morning we have some boxes we have to deliver to the bakery and a few other places. So let's start with that.

"Since we are heading out to the mines today, I'll put in a lunch order for us at the bakery. Once the wagon is loaded for our mine deliveries, we will stop and pick up lunch on our way out of town."

Nick picked up two of the boxes for the bakery and followed Ben out the door and past the back of several buildings to the bakery. Suddenly, he felt a sharp flick on his earlobe. It startled him at first, but then he realized that Christopher had returned, and he couldn't help but chuckle. He wondered what Ben would think if he knew there was an invisible person walking with them.

Meanwhile, at the Falcon Mine, Keenan had arrived at Otis Walkins's office. He followed a miner who just happened to be going in to speak with Mr. Walkins. Mr. Walkins stood behind his large desk looking over some maps. He held a list of numbers in his right hand, and looked up when the miner entered his office.

"Yes, Parker, come in, come in!" he bellowed.

"Sir, we just broke through into another cavern. I thought you should have a look at it before we proceed," said Parker.

"Why, is there a problem?" Mr. Walkins asked.

"Sir, there's a large hole in the middle of the floor there—it may lead to a secondary cavern. The guys can't see the bottom so they've been calling it a bottomless pit. I don't believe that it's a stable enough area for the men to work in," Parker replied.

"I see. Round up Slim. He'll need to take a good look at it," said Mr. Walkins.

"Sir, Slim is still in Cartersville and won't be back until the weekend."

"Oh, that's right. Then call for Stanley Watts. He'll have to do. I want you guys to have a look around down there and collect some samples, and then we'll close it up until Slim returns. He can do a complete safety assessment of the area then."

"Yes, sir," said Parker.

"I'll meet you at the main entrance in fifteen minutes. I have some things I need to finish up here first," said Mr. Walkins.

When Parker left the office, Keenan, still in his invisible state, stayed behind and moved closer to Mr. Walkins's desk. The mine owner made a note on one of the maps. He placed an *X* on one of the tunnels. "We'll see," Otis whispered. "Maybe we'll find a new vein of gold." Then he grabbed his overcoat and a lantern and headed out the door of his office, unaware that Keenan followed him.

They approached the entrance of the mine, and Keenan saw Parker and another man waiting there.

"Stanley," boomed Mr. Walkins, "you are going to have to cover for Slim today. This new area might be unstable. We need to retrieve some samples for Slim so he can analyze them before we send miners in."

Stanley Watts was tall, lanky, and weathered in the face. He appeared to wear a permanent frown.

"Stanley," Parker said, "there's a large hole in the floor of the cavern. We're going to lower you down into it to see how deep it is and find out if there's water at the bottom. You can retrieve the rock samples from the walls."

As Parker was talking, all of the color drained from Stanley's face.

"Don't worry. We've never had a single accident at the Falcon Mine. Slim has done this sort of thing many times. Now, let's head out," said Mr. Walkins.

Keenan noticed a strange look pass between Parker and Stanley. The two of them turned and trailed after Mr. Walkins.

The three men entered the main cave and walked down the natural corridor. Little had been altered here since its original discovery, with the exception of the beams shoring up the ceiling for stability. The miners used the central corridor to make their way to all the different mineshafts, as well as to move equipment. As they walked deeper into the mineshaft, they passed openings in the walls. These led to new tunnels being dug by miners looking for signs of gold or silver ore.

The group made their way into one of the farthest openings and approached the lift equipment used to lower the men into the deeper tunnels. There were a couple of miners waiting for their turn on the lift, so Mr. Walkins's group waited patiently until everyone had been lowered into the different tunnels. Finally climbing onto the lift themselves, they descended down into the deepest tunnel. Once they emerged from the lift, they walked down a rough new tunnel that had only been partially carved out. They didn't have far to go before they entered a large cavern and saw a yawning pit appear in front of them.

Some of the men had already tossed rocks in and listened for sounds. The biggest problem with the hole was that its width did not give the workers any room to maneuver, so virtually all work had stopped.

The miners had managed to run a long, thick timber beam across the mouth of the hole so they could get to the other side. They attached a pulley system to the middle of the beam so a man could be lowered down in a harness. None of the miners had volunteered to be lowered into the pit, because its depth was intimidating. Parker picked five men from the group of miners to work with him.

"All right, all right, I'm not paying you to stand around and watch," bellowed Mr. Walkins. "Anyone not willing to help should head back up and check in with the foreman. You'll be assigned to another tunnel until further notice."

After some of the men left, Parker took the end of several of the longer ropes and tied them to his waist. He straddled the beam in a sitting position and shimmied slowly out to the middle, where the pulley was. Parker untied one rope, secured it to the beam, and then followed suit with another rope. He threaded a rope through the pulley and secured it, then carefully crawled back across the log, bringing several secure ropes with him.

Parker took one of the rope ends and turned to Stanley, who had been fitted by the other workers with the harness. They threaded the pulley line through the back of the harness several times and tied it off.

Stanley didn't say anything, but Keenan could tell by the ashen tone of his skin that this man was scared to death. He wished he could go down with him, but he knew he could not, because any additional weight on the line could put Stanley at risk.

The men placed tools and a leather pouch into Stanley's pocket as he stood on the lip of the hole. They tied a lantern to the rope a few feet away from the harness. After checking the line one more time, the men lined up and took their place on the rope. Stanley shimmied out onto the beam, stopping at the pulley. He swung his leg over and the men began to pull on the rope as he lowered himself below the beam.

The pulley gave a groan, and a second later Stanley was suspended in the hole.

Parker shimmied back across the beam to the middle where the pulley was. A second miner tied one of the ropes around himself and followed Parker out to the middle of the beam to help, just in case.

As the two men adjusted their positions on the beam, Mr. Walkins yelled at Stanley. "Snap out of it! You look like you've seen a ghost. Parker, lower when ready."

Stanley gulped as he was lowered deeper into the hole. His hands shook.

"What do you see, Stanley?" called Mr. Walkins.

Stanley had closed his eyes as he descended. Mr. Walkins's loud voice echoed loudly through the cavern, prompting Stanley to finally open his eyes and look around. The walls were covered with jagged rocks. "I see a lot of rocks!" Stanley yelled back.

They continued to lower Stanley slowly deeper into the pit. Suddenly Stanley stopped descending. There wasn't enough rope to go any further.

"Can you see the bottom?" Walkins shouted.

Stanley reached up and untied the lantern from the rope above his head. He held it out, bending forward slightly to look for the bottom. To his surprise, he saw it about twenty to thirty feet below him. As he moved the lantern back and forth, something glittering caught his eye. He brought the lantern in closer so that he could turn up the flame, then held it out at arm's length and swung it around the cavern. The cavern floor and walls exploded in sparkling light, shimmering in different colors, jumping like rainbows before his eyes. He could not quite make out what it was, but it seemed like a prism of light surrounded him every time he moved the lantern.

"Stanley!" Mr. Walkins voice echoed down. "Can you get some samples?"

Stanley knew that he wouldn't be able to get any from the floor, so he turned toward the sparkling wall. A ledge of rock jutted out not too far away from him.

Lifting his head, he yelled up, "Can you help me swing toward the wall?"

A faint voice answered back. "Yeah, but take it slowly."

Stanley began to swing sideways. It took several tries before he was finally able to grasp the ledge. He pushed himself away from it and used the momentum of the swing to haul himself onto the ledge.

Stanley sat there for a moment breathing deeply. He was grateful that the ledge was strong enough to support his weight.

Again, he heard the faint voice calling from above asking for samples.

"If they want it done faster, they should come down here and do it themselves," he grumbled.

Turning slightly to his left, he set the lantern on the ledge and grabbed the small pick from his pocket. Light bounced and reflected off the wall.

Crystals of different sizes sparkled all around him. He released several stones from the wall with his pick and placed them in his pouch. He also took samples of the rock that the crystal stones were embedded in and added them to the pouch. Stanley was nearly finished when a thought occurred to him.

He used his pick several more times and knocked a handful of the crystal rocks into his hand. He placed these stones into his pocket for his own personal project. Raising his voice, he let the guys know that he was done.

Pushing off the ledge and dangling once more in the air, he relaxed and enjoyed the light show as he moved his lantern back and forth. He felt the rope tighten and he braced himself as he started the long journey back up to the top of the hole.

It took longer to raise him than it did to lower him. When he was finally within an arm's length of Parker and the other miner, they grabbed his harness and pulled him up so he could straddle the beam. Then, very carefully, each one of them shimmied slowly back across the timber to the edge of the pit, where the other miners helped them back onto solid ground.

Mr. Walkins walked over to Stanley, and snatched the leather pouch protruding from his front pocket. He walked away quickly to open it alone. He tipped the bag into his hand and several stones rolled out into his palm. The crystal-like rocks that sparkled softly in the dim light puzzled Mr. Walkins. He swiftly slipped them back into the leather pouch to hide them from everyone.

"Does it look promising?" asked Parker.

Ignoring him, Mr. Walkins turned toward Stanley. "Was there a bottom to that hole?"

"Yes, sir. But it was about twenty to thirty feet further down from where I stopped," answered Stanley.

"Okay, then. Parker, I want this shaft closed until further notice. Slim will be back soon and he can take a look at these samples. He'll decide if it's worth it to continue mining here," said Otis. "Stanley, get cleaned up and then head back to work. That's it for today, everyone. Thank you all for your help."

Keenan watched everyone leave and head back to the lift. He shook his head as he followed the group. He hadn't gotten to see the contents of the pouch, so he would have to continue following Mr. Walkins.

Back in his office, Otis sat down behind his desk with a loud sigh. "What a waste of time," he muttered. "No sign of gold anywhere." He threw the pouch onto the desk.

The leather bag fell open and out spilled its contents into the sunlight. The samples exploded with light, casting prisms of color onto the desk and around the room. Startled, Mr. Walkins bent forward and picked up one of the crystals. He held it up to the light. Mesmerized, he picked up another and studied it closely. Keenan was just as stunned as Mr. Walkins.

Otis shook his head and whispered, "Jumpin' Jehoshaphat, could these be diamonds?"

Chapter Fourteen
THE UNUSUAL STONE

Mr. Walkins was startled by a loud knock at the door. He quickly scooped up the sparkling rocks and poured them back into the pouch, then slipped the pouch into his pocket. "Come in!" he yelled.

Parker opened the door and walked in. "I just wanted you to know that the tunnel has been closed and is off-limits until further notice."

"Good. I don't want anyone in there. It's not safe right now, and I want Slim to take a good look at it. Have all the men been reassigned to other tunnels?"

"Yes, sir," answered Parker.

"Good. Now go and get Stanley. I want to talk to him."

"Yes, sir," said Parker. He turned around and left Mr. Walkins's office, slowly making his way back across the yard to the tunnel entrance.

Since Mr. Walkins wasn't going anywhere, Keenan decided to follow Parker. He seemed to remember him from old times. Keenan tried and tried, but he couldn't remember the position Parker held under Mr. Billings's ownership of the Falcon Mine.

Entering the mine, Keenan could hear the banging of picks echo in the distance. Parker went into the right tunnel and yelled Stanley's name.

There was silence for several minutes until a voice echoed up. "He's coming."

The glow of a lantern appeared in the darkness, and after several minutes, Stanley appeared.

"Now what?" growled Stanley. "Another fill-in for Slim?"

"No," Parker said, "Mr. Walkins wants to see you now. So come on."

Stanley fell into step beside Parker as they walked through the tunnel. Just ahead of them, another miner had pushed a full cart of ore to a standstill while he took a moment to catch his breath. In the low light of the narrow tunnel, Stanley accidentally tripped over the miner's foot as he and Parker passed by and fell to the ground.

The startled miner bent over to help, but Parker waved him on. He bent down to help Stanley up. Several of the rocks from the pit had fallen out of Stanley's pocket. They sparkled in the light of the lantern and caught Parker's attention. "What are these?" he said as he scooped them up.

"Oh, those are mine. They're nothing," said Stanley nervously.

"What do you mean, they're nothing?" asked Parker.

Parker turned one of the crystals in front of the light. It splashed a prism of color onto the wall. "Wait a minute, where did you get this, Stanley?"

Stanley didn't say anything.

"Did you get this from the pit?" Parker asked.

Again, Stanley was silent.

Parker grabbed his shoulders. "Stanley, I asked you a question."

The other man sighed. "I just thought they were pretty, and I only wanted to keep some as a souvenir."

"That's fine, but this looks like something that I need to send to Cartersville to have analyzed," said Parker.

"Don't worry. There are some of these in the leather pouch I gave to Mr. Walkins. Knowing him, he probably sent them out to be analyzed already," said Stanley.

Parker stood there for a moment and stroked his chin thoughtfully. "Stanley, I'd like to keep a few of these. I won't tell anyone that you took these from the pit."

"You can have those," said Stanley. "I have a few more. I'm going to carve them into beads and make a necklace for my oldest niece."

"Thanks," said Parker, as he pocketed the three stones. "Don't tell anyone about this. We'll keep this just between the two of us. I want to conduct my own investigation on these."

"Okay. Thanks for not telling Mr. Walkins, Parker. I can't afford to get fired."

"Don't mention it, Stanley. I believe that there are some things Mr. Walkins doesn't need to know."

Keenan stood leaning against one of the walls, watching the strange exchange. He realized that the crystals in Parker's hand were possibly the same as those Nick said he had found in the pouch in the pool. Things were getting more interesting by the minute.

Keenan followed the men back to Mr. Walkins's office. He strolled in behind them and had to jump out of the way as Mr. Walkins sent Parker right back out again. Stanley was alone with Mr. Walkins, but an invisible Keenan watched over them.

Over at the Black Stallion Mine, Michael had wandered unseen through the tunnels checking out the working conditions and the men. Michael could tell that tensions were running very high. He overheard the men talking about a recent partial cave-in, in which two good miners had been hurt.

As Michael walked around, he checked the safety features of the mine tunnels. He found that the wrong amounts of dynamite were being used for blasting, and the support beams in several critical areas needed to be replaced. Miners were also digging in several unstable areas. Michael knew that in a few short months the support beams would collapse beneath the pressure of tons of water from an underground river. In another part of the mine, an explosion would open a river into the main tunnels. The rushing water would kill many miners—including Christopher, Keenan, and himself.

Mr. Billings did not spend the morning at the Black Stallion Mine Company offices as he normally did. Slim followed him to the bank after he left the town's hotel, where he had spent the previous evening playing cards and drinking. He was tired and irritable, and his meeting with the investors did not go well.

The Black Stallion Mine was in serious trouble, and according to the paperwork Slim saw that morning, the bank was planning to close them down in a month. A troubled Mr. Billings spent the rest of the morning pacing the entire length of the boardwalk several times with his head down. Around noon, he sighed and headed toward the saloon.

He approached Ike at the bar and ordered a drink. Mrs. Corrine saw him from her office and walked over to talk to him. After several minutes, Slim realized that Mr. Billings was going to unload all of his problems on the unsuspecting saloon owner. Corrine could see that something was up, so she offered to take Billings to lunch. After gulping down his drink, he followed her out of the saloon and down the boardwalk to the hotel for a meal. Slim, having no desire to hear Mr. Billings's troubles for a second time that day, decided to take a break and check up on Nick.

Nick and Ben were just arriving at the Black Stallion Mine. Ben brought the wagon to a halt in front of the office. He jumped down, asked Nick to keep an eye on the wagon, and walked up to the office to check in. Nick waited in the wagon and watched as tired, dust-covered miners walked back and forth with picks and shovels. Ben emerged moments later from the office, followed by a tall, bulky man whom Nick did not recognize.

"Nick," Ben said, "this is Jeb Larkey. He's the senior foreman here at the Black Stallion Mine. Mr. Billings is in town at a meeting with the bank, so I guess you won't meet him until next time. But if the owner of the mine is not available, then you need to locate the senior foreman. He's the only other person who can sign off on our order forms."

"Nice to meet you, Nick. I understand you're going to be taking over for Ben here while he takes a long holiday," said Jeb.

"Yes, sir," Nick replied.

"I'm sure I'll be seeing a lot of you. Say, Ben, you know your way around here, so why don't you give Nick a tour after you unload our supplies? If you have any questions, Nick, never hesitate to come find me. I'll help in any way I can. Well, Ben, did I sign everything you needed me to sign?"

"Yes, Jeb. All the paperwork is taken care of. Thanks for your help," said Ben.

"Not a problem. You guys have a good day." Jeb flicked his hat in a farewell salute, then turned and headed back to the office.

Ben crawled back onto the wagon and nudged the horses forward. "We'll unload our supplies at that stone building over there. I'm sorry," he added, "but we won't have time for a tour today because we need to get moving to make it over to the Falcon Mine. Besides, these guys aren't stupid. If we leave the wagon alone for any amount of time, all the stuff for the Falcon Mine will be gone. The competition between the two mines is pretty intense, and we want to avoid getting in the middle of it."

It didn't take them very long to unload the order for the Black Stallion Mine. It was much smaller than the Falcon Mine order, so Nick could understand Ben's concern.

After they finished, they got back into the wagon and made their way down the mountain. By the time they got to the bottom, it was early afternoon. They stopped by a river and ate their lunch quickly. Then they pushed on so they could get to the Falcon Mine early enough to unload and get back to town before dark.

The ride up both hills was bumpy and steep, but it provided a dazzling view of the forest that lined the mountainside. When they pulled in to the Falcon Mine entrance, Nick could sense immediately that the atmosphere here was different. The miners were talking, laughing, and waving to people as they came into the yard.

Ben stopped the wagon in front of a large log cabin that served as the main office. He got off the wagon and tied up the horses. "Come with me, Nick. We don't have to worry about the wagon here." Nick climbed down and followed Ben up to the cabin.

Ben knocked three times on the door. A booming voice called out, "Come in!"

Ben opened the door, revealing a large office with a small kitchen to the left. On the right side there was a small desk surrounded and covered with books and maps.

"That's Slim's desk," whispered Ben as they passed.

In front of them, behind a very large desk, sat a tall man of medium build. In front of the desk a very thin, dust-covered man sat in a small chair, looking ill at ease.

"Ben!" said Mr. Walkins. "I'm always glad to see you, my boy!"

Ben walked forward to the desk with Nick at his heels. They stopped right next to Stanley Watts.

"Mr. Walkins, sir, I'd like to introduce you to Nick. He's my replacement for the next several weeks."

"Replacement? Where are you going?" asked Mr. Walkins.

"On a much-needed holiday, sir. I'm heading out to visit my sister and her kids," replied Ben.

"I see," said Mr. Walkins. "Well, Nick, it's nice to meet you. Let me introduce you to one of my miners. This is Stanley Watts. Stanley graciously covered for Slim Marano this morning and explored a pit that we just recently stumbled upon."

"A pit? Did you find any bones or a treasure chest?" asked Ben.

"Whoa, boy! You have quite an imagination!" said Mr. Walkins. "No, the pit was just exposed recently in one of the tunnels. It's like a large fissure in the ground. From the looks of it, it is very deep—the men are calling it the bottomless pit—and unsafe, so we've closed off that tunnel."

"Wow! I wish I could have been lowered down there!" exclaimed Ben.

"It's very dangerous down there, young man. You might have gone down looking for a chest full of gold coins, and never come back up again," replied Mr. Walkins.

"Yeah, but think about it: Wouldn't it be the perfect place to hide some great treasure?

Mr. Walkins just smiled indulgently, and then turned his attention to Stanley.

"I think it's time to tend to these boys and our supplies," Mr. Walkins said, "Stanley, why don't you head back to work? Thank you for your information and for being such a good sport this morning."

Stanley got up from his chair. "You're welcome, sir."

Walking Stanley to the front door, Mr. Walkins whispered, "Stanley, everything concerning the pit must remain confidential until we get reports back and talk to Slim. I can count on your silence, right?"

"Yes, sir," Stanley responded. He turned and walked out of the office.

Nick watched Stanley leave as Mr. Walkins and Ben chatted about horses. *Something just doesn't feel right. He has to be a link in this mystery,* he thought, trying to trust his instincts. Nick turned his attention to the conversation between Mr. Walkins and Ben.

"Ben," said Mr. Walkins, "when you and Nick are done unloading the supplies, go ahead and take Nick on a tour around the grounds. I have a special assignment for you that I need to prepare. I'll need you to head over to Cartersville tomorrow morning and take some rock samples to Lucas Marley. All my instructions for him will be in the box that I give you later. Please tell him that I need the results back as soon as possible."

"No problem, sir," replied Ben. "I can have it there first thing in the morning. Nick can handle deliveries in the morning, since most of them will be in town."

"Good! Well, you probably need my signature now, don't you?"

Ben pulled the order form out of his pocket and held it out. Mr. Walkins looked it over and signed it.

"Nick, welcome aboard. If you have any questions, just ask," Mr. Walkins said. He reached out and shook Nick's hand.

His handshake was very firm and strong. Still, Nick couldn't help but shiver with the knowledge that Mr. Walkins would be murdered in just a short time. *One thing at a time,* he told himself. *One thing at a time.*

Ben and Nick left the office to unload the wagon. They climbed back on board and moved the wagon to the supply building. There were a couple of miners that Ben knew standing around, and they pitched in and helped the boys unload the supplies into the building.

Once they were done, Ben said they had enough time to take a short tour of the mine with a friend of his named Horace. The three of them headed to the mine entrance.

The miners were using a natural cave as the main entrance. Nick realized that it looked similar to the cave that he had entered before the cave-in in his own time. As Nick stood in the entrance, a flood of memories engulfed him. He could almost hear the sounds of the cave-in.

Ben's voice cut through his churning thoughts, "Nick, are you coming?" he asked.

"Yes, of course," he said. He ran to catch up with Ben and Horace. "Sorry, this cave just reminded me of another cave I was in not too long ago."

"Honestly, I can't tell one cave from another," said Ben.

"After you've been in them as long as I have," Horace chuckled, "they all seem very different, and they each have their own personalities, as well as their own stories and secrets."

They continued down the main shaft and then came upon a fork in the tunnel that separated into three shafts that looked familiar to Nick.

"The two on the right are working tunnels. The tunnel on the left with those barrels in front of it is currently closed because it's unsafe," said Horace.

"Is that the tunnel where the pit is?" asked Ben.

"Yes. That corridor leads to the lift. The actual tunnel is much farther down below, and I'm not allowed to take you or anyone else down there. Mr. Walkins has put out the word that the pit is off-limits until Slim gets back this weekend and takes a look at it. He'll have the final say as to whether it will be reopened or closed for good. But enough about the pit. Let's go!" said Horace.

The three of them turned, started down one of the tunnels to the right, and arrived at another lift. They climbed on board the lift and were lowered down to the next level. Nick couldn't stop thinking about the closed tunnel. He vaguely remembered that one of the guys had said something about a tunnel shaft that was closed and guarded after Slim's death, when the mine was taken over by Mr. Billings. He couldn't shake the feeling that this could be the tunnel the guys were talking about.

The tour through the mine really helped Nick understand how much work was involved in finding and extracting gold and silver ore. Horace was right. The cave really did seem to have its own personality. Nick and Ben got the opportunity to talk to several miners and watch them as they worked. Horace walked up with his pick and pointed to the wall that he was working on.

"This is a rich vein we're digging out here," he said. "We aren't sure how far or deep it is yet. Down here, the gold veins can be seen spreading through the rock itself. Look, I'll show you."

Using his pick, Horace hit the wall several times, breaking rock free. He picked some up and handed a piece to Ben and to Nick. Nick rolled the rock in his hand. The light played over the surface and reflected off rich golden streaks.

"This is the type of stone most people hope to find," Horace said. "Now this one was found closer to the surface," he added, pulling a small round piece of pink quartz out of his pocket. It not only had threads through it, but also had a large chunk of gold attached to its surface.

"Wow, where did you find that?" whistled Ben.

"Don't tell anyone, but I found it down by the creek the other day when I was wandering around during my lunch break," said Horace. "When I have time, I might go back down and pan some to see what I come up with."

After a few more minutes, Horace said, "Well, I better get the two of you back up top. Didn't Mr. Walkins want to see you again, Ben?"

"Yes. We'd better get going. I'm supposed to pick something up for a delivery to Cartersville tomorrow."

Horace pocketed his stone, then took the rocks from both Ben and Nick and threw them into a bin. "Okay, let's go!"

They retraced their steps through the long tunnel back to the lift, then rode up to the main level and walked back to the fork. Ben and Horace were busy talking, so they did not notice when Nick turned his head and glanced back. He was dying to go down the tunnel with the barrels in front of it. *There has to be a way to get in there*, he thought.

The three of them continued on to the entrance of the cave. Horace shook hands with them, and turned to head back to work.

Ben and Nick returned to the Falcon Mine office. Ben knocked on the door three times. As if on cue, Mr. Walkins's booming voice yelled, "Come in!"

To the surprise of both Ben and Nick, Mr. Billings from the Black Stallion Mine stood in the middle of the office.

"Come in, boys. I'm sure you know Mr. Billings. He just arrived."

"Mr. Billings," said Ben, "we just delivered your supplies to the Black Stallion Mine. I'd like to introduce you to Nick. He's going to be replacing me for a couple weeks while I visit my sister."

Mr. Billings shook Nick's hand firmly. "Nice to meet you, Nick. Sorry I missed you earlier," he said.

"Nice to meet you, too, Mr. Billings," said Nick.

"Pernell, will you excuse me while I take care of these boys?" asked Mr. Walkins.

"Of course. Go ahead. I can wait," replied Mr. Billings.

Picking up a small strongbox on the edge of his desk, Mr. Walkins turned and ushered the boys outside, shutting the door behind him.

"Did you enjoy the tour of my mine, Nick?" Mr. Walkins asked.

"Yes, sir. I learned a lot about mining."

"Enough to come and work for me someday?" asked Mr. Walkins.

"Um, I'm not too fond of caves. I got trapped in one recently," said Nick.

The three of them walked back to the general-store wagon. When Nick and Ben climbed in and were settled, Mr. Walkins handed Ben the strongbox. "Get this to Lucas Marley in Cartersville tomorrow. I'm trusting you boys to keep this totally confidential. I'm not sure what I have here, so the fewer people who know about this, the better."

"Yes, sir. You can count on me," said Ben.

"Good. Now get going. I have to go and find out what Pernell Billings wants," said Mr. Walkins.

Ben pulled the reins and slowly backed up the horses. He turned them around and guided the wagon toward the main road that took them down the mountain.

Nick turned around to catch a glimpse of Mr. Walkins as he walked back to his office. Just beyond him, Nick noticed a man who looked familiar. Nick stared at him for several minutes, but the distance was too great. He couldn't be sure, but it looked like the prospector from the saloon. But why would he be at the Falcon Mine? Squinting to get a better view, he could only watch as the figure turned and entered the main cave entrance.

Chapter Fifteen

COLLECTING CLUES

It took about an hour to get back down the mountain and into town. Ben steered the wagon around to the back of the general store. He dismounted and went ahead to check in with Mr. Guillot, while Nick detached the horses and led them to Mr. Green's to be watered, fed, and stabled.

When Nick finished, he returned to the general store. Suddenly, a soft voice spoke in his ear. He jumped at first, but then he realized it was Christopher. He calmed down and listened.

"Nick," whispered Christopher. "I'm going to go and get our horses. I'll meet you in front of the store when you're done."

Nick nodded his head slightly and kept walking. Upon reaching the back door of the store, Nick entered and looked for Ben. He heard voices coming from the front, so he made his way up there.

Mr. Guillot and Ben were talking at the bottom of the steps when Nick rounded the corner.

"So, Nick," asked Mr. Guillot, "how was your first day?"

"Good, sir. I learned a lot about the mines."

"Ben just told me that he has to run to Cartersville tomorrow for Mr. Walkins," said Mr. Guillot. "Tomorrow morning will be fairly easy, with just a couple of deliveries. But later in the afternoon, we should have a couple of shipments coming in by coach, so we might be a bit busier then."

"I'm up for it, sir," replied Nick.

"Good. Well, I had better get back to the books. Ben, show him what we do with the inventory sheets. Here's the book."

"Come on, Nick, we'll do this at my desk," said Ben.

They sat there for about twenty minutes as Ben showed Nick how to log new orders in the book, balance the numbers with the actual merchandise, and ready an order and double-check it. Then he showed him where to place the finished, signed invoices and where to get new ones.

"See, it's pretty easy. And if you have any questions, Mr. Guillot is always available to help. He's really nice to work for," Ben assured him.

"That's good to know," said Nick.

"You did fine today. Do you think you could make your way back to both mines on your own if you had to?"

"Yeah, sure."

"Great! Well, my friend, it's quitting time. I'm just going to run this book back up to Mr. Guillot's office and then head on out. Have a good evening, and I'll see you sometime tomorrow afternoon when I get back from Cartersville," Ben said. He patted the small strongbox that sat on his desk.

Nick eyed the box after Ben left. He ran his hand lightly over the top of it, wishing he could pick the lock and open it.

Hearing Ben's voice in the distance, Nick decided not to tempt fate, so he quickly scooted through the store and out the front door. *Maybe one of the guys could go to Cartersville and find out what's in the box. But then again, maybe I'm overreacting and it's nothing after all.*

Sorting through his scattered thoughts, Nick stopped in front of the store. He watched people as they passed by. Finally, he saw Christopher riding down the street leading his horse. Nick walked over, took the reins of the horse, and mounted. Side by side, they made their way out of town.

When they cleared the town, Christopher turned to Nick and asked, "So, what did you find out today?"

"I saw a few things I'm questioning. But what about you, did you see anything strange?" Nick asked.

"By the sounds of it, most of the activity today was at the Falcon Mine. Keenan and Michael are going to meet us at the ranch, but Slim is still at the Falcon office observing the meeting between Walkins and Billings. He should be arriving later. It looks like we have a lot to talk about tonight. I hope you're keeping notes, because this is becoming much more complicated than any of us thought!"

"Wish I could have somehow gotten a peek into that box that was sitting on Ben's desk. He's supposed to take it to Cartersville to Lucas Marley tomorrow," said Nick.

"Lucas Marley, huh? He specializes in the identification of all sorts of stones. When Slim has a question about a grain in a rock formation, he sends it or takes it to Lucas himself.

"Slim will probably have Michael follow Ben tomorrow and see what happens in Cartersville. Remember, Nick, in our time, the real Slim was completely baffled by this situation. It seems that Mr. Walkins never told him about sending any samples to Cartersville, let alone what the results were. He found out about the pit only after he returned from Cartersville, but Otis placed him on another project, so he never got down there to check it out himself."

Nick and Christopher were quiet as they turned onto the road that took them back to the ranch.

When they could see the house, Christopher broke the silence. "Nick, after we get the horses settled, go and update your journal while the events of today are still clear in your mind. Make sure you write down everything.

At this point, no detail is unimportant. Keenan, Michael, and I will handle getting dinner ready."

Nick nodded his head as his mind raced. What about the prospector he saw at the Falcon Mine . . . and what about that foreman, Jeb Larkey? Nick sighed deeply. *So many questions with no answers in sight.*

Christopher and Nick arrived at the ranch as the sun was casting long shadows across the valley. They dismounted and led their horses into the barn. Nick was still deep in thought as he removed the reins and saddle from his horse. When he was done putting everything away, he walked up to his horse, reached into his pocket, and pulled out several cubes of sugar. Rusty eagerly gobbled up the sugar and turned to rub his nose against Nick's arm.

"Ah, so you'll be my friend for a couple cubes of sugar, huh? That's okay. I would be your friend just for spending time with me."

Nick had just started brushing his horse when Christopher rounded the corner.

"Nick, go ahead in. I bet you have a lot of writing to do. I'll finish up here."

Nick nodded and patted his horse one last time. Then he handed the brush to Christopher.

"All right. I'll see you inside, then," Nick said. He turned and ran across the yard. His mind was spinning. *Maybe if I write it all down, it will make some sense,* he thought.

Nick entered through the back door that led directly into the kitchen. Michael was leaning against the counter and Keenan sat at the kitchen table drinking a cup of coffee. Michael looked up when Nick entered.

"How was your first day on the job?" he asked.

"Good. I ended up going to both mines today. Tomorrow I'm on my own in the morning with all the deliveries."

"Where is Ben going to be tomorrow morning?" asked Michael.

"Ben has to go to Cartersville tomorrow to take some rock samples to Lucas Marley," said Nick.

Nick did not miss the worried look that quickly passed between Keenan and Michael.

"I have to go write in my journal before dinner," Nick said, about to duck out of the room.

"Hey, Nick, bring your journal to dinner tonight," said Michael. "Between all of us, you'll have lots to add to it."

"And Nick, before you take off, what would you like for dinner?" asked Keenan.

"If I had my choice, I would have to say Mexican," said Nick.

"Any particular restaurant?" asked Keenan.

Nick laughed. "Keenan, are you kidding me? There's no Mexican restaurant around here."

"That's true. But what if Keenan was talking about your time?" replied Michael.

"Well if you're going there, then the restaurant I like best is called The Little Hombre." He sat down at the table and pulled a piece of paper out of his pocket.

"I can make a list for you that would probably make things a lot easier," said Nick. Within five minutes, Nick listed all the foods that he thought that everyone else would like. He handed the list to Keenan, who looked it over with interest.

"You know, I have no idea what any of this is," Keenan said.

"Don't worry, it's all on the take-out menu. All you have to do is hand the list to whoever is working at the counter and they'll prepare everything and load it all into bags. You may want to ask for paper bags. I doubt they had plastic bags in 1866. But you're probably going to need help carrying everything back," said Nick.

"Well, Michael, since you're the only one available, you're it," said Keenan.

Michael got up and stood by Keenan. "This is the address, right?" asked Keenan. He pointed to the top of Nick's list.

"That's right," said Nick.

"Okay, then, we'll see you later," said Keenan.

Nick watched as they slowly began to fade away.

"Cool!" whispered Nick. "I wish I could do that!"

Nick went to his room and pulled his journal out of his back pocket. After propping himself up on the bed, he began to write using the light that streamed through the window from the setting sun. He lost track of time and had to stop writing at one point to light the lamp by his bed.

Some time later, he heard Christopher enter the kitchen from outside. *He has such a distinctive footfall,* thought Nick. It took several minutes, but Nick could tell by the sound of Christopher's boots that he was heading toward his room. Christopher appeared in the doorway, and Nick stopped writing and looked up.

"Hey, bucko. Where are the guys?" asked Christopher.

"Michael and Keenan are out rounding up dinner," said Nick.

"Have you seen Slim yet?"

"No, not yet," replied Nick.

"It's getting late, and I'm anxious to find out what happened with Billings and Walkins," said Christopher. "Well, I'm going to get washed up. Holler at me if any of the guys get back."

"Okay," said Nick. He wrote for another ten minutes, finally finishing his notes for the day. Then he closed the journal, tapped his pencil on the cover, and slipped into deep thought. *I've only been here for a few days and already it feels like I've been in this time and place for a lifetime.*

He looked out across the yard from his bedroom window. The last glimmer of light was slipping behind the mountains. In a few moments, it would be totally dark. *I wonder what my dad is doing,* he thought. *Is he worried about me, or relieved that I'm finally out of the picture?* Nick's thoughts kept him occupied until he heard a sound echo from the direction of the kitchen.

He hopped up, went to the washroom door, and knocked.

"Yeah?" Christopher answered.

"Someone just got back. I heard a noise in the kitchen, but I don't know who it is yet," said Nick.

"Okay, I'll be there in a minute," said Christopher.

Nick strolled down the hallway and across the main room, peeking into the kitchen.

As he peered around the doorframe, he heard a spoon clatter to the floor, followed by a huge sigh.

Nick saw Slim bend over to pick up the spoon.

"Nick!" Slim exclaimed as he straightened up. "How are you, and where is everyone?"

"Hi, Slim. I'm fine. Christopher's getting cleaned up. He'll be here in just a moment. Keenan and Michael went to get dinner."

Nick barely finished his sentence when he saw the wispy figures of the two cowboys begin to appear. They slowly materialized, holding paper bags stamped with the logo of The Little Hombre.

"Hey, Slim," said Keenan. "Hope you're hungry."

"What in the world do you have there?" asked Slim.

"It was Nick's idea. He sent us to one of his favorite Mexican restaurants. They do takeout, so Michael and I got dinner. Let's eat!"

"It smells wonderful!" said Christopher, taking a deep breath as he appeared behind Nick in the kitchen doorway.

"Well, now that everyone's here, I think it's time to eat and talk," Slim agreed.

Keenan unloaded the food on the main table while Slim looked everything over.

"I've never had anything like this before," he said.

When dinner was over, Keenan got up and fixed coffee and hot chocolate, and they all retreated to the main room, where Michael started a fire in the fireplace. Christopher and Nick gathered up all the cardboard cartons and paper bags and dumped them into the fireplace. Then Nick ran to get his journal and rejoined everyone.

Slim began explaining the current problems that the Black Stallion Mine had, adding that the bank was planning to close the mine in a month. He had witnessed a heated discussion between Mr. Billings and Mr. Walkins at the end of the business day.

Mr. Billings had approached Otis Walkins to find out if he was interested in buying the Black Stallion Mine. Walkins told Mr. Billings that at this point it would not be a good investment for him to purchase the mine in its present state of disrepair. This angered Mr. Billings and a full-fledged argument broke out. Several miners outside the office heard it quite clearly.

"Mr. Billings threatened Otis," Slim said, "and then Otis turned around and threatened Mr. Billings. It was a toss-up as to whose ego was bigger. I have never seen Otis this way before. And there were imps all over that office." Slim threw his hands in the air with a groan, and then turned the conversation over to Michael.

Michael began to explain his findings at the Black Stallion Mine. "It's a miracle that the river that will flood the mine next month hasn't ruptured by now. There are several weak areas in the main wall. I investigated and found a rich area of gold ore on the back side of the mine, and they haven't even surveyed that area at all. It's frustrating to know that they wouldn't be having their current problems if Mr. Billings had listened to his first foreman instead of firing him. He doesn't know what he's doing, so the decisions he makes are entirely ego-based." Michael paused. "That's all I've got. Keenan, it's your turn."

Keenan explained how the Falcon Mine workers had sent Stanley down on a rope into the pit, and how Stanley had finally come back up with some samples that he had put in a leather pouch to give to Otis.

"Later, Otis had Parker retrieve Stanley for a private talk in his office, where he grilled him for details concerning the pit. Stanley seemed a little taken aback by all the attention. I'm not sure how forthcoming he was. Just saying that there were a lot of rocks is a little vague. When Otis opened the pouch with the rock samples, I noticed they were quite a bit different from anything I have ever seen. Several of them were crystals."

Nick's head snapped up. "Say, I have something that might help," He bolted from his chair and into his room. He reached under the bed and pulled out his backpack, removing the small leather pouch he'd found in the cave. He rushed back into the main room, opened the pouch, and poured out the contents. Among the gold coins, gold nugget, and watch fob was the sparkling crystal. Nick picked it up and handed it to Keenan.

"This is what I was talking about earlier. Did it look like this?" Nick asked.

Turning the rock round and round in his hand, Keenan held it up to the light of the burning fire. It exploded in a prism of color that sparkled throughout the room. "Nick, I don't know where you found this, but this looks exactly like one of the crystals that came out of the pit," he said. He handed the crystal to Christopher, who passed it around the room.

"Ben is taking several samples to Lucas Marley in Cartersville tomorrow morning for Mr. Walkins. I'm assuming the box contains these crystals. Mr. Walkins also put a note in the box. I'm guessing it says that he wants the findings to be kept secret and rushed to him as soon as possible," said Nick.

Slim stroked his chin as he stared at the crystal. Finally he got up and walked over to Nick, reaching out his hand. "Here, Nick. Take good care of this and don't let anyone know that you have it."

Nick took the stone, placed it back into the pouch, and retied the strings.

Slim paced in front of the fireplace as the others watched silently. After several moments, he finally spoke.

"Okay, first things first. Michael, you need to head to Cartersville and keep an eye on Lucas Marley. Let's confirm what's in that box before Otis finds out. Christopher, I have the feeling we will need to keep an eye on Stanley and probably Parker, too. Between you and me, we should be able to handle those two. Keenan, keep an eye on Otis and any movements toward that pit.

"Guys, I think we need to have a look at the pit and see firsthand what's really down there," Slim said firmly. "Otis may have stumbled onto something too big for him to handle. This may be the very thing that led to his death."

Keenan, bring Nick to the Falcon Mine tomorrow night after he's finished at work. I'll figure out the details later, but we're going into the pit."

"What do you think is going on?" asked Keenan.

"The pit area where the guys have been digging is new, so I'm guessing that excessive heat and pressure from ancient volcanic activity may have changed the rock formation. If that's true, then I believe that Otis's group might have stumbled onto a diamond deposit. The fact that Otis never let me investigate the pit when I was alive and that he kept all the information to himself makes me think that it could be a large deposit. But I need to see it for myself."

"If he really did find diamonds, Walkins's murder could involve any number of greedy people," said Christopher.

"This information never came out in the sheriff's investigation, so that means whoever is ultimately involved covered it up good. Now we'll just have to figure out who all the players are without them discovering any of us. We'll have to stay on our toes!" Michael said.

"Okay, so who's on our list?" asked Keenan.

"So far I have Parker, Stanley, Mr. Billings, Jeb Larkey, and the prospector I saw talking with Mr. Billings in the saloon," said Nick.

"A prospector? When did he appear in the picture? Do we have a name?" asked Slim.

"No name yet," said Nick. "The first time I was in town, I saw him in the claims office having a disagreement with one of the tellers. The second time I saw him was when I met Mrs. Corrine and Miss Terri. He was at the bar. I saw Mr. Billings join him. I couldn't hear their conversation, but I did see Mr. Billings give him a gold nugget and a small bag of coins before leaving. And today when I was leaving the Falcon Mine, I thought I saw him again, walking toward the mine like he worked there."

"Hmm . . . This is not good. We've got to figure out who this guy is," said Keenan.

"Well, we aren't going to solve this mystery tonight, and it's getting late. Let's look at this again in the morning. I think we all had a rough day, and tomorrow is going to be much longer. So get some sleep, everyone; we're going to need it," Slim said.

"Sleep well, Nick!" called out Keenan as he rose from his chair and headed toward his room.

"Good night," echoed Michael and Christopher as they too rose from their chairs and followed Keenan.

"Did everything that happened today surprise you?" Nick asked Slim as the guys left the room.

Slim walked over to Nick and draped his arm over his shoulders. "Come on, it's time for bed. To answer your question, yes. It's interesting to follow people around and learn things that you never knew before. But on the other hand, it's a wonderful opportunity to solve the mystery of Otis Walkins's death and to be put in the position to possibly save the lives of all those miners in the Black Stallion Mine—including Michael, Keenan, and Christopher. The only reason the guys all ended up working at the Black Stallion Mine was because they were trying to clear my name. They were just in the wrong place at the wrong time. It was not their time to go. I would like to see the guys get a chance to live the lives they should have had, instead of dying before their time. I would like to see them get married and have kids."

Pausing by Nick's door, he continued. "You see, Nick, it all starts from a spiritual connection with the Almighty and knowing what you truly believe in. What we accomplish in this life stretches throughout eternity. That good power that lives in you makes it possible to go through this life and help others. Something for you to ponder, young man. But for now, enough talk, off to bed with you! I'll see you in the morning," said Slim.

Chapter Sixteen
THE UNHOLY ALLIANCE

The next morning, Nick woke up before the rooster crowed. Glancing at his pocket watch, he realized that he had awakened an hour early. He dressed quickly and joined the others in the kitchen. Nick was hard-pressed to contain his excitement about the adventures the day promised: sneaking into the Falcon Mine, climbing into the pit, and seeing first-hand what all the mystery was about.

Bright sunlight and the aroma of coffee filled the kitchen. The guys sat at the table reviewing a hand-drawn map that was similar to the maps Nick remembered seeing on the wall of the Land Claims and Patent Office in his time.

Keenan looked up first. "Hey, Nick, you're up early this morning."

"I couldn't sleep—too excited," replied Nick.

"Well," said Slim, "it's good that you are up early. We were just going over this map and the plan for tonight."

Nick sat beside Slim, and Keenan brought him a mug of hot chocolate and a tray of blueberry muffins he had just pulled from the oven. Michael got up and filled the cowboys' mugs with coffee.

"Okay," Slim said between bites of muffin. "Let's make sure we understand today's plan. Michael is going to follow Ben to Cartersville to get a look at the note Otis Walkins wrote to Lucas Marley. He'll wait there to find out the results of Lucas's analysis of the samples. I want the advantage of knowing what the samples are before Otis finds out.

"Christopher and I are going to do split duty on Parker, Stanley, and Mr. Billings to find out how much they know, or how they are involved. Keenan is going to keep an eye on Otis and the pit during the day. In the evening, Keenan will meet Nick after work and bring him to the quarry. Guys, stay on your toes! We need to closely track these people's activities, and we need to know where they are around closing time at the Falcon Mine, since we are heading into the pit," explained Slim.

"What is the plan with the pit?" asked Christopher.

"We'll meet in the woods by the quarry on the backside of the mountain near the river at about half past five. Nick, put in an early order at the bakery for sandwiches. Pick them up when you and Keenan are heading this way. At about eight o'clock, when it's dark, Christopher will transmigrate into the tunnel from the quarry to make sure it's clear and safe. Then, we'll take Nick into the tunnel," said Slim.

Nick tilted his head. "How am I going to get into the tunnel with you guys? I can't transmigrate."

"You can travel with me," said Keenan.

"But how?"

"It's a little trick we call porting. We just hold on to you and we're able to move you to where you need to be. It's different than transmigrating because we're actually moving the matter that makes up your body," replied Slim. "We can transmigrate with inanimate objects, but not with living beings."

A worried frown pulled down the corners of Nick's mouth. "Uhmm . . . OK, I guess."

"Don't worry, Nick," Keenan reassured him. "It will be a little weird your first time, but then I think you'll like it. I'll take you in, and Michael or Christopher will take you out."

"Why can't you take me both ways?" asked Nick.

"It takes a lot of energy to port a human. We don't do it very often. It's easier if we take turns," said Keenan.

Slim chuckled softly. "You see, Nick, even in our world we have limits."

"Now, we won't be able to use their rope," continued Slim. "Keenan said it didn't reach to the bottom, and we have to hit bottom. I have a barrel of rope in the barn. It's about two hundred and fifty feet long. I'll swing back here and pick it up on my way to the quarry."

"We could use several lanterns, too," suggested Michael.

"There are a few in the barn, but we may be out of oil. We could use some of the lanterns at the mine. There should be some by the lift that we can borrow," said Christopher.

"Well, then, I guess we're ready. This is an old map I drew before I left for my trip to Cartersville," Slim pointed at the map lying on the kitchen table. "I drew this before the miners broke through the tunnel and discovered the pit. This black star indicates that section of the mine network. These black dots indicate locations that are good prospects for gold. This red mark is the site where I discovered old volcanic rock and some other material.

"I never showed this to Otis before I left town. I kept it in the back of my journal. When I left for Cartersville, I forgot my journal at home. I was pretty annoyed about that. I wonder if someone found out about the map and stole my journal, hoping to get some ideas about where to look for gold? Everybody knew that I documented every detail of the mines in this journal," said Slim.

"And in my time," Nick said, "your journal was stolen from the museum by some kids. They seemed to be working with someone who worked at the museum. Why would they be stealing it again?"

"Wow, Slim! You're popular in the future, too," chuckled Keenan.

"Maybe people thought you knew more than you did," commented Michael.

"Slim," Christopher asked. "Could it be that your journal is getting so much attention in Nick's time because someone is thinking about reopening the mine?"

"Christopher, you might be on to something. But in Nick's time, the information in my journal wasn't any big secret; most of the gold deposits I'd discovered were mined after my death. So what could they be looking for?" sighed Slim.

"You know, guys, I need to get going," said Michael. "I'm supposed to be following Ben. I'll be back as soon as I have more information." He put his dirty dishes on the counter, and then saluted everyone as he walked into the living room.

"Michael's right. Let's go. Everything is set for the quarry tonight. Nick, have a good day today. Keenan will meet you tonight, so wait for him after you're done with work," reminded Slim.

Nick nodded. He and Keenan headed out the back door to the barn. They tacked up their horses and rode into town.

Michael stood, invisible, behind a storage shed at the edge of Cartersville. He could see Ben in the distance, riding into town on his new horse. Reassured that Ben was on schedule, Michael transmigrated to the front door of the offices of Lucas Marley, Geologist.

Ben slowed his horse to a trot as he entered town. Cartersville was larger than Silverado—and much more crowded. It was a major trading hub filled with storefronts offering specialized services and goods brought in by the trains. Ben guided his horse through the traffic and headed to the opposite side of the town, where the geologist's office was located. He dismounted in front of the office and tied his horse to the hitching post. Taking the strongbox from his saddlebag, he walked into Lucas Marley's office.

Ben was immediately fascinated by the incredible display in the glass case that served as a counter. Lanterns cast beams of light onto small bits of ruby, emerald, garnet, sapphire, gold, silver, and other stones that Ben did not recognize. Lining the walls was a huge selection of hand tools for extracting gems and precious metals from the earth. Before Ben was done exploring, a man emerged from the back room to stand behind the counter. He had the slightly hunched shoulders of a man used to bending over a table to peer closely at small bits of treasure. A pair of glasses pinched the bridge of his nose, and a magnification glass hung around his neck.

"Can I help you?" he asked.

"Yes, sir, I'm looking for Lucas Marley."

"I'm Lucas Marley. What can I do for you?"

"I'm Ben Miller from Silverado. I am here on behalf of Otis Walkins, owner of the Falcon Mine. He asked me to deliver this box of samples," explained Ben. "There is a note inside with further instructions." He handed the box to Mr. Marley.

"Hmmm. Good ol' Otis. Between him and Slim, they keep me very busy. How soon does he want this?"

"Today," replied Ben.

"Why so soon?" asked Mr. Marley, clearly surprised.

"Couldn't tell you, sir. My instructions are to wait for the results and bring them back today," responded Ben.

"Really? Well, okay, I'll need the rest of the morning to work on this. Come back after lunch and I will have everything ready for you," said Mr. Marley.

"Thanks, Mr. Marley. See you then," said Ben. After a last glance at the glass counter, he turned and left the office.

Lucas looked at the strongbox. "I know Slim's in town this week. What could be so important that Otis can't wait until Slim returns?" he whispered.

Lucas started sifting through the drawers of the counter, searching for the spare key for the Falcon Mine strongboxes. Finally, he found it and inserted it into the lock. Lucas found the note tucked into the lid of the box. He pulled it out and, recognizing Otis's handwriting, began to read:

Lucas,

We retrieved this rock sample from a deep pit we discovered in the floor of a cavern we recently broke into. This could become a major problem for the Falcon Mine Co. These samples and your findings must be completely confidential, even from Slim Marano. Please return your results and the samples today in the strongbox. Ben will bring it directly to me.

Your understanding, cooperation, and confidentiality are greatly appreciated.

Sincerely,

Otis Walkins

The note piqued Lucas's curiosity, and he began to examine the samples immediately. He picked up one of the rocks, turning it slowly in his hands several times. His brow furrowed in a slightly perplexed expression. He grabbed another rock and rolled it around on his palm. Then, holding it between his thumb and forefinger, he held it up to a beam of sunlight coming through a nearby window. A prism of color burst forth onto the counter, ceiling, and walls. Turning the crystal back and forth, his eyes opened wide and the air rushed from his lungs.

"Oh my . . . you certainly do have a problem, Otis," whispered Lucas.

Lucas gathered the rocks and the note in the strongbox, and headed to his lab. A few hours later, he had finished his tests and had the amazing results written into a full report. Returning the rocks to the strongbox, he took out a clean sheet of paper and began to write:

Otis,

If your concern is that these samples are diamonds, then I confirm that your suspicions are correct. The stone encasing the crystals is called kimberlite and is usually present when diamonds are found. The diamonds I have reviewed are of very high quality. In fact, these are some of the purest stones I have seen in a long time. I've included a full report on my analysis.

Your secret is safe with me. Whether or not to tell Slim is your business, but I do recommend that you have Slim look over the pit carefully. Slim can re-register the operation of the Falcon Mine to include mining diamonds. Obviously, mining diamonds is different from digging for gold. I believe he is qualified to supervise the work. Other than Slim, I agree that the fewer people who know about this discovery, the better off you will be."

Sincerely,

Lucas Marley

Lucas folded his report and his note and placed them into the strongbox. Locking it, he returned the key to the drawer, then slipped the strongbox into his desk drawer. It was almost lunchtime, so Lucas grabbed his office keys and walked out the front door, locking the office securely behind him.

A low whistle echoed throughout the empty room. Michael's voice came out of thin air: "Wow," he whispered. "I'll say we have a problem!"

★ ★ ★

Back in Silverado, Slim was keeping an eye on Mr. Billings. At about noon, Mr. Billings left his office to have lunch in town. Slim went on ahead of him to check on Nick.

Christopher was hopping back and forth between Stanley and Parker at the Falcon Mine. Nothing unusual had happened all morning. As lunchtime approached, Parker left and rode into town. Christopher found Stanley eating with the other miners, so decided to follow Parker.

Nick had spent the morning delivering orders to businesses up and down the main street. He was proud of himself for finding every shop and getting the deliveries completed on time. He was feeling more comfortable with the layout of the town and the names of the shop owners.

Nick had just finished checking in an order of towels for the hotel when his stomach growled loudly. Glancing around, he realized that the general store was empty. *It must be lunchtime.* Nick headed to the washbasin to clean up. Mr. Guillot was taking him to lunch.

Suddenly, Slim appeared at Nick's left elbow, making him jump.

"Hey, Nick," whispered Slim. "Keenan, is that you?" he asked the air directly behind Nick.

"Yeah," came an answering whisper, and Keenan appeared.

"Otis Walkins and Pernell Billings are in town, I am assuming for lunch. I doubt they are together, so I need some help," requested Slim.

"Hey, guys." Another voice came out of the air as Christopher materialized. "Parker left the Falcon Mine. He's in town, too."

"That makes keeping tabs on everyone a little easier," said Slim. "I'll take Otis. Christopher, stay with Parker. Keenan, you take Pernell Billings, and we'll try to figure out what's going on."

"Has anybody heard from Michael yet?" asked Keenan.

"No, not yet," answered Slim.

"Ben's not back yet from Cartersville," offered Nick. "He didn't think he'd be back until late this afternoon. He's supposed to take the sample analysis directly to Mr. Walkins at the Falcon Mine office first."

"Nick, are you ready?" yelled Mr. Guillot.

"Yes, sir. I'll be right there!" Nick yelled back. "Sorry, guys, I have to run. Mr. Guillot is waiting to take me to lunch."

"Go on—we'll catch up with you later," said Slim.

Nick turned and walked down an aisle toward the front of the store. Keenan, Christopher, and Slim disappeared to follow the three men.

Mr. Pernell Billings arrived in town on horseback and rode straight to the Grand Hotel. Several carriages blocked the entrance, so he continued down the street to the nearest hitching post. After securing his horse, he walked toward the hotel for his lunch meeting with Parker from the Falcon Mine. He was not sure why Parker had sent a note asking to meet with him, but he was certainly curious.

Billings started to cross the street, but stopped short when he saw Otis Walkins enter the hotel. He paused to let Walkins get into the lobby, then continued across the street and down an alley to the back of the hotel where the restaurant was located.

Carefully concealing himself, Mr. Billings peered through the restaurant windows. He watched as Otis Walkins was escorted to a quiet corner table. Otis was reviewing the menu when a man Billings recognized well was seated at Otis's table—it was Angus Jenkins, Mr. Billings's primary investor. "Didn't take him very long at all to set up a meeting with Otis Walkins, did it?" grumbled Mr. Billings.

Billings left his post and made his way back to the front of the hotel. He walked to the front desk and requested a piece of paper, an envelope, and a pen. After writing a quick note and tucking it into the envelope, he wrote Parker Owen's name on the front and handed it to the young lady behind the desk. Smiling, Billings gave her a few coins, then left the hotel and hurried to the saloon. Bursting though the swinging doors, he went directly to Mrs. Corrine's office and knocked several times.

"Come in," called out a voice.

Mr. Billings opened the door and walked in. "Afternoon, Corrine. I've come to ask a favor. I was supposed to have a private meeting with someone at the hotel restaurant, but Otis Walkins and Angus Jenkins are currently dining there. Do you have a private room I can use for my meeting?"

"Well, of course, Pernell. Upstairs, the next to last room on the right is very private and has a door that leads to a separate stairwell in the back. You can go on up and I'll route your guest around the back. I can bring up some sandwiches for you."

"Thank you, Corrine. I appreciate your help," said Billings.

"Who am I going to be looking for?" asked Corrine.

"Parker Owen. He sent me a note requesting a meeting with me," replied Mr. Billings.

"Hmm, I can see why it would have been a problem to meet him at the hotel with Otis there. I'm assuming Otis would not be happy about Parker having lunch with you," said Corrine.

"That's an understatement. I left a note for Parker at the front desk to meet me here. But, to be honest, I have no idea why Parker would want to meet with me. I thought he was happy at the Falcon Mine," said Billings.

"I'll go outside and look for him," offered Mrs. Corrine. "Go upstairs and make yourself comfortable. I'll be up in a few minutes with food."

Mrs. Corrine walked up to the bar and wrote down an order on a piece of paper, which she handed to Ike. She leaned over and whispered something to him, then left to keep watch for Parker from the boardwalk in front of the saloon.

When Parker arrived at the hotel, the young lady whom Mr. Billings had spoken to earlier smiled at him.

"Are you Parker Owen?" she asked.

"Yes," he answered.

"A gentleman asked me to give this to you," she said, handing him the envelope.

"Thank you," Parker said. Taking the envelope, he walked to the corner to read the note in privacy. When he had finished, he stuffed the note in his pocket and scanned the lobby with a worried frown. He walked quickly to the front door and almost ran across the street to the saloon.

Corrine, who was standing by the hitching posts, spotted Parker crossing the street and intercepted him.

"Parker," she called. "Take the outside stairway behind the saloon. Mr. Billings is in the second room from the left. He's waiting for you there."

"Thank you, Mrs. Corrine," said Parker. Shifting direction, he cut through an alley. Mrs. Corrine headed back into the saloon and walked up to the bar, retrieving a tray of food and drinks Ike had prepared. When she had made her way up to the room, she knocked and Mr. Billings let her in. "He's here. He'll be up in a minute," she said as she set the tray on the table. "You can stop by my office later to settle up."

"Thanks for your help, Corrine," replied Mr. Billings.

"You're welcome, Pernell," said Corrine as she left the room.

Parker entered through the door on the back wall, shutting it tightly behind him.

"Have a seat, Parker. I ordered us lunch, so help yourself."

"Good afternoon, Mr. Billings," replied Parker, shaking Billings hand. "Thank you for changing the location of our meeting. I think it's best if Mr. Walkins doesn't know about this," said Parker.

"I have to be honest," said Mr. Billings. "Your note really piqued my curiosity, particularly because it was so vague. What can I do for you?"

"Well, sir, it's no secret that the Black Stallion Mine is in trouble and that the Falcon Mine is doing well. The whole town is aware of that at this point. But, despite the Falcon Mine's success, I keep getting overlooked for promotions, and Slim Marano keeps moving up. He's Mr. Walkins's golden boy. At this point, the only move left for him would be to make him a partner in the Falcon Mine Company. The rest of us foremen are ignored.

"A few days ago, we were digging a new tunnel that Slim had mapped out. When we broke through the main wall, we found a cavern with a large pit in the floor. It's deep, so the rumor among the crew is that it's a bottomless pit. Slim is currently working on a project in Cartersville and was unavailable to check it out, so Mr. Walkins had Stanley Watts lowered down into the pit to see how deep it was and to retrieve rock samples. None of us got to see any of the samples that Stanley brought up. As soon as Stanley was on solid ground, Mr. Walkins snatched the pouch with the samples out of Stanley's pocket and we all headed back to work.

"Later, Mr. Walkins sent me to fetch Stanley again. He wanted to talk to him privately in his office. On the way there, Stanley tripped and some crystal-like stones fell out of his pocket. I picked them up and had a good look at them. Now, I don't know a lot about rock formations, like Slim does, but I know enough to realize that these were no ordinary rocks. Stanley confirmed they were from the pit, and he was pretty scared that I was going to tell Mr. Walkins. So, for my silence, he gave me a few of the samples to keep," explained Parker.

"Has Otis sent anyone else into the pit since then?" asked Billings.

"The pit is closed for safety reasons until further notice," replied Parker.

"What did Otis do with the samples?"

"Well, usually Slim gathers the samples and heads to Cartersville for Lucas Marley's help. But with Slim already in Cartersville, there was no one to take the samples. Knowing Mr. Walkins, he probably found another way to get those stones to Lucas Marley. He was seen talking to Ben and another kid from the general store later that day. There is a rumor that Otis gave Ben a box, but I don't know for sure. I'm checking into it when I get back."

"Did you bring some samples with you?" asked Billings.

"Yes, sir. They're right here," said Parker. He reached into his pocket and brought out two crystal stones.

Mr. Billings stared at the stones that Parker held out to him. He selected one and held it toward the light streaming in from the window. A rainbow of color burst out of the stone.

"This can't be what I think it is," muttered Mr. Billings, with an astonished stare. "This just can't be!"

Parker, picking up on Billings's excitement, began questioning him. "What is it Mr. Billings? Is it worth something? Is it worth a lot?"

"Hold on, Parker," replied Billings, turning toward Parker with a calm demeanor. "I don't know anything. Without an analysis, I couldn't tell you what this is."

"Well, I'm hoping to send out my own sample for analysis and confirm what it is. Or, if Mr. Walkins did in fact send out his samples with one of the boys, then maybe I can get to the report after Mr. Walkins receives it," said Parker.

"Do you know how much of this is down in that pit?" asked Mr. Billings.

"No, sir. When we sent Stanley down into the pit, we didn't know how deep it was. Stanley said he never hit bottom, so we think that it's at least two hundred feet to the bottom. But Mr. Walkins has that tunnel closed off, so no one is allowed in the area. We can't send anyone back down there to get a good look," said Parker.

"If Otis closed the tunnel off, he knows he has something big," reasoned Billings. "So, Parker, what do you want from me?"

"I'm tired of playing second fiddle to Slim, and I believe you're tired of playing secondary fiddle to Mr. Walkins. So, I figure, two fed-up men should partner up and figure out how to at least get a piece of this find," said Parker.

"Well, it's interesting that we share similar feelings. The real question, Parker, is how fed up are you? People could get hurt. Would you be willing to accept those circumstances, to live with that knowledge?" asked Billings.

"I'm fed up, Mr. Billings. I couldn't care less who gets hurt. I want to be rich."

"Interesting proposition, Parker. I'm not moving on this until I get confirmation on this sample and see how big a find this is. It has to be worth the risks I'll have to take," said Mr. Billings.

"That's fair," said Parker. "I'm supposed to be the foreman one night this week. I'll send you a note as soon as I know the schedule. You'll need to be ready to move quickly. Attention is the last thing we need."

"Of course. Let me know as soon as you can. I am going to brief my foreman, Jeb Larkey, and bring him with me."

"I'm not too comfortable with that, Mr. Billings."

"That's understandable, but I don't think you could lower me into the pit alone. Jeb is very strong. Besides, I would trust him with my life, and I trust him with this secret."

"All right, Mr. Billings."

"Good, Parker. Once we know how big of a deposit is in that pit, I will be able to start making plans. In the meantime, let's eat. I believe Mrs. Corrine went a bit overboard for us," said Mr. Billings, eyeing the large plate of sandwiches.

After lunch was finished, Parker got up and shook Mr. Billings's hand. He left the saloon by the back stairwell.

Mr. Billings gazed out the window, considering everything he had just heard. He waited several minutes before he headed down the front staircase. Once he reached the main floor, he proceeded toward Mrs. Corrine's office to settle the bill.

"Did everything go okay with your meeting?" she asked.

"Yes," he replied with a huge smile, handing her some bills. "Thank you for your help. It was very interesting. Forgive me for not being able to stay and talk, but I do need to get back to the office." He touched his finger to his cowboy hat, then turned and strolled out of her office.

Chapter Seventeen

INTO THE PIT

Nick, who had lunch with Mr. Guillot at the hotel restaurant, had also seen Otis Walkins having lunch with Mr. Jenkins. Nick thought it was probably business related, but something about the meeting seemed suspicious. While he was listening to Mr. Guillot explain the intricacies of managing inventory, he caught a faint movement out of the corner of his eye. When he was finally able to turn toward their table, he was surprised to see three imps circling the two men.

Nick was puzzled. The last time he had seen the imps, they were circling a very angry Mr. Billings and Mr. Jenkins. But now they were focused on Mr. Walkins and Mr. Jenkins, and neither man seemed to be angry. They were just sitting calmly, having coffee. Nick returned to his conversation with Mr. Guillot, still wondering why the imps were nearby.

Nick and Mr. Guillot finished their lunch and headed back to the general store. Nick spent the rest of the day helping unload supplies and merchandise from the afternoon coach. He had finished unpacking boxes and was in the process of updating the log books when Ben entered through the back door. He looked dirty, windblown, and very tired. But from the grin on his face, Nick could tell that Ben had enjoyed the trip.

"Hey, Ben," called out Nick. "How did it go? Did you find out what was in the box?"

"Hey, it went really well. I had a lot of fun breaking in my new horse. He responds quickly and runs faster than any other horse I've been on before. But, no, I did not find out what was in the box. I did my best to try to get Lucas Marley to give me some idea, but he would not budge. When I was leaving, I took a good look at the box itself. I thought I might be able to get into it, but it had been relocked. Lucas must have had a spare key. When I gave the box to Mr. Walkins, he seemed really excited. He didn't open it in front of me, though. He just paid me really well and shooed me out of his office. So it's my guess that the samples are really important—either to Mr. Walkins personally or to the mine."

"I wonder what it could be," mused Nick. "It seems strange for Mr. Walkins to be so secretive when his business is a gold mine. Finding gold shouldn't be such a secret. It seems like it would be a normal daily event."

"I agree," responded Ben. "I've been here for several years, and a new gold vein is no longer a big deal. I know Mr. Walkins said that he was sending rock samples to be analyzed, but maybe they found some kind of priceless artifact. Or maybe they found a chest full of gold coins or treasure that some outlaw stashed."

"Ben, has anybody ever told you that you have a very active imagination?" chuckled Nick.

"Yeah, yeah. Say, how did you hold up today, Nick?" asked Ben.

"I completed all the in-town deliveries early this morning with no problems, and then Mr. Guillot took me to the hotel restaurant for lunch. This afternoon, a supply coach came in. I have been unpacking boxes and logging the shipment in the inventory book," said Nick. "I would feel better if you checked my numbers, though."

"No problem. I have to brief Mr. Guillot first, and knowing him, I probably have to help with the accounting. I'll be here awhile, so I'll double-check your numbers before I help Mr. Guillot. Say, it's almost quitting time for you. What are your plans for tonight? Would you like to come to my house for dinner?" asked Ben.

"Uh . . . I'm busy tonight. I'm going out with some friends of mine. Maybe we can do it another night," replied Nick.

"Sure, no problem. Can you stay here a little longer and help me crunch numbers with Mr. Guillot?" asked Ben.

"I think I've had enough work for today," sighed Nick. "I am looking forward to spending some time with my friends."

"Suit yourself then. But keep in mind that Mr. Guillot pays us extra when we work over our normal hours," said Ben.

"I'll remember that the next time," said Nick.

"Ben!" yelled Mr. Guillot. "Are you back?"

"Yes, sir!" Ben called out. "I'll be right there."

"Well, I've got to go, Nick. I hope you have a good night with your friends. Don't get into any trouble, or do anything I wouldn't do," warned Ben with a big grin as he turned toward the stairs that led to Mr. Guillot's office.

Good thing he doesn't know anything, thought Nick as he left for the night. He stepped through the front door onto the boardwalk and squinted as the warm sunlight hit his face. He looked around for Keenan, but did not see him. After waiting a few minutes, he decided to head over to the bakery and pick up the order he had placed earlier that morning. But when he left the bakery, he still did not see any sign of Keenan. After loitering in front of the bakery for a while, Nick headed to Mr. Green's Blacksmith Shop and Stable. The smithy was empty, so he headed for the stables behind the shop. Mr. Green leaned against the paddock fence talking to someone. He could tell by the cowboy's stance that it was Keenan.

Nick walked up behind him unnoticed and poked him in the ribs with his finger. Keenan jumped, startled.

"Nick! You spooked me!" said Keenan.

Nick chuckled. "Sorry."

"Yeah, yeah, I'll bet you are," said Keenan, with a slight grin. "Are you ready to go?"

"Yes," replied Nick.

"It's always a pleasure talking to you, Mr. Green," said Keenan.

"I'll see you again soon," said Mr. Green. "Goodnight, y'all."

Nick and Keenan retrieved their horses, saddled up, and rode out of town toward the Falcon Mine. Keenan asked Nick about his day, so Nick told him everything that had happened, including his conversation with Ben about the box and his lunch with Mr. Guillot. He also told him about seeing Otis Walkins and Mr. Jenkins at the restaurant. Nick was just winding down when Keenan raised his hand and pointed to a grove of scrubby trees. Keenan slowed his horse and turned to pick his way through the stony debris between the road and the trees. Nick followed.

They traveled a couple of miles into the thickest part of the forest, and then slowly worked their way around the base of the mountain through jutting boulders. The path led them closer to the quarry. The terrain was getting rougher and rougher when suddenly Nick heard the roar of the river in the distance. *No wonder Slim wanted to meet here,* he thought. *It's very secluded and totally confined.*

They cleared a bank of trees and found the way blocked by a huge wall of rocks at the base of the mountain. Keenan swung down from his horse, cupped his hands over his mouth, and whistled. Nick dismounted from his horse and listened. Shortly, he heard the return whistle.

"Okay, Nick, follow me," said Keenan. Nick followed him as he picked his way around the wall of rock, leading his horse, and entered an open quarry. Nick spotted a small cave in the side of the mountain, just as Slim, Christopher, and Michael emerged from its dark entrance.

"Hey, guys. We have a little more than an hour before the sun goes down, so let's make ourselves comfortable and have some dinner," said Slim.

Nick and Keenan tied up their horses. Nick grabbed his saddlebag off his horse and went to sit by a small fire burning just inside the entrance of the cave. He passed out the sandwiches he'd brought as the conversation turned to the day's events.

Michael had the biggest news, confirming that the samples Mr. Walkins had sent to Cartersville were in fact diamonds, and were very pure. He also described Walkins's letter, particularly the request to keep the information from Slim.

Christopher and Keenan took turns telling their stories of the conversation between Mr. Billings and Parker Owen. Of course, they'd both been in the room at the saloon as the two men had discussed their plans. Slim wrapped up the discussion by describing the conversation between Otis Walkins and Mr. Jenkins.

"Jenkins called the meeting with Otis, but Otis didn't jump at Jenkins's interest in becoming another primary investor in the Falcon Mine. Mr. Jenkins looked somewhat surprised at Otis's lack of enthusiasm over his offer," said Slim.

"Otis went over numbers and explained about future tunnels that were slated to be drilled. He pretty much covered everything except the pit. Otis is sitting on the most important find of the century and seems to want to keep it a secret from everyone. Mr. Jenkins is the chair of the Falcon Mine financial board, and is the wealthiest man in town. He's offering to totally finance the Falcon Mine Company, and Otis has turned him down. I don't know what Otis thinks he's doing, but I believe whatever it is, he's getting in way over his head. Not telling Jenkins about the pit will come back to haunt him," explained Slim, anxiously rubbing the calluses on his knuckles.

"What do you think Mr. Jenkins will do when he does find out?" asked Nick.

"Not too sure. But I do know that Jenkins has quite a temper, and he will not be happy about Otis trying to shut him out of such a significant find.

And keeping the information from the financial board will create legal problems, too," said Slim.

"Hey, I've got a question," said Nick. "When Mr. Walkins and Mr. Jenkins were having lunch, I saw imps around the table. But neither of them seemed angry. Why were the imps there?"

"Well, the imps aren't attracted to only anger," replied Slim. "What imps are really attracted to is fear, and anger is just a result of fear. And there was probably a fair amount of fear at that table: Mr. Walkins's fear that Mr. Jenkins would find out about the pit, Mr. Jenkins's fear that Mr. Walkins didn't need his money and would be successful without him, and other kinds of fear. Actually, Nick, fear is the reason that most people make bad decisions. And that's when the imps get really interested."

The guys began swapping ideas and opinions about the day's events. Nick wished he had something else useful to add, but his day had been pretty normal at the general store. So, to kill time, he took out his journal and started writing down the names and the activities of all those involved in the mystery.

Slim turned to Christopher. "Check out the guard situation and see if it's safe for us to head in," said Slim.

"Okay, I'm off," said Christopher, and faded into nothingness.

The conversation continued as the sun sank lower and lower behind the mountain. As darkness came, everyone fell silent, listening to the chirping crickets and the forlorn howl of a coyote as it cried to the moon.

"A lot happened today," mused Slim. "As soon as Mr. Billings gets to see the pit, I'm guessing things are going to start accelerating."

"Well, speaking of the pit, are we ready to head out yet?" asked Michael.

Christopher suddenly reappeared. "Hey guys, there are guards at the main entrance and in the tunnel leading to the lift that gets you to the pit. There are none down on the pit level."

"All right, I think we're ready," said Slim.

"Nick, come over here," said Keenan.

Nick stopped writing, closed his journal, and stuffed it in his pocket. Michael kicked the fire out, and the dying embers cast a warm glow. The guys stood in a group, with Slim and Christopher holding an enormous bundle of rope between them. Nick stood in front of Keenan.

Slim turned to Keenan and said, "You should go first since you're taking Nick."

"Couldn't we just walk in?" asked Nick, feeling a bit nervous.

"I wish we could, but you heard Christopher. We can't chance being seen," said Slim.

"Okay. What do I need to do?" asked Nick.

"Turn around and stand on my boots," Keenan said. "I'm going to put my arms around your waist. Grab my belt and hang on tight."

Nick got into position. He looked up to find the guys smiling at him. Nick felt a little ridiculous, but was excited and uncertain what to expect next.

"Enjoy the trip, Nick. We'll see you in a few minutes," said Christopher.

As he watched, the guys faded from his view, as if a misty curtain was being pulled around him. But then his vision returned, and he was able to see through the curtain. Nick felt himself floating upwards with Keenan, and he was in awe as he stared at the trees and sky around him. He could feel Keenan, but he couldn't see him. He looked down and was shocked for a moment when he couldn't see his feet. *I must be invisible, too,* he realized.

They approached the side of the mountain. Closer and closer it came, and before Nick could say a word, he found himself inside the mountain, totally surrounded by rock. They moved through the rock as if it were water—slowly and steadily. Then they began to drop. Down and down they moved, giving Nick a chance to examine the rock around him.

All of a sudden, he found that he was passing though a tunnel, then another, and yet another. *We must be close,* Nick thought. Nick felt them slowing down. They passed through another tunnel ceiling, then slowed to a stop and softly touched the ground. They were in a rough tunnel next to the lift. Lanterns were clustered on the floor next to the lift, and one hung on a peg in the tunnel wall, glowing very dimly.

Nick's floating feeling began to wear off. When he looked down, he could see his boots again, and then Keenan asked, "How did you like the ride?"

"Wow! It was awesome. Totally unbelievable!" said Nick. Keenan's arms released him, and he stepped off Keenan's boots. Keenan leaned heavily against the lift. Nick could tell by his face that he was drained. "Are you okay, Keenan?"

"Yeah, I just need a few minutes. While we are waiting for the others to arrive, could you light those lanterns over there?" asked Keenan.

Nick was lighting the last lantern when Christopher, Slim, and Michael materialized a few feet away from him.

Slim walked over to Keenan. "Are you okay, Keenan?" asked Slim.

"Yes, I'm fine. It was just a short trip, but it did take quite a bit out of me, particularly moving through all that solid rock."

"Okay, everyone grab a lantern and move out," said Slim. He led the way down the tunnel to the cavern. Toward the back wall of the cavern stretched a dark, foreboding hole. A long hewn log stretched across the width of the hole. Rocks anchored the log on both ends.

"There it is. Wow, it is big!" exclaimed Slim.

Christopher pointed toward a pile by the log. "There's the rope they used," said Christopher. "It's not that long."

"I'm glad we brought our own. Let's get started guys," said Slim. Christopher shimmied out onto the log and set up the rope they had brought.

"Nick, how would you like to go down with me?" Slim asked.

Slightly nervous, Nick looked at the yawning mouth of the pit before him. He finally found his voice. "Yeah . . . OK."

"Let's go. Hook Nick up in a harness. I'll use a foot loop and go down with him," said Slim.

"Why don't you just transmigrate?" asked Nick.

"Because I've never seen the bottom of the pit, so I can't picture it," replied Slim. "And I should accompany you on the rope in case there are any problems."

Keenan secured the harness around Nick's body. "Okay, Nick, listen. Since you are going first, you need to straddle the log and inch your way out to Christopher in the middle. Move slowly. Do you understand?" asked Keenan.

"Yes," said Nick.

Trembling, Nick climbed onto the log and shimmied out to Christopher. Glancing down, all Nick could see was darkness. Christopher hooked him up to the main line and double-checked his harness. "Now, Nick, don't worry. I have you. I want you to throw your leg over the log and sit sideways. When I tell you, slowly slide off. Now remember, I have a solid hold on you, so don't worry, but move slowly."

Nick followed Christopher's instructions and moments later found himself suspended under the log. Dangling at the top of the hole, Nick felt uncertain, searching the darkness below him. But the tight harness made him feel secure.

Slim crawled out on to the log above him. "Are you okay, Nick?"

"Yeah, I'm ready to go," Nick replied.

"Okay, I'm going to hand you a lantern, and Christopher will begin to lower you. Then I will climb on just above you using foot and hand loops. The guys will lower us down until we hit bottom," explained Slim.

Nick nodded and grabbed the lantern. Then, very slowly, he felt himself being lowered. He looked around, trying to take it all in, but all he could see was smooth rock on all sides and darkness below. In a few moments, his descent stopped. Nick could feel Slim getting on the rope. Then he felt himself moving downward again. They moved further and further into the pit for what seemed like an eternity, with nothing to look at but rock. But then Nick's lantern caught a flash of color.

"Slim, I must be close. My lantern light is reflecting off the walls," yelled Nick.

"Excellent. Take a good look around you. Is it reflecting on the entire wall and below you?" echoed Slim.

"Yes," said Nick. "But not a lot at this level. The walls twinkle like stars."

"Okay wait and tell me what you see when we are lower. Let me know when you see the bottom, too," echoed Slim's voice.

Deeper and deeper they went, and the pit got brighter and brighter. Nick's lantern light was reflecting everywhere. The entire cavern seemed to be glowing with the twinkling lights. Nick looked below and could just make out the bottom.

"Slim!" Nick yelled. "I'm close to the bottom. It's about another ten feet or so."

"Good," said Slim.

Within a few minutes, Nick touched down. "I'm on the bottom!" he yelled.

"Christopher!" Slim yelled. "Nick's down. It's just about another five feet for me now."

"Okay," echoed a faint voice.

Nick moved aside the length of coiled rope so they would not trip on it. He could see Slim's figure creeping down toward him out of the darkness. The opening in the cavern floor above looked no bigger than a pizza. Slim touched down and detached himself from the rope. He yelled up to Christopher to let him know he was down.

"You okay, Nick?" asked Slim.

"Yeah. What do you think about this pit?" asked Nick.

Slim looked around, raising the lantern above his head. He touched the wall with his hand and then stared down at the floor. "I can't believe this."

Nick followed Slim's gaze around the small cavern. The floor and walls sparkled with iridescent colors as the lantern bathed the cavern in its warm light.

"Nick, you are looking at the result of millions of years of geothermal heat and pressure," Slim whispered, sounding awestruck. "This is a fortune in diamonds. No wonder Otis didn't want me to know about this. I would have written up a report for the Falcon Mine financial board, complete with maps and estimates of value and profits. Now that I've actually seen the diamond deposit, I'm sure that Otis is in way over his head. There's no way he can keep something this big a secret." Nick touched the wall in wide-eyed wonder, amazed at the fortune and potential ruin displayed before him.

"Well, there is one more thing I need to do while we're down here. I need to see how far this deposit spreads in the rock around us," said Slim.

"How are you going to do that?" asked Nick.

"The same way we're bringing you in and out of here—porting. I don't even have to become invisible to do it, actually, just transparent. I'll let you watch me walk in," said Slim with a grin, as he faded into transparency. He took on the greenish aura that Nick remembered. "I'll be right back," he said as he walked into the wall, disappearing nose first. Nick placed his hand on the wall where Slim had disappeared. It felt warm, and seemed to vibrate in an almost imperceptible way.

While Nick waited, he explored the small cavern more thoroughly. He spied a piece of rock jutting from the wall at an odd angle. Curious, he reached up, put his finger under the lip of it, and gently pulled it forward. To his surprise, it popped out and debris cascaded down upon him. Nick raised his lantern up to the fist-sized hole the rock had left. Diamonds sparkled brightly within, reflecting his lantern light. He lowered his lantern and squatted down to explore the chunks of rock that had rained down upon him. Most of them were diamonds interlaced with what looked like regular brownish-gray rock. Nick picked up a few pieces, each about the size of a nickel, and rolled them around in his hand, admiring the rainbow of colors they created.

A sudden noise startled Nick. He jumped up and whirled around. Slim was standing in front of the wall, back in solid form. "Sorry, Nick, I did not mean to startle you. You seemed mesmerized, so I tossed a rock to get your attention," he said with a sheepish grin.

"I knocked a piece of rock from the wall and a bunch of stuff fell down on my head. I picked these out of the rubble." Nick showed Slim the chunks of diamond in his hand. "Should I leave these here or take them with me?" asked Nick.

"Hmmm . . . bring them with you, Nick. I don't want anyone else to find the debris or that rock and realize that someone was down here snooping around. I'm done here. I believe we've stumbled on an unusual geo-thermal fissure that has been pushed up through the ground over many thousands of years. I need more information, though. Are you ready to go back up?" asked Slim.

"Sure," said Nick.

Looking up, Slim gave a loud whistle and a tug on the rope. The rope began to rise slowly. Slim grabbed it, placed his boot into the foot loop, and rose with it. Nick felt the tug of his harness as the rope began to pull against him. His feet left the ground, and he was suspended in the air. Nick took one last look around at the sparkling cavern, and then focused on the opening above him. The ride back up was definitely less nerve-racking than the ride down—even enjoyable—but Nick still hung on for dear life.

When Slim reached the top, he climbed back onto the log and waited to help Nick. Slim stretched out his hand and helped Nick swing his leg over the log. Once Slim and Nick were safely seated, Christopher untied the rope from the log, wound it up, and looped it over his shoulder. All three crawled slowly back across the log to Michael and Keenan, back onto solid ground.

"So how did it look down there?" asked Keenan. "Is it what you expected?"

"It's big, but the deposit doesn't stretch too far beyond the walls of the pit. It's a good fortune in diamonds, though. Once Mr. Billings gets a look, he is going to be hooked," said Slim. They picked up the lanterns and Slim and Christopher gathered the rope. As they were heading down the tunnel toward the lift, Slim stopped suddenly and raised his hand, signaling for them to stop. "I thought I heard something," he whispered. They all listened intently, and for a moment there was only silence. They had resumed their march toward the lift when they heard its gears start up—it was being called to one of the tunnels above. They froze, with wild eyes searching for places to hide.

"We might have unexpected visitors," whispered Christopher.

Everyone stood still, holding their breath as they listened. There were footsteps and the voices of several people getting onto the lift. The lift started its descent, slowly making its way down the shaft. But it was not stopping. They heard it reach the tunnel above . . . then pass it.

"Quick!" called out Slim. "Put those lanterns out and leave them here. Then get against the wall!"

The light disappeared abruptly as the lanterns were extinguished. Someone grabbed Nick's hand and led him to the wall. Nick's heart was beating hard, and he could feel sweat drip down the side of his face. He was being pushed gently against the cold, damp stone wall of the tunnel. Two of the guys backed up against him, covering him with their bodies. Nick tried to control his breathing, but he had started to shake.

"Nick, calm down," whispered Keenan. "Michael and I have you covered. They can't see you—you're invisible."

Nick quietly blew his breath out, trying to calm down. The whining of the lift grew louder as it slowly descended to their level. When the lift finally stopped, it was within arms reach of where Nick stood with his eyes closed. He saw light through his lids and opened his eyes to see who had arrived. Nick had to hold back a gasp as he recognized three faces illuminated by the lantern light—Mr. Billings, Parker Owen, and Jeb Larkey. Two miners stood behind them, and slithering around the group were the shadowy forms of imps.

The men stepped off the lift and Parker said, "This way, gentleman," gesturing in the direction of the cavern. The group started down the tunnel, but Mr. Billings suddenly stopped and backtracked a few steps.

"Parker," Mr. Billings drawled slowly, "I believe you have a problem, my boy."

"What are you talking about?" asked Parker.

"Does your nose work at all? I smell smoke. Jeb, there are some lanterns over there by the lift. Check them out, please."

Nick held his breath as Jeb walked toward him. Jeb stopped just a few feet from an invisible Nick, dropped down on one knee, and placed his hand on the base of one of the lanterns. The imps were becoming agitated, circling Jeb, Mr. Billings, and Parker faster and faster. Nick tried to think the most non-frightening thoughts possible. He wasn't sure if the imps could see him or not.

"You're right, Mr. Billings," said Jeb. "Someone has been here recently. These lanterns are hot."

"That can't be," exclaimed Parker. "Everyone knows this tunnel is off limits. Only the miners who were with us know about the pit. And Stanley is the only one who knows what's down there."

"Well, Parker, there are five lanterns here that have been used recently. That is a pretty good indication that someone has been snooping around. Could it be that Stanley and some of his friends decided to do some exploring?" asked Mr. Billings.

"No, not Stanley. He couldn't pull off anything like this. I've been watching him like a hawk since we found the pit, and he has not talked to anyone. He doesn't even know what he found in the pit, let alone that the few stones he kept could be worth a small fortune."

"Well, either he spilled the beans to someone, or Stanley is smarter than you think. Either way, we need to find out who was here and what they know. The stones that Stanley has—we need to retrieve them. We cannot have any stones floating around that could draw attention to this situation. But first things first, Parker. Let's deal with the task at hand. Show us this pit," said Mr. Billings, slapping his hand on Parker's shoulder.

Parker looked anxious and uncomfortable as he moved out from under Mr. Billings's hand. He turned around and led the group down the tunnel. As they walked around a bend, the area around the lift was thrown into darkness again.

Nick felt Michael and Keenan step away from him.

"Christopher, Keenan, follow those guys. I'll join you in a few minutes," whispered Slim. "Sorry, Nick, but we cannot shed any light for you to see by. We don't want to draw any attention. Michael, get Nick out of here. It is way too dangerous. Take him directly back to the ranch. We will pick up the horses after we are done here."

"Slim, what happened? Parker was not supposed to give this tour until later this week," said Michael.

"I don't know," replied Slim, sounding worried. "Parker was not scheduled for night duty tonight. He's on the schedule for tomorrow night. My guess is that he switched nights and contacted Mr. Billings earlier this evening while we were on our way here. Regardless, we have to make sure they don't identify Nick as the person who was here," said Slim.

There was an urgent sound to Slim's voice that told Nick that he was in a very dangerous situation, and everyone around him was concerned. For the first time, he realized that the guys could not protect him completely.

"Get going," said Slim. "We'll see you later." Then Nick could tell that Slim was no longer standing next to him.

Michael grasped Nick's arm and guided him into position in the darkness. Michael's arms came around him, tight and secure. Nick grabbed hold of the sides of Michael's jeans and stepped onto his boots. The floating feeling returned, and Nick could tell that they were rising toward the ceiling of the tunnel.

Despite the urgency and danger, Nick began to relax, watching the rock flow by and then disappear as they emerged from the mountain into the night air. Michael carried them above the trees, giving Nick a bird's-eye-view of the world. As they passed over the town, a brawl spilled out from the saloon and into the street. The spectators and Mrs. Corrine were yelling at the brawlers. Nick chuckled, so Michael paused to let Nick watch for a moment. Then they were off again toward the ranch, which came into view very soon. Nick let out a small sigh of relief.

The light of the moon illuminated the main room as they materialized in front of the fireplace. Nick stepped off Michael's boots and looked up at him. Michael looked haggard and completely worn out. He gripped the back of a chair and leaned wearily on it.

"Are you okay?" asked Nick.

"Whew! Keenan was right. It does take a lot of energy," replied Michael.

"Is there anything I can do?" asked Nick.

"Yeah," replied Michael. "Would you go around and light some of the lanterns and start a fire. We need some light and warmth in this cold house." He let go of the chair and began to move around it to sit, but stumbled. Nick grabbed Michael's arm and led him to the chair, supporting him as he slumped into it.

Nick turned his attention to the fireplace. He stacked logs on the pile of ashes from the previous evening's fire and added kindling. He struck a match and lit a few of the sticks, watching the flame spread, slowly at first, then up over the logs. The fire created a warm glow throughout the room. After lighting a stick from the fire, Nick lit the lanterns in the room and then moved to the kitchen, driving away the darkness. He brewed a pot of strong coffee, filled a large mug, and carried it out to Michael. Michael grasped the mug and took a long sip.

"Where did you learn to do this?" asked Michael.

"My mom taught me. Dad's a real coffee drinker, and if Mom was away in the morning, it was my responsibility to make the coffee," said Nick.

"She taught you well, then," said Michael, mustering a little smile. "This is much better than Keenan's, but don't tell him that."

"How long do you think they will be?" asked Nick.

"Hard to tell at this point. It could be awhile. We weren't expecting Parker and Billings to show up tonight at the pit. If they had been just a few minutes earlier, we would have had a major problem. You could have still been down in the pit, and there's not much room to hide down there."

"But we could have just become invisible, right?"

"Yes, but getting you out of there without alerting the imps would have been very difficult. You see, Nick, it isn't normal for a human to become invisible, so a certain amount of energy is used. The imps would have noticed. It would have only taken a few minutes for them to locate your position," explained Michael.

"Then why didn't they detect me when we were by the lift?" asked Nick.

"We were fortunate that they were more interested in Mr. Billings and Parker. You did a good job of controlling your fear, and Billings and Parker were very frightened by the prospect of somebody else trying to investigate the pit. Their fear became the imps' focus. But it was a very close call."

"Whoa!" whispered Nick, suddenly frightened again.

Michael finished his coffee and sat his mug down on the small table near his chair. He watched the flames dance around the logs.

"I think I'm going to make some hot chocolate," said Nick, feeling the need for something warm and cheerful. "Do you want any more coffee?"

"No, thanks, I'm fine. I'm just going to sit here and relax," said Michael.

"Okay," said Nick as he picked up Michael's mug and headed back to the kitchen. It took only a few minutes for Nick to make a steaming mug of hot chocolate. He cleaned up the kitchen, returned to the main room, and found Michael fast asleep in the chair.

Nick set his mug on the table and went to his bedroom to grab an extra blanket. He returned and spread the blanket over Michael. Michael did not stir and continued to snore softly. Nick sat in the chair next to Michael's and pulled out his journal. He began to write as he sipped his hot chocolate. After finishing his hot chocolate, he turned his attention to several small drawings he had added to his journal. He enjoyed drawing, and spent some time enhancing the details in each of the sketches. As the night wore on, Nick drifted off to sleep with his journal open on his lap.

Keenan walked through the kitchen door at about two o'clock in the morning and headed for the main room. Nick and Michael were sound asleep, so Keenan retreated into the kitchen, heated the coffee, and poured himself a cup.

Slim and Christopher transmigrated into the main room soon after. Keenan was standing in the kitchen doorway and motioned for the two of them to join him. They walked quietly into the kitchen.

"Coffee?" asked Keenan.

"Thanks," said Christopher, and Slim nodded in agreement.

Slim reached for the cup Keenan offered and let out an exhausted sigh. "Wow, what a night."

"What happened after I left?" asked Keenan.

"Not much," said Slim. "Mr. Billings sent Parker back up first, and then helped himself to a couple handfuls of stones before Jeb and the other men pulled him up. Billings is eager to get control of the Falcon Mine. I don't believe he wants to help Parker, though. He's only interested in helping himself.

"They left soon after that, and Billings told Parker that he would get in touch with him in a day or two with a solid plan. Christopher followed Parker back to his house. I followed Mr. Billings and Jeb back to the Black Stallion office. Billings emptied the stones from his pockets and showed them to Jeb. He asked Jeb for a rough estimate of how much they could be looking at overall. Jeb's estimate was high, but close enough."

Slim drained the last of his coffee in one gulp and set his mug in the sink. "They talked about taking ownership of the mine from Otis. So far, though, they haven't come up with a concrete plan. To be successful in taking it over legally, they're going to need some more help. Regardless, we are going to have to keep a tight watch on them this next week. It's just a matter of time before they hatch a plan they can carry out," explained Slim.

"Whew," whistled Keenan. "This is shaping up to be a major mess. It's becoming so unpredictable."

"Yeah," said Christopher. "Well, guys, it's really late. We are not going to figure this out tonight. Let's get Nick and Michael off to bed, and then get some sleep ourselves."

Keenan extinguished the lantern in the kitchen, and they walked into the main room. Keenan shook Michael's shoulder gently, and Michael opened his eyes.

"Time for bed, sleepyhead," said Christopher.

"How'd it go?" mumbled Michael.

"We'll tell you about it in the morning. You need to get to bed now," said Keenan.

"Okay . . . Where did this come from?" asked Michael as he pulled the blanket off his shoulders.

"Nick probably put it on you," whispered Keenan.

Slightly disoriented, Michael looked around with a worried expression. "Where is Nick?"

"Shh . . . he's fine, he's right over here. Now be quiet, or you'll wake him up," whispered Keenan.

Christopher picked up Nick's journal and handed it to Slim. Then he slid his arms under Nick and picked him up, following Slim to Nick's room. Keenan followed, guiding Michael into his room. Michael fell across the bed, sound asleep again. Keenan pulled Michael's boots off, then left the room, closing the door after himself. He walked back down the hallway and looked into Nick's room. Slim and Christopher put Nick to bed, removing his boots first, then turned and left his room.

"Get some sleep, guys," said Slim. "Tomorrow is another day, and we still have a lot of work to do."

"Okay, Slim, see you in the morning," said Christopher.

"Goodnight," echoed Keenan.

They headed to their rooms. "What a night," Keenan muttered as he climbed into the bedroll on the floor.

Chapter Eighteen
MISS JUDITH'S NECKLACE

Sunlight filtered through the shades of Nick's room and stretched its long fingers across his face. Groaning, Nick opened his eyes, then squinted as he tried to adjust to the brightness. He rolled over, stretched, and sat up, only to realize that he had slept in his clothes. "Last night . . ." he mumbled, as his mind kicked into gear. Memories of the pit, Mr. Billings, Parker, and the imps came flooding back.

Grabbing clean clothes, Nick got cleaned up and dressed. Then, he quietly tiptoed to Slim's closed door and placed his ear against it. It only took a second for Nick to detect the distinctive sound of Slim's snoring. Nick headed to the kitchen and made his own breakfast and a fresh pot of coffee. He had to be at work early because Ben was going to leave for his vacation, and he wanted to be there when Ben stopped in to say goodbye.

Finishing his breakfast, Nick wrote a note to the guys and left it on the kitchen table. He slipped out the kitchen door and headed to the stable. He tacked up Rusty by himself for the first time, checking his work twice with the hope that the saddle wouldn't slide off on the way to town.

He made it to town still in the saddle. Signs of morning life were materializing all around him. Store windows were opening, shopkeepers were sweeping their entryways, and patrons were arriving in carriages and on horseback.

Nick took his horse to Mr. Green's stable, and walked back to the general store to meet up with Mr. Guillot. Nick helped open the store and arranged boxes that were supposed to be delivered that day. Checking the list, Nick found that no deliveries were scheduled for either the Falcon Mine or the Black Stallion Mine. Nick was disappointed; he was eager to head back to either mine to do some more investigating. Nick had just finished checking the boxes against the list when Ben came bursting through the back door.

"Hey there, Nick!" he exclaimed.

"Morning, Ben. Are you all ready for your trip?" asked Nick.

"Sure am," replied Ben, and launched into a detailed description of the route he was going to take, how long it would take him, and the gifts he was bringing. His excitement made Nick grin.

The jingling of the front door bell drew their attention. They walked to the front to see who had came in so early in the morning. Mr. Guillot came out from behind the counter to help a young girl who had headed straight for the bolts of fabric on one wall. Nick did not know who she was, but Ben clearly did. He was straightening his shoulders and running a hand through his hair when he caught Nick looking at him.

"That's Miss Judith. She is the prettiest gal in town," he said, a little defensively.

Chuckling, Nick responded, "Sounds like you're in love."

"Wait till she turns around, Nick, then tell me about love," said Ben.

Nick just smiled and watched Ben try to stand taller. He was about to return to the back room when Miss Judith turned around and greeted both of them. Nick had to admit that the petite blond was stunning, and he figured

Ben was not her only suitor. As she floated toward them with her bright smile and her perfect hair, Nick caught sight of something more shocking than her beauty and his mouth fell open. Hanging around Miss Judith's neck was a beautiful necklace of sparkling stones. They looked just like the stones that came out of the Falcon Mine pit.

"Good morning, Miss Judith. How are you this lovely morning?" asked Ben.

"I'm fine, Ben. And who is this gentleman? I don't believe I've met you before," said Miss Judith, holding her hand out to Nick.

"My name is Nick. Uh . . . it's a pleasure to meet you, Miss Judith," said Nick as he took her hand, uncertain what to do with it. He gave it a little shake before dropping it. "I'm here visiting some friends and covering the store so Ben can go on vacation. Miss Judith, could I ask you where you got that stunning necklace?" asked Nick.

She blushed and tucked a piece of hair behind her ear. "Oh, this little thing? My uncle gave it to me for my birthday," cooed Miss Judith.

"Do you know where he got it?" asked Nick

"He made it for me. As you can see, he is quite talented," replied Miss Judith, fluttering her eyelashes at Nick.

"Do you know where he got the stones?" asked Nick.

Miss Judith's sweet smile faded and she gazed at Nick coolly. The direction of the conversation was no longer to her liking. "Well, aren't you full of questions. If you must know, my uncle found the stones. He works at the Falcon Mine, so he is always coming across interesting stones that he uses to make beautiful jewelry. Now, if you will excuse me, I think I will finish my shopping. It was good to see you, Ben. I hope you have a good trip," said Miss Judith with a smile that was once again warm and open.

"Thank you, Miss Judith. May I come to call on you when I return?" asked Ben.

"You may," answered Miss Judith.

Ben grinned from ear to ear as Miss Judith returned to Mr. Guillot and the fabric. Nick just smiled as he watched his friend try to expand his chest further. He had turned toward the back room when the bell above the front door jingled again. Mr. Jenkins walked in and Ben walked over to help him. But the door had barely closed when it was pushed open again—this time by Mr. Billings.

Nick walked toward Mr. Billings with his mind racing. *What a mess,* he thought. With Miss Judith parading around with that diamond necklace in front of Mr. Jenkins and Mr. Billings, the situation was getting a bit hair-raising.

Nick reached Mr. Billings and smiled. "What can I do for you this morning, Mr. Billings, sir?"

"Ah, yes. You're the new kid. What is your name again, son?" asked Mr. Billings.

"Nick, sir."

"Ah, Nick, my boy, I am bringing my order to you instead of waiting until you have a delivery for the mine. I'm sure Mr. Guillot will be very happy," replied Mr. Billings.

"I'm sure he will," replied Nick. "Let's go over to the counter, and I'll get this written up real quick for you."

While Nick talked to Mr. Billings, another customer walked in, and Mr. Guillot left Miss Judith to help the lady. It only took a few minutes for Miss Judith to make her way over to where Mr. Jenkins and Ben talked. Mr. Jenkins glanced up briefly, then returned to his conversation. When Miss Judith reached out and touched Ben's arm, Mr. Jenkins looked up in annoyance. But this time he saw the glittering necklace that hung around her neck, and his expression immediately changed.

"My dear, dear girl, where in the world did you find that beautiful necklace?" Mr. Jenkins asked excitedly, loud enough to make Mr. Billings turn and look.

Nick could tell from the look on Miss Judith's face that she did not enjoy having her necklace be the focus of attention. But her demeanor changed suddenly when she noticed that everybody had stopped what they were doing and were now looking at her.

"Why, Mr. Jenkins, this little old thing? How delightful that you should notice it," she simpered.

"I must know where such a beautiful necklace came from? Was it a gift from a suitor?" asked Mr. Jenkins.

"My goodness, Mr. Jenkins, you flatter me. It is only a birthday gift from my uncle," answered Miss Judith.

"Oh, and who is your generous uncle, my dear?"

"Stanley Watts," she replied.

The mention of Stanley Watts made both Nick and Mr. Billings jerk. Mr. Billings left Nick to quietly stand behind Mr. Jenkins, looking over his right shoulder. Nick had to see what was happening, so he slowly crept up and stood to Mr. Jenkins's left.

Mr. Guillot watched the unfolding scenario in confusion. He seemed to feel that Miss Judith might need protection, because he left the woman he was helping to stand behind Miss Judith.

"Is there a problem, gentlemen?" asked Mr. Guillot.

"Oh, no, no problem at all. I was just interested in this lovely lady's necklace," answered Mr. Jenkins. "Do you have any idea where your uncle bought this for you my dear?"

"He made this necklace for me. Uncle Stanley is quite talented when it comes to designing jewelry. Why, he has made several beautiful pieces for my mother and her sisters," replied Miss Judith.

"Where does your uncle work? I might like to commission a necklace for my wife," said Mr. Jenkins.

"He's a miner at the Falcon Mine Company," answered Miss Judith.

Nick held his breath as Mr. Billings, with an amused look on his face, leaned over Mr. Jenkins' shoulder and whispered, "Isn't it amazing what can be found in the ground and become absolutely beautiful in the hands of a miner?"

Mr. Jenkins jumped slightly, not having realized that anybody was behind him. He glanced over his shoulder, pursing his lips when he realized that it was Mr. Billings. He didn't respond to Mr. Billings comment, but returned his attention to Miss Judith, bowing his head toward her. "Such a lovely necklace on such a beautiful young lady. It helps make you sparkle like a star, my dear," he said as he picked up her hand and gently kissed the top of it.

Finally, Miss Judith was getting the attention she had been seeking. She blushed slightly, nodded her thanks, curtsied, and then turned back to Mr. Guillot. He retrieved her packages for her, and she gave Ben a last smile over her shoulder as she left the general store. Nick breathed a sigh of relief and returned to the counter to complete Mr. Billings's paperwork, thinking the incident was over. But Mr. Jenkins had turned to face Mr. Billings.

"You seem to be insinuating that you know more about that necklace, Pernell," said Mr. Jenkins.

"Maybe I do, Angus, maybe I do," replied Mr. Billings with a sly grin.

Mr. Jenkins stood there for a moment, staring at Mr. Billings's face. Nick tried to look like he was busy and not listening to the conversation, but every fiber of his being was straining to hear.

"So, are you going to share this information?" asked Mr. Jenkins.

"Well, I might be interested in having a conversation with you, Angus," stated Mr. Billings. "In fact, you might be the very person I should be talking to."

"All right, Pernell, you've got me interested. So let's talk," said Mr. Jenkins.

"Meet me for lunch at the saloon," replied Mr. Billings. "Mrs. Corrine has a nice, private room that she rents out for meetings."

"Fine then," answered Mr. Jenkins, then turned and went to the counter, paid Mr. Guillot for the packages Ben had prepared, and left.

Mr. Billings walked back to the counter toward Nick, looking pleased with himself. "Got that paperwork ready for me to sign, boy?" he asked.

"Yes, sir. Sign right here on the bottom, and your order will go out this morning. It will probably be here within two days," said Nick.

"Good. That works out fine. You'll bring it up the same day, won't you?" asked Mr. Billings.

"Yes, sir. Same day delivery," answered Nick.

As Mr. Billings signed his name on the documents, he asked, "So, my boy, how long have you been in this town?"

"Only a week, sir. I'm still trying to figure out where everything is and who the important people are," answered Nick.

"Well, mark my words. I'm going to be a very important person in this town, and you will do well to remember that," said Mr. Billings.

"Yes, sir, I believe that," said Nick.

Mr. Billings handed Nick two gold coins. "I like you, son. You seem like a smart boy. This is for you. Spend it wisely."

"Thank you, sir," said Nick.

Picking up his copy of the order form, Mr. Billings turned and left the general store with his head held high. Mr. Guillot and Ben walked over to the counter where Nick was standing with a slightly stunned look on his face.

"What was that all about?" asked Ben.

Before Nick could come up with an answer, Mr. Guillot spoke up. "For some reason, I have the feeling that it would be safer if we don't know a whole lot about what's going on."

Nick nodded his head in agreement, trying to look as confused as Ben, then picked up the order form and handed it to Mr. Guillot. He turned and walked back to the storage room, whispering "You don't have any idea how right you are."

Nick did a last check of the delivery list and found that he had a delivery for Mrs. Corrine at the saloon. Nick decided to take the box over just before the lunch hour. If he timed it just right, he could arrive during Mr. Billings and Mr. Jenkins's meeting and maybe find a way to eavesdrop.

The rest of the morning seemed to drag on slowly as Nick made a few other deliveries and helped Mr. Guillot and Ben wait on customers. At half past eleven, Mr. Guillot announced that Ben could leave to start his vacation. Ben's face lit up with a big smile. He walked over to where Nick was sweeping the main floor, extended his right hand, and said, "Thanks for your help with the horse, Nick. He's great! And thanks for the vacation."

Shaking Nick's hand, he leaned closer and whispered. "Listen, I'm not sure why you really need this job, but if it has anything to do with what happened this morning with Mr. Billings, then you need to be extremely careful. Mr. Billings is known to be a dangerous man and you do not want to be on his bad side."

Nick grinned and released Ben's hand, but did not say a word.

"I see you're keeping your mouth shut. Will you at least fill me in if anything interesting happens while I'm gone?" asked Ben.

Nick grinned slyly, "We'll see. I can't promise you anything at this point. But the important thing is for you to have a good time and not worry about what's going on here."

"Then I will see you later," said Ben.

"Have a great time," said Nick.

Ben smiled and turned to say goodbye to Mr. Guillot, then headed out the front door to start his vacation. Nick watched through the window as Ben disappeared into the wandering crowd. Glancing down at the pocket watch Slim had loaned him, Nick realized it was almost noon. Rushing to the back, he put the broom away and picked up the box that needed to be delivered to the saloon. He called out to Mr. Guillot to let him know he was heading out for a delivery and then to lunch, then quickly scooted out the back door.

Nick walked fast behind the buildings and tried not to draw too much attention to himself. He slowed down as he came up the alley next to the saloon and entered through the saloon's front doors. Ike was behind the counter cleaning glasses. He grinned when he saw Nick enter. Nick placed the large box on the bar.

"Hey, Nick. How are you doing, bucko? Is the general store running you ragged yet?"

Nick sighed. "It wouldn't be so bad if some of the boxes that have to be delivered weren't so heavy."

Ike chuckled as he wiped out a glass. "Feel like some lemonade?"

"That would be great," said Nick.

Ike poured Nick a large glass of lemonade. He and Nick both jumped a bit when the booming voice of Mr. Billings filled the saloon.

"Good afternoon, Ike," said Mr. Billings in an almost jolly tone. "Sorry. Didn't mean to scare you," he chuckled, when he saw Ike and Nick jerk. "Is everything ready for my meeting, Ike?"

"Yes, sir, Mr. Billings. Feel free to head on up. I believe Mrs. Corrine is making sure it's clean and tidy," said Ike.

"Has my guest arrived yet?" asked Mr. Billings.

"No, sir. But I'm sure that when he does, Mrs. Corrine will escort him up to the room."

"Very good, then," said Mr. Billings. "Nick, it was good to see you again," said Mr. Billings. He reached out and tousled Nick's hair into a mess and then turned and walked up the main staircase.

Ike shook his head as he continued to wipe the inside of the glass he was holding. "There is something big going on with Mr. Billings," whispered Ike. "He's been courting some meetings here in the last couple of days with some very interesting people."

"Really?" asked Nick, trying not to look too excited. "Who?"

"Well . . . a foreman at the Falcon Mine. I shouldn't be talking about this, so don't say anything to anyone."

"Any idea what's going on?" asked Nick.

"Nope, but Mr. Billings has had some business difficulties in the past, so his reputation is shaky," said Ike.

Ike shut his mouth quickly when Mrs. Corrine's voice drifted across the room as she descended the stairs. Ike pulled the paperwork off the box that Nick had delivered. He grabbed a pen, signed the invoice, and handed it to Nick as Mrs. Corrine walked toward them.

"Well, hello there, Nick. I haven't seen you in a couple of days. Are things going well for you?" she asked.

"Yes, ma'am," said Nick.

"Nick brought this order to us," said Ike. He nodded his head toward the large box on the bar.

Mrs. Corrine glanced at the box and then put her hand on Nick's shoulder. "Thank you, Nick." Turning to Ike, she said. "Ike, that's the order of spare glasses. They need to go upstairs in the storeroom."

"Yes, ma'am," Ike said. He glanced at Nick with a slight smile and started to say something else to Mrs. Corrine, but Mr. Jenkins walked into the saloon at that moment. Mrs. Corrine turned and greeted Mr. Jenkins, then looped her arm through his and escorted him up the stairs.

Ike resumed wiping down the glasses. He nodded and whispered to Nick, "Mr. Billings's guest for his lunch meeting."

Nick watched as Mrs. Corrine and Mr. Jenkins reached the top of the stairs and headed to one of the rooms. A few minutes later, Mrs. Corrine reappeared and called down to Ike to bring up the tray from the kitchen.

Ike sighed, "Well, Nick, I have to get back to work. It was nice talking to you."

"See ya, Ike," replied Nick.

Ike disappeared into the kitchen, leaving Nick to finish his glass of lemonade. Nick tried to figure out a way to get upstairs without drawing any attention to himself. He took his last gulp of lemonade and decided it was too risky to go upstairs. He just could not think of a good excuse to get up there. He was ready to leave when Ike backed through the kitchen door carrying a tray full of food and drinks.

"Thanks for the lemonade, Ike. I'll see you later," said Nick.

"Nick, since you are still here, could I ask a favor?" asked Ike.

"Sure, what do you need?"

"Could you carry that box to the storage room upstairs for me? It's the next to last door on the right. You can scoot out the back once you have put it away. The door to the back stairway is the one at the end of the balcony. I need to get back to the counter right away because the lunch crowd is arriving," said Ike.

"Sure!" Nick could not believe his luck as he picked up the box from the counter and followed Ike up the stairs.

As they moved along the balcony, Nick could hear voices coming from one of the rooms. Mrs. Corrine talked with the two gentlemen, waiting for Ike to appear with lunch. Nick kept a slight distance from Ike so that when Ike entered the room, Nick was able to slip past unnoticed, as all attention was on Mrs. Corrine and Ike setting out lunch. By the time Mrs. Corrine and Ike left the room, Nick had already slipped past them, grabbed a lantern from a wall peg, and entered the storage room, closing the door behind him.

Setting the box down on the floor, Nick turned up the lantern, creating enough light to explore the room. He lifted the box and placed it on an empty shelf. Hearing muffled voices in the hall, he quickly placed the lantern on a peg next to the door and turned the flame down very low.

Nick reached out and touched the wall shared with the meeting room. He moved closer and crouched down next to it, then placed his ear against the wall, hoping that he could hear something from the room next door. He was in luck. The walls were thin, and he could make out most of what Mr. Jenkins and Mr. Billings were saying.

"All right, Pernell, you've got me here. Now I want some answers," said Mr. Jenkins.

"Very well, Angus," said Mr. Billings. "I want to discuss how you and I might partner up and seize the opportunity a diamond deposit offers."

"What are you talking about?" asked Mr. Jenkins.

"The stones you saw in Miss Judith's necklace are from the pit that was just discovered at the Falcon Mine."

"What pit?"

"Wait a minute, Angus. Didn't Otis tell you about the pit yesterday at the hotel?" asked Mr. Billings.

There was no response from Mr. Jenkins, but Nick assumed he must have looked confused, because Mr. Billings started explaining.

"Ah, I see! Otis has failed to tell you about the cavern that they recently exposed. Well, then, I will explain. They broke through a wall in a new tunnel and discovered a cavern. In the floor of the cavern is a large pit that seems to run quite deep. They sent Stanley Watts down into that pit, since Slim is in Cartersville, you know. Stanley went down to retrieve rock samples, which Otis sent to Lucas Marley in Cartersville for analysis. He had Ben from the general store take them," said Mr. Billings.

For some moments, the room was silent except for the sound of footsteps. Nick reasoned that Mr. Jenkins must be pacing. Mr. Billings had tipped his trump card and discredited Otis.

"Are you telling me that the stones from the pit were diamonds?" asked Mr. Jenkins, sounding skeptical.

"I'm not absolutely certain, but that seems to be the case," replied Mr. Billings in a very smug voice.

"How would you know about this discovery, Pernell?" Mr. Jenkins asked. "I hardly think Otis would tell you about a find like this."

"You're right, Angus. Otis would not tell me. But one of the Falcon miners who witnessed the discovery thought that it might be to his advantage to share the information with me," said Mr. Billings.

"Do you trust this man? And why would he come and tell you?" asked Mr. Jenkins.

"Seems like Otis has repeatedly overlooked him for promotions and he's angry," said Mr. Billings. "Do I trust him? No, I don't. That is why I insisted on seeing the deposit before I made any decisions."

Mr. Jenkins gasped. "You've seen it? How much is down there? What is the range of sizes?"

"It's a good deposit, but I won't have any real information until I know more about Lucas Marley's analysis. But take a look for yourself," replied Mr. Billings, and Nick could hear the sound of rocks rolling across the table.

Mr. Jenkins gasped, then asked, "Are you sure these are diamonds?"

"I won't be sure until later today," replied Mr. Billings.

There was a long pause in the conversation, then Mr. Jenkins asked, "Who told you about the pit?"

"Parker Owen. Parker has access to Otis's office, and his assignment today is to get a look at the report from Lucas Marley."

A loud bang made Nick jump. It sounded like Mr. Jenkins had slammed his fist on the table. "So, Otis is planning to keep this to himself?" Mr. Jenkins growled.

"Yes," replied Mr. Billings. "As far as I know, he's also trying to keep Slim out of the loop," answered Mr. Billings. "But Otis does not know that Stanley Watts took some stones for himself. Parker found that out. Those stones are part of Miss Judith's necklace. We are already working on a plan to retrieve the necklace before Otis finds out about it, or before it becomes obvious to others that Stanley Watts made a diamond necklace from stones he found in the mine."

"So how do you plan to get access to the pit?" asked Mr. Jenkins.

"I'm looking for a way to legally remove Otis as the owner of the Falcon Mine. I want to discredit him on paper so that the financial board will force him out and the mine will go on the market for sale. Then I will step in and quietly purchase it. It would become part of the Black Stallion Mine holdings," said Mr. Billings. "But of course, that would take a lot of money I do not have. I need you involved for two reasons. You're the head of the financial board for the Falcon Mine, so you can influence the board and convince them—subtly—to put Otis out. And I would need your financial backing to purchase the mine."

"I see," said Mr. Jenkins. The room was silent for some time, and then he continued. "All right, my terms are simple—fifty-fifty on everything that comes out of the pit. As far as any gold you might find in the Falcon Mine, the percentage will stay at our current contract terms. In return, I will pay off the Black Stallion debt and keep you in business. I will help you on the legal front with removing Otis from the Falcon Mine, and I will put up a sizable sum to help you purchase the Falcon Mine." Mr. Jenkins's tone became forceful. "But I want to be informed about everything. If you try to hide anything from me, like Otis did, I will take both mines away from you, then bankrupt you, and leave you in jail to rot. Now, do we have an agreement?" asked Mr. Jenkins.

"We have more than just an agreement, Angus," replied Mr. Billings, "we are now full-fledged partners."

The meeting ended with the scraping of chairs on the wood floor and the shuffling of feet. A loud clap echoed through the wall, which sounded to Nick like a hearty handshake. Mr. Billings now had a financial backer, which meant all his money problems were over. The only barrier left now was the removal of Otis Walkins as owner of the Falcon Mine.

Nick straightened up carefully; he was stiff and did not want to make any noise. He had heard the door to the meeting room open and the men walk along the balcony. He could still hear muffled voices, as if the men were talking at the top of the stairs. After a few minutes, a rhythmic creaking let Nick know that the men had descended the staircase. He waited a few more moments, then carefully opened the door and peeked outside and through the rungs of the balcony banister. He didn't see the two men anywhere, so he stood and took a step to the doorway, not noticing a bucket sitting just to the side of the door.

The metal clacking of the bucket as Nick kicked it across the storeroom floor made him leap away from the door and close it quickly. He grabbed the bucket, sat it back upright, and then rested against the wall and held his breath as he listened carefully for any footsteps or voices. But there was only silence. After a few moments, he breathed a sigh of relief and quietly opened the door, grabbing the lantern from the peg on the wall. He took a tentative step out into the surrounding silence.

Looking to his left, he could see the door to the back stairway. He closed the storage room door, set the lantern on the peg, and dashed to the stairwell door. He bolted down the stairs, almost tumbling headfirst. As soon as he hit the ground, he ran around the corner of the building, through the alley, and onto to the main street, where he stopped short and tried to look calm and casual. Trying to catch his breath, he stepped into the crowd of townspeople and blended in, not realizing that he had captured some unwanted attention. The shadowy, dark figure of an imp followed him, winding its way through the crowd.

Nick breathed another deep sigh of relief as he walked into the general store. As the afternoon wore on, he relaxed bit by bit, focusing on stocking, sweeping, and waiting on the occasional customer. At the end of the day, he started thinking about the looks on the guys' faces when he shared all of his information with them that evening. He wondered why he hadn't seen them during the day, but decided they had probably slept late and then rushed off to follow the various people involved in this mystery.

He never noticed the shadowy figure that concealed itself in the dark corners and long shadows of the afternoon sun.

Chapter Nineteen

THE UNEXPECTED IMP

Back at Slim's ranch, Slim, Michael, and Keenan were hard at work in the small building behind the ranch house that Slim used as his workshop. They were turning it into living quarters, preparing for the real Slim's return from Cartersville that evening.

This was a major difficulty in this assignment. The first rule that all spirits learned when they were preparing to return to Earth on assignment was that they could never come in contact with their living selves. It would cause irreversible psychological damage, and completely change the course of the real person's life. They could not be seen, but they also couldn't come within a certain distance of their living selves. Slim was trying hard to avoid any problems, but still keep an eye on the real Slim so that they would know what he was up to.

Slim, Michael, and Keenan were assembling makeshift cots when Christopher suddenly transmigrated into the room with a worried look on his face. Slim straightened up when Christopher appeared and immediately asked, "How's Nick doing?"

"Uh, Nick's fine, but we have a problem," replied Christopher.

Michael and Keenan both stopped what they were doing and looked at Christopher, hearing the worry in his voice.

Slim approached Christopher slowly. "What kind of problem?"

"I caught up with Nick as he was leaving the saloon at about noon. He was leaving by the back stairwell. I don't know why he was there, or what he was doing, but something must have happened. I don't think Nick knows this, but he has an imp trailing him," replied Christopher.

"Uh, oh," whispered Keenan.

A low whistle came from Michael.

Slim sunk to one of the cots he had just finished putting together and dropped his head in his hands.

"Slim," Christopher said, pulling Slim out of his worried reverie. "We don't have much time. I stayed with him for most of the afternoon to make sure that the imp didn't cause any trouble. When I left, he was on his way to Mr. Green's stable to get his horse and head back here."

Keenan and Michael had been talking quietly, and Michael spoke up: "Something important must have happened, and Nick must have witnessed it and become frightened, so an imp picked up on him."

"Michael's right," said Keenan. "Nick has been really careful and responsible up to this point. I don't think he's realized what he's done."

Slim sighed deeply. "You're probably right, guys. We'll get the details later. First, we have to figure out how to deal with our unwelcome guest. Any ideas?"

The four men stood there for several moments, deep in thought. Suddenly, Christopher exclaimed, "I think I have one!"

Leaning forward excitedly, he began to explain his idea. In a few moments, all four of them nodded their heads in agreement.

"Let's get ready since we don't have much time before Nick arrives," said Keenan.

"Listen, keep your distance and stay invisible. We cannot afford to let the imp know that we're here," warned Slim.

"Okay, Slim," said Christopher as he walked out the door and headed to the stable. Keenan and Michael followed him out the door, but turned and walked toward the hay barn.

Slim sighed deeply. "Golly, I hope this works." He stood up and transmigrated to where Nick was at that moment. Slim slowly materialized on a distant ridge and watched as Nick rode out of town toward the main road that would take him to the ranch. As Slim watched Nick ride by, he could see the imp gliding leisurely in the shadow cast by Nick's horse. Slim could see the imp hiding there, but Nick was inexperienced and wasn't looking for an imp.

Twenty minutes later Nick's horse trotted past the ranch house, heading toward the stable. Nick looked around, feeling a little spooked by the dark and quiet buildings. *Where are those guys?* He dismounted and walked his horse into the stable and into the first stall.

As Nick was turning his horse around, he noticed a piece of paper attached to the wall of the stall. Letting go of the reins, he plucked the note from its position and quickly read it.

Nick, whatever you do, just act normal. You have an imp following you. Leave the horse and casually walk out of the stall and through the stable to the back door. Walk across the yard to the hay barn. Enter through the smaller door on the right. Once you close it behind you, run as hard as you can through the barn to the back wall. There is a small door there. Go through it, and Slim will meet you there.

Christopher

Nick's blood ran cold and the hair on the back of his neck bristled as he stuffed the note into his pocket. He was tempted to sneak a peek through the cracks in the wood of the stall to catch a glimpse of the imp, but Christopher's note made him realize that he was in danger, so he thought better of it. Patting the horse on his back, he took a deep breath, then turned and walked out of the stall and through the stable to the back door. Nick opened the door and went through it. As he turned to shut it behind him, he got his first glimpse of his unwanted companion. The unmistakable shadowy form of an imp was several yards behind him, flitting from shadow to shadow. He was definitely being followed.

It took every ounce of courage he had not to run across the yard to the hay barn, but he knew that he had to follow Christopher's instructions. The walk to the hay barn seemed like miles, and Nick's head was spinning with questions. *Where did I pick him up, and what has he seen? Why didn't I notice him? Is Slim really angry with me?*

He reached the side door of the hay barn and threw his concerns aside to focus on the task at hand. Opening the door, he stepped into the barn, then quickly shut the door behind him. Darkness surrounded him, but his eyes adjusted quickly, and he caught a glimpse of a glow from a kerosene lantern hanging on the back wall of the barn. He could just make out the frame of a small door below the lantern.

Nick bolted toward the lantern with everything he had. As he got closer, he saw the door open and Slim appeared, waiting for him on the other side. He leapt through and Slim quickly closed the door behind him.

"Good job, Nick. That was fast. Now stay here. Whatever you do, do not open this door! Do you understand?"

Nick was bent over trying to slow his labored breathing, but raised his head enough to nod. Slim slowly faded and disappeared.

Nick moved closer to the door and placed his ear against one of the cracks, hoping to hear what was about to happen. Through the cracks, he could see the dim glow of light from the lantern. At first, he did not hear anything, but then a stack of feed sacks tumbled over and crates were pushed in front of the door.

Nick jumped when Christopher's voice suddenly echoed loudly through the barn: "Now!" There was a loud crash followed by a lot of commotion and yelling. A high-pitched squeal, unlike anything Nick had ever heard before, filled the air. *It sounds like a trapped animal screaming,* he thought. It was ear-piercing.

The screeching muffled the guys' voices, so Nick could not understand what was going on. He could tell that something heavy was being dragged across the floor. Slim's voice grew louder, and Nick quickly stepped away from the door as Slim opened it.

"It's all clear, Nick. You can come in now," said Slim.

Nick stepped cautiously through the door, uncertain of what he would be confronting. The screeching, growling sound was still loud, but muffled. The guys were standing in the middle of the barn surrounding a squirming bag. The horrible squealing was coming from the writhing shape in the bag.

The guys were covered in dirt and hay and looking a bit ragged. As Nick surveyed the barn, he could tell that the imp must have put up quite a fight. Bales of hay had been knocked over, bags of feed had been split open, and dust from the dirt floor had been kicked up and was settling on everything.

Nick walked up to examine the bag. "So, is that the imp?" he asked.

"Yeah, the varmint is in there," replied Keenan.

Michael rubbed his upper arm. "Confound it, those things are strong," he said.

"But they're so small compared to you," said Nick.

"Don't be fooled by their size. Some of the most deadly things in life are small," said Slim. "We'll need to get it out of here pretty quick. Christopher, can you take it somewhere where it will be safely confined until this is over?" asked Slim.

"Sure, Slim," said Christopher.

Keenan spoke up. "Want some help? Safety in numbers."

"You're right," said Slim. "Let's not start underestimating our enemies. We have too much riding on this. Why don't all of you go and make sure we get it confined and secure. Nick and I will clean up here and meet you back at the workshop," replied Slim.

"Good idea," replied Michael. "Let's go, boys!"

Christopher handed the rope he had been coiling to Nick, then reached down and grabbed the rope holding the bag closed. Michael and Keenan reached forward and grabbed the rope, too. They stood around the still squirming, screeching shape and slowly faded away, leaving Nick and Slim alone.

"Whew, that was a close call," sighed Slim. He patted Nick's shoulder. "Let's get this cleaned up, shall we? Then we can fix something to eat."

It had grown dark by the time Nick and Slim finished putting the barn back together. They had worked in silence, each lost in his own thoughts. Nick put the broom in the corner as Slim moved the last sack of feed into place.

Slim stretched and looked around. "Looks much better." Nick nodded in agreement. "Let's head over to the workshop, then," Slim said as he reached up and blew out the lantern. They left the barn together, with Slim resting his hand on Nick's shoulder. Slim shut the door behind them, then turned and led the way to the workshop.

Slim was carrying a small torch, which he used to light a kerosene lantern hanging on a peg outside of the door. He propped the door open and led the way in. Nick could tell that the guys had been working hard during the day to create comfortable living quarters. The worktables had been pushed up against the wall, except for one that was set up as a dining table. All the wood projects that were not finished were neatly stacked under the tables. Barrels turned upside down served as chairs. There were five cots placed around the room.

Slim lit the large potbellied stove, which quickly warmed the room. Nick took off his boots, placed them by one of the cots, and sat down. He was concerned because Slim hadn't said much since the guys had left. It reminded Nick of his father, who always got quiet when he was angry. Suddenly, the door burst open and in walked Michael, Keenan, and Christopher, looking much cleaner and carrying two bags filled with food.

"Hey, y'all, we're back," chimed Keenan as he bounded into the room. "Sorry it took us so long. We stopped to get cleaned up and then decided to pick up dinner."

"Good idea," said Slim. "It smells good. Nick, if you go beyond that wall, there is a makeshift washroom back there."

Nick headed in that direction while the guys unloaded the food. When Nick came out, Michael poured tea, Keenan put out napkins, and Christopher gathered up the loose bags and containers. The food smelled wonderful and Nick was suddenly very hungry. He walked up to the table, unsure where to sit. Michael caught his eye and motioned to the seat—or barrel—next to his. After everyone sat down, Christopher said the blessing. As he prayed, Nick felt Michael's hand rest on his right shoulder. Michael's voice whispered gently, "Don't worry. It's going to be all right."

Dinner was chicken with mashed potatoes and gravy, green beans, rolls, and cheesecake for dessert. As they ate, the guys told Nick how they had trapped the imp.

"Slim was the decoy," explained Christopher. "He was in the corner moving feed bags and crates around. The imp could not see him clearly, so it thought he was you."

"Michael, Christopher, and I were stationed in the loft," said Keenan. "It gave us a good view of the floor. When the imp moved into the center of the room to try to see Slim, Christopher yelled and released a heavy tarp that descended down on it."

"Yeah! We all had to jump down from the loft on top of the tarp in order to pin it down," explained Michael. "That's when Slim joined the fun."

"Well, don't leave out the best part, Michael," laughed Keenan. "The biggest problem was that it was fighting back, so we had to subdue it. Michael jumped on it first and got thrown off real quick," chuckled Keenan. "It was only when Christopher jumped on top of it that the rest of us were we able to pin it down, push it into the bag, and tie it up."

"Where is it now?" asked Nick.

"It's in a special holding place where its screams can't be heard by anyone, particularly other imps," replied Michael. "We'll have to release it eventually, but we got permission to hold it there until we are finished with our assignment."

Slim leaned forward. "Nick, what happened today that drew an imp's attention to you?"

Nick pushed his plate away, rested his elbows on the table, and began to describe his day. He explained that Miss Judith had come into the store wearing a diamond necklace that she said her uncle had made for her, and that Mr. Jenkins had taken a very keen interest in it. Then he described the interaction between Mr. Jenkins and Mr. Billings and their agreement to meet at the saloon for lunch. He explained that he happened to have a delivery for the saloon, and how he had timed it so that he would be there when the men were meeting. He recounted his luck when Ike asked him to take the box upstairs to the storage room, particularly considering that the storage room was right next door to the meeting room. He told them he was able to listen to the private meeting through the wall.

"That was good thinking, Nick," said Christopher. "That's something I would have done."

"I couldn't see anything," said Nick, "but based on what I was able to hear, it seems that Mr. Billings has successfully convinced Mr. Jenkins that Mr. Walkins is purposely hiding the discovery of the pit for his own personal gain. I'm pretty sure that Mr. Billings showed him some stones he had taken from the pit. He told Mr. Jenkins that Parker was going to get into Mr. Walkins's office to look at Lucas Marley's analysis today.

"When the meeting was over, I waited until I heard the two men leave and go down the stairs. But as I was getting ready to step out of the room, I tripped over a bucket in the dark. It scared me to death when it went clattering across the floor. I closed the door and grabbed the bucket, then I waited for a few more minutes, just in case someone might have heard it and come upstairs to investigate. But I didn't hear anyone, so after checking the hallway,

I took off and ran down the back stairway and up the alley, then headed back to work," explained Nick.

"That's probably where you picked up the imp, Nick," Slim said. "He was probably in the room where Jenkins and Billings met, or in the process of following them, and heard the clatter. He likely saw you sneak out of the storage room, and your fear caught his attention. You were more interesting to follow than the others."

"So now Billings has Jenkins involved in this mess," said Michael, sounding frustrated.

"I wouldn't have suspected that Jenkins would be involved. But by getting Jenkins interested, Billings has eliminated all of the financial problems he's having with the Black Stallion Mine," explained Slim.

"You're right. That does solve the Black Stallion Mine cash flow problem, but what has Mr. Jenkins asked for in return?" asked Michael.

"Fifty-fifty of everything coming out of the pit," said Nick.

"Mr. Jenkins is a very cautious man," said Slim. "He will do whatever research he needs to do before taking any real action. And he'll probably keep a very close eye on Mr. Billings."

"Did they discuss how they were going to take over the Falcon Mine?" asked Keenan.

"Mr. Billings suggested discrediting Mr. Walkins with the Falcon Mine financial board, and then taking control of the mine. Mr. Jenkins seemed to agree, and that's where it ended. They didn't make any concrete plans," said Nick.

"Discrediting Otis might have worked, and I do remember that when I got back from Cartersville, I heard some rumors that there was going to be an investigation of the mine. But Otis was killed before the investigation started, so something must have happened that changed that plan," surmised Slim.

The room fell silent for a few minutes as everyone sat at the table, deep in thought. Slim, who had his head down drawing on the table with his finger, jumped suddenly. He jerked his head up and looked toward the front door.

"What's wrong?" asked Michael.

"The real Slim is back. He just walked through the front door of the house," said Slim.

"How do you know that?" asked Nick.

"I can feel everything he is doing. I can sense his thoughts. He is really tired right now. It's been a long ride from Cartersville."

"Can't he see the lanterns burning through the window, or the smoke coming from the stove?" asked Nick.

"No," answered Christopher. "We have been given a little help from above. There's a sort of screen around the building. Slim can see the workshop, but to him, it looks like it always does, and the screen keeps him away from the building. He won't even think about working on any of his projects. So we are totally protected. But he will be able to see us if we leave the workshop, so we have to make sure we're invisible or that he has left before we venture out in the morning."

Nick got up, walked to the window, and peered out. The silhouetted figure of the real Slim appeared in the kitchen window. He seemed to be fixing a pot of coffee.

Nick returned and sat down at the table. "How will I be able to tell the two of you apart?"

"The real Slim will be wearing a medallion around his neck. My father gave it to me. You will have to remember that he won't know who you are, though. He will not know anything that you know concerning the diamond deposit or Otis's murder, so you will have to be careful what you say to him," explained Slim.

"How does it feel, having yourself so close?" asked Keenan.

"Kind of strange," answered Slim. "I am aware of every movement, every thought, every feeling right now. The more distance I can keep between us the better. It's the only way to stay focused and work independently from him."

"What is he doing right now?" asked Christopher.

"He's in the main room reading some reports he picked up in Cartersville. He's getting ready to write an entry in his journal. The fireplace is lit, and he has a cup of coffee in front of him," answered Slim.

"What happens if you're in the same room with him?" asked Nick.

"That's not allowed, Nick. We have to maintain a certain distance from our living selves. Otherwise, we might be tempted to interfere—to prevent bad things from happening, to give hints about good things that will happen. Any interference can cause a big change in the course of a person's life, and that's what has to be avoided unless specific permission is given. It's rare that we go back in time to change things. Usually when we're on assignment, our role is to help things along on their natural course, not change things that have already happened."

"Well," interrupted Michael, "tomorrow is Sunday. The general store will be closed, so we need to figure out how we're going to set up our surveillance schedule. Now that Jenkins is in the mix and the real Slim is back from Cartersville, we're going to be spread pretty thin."

Slim sighed, "You're right, Michael. A lot more people are getting involved, and we still have a week and a half before the actual crime is committed. And it's another week after that before I am hanged," said Slim with a slightly forlorn look.

Nick pulled his journal out of his pocket and opened it to the page where he had been writing names. *All of them know something about the pit or are conspiring with other people involved,* he thought.

Christopher looked over Nick's shoulder. "Who's on your list?"

Nick read out loud: "Mr. Billings, Parker Owen, Jeb Larkey, Stanley Watts, Mr. Jenkins, unknown prospector, two unknown miners."

"Who is the unknown prospector?" asked Michael.

"You know . . . the guy Mr. Billings was talking to in the saloon after he had the argument with Mr. Jenkins in the claims office," replied Nick. "And then I saw him again on one of my first deliveries to the Falcon Mine; he was walking into the main entrance like he worked there."

"We still don't have a name for him?" asked Keenan.

"No name yet, but I can recognize him for sure if I see him again," said Nick.

Slim drummed his fingers on the table while he considered this information. "This could be significant," he said. "Nick, since you are the only one of us who has seen this guy, your assignment is to keep a lookout for him. Try to find out who he is and if he is working for Mr. Billings or Otis."

"There is a manifest for each mine that lists all the miners on the payroll. If we have a name, we can check and see which list he appears on," suggested Christopher.

"If Nick can point him out to one of us, then we could trail him and find out what he's up to," said Michael.

"It's getting late, guys. Let's just work with what we have for right now. Tomorrow we are going to have to reevaluate everything. Please remember that the real Slim is on the scene, don't assume it's me and show yourself or start talking," warned Slim.

All the guys nodded as they got up to clear the table.

Nick helped move the dishes to the sink as the guys worked on their tasks. Nick spied Slim stoking the fire in the potbellied stove. He walked over and stood by him.

"I'm really sorry about today, Slim," Nick said. "I didn't mean to mess everything up."

Slim loaded the last piece of wood into the opening. He turned, looked into Nick's eyes, then reached up and grabbed his shoulder.

"Now, don't you go worrying about that, Nick. Mistakes happen. Just be aware and on your guard, because these next several weeks are critical. Another imp could ruin everything, so be careful. Believe me, it could have happened to any of us."

Rising, Slim shut the door to the potbellied stove. "I have an assignment I want you to tackle tomorrow. The real Slim will be heading to the little white church at the end of town tomorrow morning for the worship service. I would like for you to go, too, and introduce yourself to him. Begin to establish a friendship. You are the only one of us that can contact him directly, so we need you to gain his trust. It just might come in handy in the long run. You will be on your own while the rest of us are following everyone else. But we will check on you each hour to make sure you are okay. Think you can handle that?" asked Slim.

Nick sighed, feeling relief. "Yes, sir. I can do that."

An hour later, everyone except for Nick was asleep and snoring.

Nick looked around the room at the four sleeping cowboys. He felt content for the first time since the death of his mother. He breathed deeply, closed his eyes, and yawned, "I finally belong," he murmured softly. "I really do love these guys. They're my family now," he whispered. Then he drifted off to sleep.

Chapter Twenty

THE REAL SLIM

The next morning, Nick woke up when Michael gently shook his shoulder. "Time to get up, Nick. You've got an assignment this morning."

Nick groaned as he rolled onto his back. "Okay, okay, I'm up. I just need a minute." He closed his eyes as he stretched and listened to the low voices and the occasional clatter of a pan. Finally, feeling like he had his wits about him, he rose and shuffled to the washroom to get cleaned up. Once he was clean and dressed, he reappeared in the main room to the smells of frying bacon, hot coffee, and warm rolls. All the guys were up, preparing for the day ahead.

"Hey, Nick, how did you sleep?" asked Christopher, who was setting the table. "Keenan didn't keep you up with all his snoring, now, did he?"

"Hey, now! Who snores?" yelled Keenan.

Christopher started chuckling just as a roll sailed across the room straight at his head. He ducked and caught it.

Handing the warm roll to Nick, Christopher whispered, "That's one way to get Keenan going, but believe me, there are other ways, too."

"I'll remember that," said Nick, chuckling.

"I believe we're ready to eat, y'all. We have to discuss our assignments before we head out, so let's get started," said Slim.

Everyone sat down at the table. Once the blessing had been said, plates of bacon, eggs, and rolls were passed around. In between bites of food, Slim gave out the assignments.

"I believe that Mr. Jenkins and Mr. Billings need to be watched. I also believe Otis Walkins should be closely followed. He is trying to keep the pit a secret, and he doesn't realize the number of people who know about it already. Any one of them could be the person who kills him," explained Slim.

"Michael, you take Mr. Jenkins. Christopher, you take Mr. Billings. Keenan, you take Otis Walkins. Nick, you take the real Slim and keep an eye out for the unknown prospector. I will split my time between Jeb and Parker. Guys, I don't care how you split it up, but since Nick is going to be with the real Slim, he needs to be checked on at least once an hour, and obviously, I can't do it."

"Oh, Nick, you're going to have to travel with us from now on. Christopher had to return the horses to his friend Black Feather last night after we stowed the imp. We don't have any place to keep them with the real Slim back in town. When we check in with you, you'll need to let us know when you'll get off work so that we can transport you back here," said Michael.

Nick nodded and stood to help Keenan and Christopher clear the dishes. It did not take long to get everything cleaned up. Once finished, they stood in the room in front of the cots and waited for Slim.

Slim rounded the corner from the washroom and stood among them. Clapping his hands in front of him, he took a steady breath. "Okay, guys, we are coming down to the wire. We have a lot of suspects, but nothing definite. Everything is a lead—any comment, any situation, any person.

Michael will take Nick to the church and you guys rotate and check up on him every hour. That pretty much covers everything. Any questions?"

"I think we got it," said Keenan.

"We'll be keeping an eye on you, Nick. Just be careful," said Christopher.

Then, with a smile and a wave, Keenan and Christopher faded away and disappeared into thin air.

"Are you ready, Nick?" asked Michael.

"Yep," responded Nick. He moved to stand on Michael's boots. He looked over at Slim as Michael's hands gripped his shoulders.

"Remember, Nick, be careful what you say to the real Slim. He knows nothing," reminded Slim.

"I won't forget," Nick said. He and Michael began to fade and then disappeared, leaving Slim alone in the room.

The trip to the little white church did not take as long as the trip from the mine. So before he knew it, Nick felt the ground beneath his feet. He looked around and found himself behind the small white church.

Stepping off Michael's boots, he turned and looked up at him. "Are you okay?" he asked.

"Yeah. Shorter trips are easier, particularly when we don't have to move through much solid material," said Michael. "Now, all you have to do is go around the building and enter the front door. Slim usually sits in the middle on the left side. He isn't here yet, but I saw him on the way, so he should be here soon. Christopher, Keenan, and I will check on you throughout the day. As long as you are near the real Slim, we can't approach you. But we'll try to catch you when you are alone. Remember, the real Slim wears a medallion around his neck. That should make it easier to tell the two Slims apart."

"Thanks for reminding me," replied Nick.

"Okay, I'll see you later. Be careful, there will be a lot of imps around, too. They don't know that you can see them, so don't let on that you can," reminded Michael.

"I'll be on my guard," Nick promised. He waved, then turned and walked around to the front of the church.

Standing at the corner of the church, Nick watched the townspeople walking up the path or milling around the courtyard, socializing with their neighbors. He straightened his shirt, then strode across the yard, unnoticed until he came upon a small crowd. He planned to skirt around them and head up the stairs, but he heard his name being called. Nick whirled around to see Miss Judith standing at the edge of the group. A ray of sunlight hit the necklace she wore, sending twinkling, colorful lights dancing on every nearby surface.

"Well, well, fancy seeing you here, Nick. You did not strike me as the churchgoing type," said Miss Judith.

"I have always gone to church, Miss Judith," replied Nick. "My mother used to take me every Sunday—that is, until she died. I only got into town last week."

"Well then, since this is your first time here, come and sit with me. Ben is still away, and I could use the company," said Miss Judith.

Nick considered Miss Judith's proposition for just a moment before deciding it was probably a good idea. He'd be happy to have the company, but more importantly, with that necklace on, Miss Judith was sure to draw a lot of attention from all of the people he wanted to keep an eye on. He fell into step beside her as she climbed the stairs to the doors of the little white church.

As they entered the building, Miss Judith linked her arm through Nick's and walked proudly across the threshold. They walked halfway down the aisle and sat on the left-hand side. Nick looked around as people were filing in and taking their places. The pastor walked to the pulpit and lay down his sermon notes and Bible. When he looked up to survey his parishioners, he smiled as if he recognized someone he had not seen for some time. He left the pulpit and walked back down the aisle toward Miss Judith and Nick.

Nick watched as the pastor hurried past him. Turning slightly to look over his shoulder, he heard the pastor say, "It's good to have you back. How was your trip?" Twisting further to get a better view, Nick's heart leapt when he saw who the pastor was talking to—it was the real Slim.

Slim and the pastor talked for several moments as the parishioners took their seats. Nick tried to watch them without being too obvious. The real Slim looked just like his spirit—except that he was wearing different clothes. He talked just as animatedly as the spirit Slim. Nick noticed a bruise on the left side of his forehead, and as Slim turned, Nick caught a glint of light on a gold chain that hung around Slim's neck. It was mostly hidden beneath his shirt.

The crowd settled down as the pastor left Slim and headed back to the pulpit. Slim walked past Nick and Miss Judith and took a seat two pews in front of them. Nick cautiously surveyed the parishioners, quickly finding Mr. Billings, Jeb Larkey, Parker Owen, Otis Walkins, Mrs. Corrine, and Miss Terri scattered throughout the crowded church. As the pastor spoke, Nick angled himself into different positions to keep an eye on everyone. He noticed Mr. Billings scowling in Slim's direction. Nick could tell that he was not pleased that Slim was back in town. Nick also caught Otis Walkins glancing at Slim several times. Most of the key players also seemed to be aware of Miss Judith's presence, judging from the looks Nick saw directed at them. *They're probably not speculating about Miss Judith's new suitor—not that I'm a suitor—so they must be interested in the necklace,* he thought. Those who knew about the pit were probably concerned about Mr. Walkins or Slim noticing the necklace and questioning Miss Judith about it. Nick could feel the tension heighten in the church as the service continued.

The service lasted a little longer than an hour. As the last prayer was said, everyone stood for a moment in silence. As the congregation slowly began to exit the church, Nick was torn between wanting to try to make his way over to Slim and wanting to stay close to Miss Judith to see who came her way. To Nick's surprise, Slim was the first to reach them. Reaching out to Miss Judith, he took her hand and raised it to his lips, causing Miss Judith to blush.

"You look beautiful today, Miss Judith. What a lovely necklace you have, my dear. It makes you glow," said Slim.

Miss Judith's blush deepened. "Thank you, Mr. Marano. It is good to have you back in town. You've been gone for some time. So, you like my necklace? It was made for me by my uncle," she said.

"Miss Judith, do you know where your uncle found such beautiful stones?" Slim asked as he gently reached forward and touched the necklace around her neck. She was about to answer him when a shout interrupted her.

"Slim!" exclaimed Otis Walkins.

Slim's attention was wrenched away by the sound and a sharp pain as Otis slapped his shoulder. His hand dropped away from Miss Judith's necklace.

Otis grabbed Slim's hand and shook it vigorously. "Slim, it's good to have you back," he said.

"Thank you, sir. It is good to be back," replied Slim.

Nick studied the small group that suddenly surrounded them. Everyone on his list of suspects was present. They all seemed to be playing a part in this elaborate homecoming welcome. Nick knew that most of them were trying to keep Mr. Walkins and Slim from noticing the necklace, which was almost impossible, as it sparkled with the changing light from the windows. So keeping Slim and Mr. Walkins occupied seemed to be the plan of action. The antics of the group amused Nick. There was much handshaking and many inane questions about the trip to Cartersville. Nick wondered what Otis would do if he knew how many people in this group actually knew his secret, or if he realized that Parker was responsible for the leak.

Realizing she was no longer the center of attention, Miss Judith became bored and quietly slipped out the other side of the pew. Nick stood where he was, hoping to be introduced to Slim. It took a few minutes for the group to realize that Miss Judith and the necklace were no longer present. All eyes searched the immediate area, and as soon as they discovered she wasn't in the church, each person made an excuse and dashed off. The pastor was the only one left standing with Slim and Nick after the others had disappeared.

"I've never had a welcome home like that before," said Slim.

"Yes, that was quite peculiar," said the pastor. "I've heard strange things are going on in the mines these days. Slim, did you realize that you had people from both mine companies in the group?"

"I know," said Slim, scratching his chin. "That's what made it even more strange." Sliding his glance toward Nick, he asked, "Well, now, who do we have here? This is a face I don't know."

"My name is Nick Stewart, sir. I work for Mr. Guillot at the general store with Ben, but he's on a holiday. I make deliveries."

"You are new to town, aren't you? I don't remember seeing you around before," said Slim.

"I've been here for about a week, sir. I've heard quite a bit about you from the miners, of course," replied Nick.

"Call me Slim. 'Sir' sounds so formal. So you've heard of me, huh? Well now, you're going to have to tell me what they are saying behind my back, aren't you?" Slim said with a chuckle.

"Yes, Slim," said Nick with a smile.

"You make deliveries to the mines, right? Maybe you can tell me what's been going on in this town since I've been gone. Why don't you join me and Pastor Greg at the hotel for lunch? That way we can find out more about you. You and Pastor Greg can fill me in on what has been happening while I've been gone," suggested Slim.

"I'd like that," said Nick.

"That sounds good, Slim," responded Pastor Greg. "Give me a few minutes. I'll meet you both outside."

"Okay," replied Slim. "Come on, Nick, let's go."

Nick eased out of the pew and fell into step with Slim as they exited the church. They stood in the courtyard and waited for the pastor.

Behind a tree near the church, Michael watched the scene with invisible eyes. He smiled as he watched Nick talk to the real Slim. Pastor Greg joined them, and the three of them wandered down the hill toward the hotel. Michael sighed. "So far, so good," he whispered, then departed to continue his assignment.

It turned out that lunch at the Grand Hotel restaurant was almost as tense as the church service. Many of the same people had arrived for lunch, and Nick noticed that the room seemed to quiet down when Slim entered the restaurant. They were directed to a table near one wall, and Nick tried to choose a seat that gave him the best view of the room. Otis Walkins sat at a table nearby with several gentlemen Nick did not recognize. On the other side of the room, Mr. Billings was seated with Jeb Larkey, who watched them over the top of his menu. Several tables over, Mr. Jenkins sat with Stanley Watts, a woman Nick did not know, and Miss Judith with her sparkling diamond necklace. And near these tables danced the dark forms of imps.

Nick rolled his eyes and turned his attention to the menu that the waiter handed him.

"Is everything okay, Nick?" asked Slim.

"Oh, it's nothing. I just saw Miss Judith," said Nick.

"Would you rather join their group?" asked Pastor Greg, with a wink at Slim.

Nick thought quickly, not wanting to bring the focus on Miss Judith's necklace. "Oh, no, I'm not interested in her in that way. Besides, Ben really likes her, and I would not want to get in the way of true love."

"You're a good friend, Nick. Most young men would not have given it a second thought. Isn't that right, Slim?" said Pastor Greg.

Slim gazed lazily at Miss Judith's table. "That's right. Most young men wouldn't take such care to protect a friend. But I have to say that what is more interesting and puzzling to me right now is the fact that Mr. Jenkins is sitting with Stanley Watts."

"You're right, Slim," said Pastor Greg. "Why would Mr. Jenkins lower himself by having lunch with someone he considers to be a second-class citizen? Unless he has something to gain from it, of course. Stanley is quite good at making jewelry, though. I believe his talent is being wasted by working in the mine."

Slim surveyed the room. "I believe that Stanley has risen through the social ranks with the creation of Miss Judith's necklace. Their table is getting a lot of interesting looks. But the real question is, where did he get those stones in the first place? I'm sure that's the question on the minds of most of the people in this room. They look ready to pounce on Stanley to get the answer."

Nick sat silently, uncertain of how to respond. The real Slim was obviously observant, but he certainly didn't know the whole story. The waiter came and took their lunch order, interrupting Slim's observation of the room. The conversation turned to the good old days when the pastor and Slim were young men growing up in Cartersville. The pastor and Slim told story after story about their childhood pranks and had Nick laughing until his sides hurt.

After they had finished their lunch, a wide, bulky man walked into the restaurant and up to their table. There was a metal star pinned to his shirt, and Nick recognized him from the old black and white photo he had seen in his time—this was Sheriff Artemus Chamberlain, Slim's best friend.

"Howdy, partner," drawled the sheriff. "I hope you guys haven't eaten dessert yet."

Slim rose and vigorously shook the sheriff's hand. "Good to see you, Artemus. I was going to stop by to see you after we were done here."

Pastor Greg rose, too, and shook the sheriff's hand. Slim looked in Nick's direction. "Artemus, meet my new friend, Nick. He's new in town and filling in for Ben over at the general store. Nick, this is one of my best friends, Sheriff Artemus Chamberlain."

"Glad to meet you, sir," Nick said, rising and shaking the sheriff's hand across the table.

"Take a seat, Sheriff, and have something to eat while we have dessert," said Pastor Greg.

Nick could tell that these three men had a strong bond, a true friendship established by their shared history. They had grown up together, playing practical jokes, getting into trouble, getting out of trouble. As Artemus finished telling another story about one of their amazing adventures in the caves, he turned to Nick, winked, and asked, "Now what do you think?" The look in the sheriff's eye made Nick question how true their stories were.

The stories went on until the other lunch patrons were long gone. Slim was the first to notice that the staff was changing the tablecloths and setting up for the dinner crowd. He insisted on paying the bill over loud opposition from the pastor and sheriff. Once the bill was paid, the four of them rose and headed out of the restaurant, still laughing about the last tall tale.

Pastor Greg had to return to the church to prepare for the evening service. After shaking Nick's hand vigorously, he walked up the path that led to his church. The sheriff invited Slim and Nick to join him in his office for coffee. They turned and headed back down the boardwalk into town. As they walked through town, something across the street caught Nick's eye. When he turned his head, he saw Christopher standing a few feet down an alley between two buildings. When he caught Nick's glance, he waved at him then turned and quickly walked deeper into the shadows of the alley. It was comforting to know that the guys were checking up on him. Nick's assignment was to get close to the real Slim, and he felt good that he had been able to accomplish the task. And spending the day with Slim and his friends was a lot of fun, too. Ending this day on a positive note meant a lot to Nick, particularly after the imp incident.

He felt totally at ease with the real Slim and the sheriff. Conversation between them flowed comfortably as they walked. It felt like he had known them all his life, and they made him feel that they thought highly of him, too. As the sheriff opened the front door to his office, he said to Nick, "You're welcome to stop by here anytime, Nick. Any friend of Slim's is a friend of mine."

Nick smiled broadly as he walked into the sheriff's lobby. The sheriff and Slim continued through the lobby and down the hallway, but Nick stopped short, staring around the lobby. He was struck by how little had changed since the last time he had been here—more than 150 years in the future. It made his skin crawl to realize that the past and the present were connected by a single thread of time.

Aside from different pictures of outlaws posted on the wall, everything else seemed to be pretty much the same as when he had first seen it. A desk sat to one side with paperwork piled on it. The sheriff turned back and saw Nick staring at the desk, so explained that his deputy was off for the day. Nick pulled himself out of his reverie and followed Slim and Sheriff Chamberlain as they walked down the hallway. The sheriff passed the small kitchen off to the right and then turned into the next doorway. Just as Nick remembered, the door said SHERIFF in big black letters.

"Just had that painted on there this past week," said the sheriff. He waved his hand toward it as he passed by and headed toward the chair behind the big desk.

"Looks really official now," responded Slim.

"Come on in and make yourselves at home," said the sheriff as he sat down, leaned back, and propped his boots on the corner of his desk.

Nick let his eyes wander around the room as he headed to one of the chairs in front of the sheriff's desk. There were a lot more personal items in the room than there were in his time. There was a gun rack hanging behind the desk that was filled with rifles and pistols. A worn saddle leaned against the wall in the right corner. On the sheriff's large desk, there were piles and piles of papers, along with an ink bottle, an empty mug, and a pocket watch with its cover open.

As Nick sat down, he noticed a small table tucked into the opposite corner of the room. On it sat an assortment of glass jars. Curiosity drove Nick to rise and walk over to the table to examine the contents of the jars. He was surprised to find that they were full of bullets of all different shapes and sizes.

"Interesting, isn't it?" asked the sheriff. "You can pick 'em up and look closer if you want."

"What are they?" asked Nick.

"They're all the bullets we've confiscated. Every once in a while we have a few wild people come into town. They have a few drinks, and then they figure they need to stir up some excitement. So, I gather a small group of men and we go out, round them up, take away their guns, and throw them into jail until they sober up. Then, we give them back their guns, but without the bullets," explained the sheriff.

"I've never seen so many different bullets," said Nick.

"You haven't been around much, have you, Nick?" asked Slim, with a chuckle and wink at the sheriff.

"Nope. Spent most of my time working with my father. The only action we saw was with picks and shovels. Then my mom died. Now he's a teacher," replied Nick.

"Hmm, teaching is a good occupation," said the sheriff. "Oh, and before I forget, Slim, I confiscated something that I think Keenan is going to want to have back."

At the mention of Keenan's name, Nick's heart skipped several beats. He placed the bullet he had been rolling around in his hand back into one of the jars and quickly returned to his seat next to Slim.

The sheriff reached into one of his lower desk drawers and pulled out what looked like a coil of dark rope. He tossed it Slim, saying, "I believe that this is Keenan's bullwhip."

"Where did you find it?" asked Slim. "Keenan thought he lost it on the ride back to Cartersville last month."

"Well, tell Keenan when you see him that he didn't lose it after all. That boy Will Henley admitted to lifting it from Keenan's saddle. I found him and some of his friends playing around with it behind the hotel last week. I thought it looked like Keenan's, and then I saw his initials on the handle."

"Well, he'll sure be glad to get it back," said Slim, running his thumb over the whip. "Ever used a whip before, Nick?"

"Nope," answered Nick.

"Here. Get a feel for it while I get a cup of coffee. You do have some hot coffee made, don't you, Artemus?"

"Of course. This office doesn't work without lots of coffee going day and night. Help yourself, Slim. I don't figure you drink coffee, do you, Nick?"

"No, sir, I don't," Nick said. Nick turned the coiled leather whip around in his hand, and then grasped the long, leather-wrapped handle, imagining Keenan unfurling it into the air with a loud crack.

"Get me a cup, too," called the sheriff after Slim had left the room. "Keenan's pretty good with that. He can knock bottles off a fence with just a flick of his wrist. I'm waiting for the day he can flick a horsefly off the backside of a cow without spooking the cow," laughed the sheriff.

"Can you be that precise?" asked Nick.

"Oh yeah. If you are really, really good, you can snatch a gun out of a man's hand from several feet away. Keenan is really good. He did that trick once in practice. Unfortunately for Christopher, it popped his hand pretty good. Gave him a nice bruise," reminisced the sheriff.

"You sound like you know Keenan pretty well then," said Nick.

"Yeah, I grew up with Keenan and two other friends, Michael and Christopher, in Cartersville. Slim moved there with his family from Boston when he was ten. One night we got into some trouble with several older men who had been drinking. They might have given us a good whippin', but Slim showed up and interrupted them. He told them that another round was waiting for them at the bar, and when they left, he hustled us away. He's been part of our group ever since."

"After that we became, in some ways, a holy terror to the townspeople. It is a miracle we never got put in jail for some of the pranks we pulled. We never hurt anyone, but we sure did cause trouble," said the sheriff. He leaned back in his chair, staring at the ceiling and grinning broadly, lost in his memories. "I miss those days. Life seems so much simpler when you're a kid. The older you get, the more complicated it becomes. Now I have lots of responsibilities, and a lot of expectations from the townspeople to live up to. So Nick, my friend, my advice to you is to stay a kid as long as you can. It's easier," said the sheriff.

Nick looked down at Keenan's whip again. "Maybe so," spoke up Nick. "But when your mom dies, things get pretty complicated, no matter how old you are."

"I'm so sorry, Nick," whispered the sheriff. "You're right. Even a kid's life can be unfair, and curves like that can make you grow up overnight. But Nick, remember that you're still a kid, despite what others think or expect."

Slim walked back into the office carrying two big mugs of hot coffee. "Did I interrupt something?" asked Slim, sensing the quiet in the office.

"No, Slim. Thanks for getting me coffee," said the sheriff. He reached forward to take his mug. "Hey, I think you and I should take Nick out back and teach him what we know about cracking a whip."

"Hmm, that could be interesting, as long as one of us doesn't put the other one's eye out," said Slim.

"Nah, we'll be extra careful. What do you think, Nick? Interested?" asked the sheriff.

"Wow, I would love to learn how to crack a whip," said Nick.

"Then let's go!" Slim said. He led the way outside, cutting through the kitchen to the back door. The door opened into a small corral behind the sheriff's office and the jail. The corral was enclosed with a split-wood fence, and there was a small cluster of trees to one side.

Nick handed Keenan's whip back to Slim. Slim handed Nick his coffee cup to hold while he unfurled the whip.

"Okay, until I get used to handling this, you probably want to give me a lot of room," suggested Slim.

Nick moved several feet away and stood next to the sheriff. Slim raised his arm, then brought it down fast and hard. The whip moved through the air, making a whooshing sound.

"It's supposed to crack," drawled the sheriff to Nick. "Hey, Slim, I think you should try it again," he laughed.

"Oh, all right, so I'm not as skilled as I used to be," retorted Slim with a chuckle. "But give me credit for trying."

Slim repositioned himself and took a deep breath. He raised his arm again, and then threw it forward, finishing with a wrist flick. This time a loud crack broke the silence.

"Wow," said Nick. "That sounded great!"

"He's right, Slim. Is it coming back to you?" asked the sheriff.

"Yeah, it's coming back, Artemus. Let me give it a couple more tries and then it's your turn," said Slim.

After an hour, both the sheriff and Slim were able to flick the whip good enough to get consistent cracks, so they began to take turns showing Nick how to do it.

Nick's attempts were all over the place, but after a while, he could make the whip crack and direct it to a specific area. The three of them spent the rest of the afternoon taking turns aiming at tree branches and then bottles that the sheriff set on the fence posts. By the time they finished, Nick was able to hit a bottle now and then.

"Whoa! That was your best snap yet, Nick!" laughed Slim, as one of the bottles went flying.

The sheriff tipped his hat back and wiped his brow with the back of his hand. "He's a natural," said the sheriff. "But I think we need to call it a night, or I will not be able to lift my arm tomorrow."

"You're right, it is getting late. Hey, Nick," Slim called, "can you bring the bottles here? We are going to call it a night."

Nick turned from where he was picking up the bottle he had just knocked down. "Okay!"

With Nick out of earshot, Slim turned to the sheriff with a very serious look on his face. "Hey, Artemus, it seems that some strange things are going on in town, particularly between Otis Walkins, Mr. Billings, and Mr. Jenkins."

"Hmmm, you may be right, Slim," said the sheriff. "I've seen some odd things over the past week or so—unusual meetings, peculiar behavior. Otis Walkins and Mr. Billings have been in town an awful lot, and that makes me think there's been a discovery, probably of a new vein of gold. I've heard that the Black Stallion Mine is in danger of being closed. And the rumor around town is that Mr. Jenkins was making the rounds yesterday afternoon, asking questions about Otis's competency. I'm not really sure what's going on or what was found, let alone which mine it was found in. But it must be significant, because everybody seems to be involved. I'm sure that Otis will tell you what's going on when you see him tomorrow," said the sheriff.

"Yes, I'm anxious to get to the mine tomorrow and find out more. But, ya know, I've been thinking . . . Nick has had direct access to both mine companies since I've been gone. He might be able to help me piece things together," surmised Slim. "He seems like a smart kid. I bet he could pick up information, or at least notice anything strange, at the Black Stallion Mine."

"I'm not so sure that's a good idea, Slim. He's still new to the town, and he is just a kid. Why don't we talk about this later, privately. Are you up for some dinner?" asked the sheriff.

"Yeah, that sounds good. Here he comes," said Slim.

"Nick, we are going to call it a night. Artemus and I have some things to go over tonight. Do you have a way home?" asked Slim.

"Yes, sir. I'm staying at the hotel, but I'm meeting my mother's friends soon for dinner," Nick said.

"That's good. I wouldn't want you having dinner all alone," said the sheriff.

The sun was slowly sinking behind the mountain range as the three of them headed back into the sheriff's office.

"Say, thanks for letting me spend the afternoon with y'all. I really enjoyed myself," said Nick.

Slim laid Keenan's bullwhip on the sheriff's desk and turned toward Nick. "Glad you could join us today, Nick. With you covering for Ben at the general store, I will probably be seeing a lot of you in the next few weeks. You'll still be doing the deliveries to both mines, right?" Slim asked.

"Yes, as long as Ben is still away, or as long as he chooses to let me," said Nick.

"Good, good, then I should definitely see you within the next few days. I might have a project or two for you, Nick," said Slim.

"A project?" asked Nick.

"Yes, but don't worry about it right now. I'll go over the details with you later. I just need to talk it over with Artemus first," said Slim.

The sheriff cleared his throat loudly, and Nick looked at both men curiously, not sure what to think.

"Don't worry about it. We'll be in touch," said the sheriff. He ruffled Nick's hair.

"Okay, well, I should be going," said Nick looking at his pocket watch. "I need to meet my mom's friends."

"Well, Nick. It was very good to meet you and spend the day getting to know you. If you need anything, just stop by my office, now that you know where it is," said the sheriff.

Nick reached out to shake the sheriff's hand. "Thank you, sir," he said. "I really did have a great time."

He turned to Slim and shook his hand. "Just let me know how I can be of help, Slim. I'm willing and able," said Nick.

"Thanks, Nick, I will be in touch," said Slim with a smile.

Chapter Twenty-One
THE INTRUDERS

Slim and the sheriff stood and watched from the front doorway as Nick walked down the street. "You're right, Slim. He is a very smart kid. Reminds me of you when you were his age."

"All right, all right, now you're trying to be funny," chuckled Slim. "But I wouldn't be surprised if he has information to share even now. Who knows what he's seen at this point."

"Maybe so. But we are going to have to be careful, Slim. He is just a boy, and we don't want to get him mixed up in anything dangerous," said the sheriff.

"I know, I know," replied Slim. "Let's go, Artemus. I could use something to eat."

Slim and the sheriff left the office and headed down the dark, empty street.

"You're thinking about having Nick spy for you over at the Black Stallion Mine, aren't you?" asked the sheriff.

"Well . . . yeah, basically. But then again, I wouldn't necessarily call it spying, just being more observant concerning certain people."

The sheriff rolled his eyes and shook his head, then slapped Slim on the back. He sighed deeply. "Now you are splitting hairs, my friend. I still don't think it's a good idea to get him involved in all this. But let's sort this out over the dinner table. I don't want any of the townspeople to overhear our conversation. We'll need to get a nice, quiet table at the hotel. That's all I need—to start a rumor that I'm harboring spies. That would send a wave of panic through this town like lightning."

Slim chuckled. "Remember, Artemus, it's nothing we haven't done before when we were kids," said Slim.

"Yeah, but that was a long time ago. We were less noticeable because we were kids."

"Right, just like Nick," said Slim pointedly.

Nick heard their voices as they passed his hiding spot in the shadows of the alley next to the general store. He was waiting for one of the guys to show up.

He grinned broadly when he heard what they were saying about him. His meeting with Slim went better than anyone could have expected. The real Slim seemed to be willing to listen to what Nick might tell him about everything that was going on.

Nick saw movement across the street. Stepping out of the shadows, he saw that Christopher had transmigrated to an alley on the opposite side of the street to check up on him. Nick stepped into the light of one of the few street lamps so that Christopher could see him. Christopher motioned for Nick to cross the street, so Nick headed over and followed Christopher as he ducked into the alley.

"Hey, Nick, how are you? Where is the real Slim?" asked Christopher.

"Slim and the sheriff are heading to dinner over at the hotel," said Nick.

"Good. Are you ready to go?" asked Christopher.

Nick stepped onto Christopher's boots. "Yep, I'm ready."

"Here we go then," said Christopher. Moments later, they flew effortlessly over the roofs of Main Street. A few people walked down the street, heading for the hotel for dinner. A moment later, Nick could see Slim's ranch in the distance. They soon touched down by the door of the workshop, slowly became visible, then walked in.

Keenan sat on a barrel in front of the potbellied stove, staring at the flickering flames. He looked up when the guys walked in. "Hey, Nick!" he exclaimed. "How did it go?"

"Great!" replied Nick, "I think that the real Slim wants me to spy for him over at the Black Stallion Mine. But he has to clear it with the sheriff first." Christopher and Keenan stared at Nick with their mouths open in disbelief. They looked at each other, and then they began to fire questions at Nick.

"Whoa, whoa, wait a minute," Nick finally called out. "I can only answer one question at a time, guys."

"Nick, what you just said is very significant," said Keenan, in a very serious tone of voice. "This is a major change in the original timeline of events. It did not happen before."

"Keenan is right, Nick," said Christopher. "You were not here before. There was no one in Slim's life besides the sheriff and us whom he could trust. And we were still in Cartersville at that time."

"This creates quite a wrinkle, to say the least," said Keenan. "We thought you'd meet him and be able to spend some time with him so that we would know what he was up to, but events are taking a different turn."

"So what do I do? He is meeting with the sheriff right now to discuss my involvement," said Nick.

Christopher sighed and stood in front of the potbellied stove to warm his hands. Keenan paced the floor in deep thought, stroking his chin as he walked.

"Any ideas, Keenan?" asked Christopher.

"Here is what we'll do. First off, Christopher, you go and locate the real Slim and the sheriff so we know what is going on. Nick, you stay here.

You've had a long day. I will go locate our Slim and brief him on this odd turn of events."

"Okay, I'm heading out," said Christopher, then waved his hand and slowly faded away.

"Did I do something wrong again?" asked Nick, feeling all of his happiness ooze out of him.

"No . . . no, Nick," said Keenan. He reached over and put his hand on Nick's shoulder. "Slim has always been a little too curious for his own good, which used to get us all into trouble. Too much trouble to recount, to be honest. This is just something we hadn't counted on. Tell you what. Let me fix you something to eat. You can tell me everything that happened today before I take off to talk to our Slim," said Keenan.

Nick followed Keenan over to the makeshift kitchen and sat down at the table. He watched Keenan work as he described the day's events.

"And that's all that happened," concluded Nick.

Keenan set a plate in front of Nick and took a chair across the table from him. "Yeah, I saw Slim and the sheriff trying to teach you how to crack my whip. I'm glad you got the opportunity to try it out. Believe me, not many people can get the feel for it so quickly."

"How come you don't have it now?" asked Nick.

"Well, I got it back when Michael, Christopher, and I came down for Slim's trial. I still had it with me the day we were working in the Black Stallion Mine and the accident happened. I guess it's still somewhere in the mineshaft, because it wasn't on me when they finally found my body. Now, I have a new one that I still mess around with. But I do miss my old one. Lots of memories there," explained Keenan.

"Will you teach me some tricks if I can find one at the store?" asked Nick.

"Sure, I'd be happy to," replied Keenan. He paused for a moment before changing the subject. "So Slim wants you to spy for him," he sighed.

"How big of a problem is this?" asked Nick.

"Not too sure at the moment. You see, what happened today could be a wrinkle in time. Up to this point, everything has happened exactly as it happened in the original timeline, with the exception of Ben getting his horse and taking a vacation. But even that was carefully planned to minimize the long-term consequences.

"Our potential problem is with the real Slim's overactive curiosity. Now he has found a possible willing participant in his investigation. The question is, how far is Slim willing to go with this? And how do we control the information he discovers so that he does not jeopardize our assignment?

"He's been kind of lost since his kids grew up and left home. And then his wife passed away last year. I wouldn't be surprised if you kind of remind him of his son or maybe even himself when he was your age," said Keenan.

Nick listened intently while he ate. When he finished, he pushed his plate forward and leaned his elbows on the table. "So what if I just come up with some sort of excuse for not being able to help him?" asked Nick.

"Well, I'm not sure that would work, and Slim can be very persuasive. If you turn him down, it might just make him more suspicious and curious. Besides, I've been thinking . . . this might benefit us in the long run. We do have to keep a close eye on Slim, and we could control the information he has access to. So in the end, you working for him might work out just fine. But I really need to talk to our Slim about this before any decisions can be made, so I'd better scoot out of here and find him."

Keenan jumped to his feet. "Okay, Nick, I should not be too long. Why don't you take it easy and just relax. Whatever you do, though, do not leave this barn. Slim can't see us in this building, but he can see us once we're outside. We have to be careful, particularly when our Slim isn't around to tell us where the real Slim is."

"That's fine, I'm not planning to go anywhere," yawned Nick. "I'm pretty tired, and I need to write in my journal."

"Okay then, I'm off," said Keenan, and slowly disappeared.

Nick let out a sigh as he looked around the workshop. It was so quiet, he could have heard a pin drop. He realized that this was the first time that he had been totally alone since coming to Silverado. He paced around the barn, letting his thoughts wander through the day's events. He stopped sporadically to look at some of the woodworking projects that the real Slim had started before he left for Cartersville. He had just picked up a beautiful hand-carved wooden horse and was admiring the detail when his thoughts turned back to a comment that Keenan had made. Why did the flooding at the Black Stallion Mine happen so soon after Slim's hanging? Nick shook his head as he jumped from one thought to another. He stared off into the distance, absent-mindedly stroking the carved horse he held in his hand. He continued to wander about the room, thinking about the flood and what might cause something like that to happen. Suddenly, a memory leapt to the surface—the memory of the invoice he had found in the general store on his school trip to Silverado. He remembered that there had been a lot of explosives in that order. He wished he could take a look at it again.

But I can! he thought, realizing that he had a copy of it in his backpack. He began searching the workshop for his backpack. He looked everywhere, under and behind everything, but couldn't find it. Then his heart dropped into the pit of his stomach as he realized where his backpack was—beneath the bed in his bedroom in the ranch house. "The guys must have missed it when they moved all our stuff over here," groaned Nick.

Biting his lower lip, Nick tried to shake the fear that the real Slim would find his backpack. That would be a disaster. He paced for several minutes, examining his options. He kept returning to the order form—he just knew it was important.

Suddenly a horrible thought struck Nick. *What if the flooding in the mine was not an accident at all? What if it was planned? What better way to get rid of evidence—or people, for that matter?* Nick felt a little sick to his stomach and tried to shake the thought, but he could not. He had a gut feeling that he was right. Getting another look at that order form seemed very important.

With the real Slim occupying the ranch house and with Nick due at the general store early in the morning, there didn't seem to be any time to retrieve the backpack. He had to do it now, even if it meant breaking his promise to Keenan.

Nick walked to the front door and cracked it just enough to peer across the yard at the ranch house. It was dark, so Slim probably had not returned yet. Knowing he was taking a huge risk, Nick took a deep breath and slipped out of the workshop door. Hiding in the shadows against the wall, Nick could hear his heart beating loudly. "Okay, you know where it is. You just have to run to the house, grab the bag, and run back. Simple," he reasoned quietly. He counted to three, then dashed across the yard to the ranch and quickly hid in the shadows next to the kitchen door.

Praying that it was unlocked, Nick reached up and placed his hand on the knob. He sighed with relief as it turned easily in his hand. He slipped in and closed the door behind him, then leaned against it for a few moments to catch his breath and let his eyes adjust to the darkness.

Once he could distinguish the dark shapes of furniture, Nick made his way to the room where he had been staying. He opened the door and slipped into the room. Scooting quickly across the room, he reach the foot of the bed, got down on his knees, and began groping in the darkness. His hand hit the backpack, and he grabbed it and pulled it out. He felt along the top to reassure himself that it was still zipped closed. Breathing a deep sigh of relief, he slung it over his shoulder and headed toward the door.

Nick had just placed his hand on the doorknob when, suddenly, he heard the shuffling sound of footsteps coming from the main room of the house. An unmistakably male voice spoke, but Nick couldn't make out the words.

Nick's heart pounded and he began to sweat. *Slim must be back,* he thought, trying not to panic. *How am I going to get out of here?* He leaned his ear against the door and listened. *Maybe I can wait until I hear Slim go to bed, then I can slip out unnoticed.*

But the low sounds of more voices destroyed that plan. *Oh no! He must have brought some friends home with him. What if they're staying the night?* Nick had to find out who was in the house. He inched the door open just a crack, hoping the hinges wouldn't squeak. The first voice he heard did not belong to Slim. To his horror, he discovered that none of them did. Nick's skin crawled. The strange voices and the sounds of doors opening and furniture being moved led Nick to only one conclusion—at least three men were searching Slim's ranch.

Nick quietly closed the door, crept across the room, then lay down and pulled himself under the bed. He was just in time. The doorknob turned and the door was pushed open as he pulled his arm in. He held his breath.

"This looks like a spare room. I doubt we're going to find it in here," a voice rumbled.

"Well, we need to look everywhere, but let's search Slim's bedroom first. It's the most obvious," another voice said.

Nick heard another bedroom door open. "Here's his room, guys. Come help me search. If we don't find it in here, we'll spread out and search the rest of the house," said a distant third voice.

Nick heard the retreating footsteps as the two men left, heading for Slim's room. He quietly shimmied across the floor to peek out from under the bed. The door was wide open. *What am I going to do?* Nick hesitated and listened carefully to the sounds coming down the hall. It sounded like they were all still in Slim's room. Deciding that this was his only chance to get out of the house, Nick crawled out from under the bed and quickly went to the door. He shut it quietly, and then crossed the room to the window. *It has to open. It has to open,* he thought.

Nick slipped his arms through the loops of his backpack to free his hands. He grasped the window frame and pushed upward. The window did not budge. Nick pushed again . . . and again . . . and still the window did not move.

Nick tried to suppress the panic that was rising in his gut. He flexed his hands and took a deep breath. He crouched down and pushed against the window frame with all of his strength. With the tiniest of squeals, the window began to move under his hands. Encouraged, Nick kept pushing. At last, the window opened and he was able to create enough space to crawl through. He listened for a moment to make sure no one was coming, then quickly pushed himself through the window and fell to the ground. He jumped up, grabbed the window frame, and pulled it closed.

Just then, he saw a beam of lantern light spread across the room as the door was pushed open again. Nick ducked behind a bush just as the lantern light fell on the window. He could hear the men discussing why the door was closed. Then the window opened. Peering between the branches, he saw a head pop out of the window and look around. As the moonlight hit the man's face, Nick recognized him immediately—it was Parker Owen, Otis Walkins's foreman and Pernell Billings's fellow conspirator. A second head appeared next to Parker's, and Nick recognized the mysterious prospector. Nick held his breath and stared at them as they looked around from the window.

"I don't see anyone. The window was not open, so no breeze closed that door. I just think you shut it and didn't realize it," said Parker with an irritated grimace. He pulled his head back into the room.

But Nick could see that the prospector did not agree with Parker. He took one more look around and grumbled as he retreated into the room. When the window finally closed, Nick sucked in a deep breath. He tried to regulate his breathing, then rose to a crouch and moved cautiously along the side of the ranch house, heading toward the back corner. He crouched down as low as he could, then peered cautiously around the corner, searching and listening for any movement or sound.

The only noise Nick heard was snorting. He searched the yard and found what he was looking for—four horses tied up in the shadow of the hay barn. *Wait,* he thought, *four horses means four men. Where's the fourth guy?* He jerked his head around to look over his shoulder, but didn't see anything. *Three in the house and a lookout somewhere outside,* he assumed. *But where?*

Realizing that he was too exposed, Nick rose slowly so that he would not startle the horses. He looked around one last time, then darted across the open space between the house and the hay barn. Holding out his hand, he gently touched the closest horse. The horse let out another snort and took a small step to the side, but after a moment, he let Nick stroke his nose. A couple of the others snorted and moved from side to side but settled down as Nick began to talk to them softly. He slowly moved between them in order to hide better. Nick felt a little better now. He was relatively hidden and he wasn't far from the workshop door.

Suddenly Nick felt the horses tense up and begin to move, pinning him between them. The sound of running feet forced him to hold his breath. A man came running around the far corner of the house, and bolted through the kitchen door.

At that point, Nick knew something was very wrong. Figuring that Slim must have been sighted, Nick realized that the men in the house were going to be coming out any second to get on their horses and flee. Instinct kicked in and Nick bolted from his position and ran as hard as he could across the yard to the workshop. Ripping open the door, he threw himself into the workshop and slammed the door behind him. He rushed to the window just in time to see the four men bolting out of the kitchen door. They jumped onto their horses and quickly moved around to the back of the hay barn.

Nick could hear the sounds of a horse approaching from the main road. A moment later, he saw Slim's figure on his horse heading to the stable, unaware of the four uninvited visitors hiding behind the barn. Nick didn't know what to do. Should he warn Slim? How would he explain what he was doing at Slim's ranch? But as soon as Slim and his horse entered the stable, Nick heard the pounding of hooves as the four thieves took off into the darkness.

Nick jumped and whirled around when somebody said his name.

"I didn't realize my arrival would be such a shock, Nick," chuckled Slim.

Nick blurted out, "There were four men on horseback. They were searching the house. They're getting away."

Keenan appeared beside Slim and caught the end of Nick's report. Slim quickly looked at Keenan and shouted, "Go! They're probably heading for town."

"How many?" asked Keenan, already beginning to fade.

"Four! All on horseback," Nick replied.

"I'll catch 'em," echoed Keenan's voice as he disappeared.

Chapter Twenty-Two
KIDNAPPED

Slim and Nick were alone. Slim turned to Nick and simply said, "Tell me."

Nick began to explain as Slim took a seat at the table. Nick described how worried he had become about his backpack being left behind in the ranch house, how he had snuck into the house, how the men's arrival had trapped him there, and how he had escaped, seeing Parker and the prospector in the process. "Then I heard the four men ride off just as you and Keenan appeared," Nick concluded. "Listen, Slim, I am really sorry I went into the house tonight. I went over there even though Keenan told me not to leave the barn. I was worried that the real Slim would find the backpack, and that would have been a big problem. I thought that tonight would be the only opportunity I would have to retrieve it."

Sighing deeply, Slim stood and headed toward the stove. "I could use some coffee," he said. "Keenan said he made some before he came to find me."

Nick took a seat at the table, while Slim poured a cup of coffee. Slim sat across from Nick, took a swig of coffee, and then raised his eyes to look at Nick.

"Nick, you sure were lucky not to get caught. You managed to stay literally one step ahead of them, but things could have happened very differently. What you did was pretty dangerous. And there were probably imps with them, but you managed to stay clear of them, as well.

"I'll be honest and tell you I'm not overjoyed that you did not follow Keenan's instructions. One option you probably should have considered is that any of the guys, except me, could have gone over there tonight while Slim is sleeping to get your backpack."

Nick was shocked into silence. He hadn't thought of that. "Oh, Slim . . . I didn't even think of that. I'm so sorry. It just seemed so important to get the backpack as soon as possible. All I could think about was the real Slim, or somebody else, finding it and the order form."

"The order form?" queried Slim.

"Oh, I forgot to tell you about the order form. That's a big part of why I went into the house," explained Nick. Riffling through the backpack, Nick found his notebook, pulled it out, and quickly flipped it open to the back. The copy of the order form was just where he had left it. He slipped it out of the pocket and placed it before Slim on the table.

"Do you know what this is?" asked Nick. Slim picked up the paper and glanced over it.

"Sure. It's an order form for the general store from the Falcon Mine."

"Read over the quantities of the supplies being ordered. Do they seem normal for a regular mine order?" coaxed Nick.

Slim examined the form more carefully, reading each line item. Slim reached the end of the list, and slowly lowered the form.

"Where did you get this?" he asked.

"On the tour through the Silverado ghost town in my time. It came out of a book that fell onto the floor in the office of the general store."

"Oh, yeah, I remember that," chuckled Slim. "I got your attention, didn't I?"

"Yeah, you sure did. But this order from the Falcon Mine fell out and it seemed odd to me, so I made a copy of it. The date of the order has been smudged, though," said Nick.

"Yes, I see." Slim paused for a few moments, looking at the list again. "Nick, these numbers are way too high. Why would Otis be ordering enough explosives for both mines, not just the Falcon Mine? And I would remember if we had placed an order this big, so I must never have seen it. You seem to have some ideas about this, Nick, so lets hear 'em," said Slim.

Nick took a deep breath. "Slim, in the history I heard of the mine, there's no mention of a discovery of diamonds. I would think that if such a large amount of explosives was found in the mine's inventory after Otis's death, some questions would be raised about what he was doing. So if this order was filled before Otis's death, then somebody must have moved the explosives . . . say, to the Black Stallion Mine."

"But what did either the Falcon Mine or the Black Stallion Mine need with all of these explosives?" pondered Slim, drumming his fingers on the table. After a few moments of silence, he said, "Well, Otis might have been ordering them to use around the pit to make it more accessible."

"Yeah," replied Nick. "So what if Otis never got that chance, because he was killed. The explosives disappeared, and they must have gone to the Black Stallion Mine. But why would the Black Stallion Mine need all those explosives? I know from hearing my dad talk that you never order more explosives than you're going to need right away. They're pretty dangerous to store, right?"

"Yes, that's right," said Slim.

"So that means that the Black Stallion Mine would have had to use the explosives pretty soon after they got them. So what did they use them for? Based on what everyone says, production in the mine is slowing down, not speeding up. Now, what if they did use them at the Black Stallion Mine, but not just for blowing new shafts? What if they were used to tie up loose ends?

What if the flooding of the Black Stallion Mine was not an accident, but carefully planned to look like an accident?" asked Nick.

Slim sat there in stunned silence. Picking up the paperwork, he stared at it, reading over the numbers again and again. After a few moments, he carefully placed it on the table and shook his head.

"Nick, I think you might have something, or at least a theory that we'll have to look at more closely. First things first, we need to find out when the order was placed, who picked it up, or if it was delivered," said Slim.

"I don't believe it's been placed yet. I can double-check that tomorrow. But if it has not been placed, then by the original timeline, it should be placed sometime this week," said Nick.

Slim stared vacantly out the window, lost in thought. Eventually, he shivered a bit, and looked at Nick again. "Nick, the outcome of this could have been much worse if you had not followed your instincts and gone over to get your backpack. Had those guys found it, they would have gotten the idea that someone was on to them, and that would have been disastrous. They might have changed their original plan, whatever that might be. But remember that we all have to work as a team, and you need to talk to us before making any big decisions."

"I will, Slim, I promise," said Nick, and then sat in silence for a moment. "Slim, what about Parker and the prospector?"

"Parker . . . that poor boy has no idea what he's gotten himself into. The prospector is still a puzzle to me, though. It looks like he's another spy for Mr. Billings at the Falcon Mine. He has to have a name and some history in Silverado. We have to find out more about him. Right now, he is our biggest wildcard in all of this," said Slim.

While they continued to talk, Keenan slowly materialized. "Good call, Nick. I caught up with the riders, and they ended up at the saloon. There were four of them, like you said—Parker Owen and three other men I've never seen before. They were searching the house for Slim's journal, and they got it."

"When did the journal actually disappear?" asked Nick.

"If I remember correctly, I couldn't find it after tonight," answered Slim. "And Keenan, if it hadn't been for Nick, they would have gotten ahold of his backpack and this copy of an order form, which would have caused a lot more problems for us than the journal."

"What is that?" asked Keenan. He took the sheet from Slim and glanced over it.

"It's an order from the Falcon Mine for the general store that Nick found in his time on a tour of Silverado. This order hasn't been placed yet in this time," explained Slim.

"Wow, these amounts are awfully high. There is no way either mine could store this, so they would have to use it right away. But this is enough to bring down a mountain," said Keenan.

"Or flood an entire mine," said Slim softly.

Nick looked at Keenan as his head snapped up. Keenan stared at Slim with a look of disbelief and horror.

"They couldn't have," he whispered softly. "Not on purpose . . . Not all those men."

Keenan sank onto one of the barrels. Placing his elbows on the table, he rested his face in his hands. "All those innocent men, Slim. All of them screaming and praying as they drowned."

"I know, Keenan, I know," said Slim softly, resting a hand on Keenan's shoulder.

"Have you told the guys yet?" asked Keenan.

"No, not yet," said Slim.

"They should be on their way here soon. I saw them briefly when I was in town. I think I should be the one to tell them about this," said Keenan.

"Are you okay, Keenan?" asked Nick.

"Huh? Oh . . . yeah, I will be. I just think I need a little fresh air. Slim, do you think I could borrow this for a little bit?" asked Keenan pointing to the paper.

"Go ahead, Keenan. The real Slim is asleep, so it's safe to go out," answered Slim.

Keenan picked up the paper and walked out the front door.

"Will he be okay?" asked Nick.

"They were in that flood, Nick. That's how they died. It will take him and the guys a little time to process this. They always thought the Black Stallion Mine flood was just an accident. There were several explosions before the water came rushing in. Having to face the fact that it might have been sabotage is going to be a shock for them. Especially considering the guys were stuck with all those other miners for several hours as the water continued to rise and the men slowly drowned."

"Oh," groaned Nick.

"They'll be okay, Nick. The guys were a great comfort to the other miners that day. They kept their spirits up as best they could with songs and stories. When the end was obvious, they all grouped together and began to pray for each other, for themselves, and their families. When the end came, it came pretty quickly, and they all went to Heaven. It was a very difficult day, though."

Slim let out at huge sigh. "Nick, I think you have had quite a day and it is getting late. You have to get up for work tomorrow, so why don't you get ready for bed while I check on Keenan?"

"But what about the real Slim wanting me to spy for him?" asked Nick.

"I need to think on that a little bit more. We'll talk about it in the morning," said Slim.

Nick rose and went to the washroom to get cleaned up and ready for bed. When he came out, he headed toward his cot and climbed in. Nick was sure that he would be unable to fall asleep; his mind was still swimming with all of the day's events.

Nick watched Slim dim the lanterns and add wood to the potbellied stove. When Slim finished, he looked over at Nick and spoke in a reassuring voice. "Nick, don't worry about the guys. They will be all right. You did a great thing tonight. You gave them the truth. Now they have the opportunity to deal with it, or maybe even correct it. So, thanks."

"Gosh, I'm glad I could help," Nick said, as relief washed over him. He yawned deeply, closed his eyes, and to his surprise, felt himself drifting off to sleep.

Slim quietly slipped out into the night and walked around the workshop. He was in deep thought when he found Keenan leaning against the wall of the main barn, staring out across the moonlit yard.

"You okay, bud?" asked Slim.

"Yeah, I will be," sighed Keenan.

Slim started to reply when Christopher and Michael materialized beside them.

"What are you guys doing out here?" asked Christopher. "Isn't it warmer inside?"

"I have some news that I think I should tell y'all," said Keenan.

"Is Nick okay?" asked Michael.

"Yes, he's fine," said Slim. "He's asleep."

"Good," sighed Michael. "Before you get started on your news, I think you should know that Stanley Watts has been kidnapped."

"Right on schedule," sighed Slim.

"And Miss Judith's necklace has been stolen," said Christopher.

Slim turned to Keenan. "Get the coffee going. It's going to be a long night, my friend. Things are starting to move pretty fast, and we have a lot of ground to cover."

★ ★ ★

Nick woke up Monday morning with the crowing of the rooster. Groaning, he rolled over and tried to go back to sleep, but that rooster would not shut up. Finally, Nick sat up and swung his legs over the edge of the cot. He leaned forward, resting his elbows on his knees and rubbing his eyes to wake himself up. After a few minutes, he stood up and stretched.

Glancing around, Nick saw that all the guys were still asleep, lying on their cots in their clothes with their boots still on. No one stirred, despite the continuing squawking of the rooster. He figured that they must have been up most of the night, and it would be best not to wake them just yet.

Nick headed toward the washroom. There was a trunk with the clothes Slim had picked up for him. He chose a shirt, socks, and jeans, and then shuffled over to the washroom to clean up and get dressed. Soon he was ready to head into town and start work.

Nick stopped for a moment, considering everything that had happened in the last twenty-four hours. A shiver ran down his spine. Though it seemed that several people had strong motives for killing Otis, the list of suspects just continued to grow. Mr. Billings seemed to be the most obvious culprit, but Nick was trying not to jump to any conclusions until all the facts were in.

Shaking himself from his thoughts, Nick heard a faint noise in the distance. He went to a window and peeked out. Nick could see that the door of the stable across the yard was now open. A moment later, Slim led his horse out of the stable, mounted him, and took off down the main road to town.

Nick turned and walked quietly over to Keenan. Bending down, he gently shook Keenan's shoulder. He had to do it several times before he finally saw one of Keenan's eyes open and look up at him.

"Keenan," whispered Nick, "I need to get to work. The real Slim just took off for town."

Keenan sat up and put his feet on the floor. "Give me just a minute," he grumbled. He yawned as he rubbed the grit of exhaustion from his eyes, and then he blinked a few times to clear them.

Nick moved out of the way, as Keenan rose from the cot. "Does Mr. Guillot have coffee made when he opens?" asked Keenan.

"Yes," answered Nick.

"Let's go. You'll need to get me a cup of coffee when we get there. Lots happened after you went to bed last night, so I'll brief you when we get to the store and I'm a little more awake. Go on outside and wait for me. I'll only be a few minutes," yawned Keenan.

Nick stepped outside and felt the cool morning air blow across his face as the sun warmed it. He closed his eyes, tipped his head back, and breathed deeply. It was a peaceful moment, and he enjoyed the silence as long as he could. Nick felt danger coming, and he knew it was up to him to do everything he could to save the real Slim, the three cowboys, and all those miners who were lost in the flood.

The noise of the door opening broke through Nick's thoughts. Keenan lumbered out. "Ready, Nick?" he asked.

"Yep! Let's go."

Keenan and Nick flew over the real Slim, leisurely trotting into town on his horse. As they continued down the main street, Nick saw the sheriff dismounting from his horse in front of the jail. Nick noticed that the sheriff looked haggard and fatigued. He watched the sheriff wave to the real Slim to get his attention, then pointed toward the office. Nick and Keenan silently flew above them as they walked inside.

"Something bad happened, didn't it?" he whispered to Keenan.

"Good observation, Nick. You are going to need that this week. Be aware of everything and everybody. We are down to the wire," said Keenan. He and Nick softly touched down behind the general store, then slowly materialized. "Why don't you go around to the front and let yourself in? Mr. Guillot is already here, up in the office. I take my coffee black."

Nick nodded and ran down the alley to the front of the general store. He let himself in and headed to the stove in the back room. He quickly poured a mug of hot coffee for Keenan, then unlocked the back door and slipped out, looking around for the cowboy.

Keenan was leaning against the wall of the building with his eyes half closed. Nick shut the door behind him and Keenan stepped forward and took the mug from Nick with a grateful smile. He took several sips from the mug, sighing with satisfaction.

"Thanks, Nick, I needed this." Keenan turned and sat down on a nearby barrel.

"What happened last night?" asked Nick.

"Last night, a group of men kidnapped Stanley Watts from his home. Also, Miss Judith's house was broken into, and her necklace was stolen from her bedroom," explained Keenan.

"Is Miss Judith all right?" asked Nick.

"Yes. She and her family were spending the evening socializing with another family when it happened. More than likely, they were being watched—the thieves just waited for them to leave the house," said Keenan. "They broke in through Miss Judith's bedroom window. She must have taken the necklace off before leaving. When she and her family arrived home that evening, they found her bedroom window broken and her room ransacked. When they located the sheriff to tell him what had happened, they learned that he was also investigating a report that a group of men had taken Stanley," explained Keenan.

"Wow," said Nick. He looked down at his feet for a moment, considering all that happened. Suddenly, he remembered something Freas had told him. He jerked his head up to stare at Keenan. "Oh no! They're going to kill Stanley, aren't they?"

Keenan paused before responding. "Well, Nick, we don't know that for sure. Yes, that is what happened in the original timeline, but things are beginning to change, and we don't know what the future holds now. If we are successful with our assignment, we may save Stanley's life."

Nick felt the weight of one more life in his hands. So many lives had been destroyed by the greed of a few powerful men. Keenan remained silent for a while, letting Nick absorb this new information. But eventually he had to pull Nick from his reverie.

"Nick, all we can do is our best. We just have to stay focused on our assignment and hope that everything works out. Now, since the real Slim has found an ally in you, don't be surprised if you get a visit from him this morning, especially once the sheriff briefs him on last night's events."

"What should I do if Slim asks me to bring him information?" asked Nick.

"Slim says this timeline is changing, so we are not sure what to expect anymore. So trust your instincts, but go ahead and do whatever the real

Slim asks. If anything he asks is too dangerous, check with one of us first. Don't put yourself or him at risk," replied Keenan. "Okay, bucko, you have been briefed. I'd better head back and see what the plans are for today. If anything changes, one of us will get to you right away." He drained his mug and handed it back to Nick.

"Okay," said Nick.

"Thanks for getting me coffee. You try and have a good day now. Michael will probably come pick you up later after work. Any questions before I go?"

"Nope," said Nick.

"I will see you later, then. Keep your eyes open."

Nick watched as Keenan began to fade and then disappeared. He turned and walked into the general store through the back door. He was in the process of washing the mug when a voice spoke up behind him.

"You didn't drink all the coffee, did you, Nick?"

Startled, Nick whipped his head around to see Mr. Guillot standing there with his empty mug and a huge grin on his face. "Oh, good morning, Mr. Guillot. There is plenty of coffee left. I only took one mug," said Nick.

"I was just kidding with you, Nick. Say, did you hear the news? Stanley Watts was kidnapped!" exclaimed Mr. Guillot.

"What? When did it happen?" asked Nick, trying to sound shocked.

"Some time last night. Stanley's wife came rushing into the saloon looking for the sheriff. A few customers overheard the conversation, and now the whole town knows," said Mr. Guillot.

The story of the disappearance of Stanley Watts was the theme of the day. Nick heard it repeated several times as he made deliveries to businesses all over town. No one seemed to know about Miss Judith's missing necklace, though. At least, no one was talking about it.

Midmorning, Mr. Guillot sent Nick to the saloon to deliver a box of supplies. Nick pushed through the swinging doors of the saloon with his shoulder, as his hands were full with a large box. He stood near the doorway for a moment, letting his eyes adjust to the dimly lit room. He was soon able to distinguish Ike's frame in the back of the room, where he worked wiping down tables. "Hey, Ike!" Nick called out. "I've got an order for you."

"Hello, Nick. Just go ahead and set it on the bar. I'll be there in a minute."

Nick walked to the bar and heaved the box up on to it.

Ike walked behind the bar, lifted the box, and put it on the floor. "Hey, Nick, Mrs. Corrine baked some biscuits. Can I interest you in some?"

"Oh, yeah," responded Nick eagerly. "I didn't eat breakfast this morning."

"Have a seat, my boy. You are in for a treat. Say, have you heard the news about Stanley Watts?" asked Ike as he dished up some biscuits.

"Mr. Guillot told me about it. Do they have any suspects, or a reason he was taken?" asked Nick as he ate.

"No, they don't. It's a real mystery. The whole town is spooked. All that they know for sure is that four men were seen removing him from his house at gunpoint. My guess is that he got himself in trouble over a debt, or something," said Ike.

"Would they really kidnap somebody just because he owed money?" asked Nick.

"You'd be surprised what people will do if you cross them. So you have to be very careful who you make friends with around here," answered Ike.

Nick nodded and finished off a biscuit as the saloon doors swung open. Nick hadn't even turned to see who had come in when he heard his name being called.

"Nick, how are you this morning?"

Nick turned around to see Slim walking toward him.

"Morning, Slim. I'm good. How are you?" asked Nick.

"Good, thanks for asking."

"What are you doing in town at this time of day, Slim?" asked Ike. "Shouldn't you be at the mine already?"

"Well, normally I would be, but I ran into Artemus this morning, and he needed to talk to me, so I'm going in later this afternoon. Say, Nick, when will you be making another delivery to the mines?"

[handwritten annotations in top margin: "B that the wagon was it com on Friday." "would that Late and it came on Friday?" "or that it came or late during Friday" "Not that thats important." "Not ext [extremely] important."]

"A wagon came late on Friday, so I should be making deliveries this afternoon to both mines," said Nick.

"If you have a few moments, could I ask you to come with me? I know Artemus would like to see you."

"What's going on, Slim? You don't think Nick here has anything to do with Stanley's disappearance, now do you?" asked Ike.

"Of course not, Ike! Don't be ridiculous. Artemus has a delivery that he'd like to add to Nick's list, that's all," explained Slim.

"I've got some other deliveries, but I can spare a few moments, Slim," said Nick, then he turned back to Ike. "Thanks for the biscuits, Ike. Tell Mrs. Corrine they were wonderful. I'll see you later."

"Okay, Nick. Have a good day. You, too, Slim," said Ike.

Nick and Slim stepped outside onto the boardwalk, then turned and walked to the sheriff's office. They entered the building and walked to the back office, where the sheriff sat behind his desk drinking a steaming mug of coffee. He looked absolutely worn out.

"Morning, Nick. Thanks for coming so quickly. I'm sure you've heard the news about Stanley Watts," said the sheriff.

"Yes, sir. It's all over town. I also heard that Miss Judith's necklace was stolen," said Nick.

"Not surprising. News around here travels faster than the wind. At this point, we believe that the theft of Miss Judith's necklace is somehow related to Stanley Watts's disappearance. After all, Stanley made the necklace for Miss Judith in the first place. Our only lead so far is Slim's opinion about the stones in the necklace—he thinks they might be quite valuable. And it seems that somebody else agrees. There is definitely something going on at one of the mines, but we're not sure which one," explained the sheriff.

"So, here is where you come in, Nick," said Slim. "We are going to ask you to keep your eyes and ears open when you are at the mines. Take note of the people who are hanging around with Mr. Billings or Otis Walkins. If you notice anything unusual, find out what you can without being noticed."

The sheriff watched Slim talking to Nick with a worried frown. When Slim finished speaking, the sheriff shook his head. "I still don't like this, Slim. He's just a kid."

"Artemus, that's the best cover he could have. They won't notice him. They'll just think he's doing his job," replied Slim. "Besides, you can't call for a full investigation unless we know for certain which mine we are dealing with."

"Then I'm counting on you to get information out of Otis today about the Falcon Mine to help us speed up that process," said the sheriff. "Nick, Slim and I talked about this last night and decided it would not be a good idea to involve you. But with Stanley's disappearance, we could use another set of eyes and ears. Slim is going to watch the Falcon Mine, and it would be a big help if you could just keep your eyes open and report back to us if you see anything strange or suspicious over at the Black Stallion Mine. Whatever you do, don't put yourself in any danger," warned the sheriff. "This has to stay very quiet. When you're at the mine, don't let on that you're watching, and don't do anything that might seem suspicious, especially to Billings. Bring any information to Slim or me immediately. We are asking a lot from you, Nick. Are you okay with what we're asking you to do?"

"I can do this, sir," said Nick. "Rest assured that I will be very careful."

"All right then," replied the sheriff. "You'd better run along now. I'm sure you have work to do, right?"

"Yep, I have to make deliveries this afternoon to both mines, so I'd best be going. I should help Mr. Guillot load up the wagon. I'll stop by later this afternoon. Don't worry, I won't let you down," said Nick as he bounded out of the office, down the hallway, and out the front door.

"I hope we are doing the right thing, Slim," said the sheriff. "I would hate to get Nick into trouble."

"I don't think we're going to have to worry about him. He's a smart kid. Besides, I don't know why, but I have a very good feeling about him, and I don't have that feeling about many people," said Slim.

"I hope you're right, Slim, I really do," replied the sheriff.

Chapter Twenty-Three
PIECES TO THE PUZZLE

Nick spent the rest of the morning helping Mr. Guillot load up the wagon with supplies for the mines. The deliveries were scheduled for the afternoon, so when Mr. Guillot left for lunch, Nick ran up to the office to check the inventory ledger for the order form he had found in his time. He quickly thumbed through the pages, but did not find the form. He closed the book and began tapping his fingers on the cover. *So the order hasn't been placed yet,* he thought. Realizing he had just enough time to get lunch before he had to head out to the mines, he put the book back on the shelf, left the office, and headed down the stairs and out of the store in search of food.

About an hour later, Nick was driving the wagon along the road to the mines. He had just reached the forested area at the base of the mountain when he heard the bench he was sitting on creak loudly, making him jump. A low voice came out of the air.

"Hi, Nick. Sorry I startled you."

Nick recognized Christopher's voice right away. "Hey, Christopher! Are you and the rest of the guys up and moving about?" asked Nick.

"Yeah. Last night was a rough night for all of us. Slim said we could sleep in a bit. He thought that the people involved with Stanley's disappearance and the theft of Miss Judith's necklace would probably keep a low profile for the next couple of days," said Christopher.

"Yeah, the whole town is talking about Stanley's kidnapping," said Nick. "It doesn't seem like a lot of people know about Miss Judith's necklace, though. Ike at the saloon seemed to think Stanley was taken because he owes somebody money. Slim found me in town and asked me to come to the sheriff's office. Of course, they think something's going on at the mines. They asked me to keep my eyes and ears open when I'm making deliveries."

"Yeah, you told us the real Slim was probably going to ask you to spy for him and the sheriff. I'll let Slim know you talked to them again. We all think it's a good thing. It will give you the opportunity to keep an eye on the real Slim and the sheriff, particularly now that they seem to be getting more involved than they were in the original timeline. But now I've got to go. Michael will be checking up on you later. Have a good day, Nick."

Nick felt the bench move a bit and he could tell that Christopher had gone. Nick was going to deliver to the Falcon Mine first today, and he had just reached the road to the mine. He turned onto the road and within a few minutes was pulling up in front of the main office. He jumped down from the wagon, grabbed the paperwork, and bounded up the stairs to the Falcon Mine office door. He was just about to knock when he dropped the order forms. As he bent down to retrieve them, he heard voices coming from the office through the keyhole. He could tell that the people in the office were agitated, because the voices were getting louder as he listened. "I'm telling you, he's too curious for his own good," a voice growled.

"Well, he's been gone for several weeks, so naturally he's going to be, especially because the shaft that he was working in before he left is now off limits to him," another voice, which Nick recognized as Otis Walkins's, responded.

"Unfortunately this situation has been further complicated because of that confounded necklace Stanley made with those stones. I should have known better than to send Stanley down. Now everyone is curious about where he found them, and if Slim finds out, we're in trouble. But don't worry about Slim, Parker. I've already talked to him and reassigned him to another shaft. That will keep him occupied for now."

"Well, I think you need to have another talk with him, Mr. Walkins," said Parker in a frustrated tone. "He was back at the shaft after lunch trying to persuade the men guarding it to let him pass. He said he had orders from you to examine the new cavern, but they told him they'd been forbidden to let anybody down unless you gave permission in person."

There was a moment of silence before Mr. Walkins began to speak again. "Hmm, you're probably right, Parker," he said with a sigh. "Slim does seem to be more of a problem than we were expecting. I will speak to him again and order him to stay away from that shaft until further notice."

"What if Slim starts snooping around, asking a lot of questions? If you forbid him to explore the new shaft, he's just going to become more curious," said Parker.

"Well, Parker, that's your problem. You chose the men to guard that shaft, so they had better follow their orders. Nobody must know about what we found in that pit. The only reason I've involved you is because I needed somebody who could help me protect the find without asking too many questions. If Slim finds out about the diamonds, then my plans will be ruined, and you won't be receiving that nice, fat bonus I promised you." Nick was still crouched by the office door, listening intently. *So now Parker and Mr. Walkins are conspiring together, too?* he wondered. He realized nobody had spoken for a few moments so he stood and knocked loudly on the office door.

"Come in!" yelled Otis Walkins.

Nick opened the door and stepped in. "Mr. Walkins, I'm here to deliver your order, sir. I just need your signature."

"Ah, Nick, my boy, come in. Parker, I see two miners heading this way. Grab them and help unload the supplies. Make sure you only take our supplies. We wouldn't want to be accused of stealing, now would we?" sneered Mr. Walkins.

Parker nodded, then turned and left. Through the window, Nick saw him stop two men on the path and walk with them to the wagon.

Mr. Walkins quickly signed his name to the order form and handed it back to Nick, who then turned to leave. "Wait just a moment, Nick," said Mr. Walkins. He opened the top right-hand drawer of his desk and rustled through a stack of papers, finally pulling one sheet out. He perused it quickly, then folded it and stuffed it into an envelope. "Nick, let Mr. Guillot know that this is a larger-than-normal order and that I will need him to put a rush on it," he said, handing the envelope to Nick. "The sooner it gets here, the better. And this order needs to remain confidential." He cocked his head and stared at Nick. "Now, I can trust you, can't I?" asked Otis.

Nick stared at the envelope in his hand, feeling his heart beat hard against his chest. *This could be it,* he thought.

"Nick?"

"Huh? Oh, sorry, Mr. Walkins. I was just wondering if we'd have to borrow a bigger cart if it's a large order. Yes, sir, you can trust me."

"Well, I'm glad to see that you're a boy who thinks ahead. If Mr. Guillot does not have a big enough wagon, I can send Parker down with our wagon to help with the delivery," said Mr. Walkins. He hesitated before continuing: "You see, we're working on a special project, but it might turn out to be nothing. We don't want to talk about it until we know what we've got."

"Yes, sir," Nick said. "Discretion is very important to us."

"Thank you, Nick. You seem like a good young man. I hope that when you're old enough, I can talk you into working for me. I always need good men of integrity and strength, and something tells me that you are going to grow up to be just that kind of man," said Mr. Walkins.

"Thank you, sir," said Nick.

"Here you go. Take this and be off. I still have a lot of work to do." Reaching his hand into his pocket, Mr. Walkins dug out a gold coin and flipped it into the air. Nick caught it, smiled broadly, and pocketed it with the envelope.

"Thank you, Mr. Walkins, sir."

"You're welcome, Nick," said Mr. Walkins.

Nick left the office, passing Slim's messy desk. There was no sign of the real Slim anywhere. Outside, Nick found Parker unloading the supplies. As he walked toward the wagon, Nick noticed that the mysterious prospector had joined Parker. Nick paused for just a moment as he watched him pick up a large crate from the back of the wagon and load it onto a cart with the rest of the mine order.

Nick was close enough to hear the man grunt loudly as he lowered the crate onto the cart. Parker walked up beside him, bent down to check the number on the crate, then straightened and started to say something to the man. But the man had noticed Nick, and he subtly raised his hand to silence Parker.

Nick pretended to be examining the wheel of the wagon when Parker turned around and looked at him.

"Okay, Nick," said Parker, "I think we have everything."

Nick quickly checked the crates against the order form, then handed a copy to Parker. "Thanks, Nick. You have a good day now," said Parker as he reached down and mussed Nick's hair. "Come on, Buck, let's get this cart up to the storage shed. The guys will be looking for this pretty soon."

Nick watched as the prospector turned his head to Parker and nodded. *Buck*, he thought, repeating the name to help himself remember it. As he climbed back onto the wagon seat, he tried to contain his excitement. The name Buck was not much to go on, but it was more than what they had. Turning the wagon around, Nick left the Falcon Mine behind and headed to his next delivery at the Black Stallion Mine Company.

As soon as he was out of visible range of the Falcon Mine, Nick opened the envelope. Nick was now holding the original to the copy he had brought with him from his time zone. Suddenly, Nick was jarred by the familiar sound of the creaking seat next to him.

This time Michael's voice came out of the air beside Nick. "How ya doing, Nick?"

"Hey, Michael, take a look," answered Nick, holding the order form out for Michael to see.

"Isn't that the same order form Slim showed us last night?" asked Michael.

"Yes. Mr. Walkins just gave it to me. So now we can be pretty sure that the order was delivered before he was killed," replied Nick.

"Right," said Michael. "And the sheriff's investigation of Otis's death was complete. There was no mention of a large amount of explosives being found in the mine's inventory. We all talked about it last night, and we think that Otis is planning to blast the cavern wider, or blast through the walls of the cavern in search of more diamonds. After Otis's unexpected death, Parker must have gotten rid of the explosives."

"Hmm," replied Nick, "that makes sense. And they would have to use it quickly, because it would be hard to safely store such a large stockpile of explosives. Mr. Billings could have used the explosives to get rid of evidence and people who were too curious, or who knew too much."

"Well, thanks to you, at least we have a theory to work from," said Michael. "Now that we are aware of the order, we can watch to see what happens. Hopefully we can prevent not only Slim's hanging, but also the unnecessary deaths of all those miners. Do you mind if I borrow this for a little bit?" he asked. Suddenly the order form was being pulled from Nick's hand by an invisible force, and then it disappeared. "I'll return it to you before you get to town. I'd like to show it to Slim."

"Sure, go ahead," said Nick.

"You're doing good work, Nick. Don't worry about this," said Michael. "We will find the truth." Then Nick no longer felt Michael's presence beside him.

Nick sighed deeply. He could not shake the awful feeling that the flooding of the Black Stallion Mine was not an accident, but deliberate. He didn't understand how anybody could do such a thing.

It was nearly four o'clock by the time Nick arrived at the Black Stallion Mine Company. Some of the miners were emerging from the entrance of the mine to go home when Nick reined in the wagon in front of the main office. Jumping down, Nick picked up the invoice and headed up the path to the office door.

He had just raised his hand to knock on the door when he heard the loud voice of Mr. Billings bellowing, and then the voice of Jeb Larkey yelling in response.

"I'm telling you that Parker cannot be trusted! He's a weasel and will turn around and bite you at the first opportunity. I can't believe you even let him be a part of this," yelled Jeb.

"Need I remind you, Jeb, that it was Parker who brought this opportunity to us? Without him, we wouldn't even know about the pit," growled Billings.

"So, what are you going to do, give him my job? And what's going to keep him from blackmailing you?" asked Jeb.

Mr. Billings hesitated for a moment, then spoke with a more controlled voice. "Don't be an idiot, Jeb. I will admit that we are going to have to watch him closely, but rest assured—I have plans for our Mr. Parker when the time is right. Now, does that make you feel better, Jeb?" Mr. Billings sneered.

Jeb hesitated before finally answering in a subdued voice: "Yes, Pernell."

"Give me a little credit for knowing what I'm doing. Now, in the meantime, tell Buck when he arrives that he has an added assignment, which is to keep a close eye on Parker. Also, let him know that when the time comes, he'll get the privilege of dealing with Parker. He seems to have a taste for that sort of work. We'll meet later to go over the plans for stealing the Falcon Mine right from under Otis Walkins's nose."

"Have you heard from Mr. Jenkins yet?" asked Jeb.

Nick did not hear Billings's response because the sound of faint voices made him jump away from the door. Knowing that it would not be a good idea to be caught eavesdropping, he quickly knocked hard on the door.

"Come in," shouted Mr. Billings.

Nick opened the door and walked in. "Mr. Billings, I've got a delivery for you, sir. I just need your signature."

"Ah, Nick, how are you today?" asked Mr. Billings as he took the invoices from Nick. A moment later, two men walked in. "Ah, perfect timing, gentlemen. Jeb, take these two out to Nick's wagon and unload our supplies so that Nick can get back to town before sundown."

"Thank you, sir," replied Nick.

"You're very welcome, my boy. Now let me get these papers signed for you so you can be on your way," said Mr. Billings.

Jeb and the two miners were unloading the wagon when Nick came out of Mr. Billings's office with the signed invoices. It only took them a few minutes to remove the crates that were labeled for the Black Stallion Mine Company. Nick thanked the men as they turned to leave. Jeb clapped Nick on the shoulder as he passed, and the three men sauntered back up the pathway to Mr. Billings's office. Nick climbed back into the wagon and headed for town.

Sometime later, after Nick's normal quitting time, he made the final turn onto the main road into town. Nick watched as miners rode past him on horseback, heading to their homes or the saloon. Many of them waved at him when they passed, while others never looked in his direction. Just before he entered town, Nick's ear caught the faint sound of the seat squeaking next to him.

"Hey, Nick, how are you doing?" came Keenan's quiet voice from somewhere beside him.

"Good, Keenan," whispered Nick, trying not to be overheard. "What's been going on with you guys?"

"Well, we've pretty much pieced together who kidnapped Stanley and stole Miss Judith's necklace. It was a group of men from the Black Stallion Mine Company, headed up by Jeb Larkey," explained Keenan.

"Any idea where they might have taken Stanley?" asked Nick.

"Not yet. They talked about taking Stanley, but they haven't gone to where he is being held. But we do know that Miss Judith's necklace was given to Mr. Billings this morning."

"Oh, before I forget," said Keenan. "Here is the Falcon Mine order Michael borrowed to show Slim. I guess you have to turn it in when you get to the store, don't you?"

"Yep," answered Nick. "Say, Keenan, do you think it would be okay if I hung out in town tonight for a little while?" asked Nick. "I kind of promised to stop by the sheriff's office after I was done with work. The real Slim will be there, and he wants the lowdown on anything that happened today."

"I don't see a problem with that," replied Keenan. "Besides, it's a good way to keep an eye on the real Slim. We're all busy following the people who were involved in last night's events. But let me double-check with Slim. I'll meet you at the back door of the store in about twenty minutes with an answer."

"Sounds good," said Nick, and within moments he felt only empty space beside him.

Nick drove the wagon behind the buildings along the main street and parked it behind the general store. He detached the horses and walked them to Mr. Green's stable, then returned to the general store. He entered through the front door and climbed the stairs to Mr. Guillot's office. Light was spilling out from the office through the partially opened door, indicating that Mr. Guillot was still there. Nick stopped and knocked gently.

"Come in," called out Mr. Guillot.

Nick pushed the door open and saw that Mr. Guillot was sitting at his desk resting his head in his left hand as he wrote in one of the inventory ledgers. He finally looked up when he heard Nick shuffling his feet.

"Oh, Nick, you're back. I thought you might be already gone for the day. How did it go today at the mines?"

"Fine, fine," replied Nick. "Oh, Mr. Walkins asked me to deliver this to you. He told me to tell you that it was urgent, and he needs it as soon as you can get it here."

Mr. Guillot reached forward, took the envelope from Nick's hand, and pulled out the order.

"My goodness!" exclaimed Mr. Guillot as he read through the order. "What in the world is Otis doing?" he asked. "This is a ridiculous amount of explosives, and he doesn't have enough room to store them anyway."

"So he has never ordered that much before?" asked Nick.

"I have filled a large order for the Falcon Mine twice now, but for about half this amount. And that was when they were blowing new tunnels. This amount could blow an entire side of a mountain clean off."

"I could be wrong, but I think they found something in one of the tunnels," said Nick.

"Well, I'm going to have to talk to Otis about this. It's going to take a few days, if not a week, to get this whole order in, and that is only if I can pull some of this order from other towns," sighed Mr. Guillot. "Well, Nick, I'll handle this. It's been a long day for you, so why don't you take off. I'll talk to Otis about this order tomorrow. We'll probably have to break it up and have you deliver it over several days. Unless Otis is in a big hurry and wants to send some of his men down to pick it up," explained Mr. Guillot. "Now scoot. Go get some supper. I will see you tomorrow morning."

"Okay. Good night, Mr. Guillot."

"Good night, Nick."

Nick turned and left the office, headed back down the stairs, and left through the back door in the storage room. He saw Keenan right away, leaning against the wall and throwing small pebbles at a fence post. He looked up when Nick came around the wagon. "Sorry I took so long. I was talking to Mr. Guillot," explained Nick.

"No problem, Nick. It's nice to have a few minutes to myself to relax."

"I guess it must get frustrating or boring sometimes," said Nick.

"Sometimes, but it's interesting to notice how trivial some of the things that I used to worry about when I was alive actually are. But then suddenly, someone will say something that makes listening in worthwhile. Anyway, I came to tell you that Slim thought it would be a good idea for you to stay in town awhile. Any chances you get to spend time with the real Slim, take them. Just let one of us know when we check in with you. Slim is concerned that the real Slim is going to get into some real trouble by snooping around, so we need to keep an eye on him, particularly now that he is more involved in finding out what Otis is hiding. Keep us updated on what is going on with him and the sheriff, and hopefully we will figure out some way of keeping them both out of trouble."

"Okay, that should be easy. They seem to really trust me at this point," said Nick. "Well, I'd better head on over, then."

"I'm not too sure who is coming to pick you up, but we will be taking turns checking on you. If you are done meeting with Slim and the sheriff, just head toward the general store at the top of the hour, and one of us will show up," explained Keenan.

"But remember, Nick, be careful what you say to the real Slim. He is now our responsibility and he can be quite a handful at times. Don't be afraid to tell us if you are having problems with him—if he's getting too pushy—and we will find a way to help."

"Okay," said Nick. "I will see you later, then."

"Yeah, and now it's back to work for me. I've enjoyed talking to you much more than listening to all these hooligans," Keenan said as he began to fade away. "Bye, Nick."

Nick chuckled softly as he waved at Keenan's disappearing form.

Chapter Twenty-Four
THE DYNAMITE ORDER

The sheriff and the real Slim were deep in conversation when Nick poked his head through the doorway of the sheriff's office.

"Hey, Nick, come in," called the sheriff, who saw him first. "I didn't even hear you come in the front door."

The real Slim sat with his back toward the door. He turned around and smiled broadly, then rose and grabbed a chair near the wall and pulled it to next to his.

"Any news concerning Stanley?" asked Nick.

"No," said the sheriff. "It's frustrating! The townspeople do not want to get involved in the investigation. Everyone knows what happened, but no one seems to have any idea why or how."

"Well, Nick," began Slim, "did anything interesting happen during your deliveries?"

Nick paused for a moment before answering, trying to determine just what information he could safely reveal. "When I delivered to the Falcon Mine, Mr. Walkins put in a huge order for explosives. I just turned in the paperwork to Mr. Guillot. And there was a heated argument going on at the Black Stallion Mine office when I got there. Parker's name came up. I heard some men coming toward the office, so I had to stop listening. I went into the office, Mr. Billings signed the paperwork, and then I left. That's pretty much it."

"Now why would Billings and Jeb be arguing about Parker?" asked Slim.

"Can you give us an idea of how many explosives Otis ordered today?" asked the sheriff.

Nick rattled off a few of the numbers he could remember. The sheriff looked at Nick blankly, uncertain what the numbers meant, and then turned his gaze to Slim. Slim sat in stunned silence with his mouth hanging open.

"Slim, what's wrong?" asked the sheriff.

Slim took a deep breath and let it out very slowly. "That's enough explosives to take down the side of a mountain, if used right. Otis knows we can't store that amount of explosives, so he must intend to use it pretty soon," said Slim.

"So what are you saying? That Otis stumbled upon something while you were gone?" asked the sheriff.

"Well," began Slim, "they have cut me off from the tunnel I was working on before I left for Cartersville, and now they have guards around it. That's a good indication that they probably found something. Seems Parker is involved in this, too. By the sound of it, he may be leaking information to Mr. Billings. And I am guessing that whatever they found ultimately has something to do with Stanley's kidnapping, as well as the theft of Miss Judith's necklace. I spoke with Otis today, and I find it interesting that he doesn't seem to be overly concerned with Stanley's disappearance."

The room fell silent as Nick watched both men ponder the unanswered questions. They were obviously frustrated with the few facts they had.

Finally, Slim spoke up. "Stanley was probably working with Parker in the shaft when I was in Cartersville. I bet the stones in Miss Judith's necklace came from that shaft. Stanley probably discovered them and took some to make the necklace without Otis realizing it.

"Now I know Otis well enough to know that if he found something he thought was even more valuable than silver and gold, he wouldn't want anybody to know about it until he was certain what it was. He would have sent a sample to Lucas Marley in Cartersville for analysis right away," said Slim.

"Mr. Walkins did ask Ben to deliver a package to Lucas Marley in Cartersville when I first got the job at the general store. He said it was a rock sample. I covered for Ben while he was in Cartersville," said Nick.

"That's it," cried Slim, slapping his knee. He jumped up and began pacing the floor. "Good going, Nick. You may have just given us the biggest clue yet."

"What do we do now, Slim?" asked the sheriff.

"Artemus, my friend, I need to go back to Cartersville tomorrow and have a heart-to-heart with Lucas. He's the only person that will be able shed some light on this situation."

"How are you going to keep this little trip from Otis? He's going to wonder what you're up to if you don't show up for work tomorrow," cautioned the sheriff.

"Hmm, Nick, would you mind delivering a note to Otis tomorrow?" asked Slim.

"Sure," replied Nick.

"They'll probably be glad that I'm out of their hair anyway, after the ruckus I caused today," chuckled Slim.

"What if your hunch is correct, Slim? What if Otis found a deposit of precious stones, maybe even diamonds? What are you going to do?" asked the sheriff.

"Well," said Slim, hesitating, "first, I'm going to have to confront Otis privately and give him a chance to explain to me what he's doing and why. Then I'll have to decide whether or not to take it to the Falcon Mine's financial board. Depending upon what I find out and what I decide to do, I may have to resign."

"Why resign?" questioned Nick.

"Because if Otis is keeping a major find from me, Nick, he's not playing by the rules, and he's putting the mine in jeopardy. There are major legal issues here concerning the investors and the banks. And on a personal level, it shows a severe lack of trust, not just in me, but in the entire crew. I can't work for somebody I know to be a liar or a cheat," explained Slim.

Nick sat silently for a moment, pondering Slim's comments. *Trust and a man's word carry a lot of weight in this time,* he thought. Nick had never encountered such a complicated situation in his time, but maybe that was because nobody treated him like an adult.

The conversation continued for a while longer, then someone's stomach growled. They all laughed and agreed to take a break and head over to the hotel to get some dinner. Dinner was subdued, with each of them lost in thought, pondering the day's events and the information they had.

After dinner, Nick, Slim, and the sheriff walked back toward the sheriff's office. Glancing at his pocket watch, Nick noticed that it was almost nine o'clock. Sensing that someone was watching him, Nick looked around. He did not see any of the guys, but he decided that it was time to go, knowing that one of the spirits would arrive soon.

Bidding the real Slim and the sheriff good night, Nick turned and headed back up the boardwalk toward the general store. As he approached the store, he caught a glimpse of Christopher standing in the shadows of the alley. Christopher waved, and then slipped down the alley toward the back of the store. Nick quickened his step and followed him.

Unnoticed by either Christopher or Nick, squinted eyes watched from across the street. A man stood hidden in the shadows, barely visible in the soft light of the moon. He took a drag from his cigar, and then slowly blew smoke rings as he watched Nick slip into the alley.

"Now what is that boy up to?" whispered a dark, sinister voice. "He seems to be awful friendly with Slim and the sheriff. And now he's walking down dark alleys alone at night?"

Stepping off the corner of the boardwalk and into the street, Buck was illuminated by light coming from a second story window. He strode quickly across the street and entered the alley. He could not see Nick, but he did hear faint voices. He slipped quietly toward the back of the general store. He was almost at the corner of the building when he heard a strange voice call out, "Ready?"

Buck hesitated for just a moment, unsure of who had just spoken. Inching forward, he lowered himself and snuck around the corner into the shadows behind a barrel. The yard behind the general store was full of empty crates and barrels and maneuvering through them was a slow process. Buck moved from shadow to shadow and then raised his head slightly to see over the rims of the barrels. But he did not see Nick, or anyone else for that matter. After several moments, he stood up and looked around. No one was there. He explored the area behind the store for a few more minutes, trying to figure out where Nick had disappeared to.

He finally became annoyed and gave up on his search. He turned and walked back down the alley to the main street. "That dirty air in the mines must be getting to me," he whispered as he walked down the street toward the hotel where he stayed.

Nick and Christopher arrived back at the ranch with Nick chattering away about his meeting with Slim and the sheriff.

"What? Are you sure the real Slim is going to Cartersville in the morning?" asked Christopher.

"Yes. Is that going to cause a problem?"

"Possibly, but it all depends on what he does there. You have to remember that the real Slim's timeline has changed, and we are doing everything we can to keep an eye on him so he won't get himself into trouble or cause us trouble in the long run," said Christopher. "Now it looks like one of us is going to have to follow him to Cartersville."

Slim, Keenan, and Michael were seated at the table when the door opened and Christopher and Nick walked in.

"Hey, Nick, how was your day?" asked Keenan as Nick and Christopher sat down.

"Good. I met with the real Slim and the sheriff after work. We talked for quite a while," said Nick.

"What information did the real Slim drag out of you, Nick?" chuckled Michael.

"Well, the fact that Mr. Billings and Jeb were arguing about Parker, and a few of the numbers from the order that Mr. Walkins had me deliver to the general store this afternoon," said Nick.

"Hmm, and how did I react?" asked Slim.

"You got awfully quiet. Your eyes looked like they were ready to pop out of your head, and your mouth fell open in shock." Nick tried to show them what Slim's expression had looked like.

The guys roared with laughter, and Nick laughed along with them. Slim just smiled broadly, as he watched the others shake with laughter.

"All right, all right!" he finally called out, waving his hands. "Enough, already. I'm sure Nick has more to tell us, don't you, Nick?"

Still chuckling, Nick could only shake his head. This brought on another wave of laughter, and Slim made an exasperated face and let out a huge sigh. After several moments, the laughter finally subsided. The spirits turned their attention to Nick, who went on to explain that the real Slim's plan was to see Lucas Marley in Cartersville first thing in the morning. Silence fell as the guys just looked at each other, wondering what this change in the timeline might mean.

Finally, Michael spoke up. "What do you think, Slim?"

"This completely changes my timeline at this point. To be honest, this is happening much faster than I had anticipated."

"How much of a problem is this going to cause for us?" asked Keenan.

Slim drummed his fingers on the table. "Actually, it depends on how successful we are at keeping an eye on me and how persuasive Nick can be. Nick, this is a big responsibility for you, but you're going to have to help keep the real me out of danger."

"That shouldn't be too hard," said Nick. "He and the sheriff seem pretty willing to listen to anything I have to say about what's going on. What's the story concerning Stanley?" asked Nick.

"Nothing yet," sighed Michael. "No one that we have been watching has gone to him or said anything about where he is, so we are still waiting for some clue."

"You don't think he's dead, do you?" asked Nick, feeling his gut tighten with anxiety.

"No, not yet," replied Slim. "Stanley is still valuable for the information he has, such as whether he told anybody else about the pit and whether he has any more of the diamonds. And if they killed him now and his body was found, then that would really heat up the investigation, and they definitely don't want that to happen."

"I find it interesting that Otis does not seem overly concerned about Stanley's disappearance. That makes me think that he was involved somehow," said Slim. "We haven't been watching him every moment, so he could have planned the kidnapping without us witnessing it. Just because Jeb Larkey did the dirty work doesn't necessarily mean the kidnapping was ordered by Billings."

"But Jeb Larkey did give Miss Judith's necklace to Mr. Billings, right?" asked Nick.

"Yes," answered Keenan. "It is locked up in his right hand desk drawer in his office."

"Well, at least we know where one thing is," said Christopher.

"I think it's important to find Stanley and figure out who planned his kidnapping. Good grief, this is getting confusing," sighed Keenan.

Nick could sense their mounting frustration as he looked around the table. They were so close, but had so many loose ends. More and more people seemed to become involved each day.

Much later, after they had decided to try to get some sleep, Nick lay awake in his cot, listening to the heavy breathing of the cowboys. He rolled over, trying to stop his racing mind, and saw Slim get up, grab his boots, and slip out into the night. Nick slipped out of bed, crept over to the window, and peered into the darkness. By the light of the moon, he could see Slim standing in the yard with his head tilted back, looking heavenward. Slim then turned toward the quiet, dark ranch house that had been his home for so many years.

Nick could not help but sigh deeply, for he could almost feel the weight of time and the unknown settling heavily on Slim's shoulders. Otis Walkins's time had come, and Slim had told Nick that, no matter what, they were not permitted to interfere with Otis's death. Nick sensed that Slim struggled with the fact that he had been sent here to possibly change his own history, but not Otis's. And they might be able to change history for a lot of the people who died in the mine flood. Slim seemed frustrated, though. Otis's life was the one life he could not save, and Otis had always been a good friend. Slim let his head drop forward, bringing his hands up to his face, overwhelmed by the strain of his assignment. Nick reached up to wipe a tear from his own face, and then headed back to his cot. He slipped beneath his blanket as several more tears fell.

A little while later, Slim crept back into the workshop. Nick pretended to be asleep, but watched as Slim sat on his cot, removed his boots, and climbed beneath his blanket. Resting his hands on his chest, Slim let out a heavy sigh. After a few minutes, his breathing slowed and he drifted off to sleep.

Nick turned over onto his back and stared at the rafters above him. "We've got to solve this," he whispered. His eyes began to get heavy, and with a final yawn, Nick drifted off to sleep for a few precious hours.

Chapter Twenty-Five

THE RETURN TO CARTERSVILLE

Several hours later a voice called to Nick from what seemed like a very great distance: "Hey, Nick, wake up!" Turning over, Nick tried to open his eyes, but found that his eyelids were made of lead. Figuring he must be dreaming, he let himself slip back into the familiar warmth of sleep. But the voice began calling to him again, this time from somewhere near his ear. He tried to ignore it, but it grew louder and louder until Nick's brain finally worked its way out of the haze of sleep, and he realized that Michael was calling to him to get up and start the day.

"Boy, Nick, you were out cold!" said Michael.

Nick sat up and swung his legs over the edge of the cot. "Sorry, I didn't get to sleep until sometime this morning."

"I understand," said Michael. "I don't think any of us will be getting much sleep from now on. The real Slim headed out to Cartersville already, and Christopher is trailing him. Keenan has left, too. He's off to keep an eye on Mr. Billings, but he made breakfast before he left. I need to get to Otis and keep an eye on him today. So, pull yourself together and I'll take you into work."

"Where is our Slim?" asked Nick.

"He's outside taking a walk. A lot is going to happen in the next few days, Nick. Some of it will probably be dangerous. Knowing Slim, he's probably praying for guidance." Michael reached down and tousled Nick's messy hair, then smiled and headed out the open door to look for Slim.

Nick sat on the edge of the cot for a few minutes, letting Michael's words sink in. *This is it*, he thought. *Time's almost up, and if I'm right, we may save more than just Slim's life. The Black Stallion Mine flood might never happen.* Nick could tell by the light outside that it was getting late, so he wolfed down some breakfast and got ready for work.

Michael returned to the workshop alone. "Slim's on his way back," he said, "but we've got to get you to work so that I can check in on Otis."

Michael ported Nick to the storage area behind the general store and left right away. Nick was about fifteen minutes early, so he headed in to make a pot of coffee for Mr. Guillot and to prepare for the day ahead. He busied himself checking the inventory list as the coffee was brewing. He counted all the boxes in the back room and then separated them into piles. He labeled each, indicating where it was to be delivered.

The sound of footsteps startled him, and he whirled around to find Mr. Guillot walking into the back room.

"Wow, you've been busy this morning, Nick. You could have waited for me, and I would have helped you sort through all of this stuff," said Mr. Guillot in awe.

"It was no problem, really," said Nick. "I got here a little earlier than I expected, and I kind of just jumped in."

"Well, it looks like you have all the deliveries ready to go. I am expecting a coach from Cartersville this morning that should be carrying some correspondence about Otis Walkins's order. I sent out a special courier last night. According to the list, there's a crate to be delivered to the Black Stallion Mine this afternoon, and I should have a letter ready for you to deliver to Otis."

Nick nodded, trying to quell his excitement. That letter could contain information that would prove his theory. He wondered if he would be able to ask Mr. Guillot about the order and the letter without raising too much suspicion. Carefully changing the subject, Nick pointed to the potbellied stove. "I made a pot of coffee. It should be ready if you want a cup."

"Well, Nick, keep this up, and I might have you replace Ben," Mr. Guillot said with a laugh. "I'm just kidding, Nick. But to be truthful, I am considering hiring you permanently. If Otis is on to a new vein, then we are going to have a lot of deliveries to the Falcon Mine Company and more in town, too. I'm going to need two delivery boys. Our town will be growing. The discovery of a new vein always attracts more people and more businesses," explained Mr. Guillot.

Nick grinned and shuffled his feet, uncertain of what to say. He found it hard to believe that he was being offered the chance to stay here and continue to work at the general store—if he had a choice about where he would live. He felt comfortable here. He felt like he was really getting to know the townspeople, and in some ways, they were like his family. The mere thought of returning to his own time brought on a wave of anxiety. He tried not to think about it, reaching out and taking the delivery list Mr. Guillot was handing to him. He headed toward the crates that needed to be delivered in town, saying over his shoulder, "I'd better get started."

The real Slim reached Cartersville in good time. He slowed his horse to a trot as he entered the town on Main Street. Lucas Marley's house was at the other end of town. Slim knew Lucas was probably awake and getting ready for work. He hoped to catch him at home and talk him into having breakfast. As Slim made his way down Main Street, three men on horses approached. He squinted into the rising sun, and then reined his horse to a stop when he recognized the riders as his friends—Michael, Christopher, and Keenan.

"Well, well, I didn't think I'd be seeing you guys this bright and early," called out Slim.

"Well, I'll be. If it isn't Slim Marano!" cried out Keenan.

"Missed us so much that you had to come right back?" chuckled Christopher.

"Now, come on, guys," said Michael. "You all know that Slim never comes to town just to visit us. Isn't that right, Slim?"

Slim laughed. "Now, Michael, surely you know me better than that!"

"What's going on in Silverado that has Otis sending his best worker back here?" asked Michael.

"Otis didn't send me this time. I'm here on my own," replied Slim, his expression becoming serious. "It seems that while I was away, something big happened at the mine. It looks like Otis found something very interesting, but he's keeping his mouth shut about it, even with me. Sunday night, one of our miners, Stanley Watts, was kidnapped. He had made a necklace for his niece with some unusual stones, and that necklace was stolen the same night he was kidnapped. Then, when I got to the mine on Monday, I found that Otis had put guards on the tunnel I was working in before I left. Even I wasn't allowed in. And it seems that Pernell Billings of the Black Stallion Mine is involved somehow, too. Artemus and I have been trying to figure out what's going on. Nick told us that Ben took a sample from the Falcon Mine to Lucas Marley for analysis a few days ago, so I'm hoping to get Lucas to tell me about the samples."

"Who's Nick?" asked Christopher.

"He's a new kid in town who's working as a delivery boy for Mr. Guillot at the general store. He's unofficially working for me now, too, gathering information as he makes deliveries to the two mines. He's a smart kid, and so far, he has been extremely valuable. He's given us enough information to make us feel pretty sure that Otis has found something big and is hiding it from everyone," explained Slim.

"Hmm, now I'm curious," said Michael. "And it sounds like maybe you could use some more help. Mind if we join you?"

"I would be grateful for any help you can give me. First things first, though. I know enough to sound convincing, so I need to meet with Lucas. I should be able to get some confirmation out of him about the samples he analyzed. Why don't you guys go pack, then meet me just outside of town in about an hour. You can come back with me to Silverado and stay at the ranch. It will be like old times!" laughed Slim.

"Sounds like a good plan," said Christopher.

"I'm in," said Michael.

"Me, too," chimed Keenan.

The three guys turned their horses and headed home to gather a few things, while Slim rode toward to Lucas Marley's house.

Invisible eyes watched the four men ride away. Christopher sighed deeply, unsure of what had just happened, but not liking what he saw. "If Slim has convinced them to come back to Silverado with him, that is going to cause all kinds of problems for us," he whispered. Then he began to follow Slim, hoping he was wrong about the guys' intentions.

Stanley Watts woke up with a start when a clattering tin landed by his head.

"Wake up, bucko," a voice cackled. "Your breakfast is finally here. Better late then never, eh?"

Stanley slowly moved his body to a sitting position on the bed of straw beneath him. Despite the straw and a blanket, the cold floor and walls of the cave made him shiver. He got up and moved around to get his blood flowing, lifting his arms high above his head and yawning. He tried to stretch the tired, cramped muscles in his back and arms.

Stanley had lost track of what day it was, having been kept in a dark tunnel since he had been taken from his home. He was under guard at all times, and was forced to work in the surrounding tunnels for long hours each day before being returned to this cave.

A man came around the corner with a pan full of steaming eggs, potatoes, a hunk of bread, a wedge of cheese, and a tall mug of hot coffee.

"Hope you're hungry. Eat up—we have a lot to do today," said the miner, handing the pan and mug to Stanley.

"Thanks," said Stanley. The miner nodded and slipped out of the only exit from the cavern.

Stanley had almost finished eating when he heard voices coming from outside the cavern. Noticing that the guard was absent from his usual post by the opening, Stanley quietly put down his plate and crossed the room. Flattening himself against the rockface, he carefully worked his way around the wall, out of the cavern, and down the tunnel. He reached a bend in the tunnel and could tell the voices were coming from just around the corner.

"I'm telling you," growled a voice, "this mine is totally dried up. We aren't finding anything but rock and dirt. It's a waste to keep digging."

"Well, keep at it anyway. Mr. Billings wants to be absolutely certain. He seems to have gotten it into his head that we're going to find something down here. Besides, you've got extra help."

"Yeah. What are we going to do with him?"

"You don't need to worry about that," said another man. "Your responsibility is to keep him here, busy and alive. Mr. Billings thinks he's useful for now. He'll let you know what to do with him when the time comes."

"He knows too much!" added a new voice that sounded very familiar to Stanley. "If he escapes, it will cause us a lot of trouble. People are already asking where he got those stones he used for the necklace."

Stanley craned his head slowly around the corner to catch a view of who was talking.

"Parker, you need to keep your mouth shut! These men will keep Stanley safe here. Mr. Billings will make the final decision about what to do with him."

Stanley caught a glimpse of Parker Owen and Jeb Larkey, who had just spoken, and the foreman who was in charge of the few men who were working in these tunnels. Stanley carefully retreated back down the tunnel and into his prison.

"Parker," Stanley whispered quietly. "Parker must have told Mr. Billings what we found in the pit. So Parker is now in cahoots with him. But how are they going to get to the pit?" he asked himself.

Hearing echoing footsteps, Stanley quickly finished off the rest of his breakfast and drained the last of his coffee from his tin mug. He rose and began to pace, pondering his predicament. He stopped pacing when he heard the footsteps coming closer. "Ready to get back to work, Stanley?" a voice called out. Stanley looked up just as the foreman who had been talking to Parker and Jeb rounded the corner. Stanley nodded, then followed the foreman out of his cavern prison and deeper into the mountain.

Just before lunch, Nick carried the last small crate he had to deliver in town to the saloon. Striding through the swinging doors, Nick walked up to the bar, set the crate down, and glanced around. It was quiet in the saloon, so Nick walked to the far end of the bar and back again, hoping to see Ike or attract somebody's attention. But he didn't see anybody. He was just about to call out when he heard the loud squeaking of the saloon doors behind him. Heavy footsteps shook the floor as Nick turned to see who had entered. It was Buck.

Walking up beside Nick, he slammed his right hand on the wooden bar and bellowed, "Service!" in a deep, scratchy voice.

Nick could hear movement in the back and the sound of rushing feet. The door behind the counter swung open as Ike rushed out from the kitchen.

"Hey, Nick," said Ike before focusing on Buck. "Can I help you?"

"I'm here for Mr. Billings, and he wants this order filled right away. Is there any problem with that?" drawled Buck, tossing a piece of paper and a small leather pouch stamped with the Black Stallion Mine's emblem onto the bar.

Ike picked up the paper and the pouch while gazing levelly at Buck. "No problem," he said in a cool voice. "It will take a few minutes though." He turned to head into the kitchen, but Nick stopped him.

"Ike, could you sign the invoice for this delivery?" Nick asked.

"Sure," Ike replied, grabbing the invoice off the crate and scrawling his signature on the bottom. "Thanks, Nick," he said, handing Nick the invoice; then he turned and disappeared into the kitchen. Nick took the invoice and turned to leave, but Buck stepped into his path.

"So, you're the new delivery boy I see up at the mine, eh?" he asked.

"Yes, sir," answered Nick.

"Hmm, you seem awful polite and proper, but you know what I think?" asked Buck.

"No, sir, I can't imagine," said Nick, getting a little annoyed.

"Boys as polite as you are usually hiding something. I think you're a troublemaker," said Buck.

"Yeah?" queried Nick, feeling his nerves start to tingle. "Well, if I'm hiding something, it must be a secret from me, too," he said in his most sarcastic voice. He tried to step around Buck, but Buck intercepted him again.

"You know, I just happened to see you outside the general store last night. I wondered, What's a nice boy like that doing creeping down a dark alley at night? So I followed you, just to make sure you were okay," he said with a sneer. "But then I heard you talking to someone, and when I came around the corner, no one was there. It's as if you just up and disappeared into thin air. Now I thought that was kind of strange. Don't you think that's strange?"

Nick's mind was whirling as he tried to control his rising anger and fear. Out of the corner of his eye he saw several imps dancing around Buck and moving to encircle both of them. Refusing to be intimated by this hoodlum, Nick responded: "You mean back behind the general store where all the empty barrels and crates are stored?" he asked.

"Yeah, I looked around all of them, and you were nowhere to be found," said Buck.

"Maybe I was meeting a friend. And maybe we heard you, and my friend didn't want to get caught out so late, so we ducked into a couple of those barrels until you left. Of course, you looked in each and every barrel, right?" asked Nick.

Buck hesitated, looking at Nick with a suspicious squint.

"Hmm, I take it that you didn't look in the barrels," Nick said. "Well, now that I've answered your questions, I think I'll be going."

Buck mumbled and grunted something Nick didn't quite hear. Just then, Ike came through the kitchen door carrying a small open crate of bottles. He placed it in front of Buck, saying, "Here you go."

Buck grabbed the crate, glared at Nick, then turned and walked toward the swinging doors of the saloon. He stopped before he reached them, though, and whirled around. "You think you're such a smart kid, don't you? Well, I know you're hiding something," he growled.

Nick could feel his anger rising. "The only thing I'm hiding, *sir*, is my dislike for adults who have nothing better to do than bully innocent kids."

Buck threw a last nasty look at Nick, turned on his heel, and stormed through the swinging doors.

"Wow, what was all that about?" asked Ike.

Nick sighed and turned to face Ike. "I just realized that bullies come in all different shapes, sizes, and ages," answered Nick. "You just can't let them intimidate you, and it was time for me to stand up for myself."

"Well I'm impressed. Say, what about lunch on the house. After that showdown, I think you need to keep your strength up," Ike said with a chuckle.

"That sounds good. I didn't have any lunch plans," said Nick.

"Good, neither did I. Let me whip up something. I'll be right back." Ike ducked back into the kitchen and Nick turned to stare at the swinging doors. *I probably made an enemy today,* he thought, feeling a tinge of regret. *I probably need to be more careful. There are traps all over the place. I can't let my temper become one of them.*

Chapter Twenty-Six
DOUBLE TROUBLE

Slim's spirit materialized on a cliff overlooking Silverado. He stared off into the distance, watching a bald eagle glide on the unseen wind currents. The eagle spiraled in a downward descent, only to rise again to catch the next current and do it all over again.

So far, it had been a productive morning. Following Parker had really paid off. They now knew where Stanley was being held and that he was alive. They had also learned that Mr. Billings had a small team of miners tunneling in a cave on the opposite side of the Black Stallion Mountain. The original cave ran deep into the mountain, and from what Slim could tell, the tunnel they were digging seemed to be running below the lowest tunnel in the main part of the mine. The new tunnel seemed to support Nick's theory. It was very damp, and Slim thought that the miners were probably getting close to an underground spring. An explosion in it could break through to the spring and the lower tunnels in the mine, causing a major flood.

Christopher returned from Cartersville and materialized beside Slim. He quickly briefed him on another impending problem. The real Slim was riding toward Silverado with the real Michael, Keenan, and Christopher, having solicited their help while in Cartersville. They would arrive at the ranch house in the early evening.

Slim just shook his head. "This is not getting any easier," he muttered as he watched the eagle in flight. Having all of their real selves in town was going to severely limit their movements. Slim let out a big sigh, "I'm going to have to give Nick more responsibility. He's going to have to keep an eye on our real selves and keep them out of trouble until we can unravel all of the tangled threads of this mess. Christopher, you can't watch Slim now that you're with him, so go and check up on Stanley and see if there are any new developments with him. Things just seem to be getting more and more complicated," groaned Slim as he and Christopher disappeared.

★   ★   ★

By the time Nick returned from lunch, Mr. Guillot had the wagon parked in front of the general store. It was loaded with one crate for the Black Stallion Mine. Walking in the front door, Nick saw that Mr. Guillot was behind the counter helping a customer.

"Thank you, Mrs. Stines. You have a nice afternoon now," said Mr. Guillot.

The older lady passed by Nick on her way out, and he opened the door for her. "Thank you, young man," she said as she left.

"Hey, Nick," said Mr. Guillot, "I have the wagon loaded and ready to go. I wouldn't normally send you out to the mines with just one crate, but I have that letter for Otis. I received some information about his order. Two of the smaller mine companies nearby dried up and closed, so all their inventory is up for grabs. I went ahead and sent a response back to them on the coach. At this point, I have been able to secure about half of what he is looking for.

It should be here tomorrow. The other half of the order will take a few more days to get here. It will be filled from the inventory of another mine that's closing, but that mine is further away," explained Mr. Guillot.

"Wow, Mr. Walkins should be really pleased with such prompt service," replied Nick.

"I hope so. But he may be just as irritated that I can't fill the full order. So be prepared for anything—Otis has been rather volatile lately."

"That's good to know. I will let you know what happens. By the way, Slim gave me a note last night to deliver to Mr. Walkins," said Nick.

"Is everything okay with Slim?" asked Mr. Guillot.

"Yep, as far as I know. He just said that he has a personal issue he has to deal with, and he won't be in to work for a couple of days. He didn't have time to notify Mr. Walkins in person."

"Then you'd better get going. I'm sure Otis will want to know where Slim is right away. Here's the other letter for Otis. Oh, and I got a letter from Ben. He asked how you were doing, and he asked for two more weeks off. His sister is due to deliver her baby any day, and since he is already there, he would like to stay and see the whole family. They're all coming down for the big event. So I know this Friday was supposed to be your last day, but I was wondering if you could stay with me for another two weeks, or until Ben gets back. Depending on what the word is from the Falcon Mine, I may be able to hire both of you on a permanent basis," said Mr. Guillot.

"Mr. Guillot, I have to be honest. I don't believe I'll be able to accept a permanent job here, though I would really like to. At some point, my father will send for me, and I'll have to go. But until that happens, I'd be happy to stay on as long as I can," replied Nick.

"I see. You're staying at the hotel, right?"

"Yes," replied Nick carefully.

"And your father's all right with you staying in town unchaperoned?" asked Mr. Guillot with a worried frown.

"Well, some of my mom's friends live nearby and check up on me."

"And where's your father?"

"He's still in Washington. After my mom died, he started working all the time. Actually, we got into a big fight, and that's why I was sent here," said Nick.

Mr. Guillot reached out and gently squeezed Nick's shoulder, saying, "Don't worry, Nick, children and parents always argue, but they always make up, too."

"I wish it were that easy," said Nick, staring down at the floor.

"Family matters are usually pretty complicated, my boy," sighed Mr. Guillot. "But believe me: It may take time, but you two will make up."

Nick mustered a smile and pocketed the letter he was holding. "Well I'd better get going now. Thanks for the words of wisdom."

"Anytime you need to talk, Nick, I'm happy to listen."

"Thanks, Mr. Guillot, I will remember that," replied Nick. He turned to leave, calling, "I'll see you when I get back," as he walked through the door.

★   ★   ★

Otis Walkins was just finishing up some paperwork when a knock came on his office door.

"Come in," he called out.

Parker opened the door and walked briskly into the room, stopping in front of Otis's desk.

"Sit down, Parker. I have a couple of things to go over with you."

"I'd rather stand," said Parker.

"Fine, then. Now, Slim did not come into work this morning, so I'm supposing he's still angry with me for preventing him from entering the new tunnel. Or it's possible that he's sick or he's had some kind of accident," said Otis.

"So what does this have to do with me?" asked Parker.

"Here's our situation. Slim is quickly becoming a bigger problem than we anticipated. Now, Slim was supposedly spotted earlier this morning by a miner who lives close to him. He said that Slim didn't look sick, and that he was heading in the general direction of Cartersville. I'm worried that he found out about the pit and that he's riding to Cartersville to talk to Lucas Marley to get some answers," explained Otis.

"But you told Lucas that his analysis was strictly confidential, didn't you?" asked Parker.

"Yes, but Slim is not stupid. He knows that if I'm keeping something from him, I've probably told Lucas to keep it quiet. He may have just enough information to convince Lucas that he knows everything and get him talking. Lucas and Slim are good friends. All he has to do is fish for the information about what we have, and the rest will become obvious, including Stanley's disappearance. I'm afraid it's just a matter of time now."

"Okay. Say he does figure out that we stumbled upon a deposit of diamonds. He's going to figure out that we're trying to keep it a secret from the financial board, the investors, and the banks. What do you think he'll do about it? And how do you want to deal with him?" asked Parker.

Otis sighed deeply and leaned back in his chair, "I don't quite know for sure. He will probably take what he finds to the investors. But he will confront me first."

"So, you've definitely decided not to notify the financial board about what we've found?" asked Parker.

"Listen, Parker, we do not know for sure if everything in the pit is in fact diamond. Further digging will reveal what's there, and how much. I want to remove everything from the pit before we start blasting it wider. We'll start on Monday. Once we remove what we can easily access, I'll make a decision about what to tell, or not to tell, the financial board. If we make an announcement now, we'll have people scurrying out of the woodwork trying to get to that pit. For now, it's better that no one knows about this. If we discover that the deposit is much bigger than we are anticipating, then I will contact the financial board and let them know about our find," said Otis. "Speaking of keeping things quiet, tell me how you dealt with Stanley. I received word from the sheriff yesterday that he'd been kidnapped. Where are you keeping him?"

"Stanley is in good hands and is being well taken care of. He will not be a problem for us," answered Parker.

"You didn't kill him, did you?" asked Otis.

"No, Otis. Let's just say that Stanley has a new occupation far away from here. The people he's working for are happy to have his help," Parker said, smirking.

"What about the necklace he made for his niece? I know it was stolen, so where is it?" asked Otis.

"It, too, is safe from prying eyes," replied Parker.

"Parker, I won't feel comfortable until it's locked up in my safe."

"Now, Otis, you will get the necklace—in time. Let's just say that, for now, it's my insurance policy for being fairly compensated for my services," said Parker.

"Parker, you and I are in this situation up to our necks. If I go down, you go down, too. Now we have to trust each other, don't we?"

Parker walked to the window and stared at the mine entrance for a few moments. "Trust, Otis? I'm not even sure you know what that word means. You've known and worked with Slim for twenty years, but have you been a trustworthy boss to Slim, or to any of us?" asked Parker with a slight smile.

Otis gritted his teeth as his face became red. "You've made your point, Parker. Keep the necklace, then, and consider it your payment for dealing with Stanley and Slim," whispered Otis.

"Slim?" asked Parker, turning quickly toward Otis.

"Yes, he has to be dealt with," reasoned Otis.

"Really now," Parker said in a hushed tone. "I don't think I can get away with putting Slim along side Stanley in his new occupation. Slim is much smarter and would do anything and everything to escape. And that would definitely ruin our plans."

"Slim will just have to meet with an unexpected accident," said Otis.

The room fell silent. After a few moments, Parker finally asked, "Then, you'll trust me with the details and ask no questions?"

Otis hung his head.

"Otis, I need an answer," urged Parker.

"Very well," said Otis, "you have my word. I will never ask or speak about this again."

Parker returned to his position in front of Otis's desk, staring at Otis's slumped shoulders and lowered head. "All right, Otis, I'll take care of this situation, too, and I'll accept the necklace as full compensation for both Stanley and Slim. You don't even have to make a final decision right now. I'll stop in at five o'clock and give you the daily report. If you say nothing about this situation, I'll take that as a sign that you want me to go ahead. But after five o'clock, there is no turning back. Plans will have been made, and even I will not be able to put a stop to them," explained Parker.

"I understand," replied Otis.

"Good," said Parker. "I'm going to take my leave now. I'll see you again at five o'clock."

"Fine. I'll see you then, Parker," said Otis, still unable to meet Parker's eyes. Parker turned and left the office.

But Otis was not alone. Michael stood near his chair, shocked by what he had just heard. He thought about how he would tell Slim about this new turn of events. Could it be possible that, even if they were successful in bringing the real killers to justice, Slim might still die? He waited and watched, hoping that Otis would change his mind before five o'clock.

★ ★ ★

Nick was walking up the path to Otis's office when he saw Parker walk out. Parker passed him, gave him a tight smile, and slapped him lightly on the shoulder.

"How are you, Nick?" asked Parker.

"Fine, Mr. Owen," replied Nick.

"I didn't think we had a delivery today," said Parker out loud.

"No, sir, you don't. Mr. Guillot asked me to drop off a letter for Mr. Walkins," said Nick.

"Oh," exclaimed Parker, then reached down and snatched the letter out of Nick's hand and quickly opened it. "I betcha this is about that order Otis put in yesterday," he purred.

"Yes," said Nick in a strained voice, annoyed that Parker had snatched the letter.

"I see," said Parker, stroking his chin as he read the letter. "Well, we should be able to start with half. By the time the other half comes in, we'll be ready for it."

"What are you working on?" asked Nick, trying not to sound too curious.

"Nothing exciting," Parker replied after a moment of hesitation. "We're just planning to blow through a wall into a cavern to see what we can find. Nothing different than what we usually do," explained Parker as he folded up the letter and handed it back to Nick.

Before Nick could ask another question, Parker ushered him toward Otis's office door. "Go on in, Nick. Otis is there. He's just working numbers," he said, then turned and hurried down the path to the hitching post. He released one of the horses, mounted it, and took off toward the main road.

Nick could not help but shiver as he watched Parker ride away. He felt like he had just given Parker some news that he had been waiting for, and that might be bad for everybody. He turned and proceeded up to Mr. Walkins's office and knocked on the door. When Mr. Walkins yelled, "Come in!" Nick opened the door.

"Good afternoon, Mr. Walkins," said Nick as he walked to the desk and held out both letters.

"What have you got for me today, Nick?" asked Mr. Walkins, taking the letters and opening the note from Slim first. After reading it, he asked, "Nick, do you by any chance know what this personal matter is that's keeping Slim from work?"

"No, sir. He just asked me to deliver that note to you. He didn't go into a lot of detail," replied Nick.

Mr. Walkins set Slim's letter aside and began to read the letter from Mr. Guillot. Otis was pleased that they could get at least half of the order so quickly. But he was also saddened by the news that the inventory came from two other mines that were closing.

"It's sad to hear that those mines finally dried up. It is just a matter of time for all of us, really. This business is so unstable," said Mr. Walkins. "Plus, the politics are enough to drive you nuts."

"Politics?" questioned Nick.

"Private, rich investors who expect to get richer. Banks get involved, offering funds to work with while you search for new veins. Then they become demanding when you're a few days late with a payment. They're all leeches, Nick. They want every ounce you bring up. You have to account for everything. They think they know how to run this mine better than I do," lamented Otis.

Nick just looked at Otis as he rambled on about the difficulties of running a mine. Finally, Otis paused, and then said, "I'm sorry, Nick. I didn't mean to bore you with all this mine talk."

"That's okay, Mr. Walkins. Actually, I find it all pretty interesting. I really don't understand how a mine company actually works. I can tell there is much more involved than just the day to day digging."

"You find it interesting, eh?" asked Otis, staring thoughtfully at Nick. "Well how would you like a real tour of the mine, sometime? I can show you all of the maps, take you into the tunnels and show you all the different types of rock and ore we find. How does that sound?"

"That sounds great, sir. I look forward to it," said Nick.

"Excellent. Maybe we can do it sometime this week. I'll have to see how things go," replied Otis.

"Yes, sir. Well, I'll see you tomorrow then with the first half of that order," said Nick, then turned and bounded out the door and down the path. He had just gotten an invitation into the mine, and if he could get Otis to give him that tour tomorrow when he delivered the first half of the explosives order, he might be able to get some interesting information out of him.

Nick climbed into the wagon and took off for the Black Stallion Mine Company. He was halfway there when something awful occurred to him—Otis was going to be murdered tomorrow night. Nick's skin crawled, and he sucked in his breath. All of his excitement faded away as he began to think. If he could get Otis to give him the tour tomorrow night, he would have an excuse to stay late at the mine and might see who visited the office later in the evening. Should he tell Slim—either Slim—about Otis's offer?

Deep in thought, Nick had reached the Black Stallion Mine before he realized he was even on the road to the office. Nick had managed to develop a plan during the ride, as well as a headache. He parked the wagon in front of the office and jumped out, deciding to take the small crate up to the office himself rather than wait for someone to come and remove it. He picked up the crate, walked up to the front door of the office, and knocked. He was still thinking about his plan when he thought he heard Mr. Billings say to come in. He hesitated for a moment, and then heard Mr. Billings swear and yell, "Come in!" Nick quickly opened the door and went in.

"I'm sorry, Mr. Billings, I . . . uh . . . I wasn't sure I heard you the first time." Nick was so shocked by the person he saw standing by the window, he could barely speak. It was Parker Owen. He tried to hide his surprise and focused on Mr. Billings, who was sitting behind his desk. "I didn't mean to disturb you, sir. I just needed to deliver this crate," he said.

Mr. Billings watched Parker and Nick with a slightly amused expression. Parker looked distinctly uncomfortable. Turning to Nick, Mr. Billings said, "Nick, that's quite all right. I was just expecting someone else."

Nick quickly set the crate on a nearby table. "I only have this one crate for you today, sir. I just need your signature on the invoice." He walked to the desk and held out the invoice to Mr. Billings.

Mr. Billings took the paperwork, signed it, and handed it back to Nick. "Now, Parker, I'm sure Nick here might be wondering why you're in my office." Parker tightened his jaw and said nothing. "I'm sorry, Nick, Parker is speechless, so let me explain. You see, my boy, Parker here just came to tell me that a miner who works for me tried to get hired on at the Falcon Mine, claiming he had access to information about new veins we had discovered in the surrounding territory. Of course, none of that is true. Now isn't it honorable of Parker to bring this to my attention?" asked Mr. Billings, smiling broadly.

Nick knew this was a lie, especially when he spied an imp creeping around in a shadowy corner. To keep up pretences, he said, "Yes, sir." Then he turned to Parker and said, "That was really decent of you, Mr. Owen."

Parker looked a bit wild-eyed, but managed a smile and nodded. "Uhh . . . thanks, Nick. I'm sure Mr. Billings would have done the same."

"Well, Nick, if you'll excuse us, Parker and I need to talk about this miner a bit more," said Mr. Billings.

"Of course," said Nick. "I'm so sorry for interrupting." He turned to leave, but as he reached for the doorknob, the door suddenly burst open, and Nick had to jump back or be knocked over. Buck, the prospector, bolted into the room.

He stopped short when he saw Nick, then turned to look questioningly at Mr. Billings and Parker. Unable to read anything from their stony expressions, he turned back to Nick. "Well, well, what do we have here?" he said, gazing at Nick with ill-disguised hatred.

"As usual, your sense of timing is way off," growled Mr. Billings. "Nick just delivered a crate to us. Parker is here to give me the news that one of my miners is trying to get a job at the Falcon Mine. Now, move your ugly body aside, and let Nick get back to his job!" said Mr. Billings through gritted teeth.

Buck shifted his gaze to Parker and a sinister smile flitted across his face. "Well now, that's big of you, Parker," he drawled.

"Buck!" yelled Mr. Billings. "Get over here and sit down, or else!"

"Excuse me," sneered Buck, with a mock bow to Nick. "Sorry to keep you from your job there, bucko."

Nick stood still for a moment while Buck turned and headed toward the desk. Then he quickly said goodbye and left the office, shutting the door behind him. Leaning against the door for a moment, Nick tried to control his racing heart. Something sinister was going on in that office, and Nick was deeply concerned that his presence was going to create a problem for the gang, or just himself, in the near future. He finally pulled away from the door, climbed back into the wagon, and left.

Meanwhile, back in Mr. Billings's office, Parker asked, "Think he bought your story?"

"For your sake, I hope so," chuckled Buck.

"Shut up, Buck! I knew your constant tardiness would cause me problems. And your inability to think before you speak may have made things worse," growled Mr. Billings. "Now, I have no reason to think that Nick did not buy our story. If for some reason he didn't and begins to ask too many questions, then he will have to be dealt with," said Mr. Billings.

"Let me deal with him now," demanded Buck. "I don't trust him. He's up to something."

Mr. Billings face took on a very stern expression. He raised himself up from the chair and leaned over his desk. "He's just a kid, and I don't think he's a threat. No one is to touch him unless I say so. Is that understood?"

Looking at Buck and then Parker, he made sure both men nodded their agreement. "Remember, gentlemen, I give the orders around here. If you disobey my orders, I will personally deal with you. Now let's get down to the real reason we're here. It seems that our old friend Otis has requested that Slim, his faithful friend, meet with a fatal accident. Hmm, interesting how quickly events turn in our favor, don't you think, gentlemen?" asked Mr. Billings with a slight smile.

Keenan, watching Billings, stood invisible in the corner of the office, shocked by the plans that were being hatched in front of him. Christopher, having checked on Stanley, had followed Buck from the cave and now stood in the opposite corner of the office, equally stunned by what he had just heard. Both spirits realized that they were not alone and that the number of imps in the office was rapidly increasing. Christopher and Keenan simultaneously transmigrated out of the office to the thick grove of trees near the road to the mine office.

"I did hear them correctly, didn't I?" asked Christopher.

"Yes, my friend, I'm afraid you did. They're going after the real Slim. So now what are we going to do?" groaned Keenan.

Chapter Twenty-Seven
THE CONSPIRACY

Nick was still a little shaken up when he arrived back at the general store. He drove the wagon to the back, released the horses, and then walked them over to Mr. Green's stable for the night. When the horses were settled, he returned to the store, entered through the back door, and made his way upstairs to Mr. Guillot's office.

The door was partially open, but Nick knocked anyway, not wanting to witness any other illicit meetings. But there was no answer, so Nick pushed open the door and went in. He laid the paperwork from his delivery on Mr. Guillot's desk.

Hearing faint voices coming from the store, Nick left the office and headed back downstairs. But he stopped behind a tall shelf when he heard a man say—

"Well, I believe some changes are going to be forthcoming for the Falcon Mine Company."

Desperate to see who was speaking, Nick quietly moved a jar and peered through the shelves. Mr. Jenkins stood in front of the counter.

"Oh, really?" responded Mr. Guillot. "I heard that the Falcon Mine has been doing really well. So what kind of changes?" asked Mr. Guillot.

"Personnel changes with the current management," remarked Mr. Jenkins vaguely. "Several miners have registered complaints, enough that I've been called in to investigate, assess the situation, and recommend a course of action."

"That sounds pretty serious," said Mr. Guillot. "Does Otis know about this investigation?"

"It is serious. The information is credible and damaging. However, I'll give Otis a chance to defend himself. And no, he does not know yet. He will be notified first thing tomorrow morning," said Mr. Jenkins.

"This seems to have happened suddenly," said Mr. Guillot.

"Well, if you think about it, lots of strange things related to the Falcon Mine have been happening. Like Stanley Watts being kidnapped in the middle of the night. And the theft of the necklace that Stanley made for his niece. The sheriff is investigating Stanley's disappearance, but there seems to be a general lack of concern on Otis's part. The family is very upset," said Mr. Jenkins.

"I see," said Mr. Guillot. "I would hate to be anywhere near his office when he finds out that he's under investigation."

"Yes, I agree with you on that one. He does have quite a temper, doesn't he?" chuckled Mr. Jenkins.

"Yes, he does," nodded Mr. Guillot. At that moment, the front door opened and another customer walked into the store.

"Excuse me," said Mr. Guillot.

"I need to get home anyway. You have a nice evening, Mr. Guillot," said Mr. Jenkins as he strode toward the front door.

"It was good talking to you, Mr. Jenkins. And thanks for the information," said Mr. Guillot.

"I might have some more for you tomorrow," said Mr. Jenkins as he closed the door behind him.

Nick waited until Mr. Guillot was done helping the other customer before he stepped out from behind the shelves.

Mr. Guillot was straightening the counter when Nick appeared. "Hey, Nick, you're back. How did it go?"

"Uh, it went okay. It was a bit strange over at the Black Stallion office. It seems like something is going on."

"The Black Stallion Mine? That is strange. Mr. Jenkins said that the Falcon Mine is having big problems. He didn't mention the Black Stallion Mine Company at all," said Mr. Guillot.

"Well, to be honest, I think they are both involved in whatever is going on," said Nick.

"Not surprising. There has always been a fierce competition between the two mines. I thought it had calmed down a bit, but obviously I was wrong. Well, whatever is going on, things should get interesting when Otis gets notification of the pending investigation."

"An investigation?" asked Nick, trying to sound surprised. "That isn't going to make Mr. Walkins happy."

"I'll say. Otis is going to be quite angry," said Mr. Guillot. "Oh, by the way, the afternoon coach came, and I got confirmation that I'll be receiving the first half of the order tomorrow morning. To make it easier, I'll ask Parker to send someone from the mine to help you with the delivery," explained Mr. Guillot.

"Okay, that sounds good," said Nick. "Well, I'm going to head into the back and start sorting the crates that came in this afternoon."

"Say, Nick, it's almost quitting time. You can wait and deal with it in the morning if you want."

"Thanks, Mr. Guillot, but I would feel better if it were done tonight and not waiting for me in the morning. Besides, working helps me clear my head," explained Nick as he headed to the back.

"Suit yourself, but let me know when you're leaving for the night," called out Mr. Guillot as he turned and headed to his office.

There was quite a pile of small crates, so Nick got busy sorting through them. He was almost done when he heard his name being called in a whisper.

"Yeah," he replied, straightening and looking around. When he didn't get a response, he called out, "Hello, anyone there?" As he turned toward the back door, the ghostly image of a human shape appeared and slowly solidified.

"Hey, Nick, got a moment?" asked Slim in a whisper.

"Yeah, is it time to go?"

"Not exactly," answered Slim. "Something has come up, and I need your help. Let's step outside for a moment and I'll explain."

Nick quickly slipped out the door with Slim. They wound their way behind a few tall crates and sat on overturned barrels to conceal themselves from prying eyes. "This sounds serious," said Nick.

"It is," replied Slim. "Now you know that the real Slim went to Cartersville this morning, right?"

Nick nodded.

"Well, it seems the real Slim ran into the real Michael, Keenan, and Christopher and solicited their help. The four of them are heading this way. They'll be staying at the ranch house."

"Wait a minute!" said Nick. "That didn't happen before, did it?"

"No! They didn't come to Silverado until I was standing trial. After my hanging, they decided to conduct their own investigation and went to work for the Black Stallion Mine Company. But now that they're helping Slim, he's probably going to get much further along in his own investigation. And to make matters worse, with them around, none of the guys can get close to the real me. We were sort of depending on being able to watch the real me in the coming days," explained Slim.

"Wow, this is a major problem!" said Nick.

"To say the least. So this is where you come in, Nick. This is going to be hard to juggle, but I need you to try to keep an eye on all of them."

"But I haven't even actually met them yet," said Nick with a worried frown.

"Well, I can help you with that. They passed the road to the ranch and are heading straight into town. Knowing me, they'll probably go to the sheriff's office first to check in. So after you're done here, you should go to the sheriff's office. The real Slim will make the introductions, and we can hope that they will ask you to join them for dinner. But we have to be careful, because having you around will be an advantage in helping them figure out what is going on. We are just going to have to keep our fingers crossed and play it by ear," said Slim.

"I can do that," said Nick. "Besides, I do have some strange things to report to the real Slim and the sheriff that should pique their interest."

"Really? Anything new for me, too?" asked Slim.

"Yes. It seems that Mr. Jenkins is going to serve Mr. Walkins with notice of a financial board investigation based on complaints from the miners."

"That's rubbish—a fabrication, no doubt. That is one way of legally taking the mine out of Otis's hands. If Otis thinks the real Slim has found out about the pit and the diamonds, he may think that the real Slim turned him in."

"That's true. Mr. Walkins will never know that Mr. Jenkins knows what's going on," said Nick, "let alone that he is involved in the attempt to take over the mine."

"Hmm," sighed Slim. "The interesting thing is that no one is planning to do Otis in at this point. They are just trying to take over the mine. So why is Otis killed, and by whom?"

Nick shuffled his feet as they stood there in silence. Then an idea popped into his head. "What if Mr. Walkins's death was not planned? What if he got into an argument with someone in his office after you left? For some reason, it just got out of hand. Maybe the person wasn't intending to kill Mr. Walkins; maybe it just happened."

"That makes sense," said Slim. "But that makes it more difficult for us to figure out who did it."

"Why?" questioned Nick. "Can't one of your guys just watch Mr. Walkins until it happens and find out that way?"

"Unfortunately, no. We are restricted from following Otis at all on his last day. As I told you, the temptation to interfere would be too great. We have to figure this out the old-fashioned way. If it happens the way you think, then someone we are following is bound to talk. They always do," explained Slim.

"Is there any restriction on me watching Otis?" asked Nick.

"Technically, no . . . except the one that I am putting on you. We have no way of knowing what the situation is, or how it will play out, but Otis will be killed—violently. I cannot, and will not, put you in that kind of danger," said Slim.

Nick sighed deeply and shook his head. *It would be so much easier if they could find out who killed Mr. Walkins by watching him,* he thought. Nick thought about the offer Mr. Walkins had made to give him a tour. *If I can just convince Mr. Walkins to do it tomorrow after the delivery,* he thought. *Is it wrong not to tell Slim if I might be able to solve the whole mystery?*

"What's up, Nick?" asked Slim. "You look like you just remembered something important."

"Uh . . . oh yeah, I did," replied Nick, trying to avoid telling Slim the idea that was forming in his head. "I needed to tell you that while I was delivering to the Black Stallion Mine Company this afternoon, I accidentally walked in on a meeting between Mr. Billings and Parker Owen. And as I was leaving, that prospector, Buck, burst into the room. Mr. Billings tried to explain that Parker was there to tell him about a Black Stallion miner who was trying to get a job at the Falcon Mine, saying that he had information about new veins that had been discovered," said Nick.

"Well, we know that is a lie," Slim muttered, with a sad look on his face. Nick didn't notice Slim's expression, and continued his story.

"Buck looked pretty unhappy to find me there. He and I had a run-in at the saloon this morning. He doesn't like me very much, and I may have made things worse," said Nick, looking a bit sheepish.

"I wouldn't worry about it, Nick," said Slim. "Buck's the kind of guy who doesn't trust anybody, because he can't be trusted himself. But we are going to have to keep a close eye on him, for our assignment and your safety. If the time is right, and he can get you alone, he'll probably come after you."

Slim sighed deeply. "Well, Nick, I've got to get going. I still have work to do. You have your new assignment. One of us will check on you at the top of each hour. If something comes up and you need us sooner, just think about one of us, get somewhere alone, and say the name of the spirit you're thinking of. We'll get to you quickly," explained Slim.

"I'll watch the time. Don't worry, I'll keep an eye out for any problems," said Nick.

Slim looked deeply into Nick's eyes. "Whatever you do, be smart about any situation that comes up. I don't want anything to happen to you, Nick."

"I understand," replied Nick, beginning to wonder about Slim's mood. "I'll be careful."

"Good, then. I'll see you later," said Slim, and he rose and began to disappear.

"See you later, Slim," whispered Nick. He jumped up and slipped in the back door of the general store. He quickly finished sorting the crates. He was excited that he had a new assignment for the evening, and with any luck, he was going to spend the evening with the real Michael, Keenan, and Christopher. He knew that they would be just like their spirits, but establishing a friendship with them in their time was important to him.

Finished with the sorting, Nick walked to the front of the store, called goodnight to Mr. Guillot, and left through the front door. He made his way down the boardwalk to the sheriff's office. Walking into the lobby, he found the sheriff's deputy sitting behind the small desk. "Hello, my name is Nick. I'm here to see the sheriff."

"Do you have an appointment?" asked the deputy, clearly skeptical about a kid asking to see the sheriff.

"Appointment?" frowned Nick. "Since when does somebody need an appointment to see the sheriff?"

"Well, you know, he could be in a meeting."

"Is he?" asked Nick, beginning to get frustrated.

"Aw, uh . . . hang on, and I'll check," said the deputy. He rose and walked down the hallway to the sheriff's office.

Nick waited in the lobby, but soon heard the sheriff's voice booming, "Nick is welcome anytime. Let him in!"

Nick smiled broadly and headed down the hallway. He passed the deputy, who looked at him with a puzzled expression and said, "He'll see you now."

Nick walked into the sheriff's office as the sheriff was moving papers off of the chairs in front of his desk. "Nick, come in, come in. How are you?" he asked, waving him into one of the empty chairs.

"Good! Tired, but good. How are you, Sheriff?"

"Not too bad. Just a lot of paperwork and lots of little complaints that are driving me crazy. So, do you have any more information for me from the mines?"

"Well, maybe," said Nick. "I think Mr. Jenkins might be involved in whatever is happening at the mines. I overheard him talking to Mr. Guillot this afternoon, and he is going to be heading up an investigation of the Falcon Mine Company. He said that miners have been registering complaints against Mr. Walkins recently."

"An investigation? Do you have any idea what it's about, or who filed the complaints?" asked the sheriff.

"No. Mr. Jenkins didn't go into detail," said Nick.

"That's really strange. I have heard more complaints concerning the Black Stallion Mine than the Falcon Mine. The only problem that I'm aware of, and am currently working on, is the disappearance of Stanley Watts," said the sheriff.

"Mr. Jenkins is supposed to tell Mr. Walkins about the investigation to-morrow morning," Nick told him.

Just then, the deputy stuck his head in the door. "You have four men here to see you, sir."

"Send them back," responded the sheriff, rising from his chair. "Now who in the world could this be?" But then he let out a holler that made Nick jump and whip around in his chair. In walked Slim, Keenan, Michael, and Christopher, and for several moments the room was filled with a blur of hugs and jostling, and lots of laughter and animated chatter as the group of friends greeted each other. "Guys, guys, settle down a minute," said Slim in a loud voice, trying to be heard. "I need to introduce you to a new good friend of mine."

Slim made his way over to where Nick sat. "Guys, this is Nick."

Nick looked up into the faces he already knew, stood, and reached out to shake the hands of the real Michael, Christopher, and Keenan.

"I feel like I already know you guys," said Nick. "Slim has told me so much about you."

Each of them shook Nick's hand with a big grin and a sparkle of mischief in his eyes.

"Any friend of Slim's is a friend of ours," said Michael.

"I hope that Slim didn't tell you too much about me. I like to have some surprises up my sleeve," said Keenan.

"Be careful not to believe everything Keenan tells you. You should check with Michael or me first. It's for your own safety," chuckled Christopher.

Laugher burst out in the room as Keenan turned and popped Christopher on the shoulder.

"Welcome to the gang, Nick. Just be careful—anything and everything can happen with these guys," warned the sheriff.

"Hey now, don't scare the boy," chuckled Slim.

"Okay, guys, have a seat—or a lean—and tell me what you're doing in town," said the sheriff. Slim and Nick sat in the chairs in front of the sheriff's desk, and the three cowboys leaned against the walls.

"We just sold our herd and drove them to the new owner. We'll start building a new herd pretty soon, but for the moment, I guess you could say we are on vacation," explained Christopher.

"They're successful ranchers," whispered Slim to Nick. "I had my chance to work with them, but I chose to work in the mine. And look where it has gotten me." He then turned to the sheriff. "Well, Artemus, I figured since we have a lot of ground to cover, we could use some more help. And since the guys were herd-less, they volunteered to give us a hand."

"Well, what did you find out from Lucas Marley?" asked the sheriff.

"Otis has discovered a diamond deposit; the stones are of good quality," Slim told them. The cowboys didn't seem shocked, so Nick figured that Slim had already told them the news. The sheriff seemed to be surprised, but also satisfied that their theory had proven to be fact. "As Nick told us, Ben brought the samples in a lockbox to Lucas. Otis included a note with the samples telling Lucas that his analysis had to be completely confidential, even from me. Lucas destroyed Otis's note after reading it. He wrote a report on his analysis and a short note to Otis and sent the box back with Ben the same day," explained Slim.

"So it is diamonds," mused the sheriff, shaking his head. "But Slim, why haven't more deposits been found? I mean, don't diamond mines usually contain lots of deposits?" asked the sheriff.

"Not really sure, to tell you the truth. I am guessing that the deposit is just one of those flukes of nature. There just happened to be enough heat and pressure in that particular area to produce diamonds. But now we know that the necklace Stanley made for his niece had to have been made with stones from that deposit. Why else would it have been stolen? Which means that Stanley helped himself to a handful of diamonds without really knowing what they were," said Slim.

"So the kidnapping and the theft were probably carried out by someone who has a vested interested in keeping the deposit a secret," reasoned the sheriff.

"Or someone found out about the deposit and wants in on it. Maybe they even plan to blackmail Otis, if he's trying to keep the discovery to himself," said Nick.

Slim nudged Michael with his elbow. "Told you this kid was smart, just like us when we were his age," Slim whispered.

"But the question is, how do we find out who knows about the diamonds? Could it be that Otis is being blackmailed? I don't think he would be too eager to tell anyone if he is, especially if he is trying to keep this whole thing a secret," said Michael.

"Nick just told me that Mr. Jenkins is informing Otis of an investigation of the Falcon Mine tomorrow," said the sheriff.

"Investigation? What investigation?" asked Slim. "I'm the one who should be notified. It's my responsibility to call the review board together. I haven't heard anything since I've been back, and there aren't any complaints to investigate that I know of."

"Well, there is one," explained the sheriff. "It was registered late yesterday afternoon by Stanley's wife. I received a copy of it this morning, so you would have received it today. Her complaint is that nothing is being done at the Falcon Mine to help in the investigation of Stanley's disappearance."

"I've been expecting one from Stanley's family, but that doesn't require an official financial board investigation. Something doesn't sound right about this, especially since Mr. Jenkins is heading up the investigation. He never gets his hands dirty with this type of thing; he always hands it off to one of his assistants," said Slim.

"But what if somehow Mr. Jenkins knows what Mr. Walkins is trying to hide?" asked Nick.

"Then I would say we have a greedy man who is possibly trying to blackmail Otis with a trumped-up investigation," said Keenan.

"Hey, let's not forget Mr. Billings. He is greed incarnate. He probably has spies at the Falcon Mine. What if others found out about the diamonds?" asked Michael.

Nick thought this might be a good time to describe what he had seen. "This might be of interest. When I made my delivery to the Black Stallion Mine today, I accidentally walked in on a meeting between Mr. Billings and Parker Owen. When I was leaving, another man I've seen at both mines came into the office. Mr. Billings and Parker were clearly expecting him. Mr. Billings told me that Parker was there to tell him that a Black Stallion miner had tried to get a job at the Falcon Mine by saying that he had information on new veins found at the Black Stallion Mine."

The room was silent. Nick's words hung in the air while the reality of the situation began to sink in.

Finally the sheriff spoke. "Whew . . . this just seems to get bigger and bigger with each passing day. Slim, I think you stumbled into the biggest conspiracy this town has ever seen."

"I have to agree. We are going to have to be very careful, because at this point, anybody could be involved," cautioned Slim.

"Listen, I think I can speak for all of us when I say that I am dirty, tired, and starving," said Keenan. "It has been a long day. We should probably take a break so that we can get cleaned up and eat."

"You're right, Keenan. It has been a tiring day for all of us. Why don't we all just head to the ranch. We can talk things over some more while we eat. Then we can at least figure out what the plan is for tomorrow," suggested Slim. "Can you join us, Artemus? And how about you, Nick? You can spend the night and we'll bring you back into the town in the morning."

"I can," said the sheriff. "I'll have my deputy take over for me tonight."

"I can, too," answered Nick. "I just have to let my mother's friends know where I'll be. It should only take me a few minutes."

"Okay, Nick. Go do what you need to do, and we'll meet you out front by the horses," said Slim.

Nick left the office and walked quickly back to the general store. Glancing at the watch he pulled from his pocket, he realized his timing could not have been better. He slipped down the alley to the back of the store. A wispy form began to appear, and Nick watched as Keenan solidified in front of him.

"Hey, Nick, what are you doing here? I thought you were supposed to be at the sheriff's office?" asked Keenan.

"I was, and I have to get back. But I needed to let you know that I will be spending the night at the ranch. The sheriff, Slim, and the guys are trying to figure out what their next move is going to be. They now know what those stones are, and they know a few of the people who are involved, but they don't know everything. I'm not sure what they're going to do next."

"Things are really popping now," said Keenan. "But at least they don't know everything that we know, and that is to our advantage. Let's just hope it stays that way. We, too, are going to meet tonight to try and figure out how to spring Stanley."

"You found him?" asked Nick, raising his voice in excitement.

"Yes, thanks to Parker. Slim followed Parker to where Stanley is being held. He's alive and well, but they're holding him at the Black Stallion Mine in a new tunnel they're digging from the back of the mountain. We aren't sure why they're digging there, especially considering there are no signs of gold or silver, but we're working on that one."

"Do you think I'll be able to help with the rescue attempt?" asked Nick.

"We'll see," said Keenan. "But for the moment, you need to concentrate on the plans the guys make tonight. What you learn is very important and will help us decide what to do next. One of us will keep you up to date with our plans regarding Stanley. Deal?"

"Deal," responded Nick.

"All right then, I've got to go. But I will inform Slim about everything. You had better scoot, too. You don't want to keep those guys waiting," said Keenan.

"Okay," said Nick.

Keenan waved as he disappeared, and Nick turned and quickly made his way back up the alley to the main street. He turned the corner and walked down to the sheriff's office, where the men were waiting on their horses.

"Is it okay for you to join us?" asked the real Slim.

"Yep," replied Nick. "Not a problem. I just have to be at work on time in the morning. I have a big delivery to the Falcon Mine tomorrow."

"Is it the order Otis put in?" asked Slim, as Nick swung into the saddle behind him.

"Yes, but only half the order will be in tomorrow. The rest of it should be arriving in a few more days."

"Interesting," murmured Slim as Nick settled just behind his saddle. "Hold on tight, Nick. Let's go, guys," called Slim as he touched his heels to his horse's ribs, and they took off in a gallop toward the ranch.

Chapter Twenty-Eight

THE SHERIFF'S THEORY

Two hours later, Keenan materialized behind the workshop alone. He could feel his real self nearby and knew that Nick, Slim, and the guys were in the house. He crept around the corner of the workshop and stared at the brightly lit windows of the house. He could hear the faint sound of laughter, and occasionally somebody passed in front of the window. He wanted to get a peek at the whole gang, so he became invisible and crept across the yard until he felt the barrier between himself and his real self repelling him. He knew what he was doing was risky, and Slim would yell at him if he found out, but he just had to take a quick look.

He stood in the yard staring hard through the window into the kitchen. It was weird to see everybody together again, talking and laughing. It was even stranger to see Nick sitting in the middle of the group, interacting with them as if he belonged there. Keenan shook his head slightly. He did not have any memory of the scene that was playing out before him, but he knew that, if they were successful, he would eventually.

Keenan watched Nick as he told a story, and he could not help but smile. He finally turned and slowly walked back to the workshop. He slipped inside and immediately began to make coffee. He was staring at the coffee pot on the potbellied stove when Michael suddenly appeared next to him.

"Hey, Keenan, I never knew a pot of coffee could be so interesting," chuckled Michael.

"Aw, you should try it sometime," laughed Keenan. "You'd be surprised what you can see."

"Christopher will be here in a few minutes. Slim is finishing checking up on something and should be arriving soon. Say, is the coffee ready yet?" asked Michael.

"Momentarily. We've got a lot to cover tonight."

"Yeah, I know. Say, where is Nick right now?" asked Michael.

"He's over in the ranch house sitting at the kitchen table talking to the real Slim, Artemus, and us. He'll be staying over there tonight. I'm a little amazed at how good Nick is with people. The real Slim and the gang have really taken a shine to him," said Keenan.

"It's probably better that he stay over there tonight, anyway," sighed Michael. "There have been some significant changes that I would feel better if we discussed alone."

"I know," said Keenan, frowning. "Christopher and I witnessed a meeting between Mr. Billings, Parker, and Buck this afternoon." Keenan was going to say more, but just then, Christopher began to materialize near the door.

"Hey, guys. Boy, I sure hope the coffee is ready."

"You couldn't have timed it better. Grab a mug, Christopher," replied Keenan.

"Grab one for me, too," said Slim, as he appeared at the back of the room. A few minutes later, all four of them were seated at the makeshift table.

"Okay, first things first," said Slim. "We know where Stanley is being held. Now it's just a question of when we should try to spring him. The problem is that we have to find a way to get him to Artemus without being seen. And we have to make sure he's well protected. Once Billings and the guys find out he's missing, they'll go after him again. And they won't just kidnap him, they'll kill him."

"Well, I know Nick is eager to help," offered Keenan.

"Yes, but with Nick responsible for keeping tabs on the real us, I'm afraid he might have his hands full," said Slim.

"Well, Nick is the only person who can really help us," said Keenan. "Timing is a major problem, too. We're going to have to keep a close eye on Mr. Billings to make sure we know about any orders he gives regarding Stanley. We may have to move on Stanley sooner rather than later."

"What about Parker?" asked Christopher. "He's playing both sides, and that makes him unpredictable—and a major problem."

"That's an understatement," said Keenan, sharing an uncomfortable look with Michael. There was a pause in the conversation and Christopher was about to continue, but Slim was the first to speak.

"Guys, I know about Otis's order," he said quietly.

"Oh . . . How?" asked Keenan, staring down at the table.

"I was following Parker for most of the day. I stayed outside Otis's office because I didn't want to interfere with Michael's assignment, but I heard Otis give Parker the order," said Slim. "And then I followed Parker to his meeting with Billings. I entered the office after I sensed you guys leave."

"Oh," said Christopher. "So . . . what do we do now?"

"Wait a minute. Could there be some mistake? Are we sure about this?" asked Michael.

Slim groaned softly and nodded. "You were there, Michael. You heard Otis."

"What else did Otis and Parker talk about?" asked Keenan.

"Well, Otis had Parker orchestrate Stanley's disappearance, but Otis is unaware that Mr. Billings is involved and has Stanley stashed away. The price for Stanley's and my disappearance is Miss Judith's necklace, which

Otis thinks Parker is holding. Again, Otis doesn't know that the necklace is sitting in Mr. Billings's desk drawer," explained Slim.

"And then this afternoon, as you know, Parker met with Mr. Billings and Buck," said Christopher. "Billings was certainly pleased when Parker told him about the order from Otis to kill Slim." He turned to Michael and continued. "The three of them talked about their plans for removing Otis from the Falcon Mine."

"It seems that Buck is helping fabricate the complaints that are at the root of the investigation Mr. Jenkins is conducting," supplied Slim.

"That certainly was an interesting meeting," said Keenan, "especially when Nick walked in on Billings and Parker."

"He did?" asked Michael, his eyebrows raised in concern.

"Nick was delivering a small crate to the office," explained Keenan. "Mr. Billings thought it was Buck, so he called out for Nick to come in. Nick walked in and saw Parker standing in the office. It was a very uncomfortable few minutes for everyone. Mr. Billings recovered and told Nick that Parker was there to report on a Black Stallion miner who was trying to get a job at the Falcon Mine by saying he had information about new veins found at the Black Stallion mine. Of course, Nick didn't buy it, but he pretended well enough to convince Billings."

"Is Nick in any danger at this point?" asked Christopher.

"No, not yet. Billings has too much to worry about to concern himself with Nick. But we need to keep a close eye on Buck. He doesn't like Nick at all, and he doesn't trust him. I wouldn't put it past him to hurt Nick," said Slim.

The room lapsed into silence for several moments as each one of them stared at the table.

Finally, Michael spoke up. "Listen, everyone, we knew from the beginning that there would be risks. Those risks haven't changed, and they will probably only get worse the closer we get to an answer. So we must decide. Do we go on from here? It's guaranteed to get tougher, and Nick's life may be at risk, but I don't think that the Almighty would have sent Nick with us to die. Or do we stop now, cut our losses, and give up?" asked Michael.

Silence again hung heavily in the room.

Keenan finally spoke. "We have come too far to stop now."

"He's right," added Christopher. "We'll do everything we can to protect Nick."

"Nick is a smart boy. We've got to trust him and his judgment, and hope that he stays one step ahead of everyone else," said Michael.

Slim agreed, "You're all right. Nick is a strong, smart kid. I can't give up on him now just because I'm afraid for him. We'll just have to get organized, stay focused, do our best to protect Nick, and see this thing through to the end."

"Say, Slim," said Christopher, "tomorrow is the day of Otis's murder. How are we going to handle that?"

"Well, remember that we are forbidden to go into Otis's office tomorrow. At this point, I'm not even going to assign anyone to him; it would just be too hard for any of us not to interfere. Michael, you take Billings. Christopher, you keep an eye on Buck. Keenan, you watch Parker. I'll keep an eye on Stanley and Jeb. Let's all take turns checking on Nick and the real guys. But remember to stay a safe distance away, we don't need to create any more problems," reminded Slim.

Meanwhile, at the ranch house, the real Slim and the gang had just finished dinner and now sat in front of the fire in the main room talking. During dinner, Michael, Christopher, and Keenan had told stories from their childhoods, and Nick could not stop laughing. Now they were discussing the discovery of diamonds at the Falcon Mine and all of the people involved. Nick had told them many things, but still held back some key information for their own protection. It was getting late, so Slim led Nick to his son's room. Nick had stayed in the same room before. Michael walked up behind them and stood in the doorway. "Hey, Slim, I have my bedroll with me. Mind if I bunk in with you, Nick?"

"Sure, make yourself at home," said Nick.

Michael joked with Nick before he drifted off to sleep. Nick felt more comfortable and safer with Michael asleep on the floor near the door. No one would be able to sneak past him.

Nick's mind raced as he thought through everything they had talked about. He could not help but think that there was something he was missing as he tried to connect all of the details in his head. Later, when the house was quiet except for the gentle hum of snoring, Nick's thoughts finally began to slow down. He found himself praying for help, wisdom, lots of strength, and the safety of his friends.

Morning came too soon, the sun rising over the mountains and cascading its warm rays through the window and across Nick's face. He woke up quickly with his heart racing, unsure of the source of his anxiety. Then he remembered. *Today is the day,* he thought. Shivering slightly, Nick sat up and leaned over to see if Michael was still asleep on the floor. Michael was on his right side breathing softly. Nick slipped out of bed, picked up his clothes and boots, and walked around Michael without waking him. He slipped out of the room, closing the door softly behind him.

He went to the washroom, cleaned and dressed himself, and then made his way to the kitchen. The real Slim and the sheriff were the only people in the house who were up. They were sitting in the kitchen at the table drinking coffee.

"Morning, Nick. You're up with the sun," said the sheriff.

"Well, I couldn't sleep, and I should get to work a little early this morning," said Nick. "There's that big delivery at the Falcon Mine this afternoon. The carriage will probably come in this morning, and I should be there to help get the wagon loaded."

"Right, Otis's big order. We still don't know what he's going to be doing with the explosives," said the sheriff.

"No, but remember, it is only half the order," said Nick.

"He must be planning to blast in the area of the diamond deposit in hopes of finding more stones," said Slim. "Unfortunately, I am guessing he hasn't tested the area for safety. It's a very deep tunnel, and doing any major blasting could cause the upper tunnels to become unstable."

"So, Slim, how many stones do you think are really there?" asked the sheriff.

"I don't have any idea," replied Slim, shaking his head. "I would bet, though, that it's just a single deposit, because we've never found any before. Lucas indicated that the deposit is probably just a geologic anomaly."

"Sounds like in order to really know what's going on, we need to find a way to get you down there to investigate. But in the meantime, what is the plan for today?" asked the sheriff.

"First thing I need to do is some general research, which I can do in town today. What I need you to do, Artemus, is try to find out who has filed the complaints against the Falcon Mine. Then, at some point today, I need to confront Otis," sighed Slim.

"You're not going to be well received if he thinks you have anything to do with this investigation of the Falcon Mine," warned the sheriff.

"I know. I hope that we'll be able to find out who filed the complaints against the mine and why they filed them. That will help me prove that I had nothing to do with it. I should be able to reason with Otis and talk him into coming clean with the financial board before it's too late and he loses the mine entirely," said Slim.

"I just don't like any of this," replied the sheriff. "Something just doesn't feel right. I think that there are more people involved than we know about. And I'm worried that somebody is going to get hurt."

"When greed is a driving force, people are bound to get hurt. The only things we can hope for are a swift resolution and to avoid hurting anyone," said Slim.

Nick considered how much information to offer at this point. He finally spoke up, "If you could get to that area and were able to retrieve some samples, you could use them as proof in case Otis or anyone else tries to keep the diamond deposit a secret."

"How could they keep the deposit a secret with a pending investigation?" asked the sheriff.

"I see where Nick is going with this," said Slim. "What if someone on the board is conspiring with Mr. Billings and is using this investigation to blackmail Otis, or even take over the mine itself. Is that what you're thinking, Nick?"

"Yeah. You already said that there have been no complaints against the Falcon Mine, so why now? That's the question I can't seem to answer," said Nick.

"Nick, I think you might have something. If we can get our hands on a couple of stones and find out who is driving this investigation, then maybe we can get Otis to come forward and tell the financial board about the deposit. Then anybody trying to blackmail Otis or seize the mine would lose all of his leverage," said Slim.

"That means breaking the law in order to solve a crime, Slim," said the sheriff. "You would have to go into that area against Otis's strict instructions, and that would be trespassing. You know I can't be involved, even though I realize that this might offer us the final proof that we need. I'm still bound to the law. So, however you and the guys retrieve some samples is between you and them. I'd like to help, but I can't know anything about it. It could jeopardize my whole investigation. Just bring me any information or proof when you have it, and I'll take it from there."

The sheriff turned to Nick, "Well, Nick, do you need a ride into town?"

"Yes, sir. That would be a big help."

"I can take him, Artemus," replied Slim.

"No, no," responded the sheriff. "You have some major planning to do when the guys wake up, and that's going to keep you plenty busy."

"You're right, Artemus—as always," chuckled Slim.

"You ready, Nick?" asked the sheriff.

"Yes, sir," said Nick.

"Have a good day, Nick!" said Slim. "I'll catch up with you later. In the meantime, remember to keep your eyes and ears open."

"Slim," said the sheriff. "Tell the guys to drop by my office this afternoon for a cup of coffee and to catch up on the latest developments."

"I'll tell them," said Slim.

Then the sheriff and Nick walked out the kitchen door and headed to the stable.

A while later, the sheriff dropped Nick off in front of the general store, turned his horse around, and went to his office. It was a very busy morning. Many people came into the store to shop and place orders, and wagons with parts of the order for the Falcon Mine began arriving early. Nick and Mr. Guillot took turns working the counter and unloading wagons. Mr. Guillot had sent word to Otis to send one of his wagons into town to help bring the order up to the mine. At a quarter past nine, a wagon with the Falcon Mine logo on the side arrived in front of the store. Nick half-expected Parker to be driving the wagon, but he did not recognize the man climbing down from the driver's seat.

Mr. Guillot came out of the store and walked over to the wagon driver. "Hey, Nick, let me introduce you to Simon Riggs from the Falcon Mine."

"Nice to meet you," said Simon as he reached out to shake Nick's hand. "I can't tell you what a treat it is to be out in the sun instead of working in the mine. I'm grateful that Parker asked me to do this."

"Where is Parker?" asked Nick, trying not to sound too curious.

"Mr. Walkins seemed to be mighty upset about something this morning. Parker stayed at the mine to try to calm him down," explained Simon.

Nick and Simon began to load crates onto the wagon. Another wagon arrived at about half past ten with the last items they were expecting. Mr. Guillot brought the general store wagon around to the front, and Nick and Simon, and occasionally Mr. Guillot, worked on loading both wagons. It was a few minutes before lunchtime when they finally finished, and Simon indicated that he wanted to take a break and grab some lunch before they left. They agreed to meet back at the store in thirty minutes, then Simon walked over to the saloon, and Nick went to the bakery.

Mr. Guillot was waiting for them when they returned. He had the invoices all prepared and he handed them to Nick. "There you go, Nick. You are all loaded up and ready to go. You'd better be off if you want to get back before dark," said Mr. Guillot.

Nick thought about what the evening held, and hoped he would be able to convince Mr. Walkins to give him a tour this afternoon. He hid his worried thoughts from Mr. Guillot, though. As Mr. Guillot waved and headed back into the store, Nick and Simon each climbed aboard a wagon and took off for the Falcon Mine.

Chapter Twenty-Nine
THE MINE TOUR

Nick did not have as much time to dwell on Mr. Walkins's imminent death during the drive to the Falcon Mine as he thought he would. The constant shouted chatter coming from Simon in the other wagon helped keep Nick's mind occupied. He tried to quiet his nerves by thinking about various ways to convince Mr. Walkins to give him a tour tonight.

They pulled up between the Falcon Mine main entrance and the office and parked the wagons. Simon stayed with the wagons while Nick ran up to the office to let Mr. Walkins know his order had arrived. Nick could see the creases of worry on Mr. Walkins's face. There was a flurry of activity as Mr. Walkins barked out orders to Parker to get some men to help unload the wagons. He quickly signed the paperwork and then headed out to the wagons with Nick to help unload the crates.

While working side by side with Mr. Walkins, Nick seized his opportunity. "Uhm . . . Mr. Walkins?"

"Yes, Nick?"

"Well, sir, I might be seeing my father very soon. I sure would like to show him how much I've learned since I've been here. Do you think we might be able to go on that mine tour tonight?"

"Well, Nick, today is a busy day," replied Mr. Walkins, hesitating. But then his expression changed and he smiled at Nick. "You know what, Nick, I could really use a break from the office for a few hours. I'd be happy to give you that tour. Once we get all this stuff unloaded, you and I can take a quick break, and then I'll give you a tour of the mine."

"That's great, Mr. Walkins. I really appreciate it," said Nick as he reached up and grabbed a smaller crate from one of the wagons.

"Listen, Nick. If we're going to be friends, I have to insist that you call me Otis."

"Yes, sir, Mr. Wal— . . . uhm, Otis," said Nick with a grin.

A little more than an hour had passed by the time the last crate was pulled off the wagon. Nick was tired, and his muscles were sore. Otis was out of breath, and he leaned against one of the wheels, wiping the sweat from his face with a handkerchief.

"Whew, I'm just not young enough to do this anymore," said Otis.

Nick just smiled, and then glanced up when he saw, out of the corner of his eye, Parker heading toward them.

"Everything has been stored in cavern three," said Parker. "The low temperature and moisture should keep the explosives stable until we're ready to use them."

"Good! Thank the men, and tell them to take a full break before they head back into the mine," instructed Otis. "I'll be busy this afternoon giving Nick a tour, so handle anything that comes up. Oh, and since Slim did not come in again today, you and I will have to do the payroll tomorrow morning instead of tonight, Parker."

Parker grimaced slightly and his expression became somewhat angry. "Yes, sir," he said, then turned and stalked away.

Otis sighed deeply as he watched Parker. "We're having a rough day today," said Otis. "I know he hates to do the payroll, but I have no choice. Slim isn't around to do it."

Otis turned and headed back up the path to his office. "Say, Nick," said a voice behind him. Nick turned around to find Simon standing by the general store wagon. "I heard that Otis is planning to give you a tour. His tours usually take several hours, so would you like me to take the general store wagon back to Mr. Guillot for you? It would give me a good excuse to stay out of the mine for the rest of the day and get off work a little early. I know that Otis has to ride through town on his way home, and I'm sure that he would give you a ride when you're through."

"Yeah, that would be great," said Nick. He smiled a bitter, secret smile as he turned to head up the path to Otis's office. Simon had unknowingly provided him with an excuse to stay at the mine late enough to find out who would murder Mr. Walkins.

"We'll start with the mines first," said Otis as Nick entered his office. "It will be easier to move around and get to different places while the men are still in there and working this afternoon. After that, we can head back here and look at some of the maps. I'm having one of my assistants bring us dinner. You are free for the entire evening, aren't you?" asked Otis.

"Yes, sir! But I will need a ride back into town. Simon took the store wagon back for me so that the horses could be stabled before Mr. Green closes up shop."

"Not a problem, my boy. I would be happy to give you a ride back into town. I think you'll find this tour very interesting, Nick. And who knows, I may be prepping you to take my place someday," chuckled Otis. He grabbed his coat and walked past Nick out the office door.

"Maybe," whispered Nick, as he followed Otis down the path and up the hill to the cave entrance.

The cave itself was dark and clammy, and the only light that penetrated the darkness came from the miners' oil lamps and the torches that were attached to the walls. The mine itself was a labyrinth of intricate winding passages that seemed to go on and on forever. Otis seemed to know every passage as he walked briskly and confidently from tunnel to tunnel, talking about removal procedures, rock formations, and the use of explosives. Nick was captivated by everything Otis told him, and Otis loved the attention. As they continued deeper into the mountain, they reached the area where the miners were currently working.

The miners stopped what they were doing when Otis entered the shaft. They let Nick take a hammer and chisel and chip away at some of the stone.

"Do you see the difference between the rock and the ore?" asked Otis.

"Yes, I see what you were taking about," said Nick.

"It's a time-consuming process," said Peter, one of the miners. "But when we hit a new vein that's rich with good ore, everybody gets excited. And there is no telling how much more we'll find."

"Yeah," said one of the other miners, "so far this old mountain has given us a lot of ore, but there will come a day when even the Falcon Mine will dry up, just like all the other mines. Then what will we do?"

"Now, Jesse, I'm the one who's supposed to worry about that," said Otis. "This mine is still producing a good amount of ore, and we still have the other half of the mountain to explore. The Falcon Mine closure is a long way off, boys, so don't even think about it."

With a big grin and a slap on each man's shoulder, Otis turned and headed toward the lift. "Come on, Nick. There is more to see!" he called out.

Nick followed Otis to the lift and climbed in. Otis was ready to push the UP button when they heard Parker's voice rising from below.

"You've got to stay awake at your post! This is the fifth time I've found you sound asleep," he shouted.

"Sorry, Parker! It's just so boring down here. Everyone knows this tunnel is off limits and probably dangerous. I don't understand why we have to keep guarding it. Why don't we just put up some barriers?"

Parker's voice began to rise to fever pitch as he yelled at the miner. Otis quickly shooed Nick off the lift, telling him to wait there for just a moment. He pressed the button and descended to the next level. The screeching gears of the lift drowned out Parker's voice. Then there was complete silence for a brief moment as Mr. Walkins got off the lift. Nick could hear Mr. Walkins talking in low, tense tones as he quickly took control of the situation.

"You're making a scene," he growled at Parker. "You need to keep your voice down. Now, where are the other guards?"

"They aren't scheduled until closing," said Parker.

"I'll have Jesse bring down strong coffee for the guards. That should keep them awake. We also need to rotate the men so that they can take breaks every two hours."

"That means that we'll have to add on two more men. I didn't think you wanted to involve any more people," said Parker.

"Include yourself and Simon in the rotation. It wouldn't hurt you to carry some of the responsibility," said Otis. "Now if you'll excuse me, I need to finish up a tour. I'm assuming we understand each other?"

"Yes, sir," chimed three male voices.

"Good." Nick heard the lift shake as Otis stepped onto it, and then the motor was running again, bringing Otis back up. Nick had been standing as close as he could to the lift opening. When the gears began to whine, he quickly moved to the far wall and pretended to be examining the loose rock on the ground.

Just as the lift came to a stop, Nick spied something on the floor of the tunnel that glittered in the flickering light of the torch. He bent down to pick it up, then rolled it in his hand. With a jolt, he realized that he recognized the stone—it was the stone he had originally found in the pouch with the gold watch fob in the pool in the cave. He was lost in that memory when Otis walked up and put his hand on his shoulder.

"What did you find, Nick? A piece of gold ore?" asked Otis.

"No," said Nick, "just this strange rock." Turning, he held it out to Otis, unsure of how he would respond.

The look on Otis's face was one of complete shock. The color drained from his cheeks as he stared at the glittering stone. He quickly composed himself, though, and reached out and took the stone from Nick. "Yes, this is strange," he said, pretending to examine the stone while turning to walk back to the lift.

Nick followed and stepped onto the lift next to him. As the lift rose Nick asked, "Do you know what it is?"

"I'm not sure," said Otis. "But I'm going to need to keep this, my boy, and send it in for analysis." Reaching into his pants pocket, Otis pulled out a leather pouch and opened it. The lift jolted slightly, causing the contents to fall out into his hand. There was a gold coin, a gold nugget, and now the glittering rough diamond.

"That's an interesting pouch you have there," said Nick.

Otis explained that the gold coin was the first coin he had ever received. The gold nugget was the first nugget that he had removed from a cave in this mountain. Nick just stared as Otis put everything back inside the leather pouch, including the glittering stone, and then put the pouch into his pocket.

The lift reached the tunnel that lead to the main mine entrance. Nick tried to remain calm as he stepped off the lift, but his heart was beating fast. The pouch from the pool in the cave was Otis's, and that meant that Otis's killer must have taken it and stolen the watch fob from the bank.

It was quitting time and getting dark when Nick and Otis finally emerged from the mine and headed to the office. Otis was back to his old self again, having recovered from the shock of Nick finding the diamond. He was chattering away as they entered his office. Nick realized how hungry he was when the smell of chicken filled his nose. There was a tray full of food on Otis's desk.

"I hope you're hungry, Nick," said Otis as he headed to his desk and settled into his chair. "Pull that chair over here and dig in. I'll show you the maps of the mine while we eat."

Nick sat down and grabbed a piece of chicken. Otis reached behind him, pulled a map down from the shelves, and rolled it out on a cleared area on the desk.

Pointing to the map, Otis said, "Here is where we were. As you can see, we explored only a small part of the mine. There were many other tunnels above us, but those are the older tunnels. We've mined most of the ore in those tunnels, but I do have men go through and double-check them from time to time, mostly for safety reasons. There are more important shafts that we're focusing on now. We've found a lot of gold ore so far, and the newest shafts are showing a lot of promise," explained Otis.

"What is this tunnel right here?" asked Nick.

Otis took several bites of his chicken, and then asked, "Which one?"

"That one," said Nick placing his finger on the incomplete line. "Were we in that tunnel?"

"Uh, no," said Otis cautiously. "We didn't go that deep."

"Say, isn't that where all the yelling was coming from?"

"Ah, uhm . . . yes, it is," answered Otis. "It's a new tunnel that we have not finished yet. For safety reasons, I have restricted access to it. That's why I have a guard down there. The guys get too curious sometimes, and I can't afford to have anyone get hurt."

"I understand," said Nick calmly.

They finished eating as they looked at the other maps that Otis had on his shelf. Nick marveled at how animated Otis was as he talked about the mine, how he got it started, and how it had become so successful. He was amazed at how easy it was for Otis to continue to lie to cover up what was really in the pit when his lies could be the downfall of the mine.

Otis's explanation of how he chose where to have the miners dig was interrupted by a loud knock at the door. "Now, who in the world could that be? Everybody should be gone for the night," he growled, then called out, "Who is it?"

"Otis, it's Slim. I need to talk to you for a minute," came Slim's voice through the door.

Nick watched as Otis's face became as white as a sheet. Otis cleared his throat, found his voice, and yelled back: "Just one minute, Slim."

"Confound it," whispered Otis, drumming his fingers on his desk. "Gone for two days, causing nothing but problems, and now he wants to talk," he mumbled.

Nick sat there, uncertain what to do. Otis's gaze finally rested on him.

"Listen, Nick. I need to talk with Slim for a few minutes. Do you mind waiting outside?" he asked.

"No, not at all. I can walk off some of that enormous dinner," replied Nick agreeably.

Otis nodded and called out, "Come in, Slim."

In walked the real Slim, then stopped short, staring at Nick.

Chapter Thirty

THE SETUP

"Uh . . . good evening, Nick," said Slim uncertainly.

"Hi, Slim," Nick said. "Otis was just giving me a tour of the mine. I'm going to take a walk and let you two talk." Then he slipped past Slim and out the door, closing it behind him. He walked quickly down the steps, but then crept quietly back up them to listen at the door.

"Well, well, Slim Marano. So nice of you to finally show up for work," Otis said in a voice dripping with sarcasm.

"All right, Otis, before you start yelling, you and I need to sit down and talk like two old friends, even if only for a few minutes," said Slim.

There was a pause, then Otis said, "Very well, then. Sit down."

Nick could hear Slim's footsteps walking away from him and then the scraping of a chair on the floor.

"Otis," said Slim, "I know what you've been hiding. I talked to Lucas Marley. I know about the diamonds. Please, my friend, tell me why you've tried to hide this from me?"

Otis did not respond right away. When he finally spoke, Nick could hear a change in the tone of his voice. It was strong, very angry, but also very controlled.

"So, when you figured it out, who did you tell? Mr. Jenkins? I got served notice this morning that the mine, specifically my management of the mine, is under investigation. Apparently, complaints have been filed. Is that your doing?"

"I have not spoken to Mr. Jenkins about this, Otis. I think you know me well enough to know that I would approach you first. The only complaint that I know of is related to your lack of interest in finding Stanley Watts."

"So . . . what complaints was Angus talking about?" pondered Otis.

"Well, if you ask me, I think it's highly possible that the complaints are false. Parker was seen at the Black Stallion Mine Company yesterday afternoon meeting with Mr. Billings and some miner named Buck," said Slim.

"Are you sure?" Otis asked, sounding shocked and frightened.

"Yes, Otis. Nick walked in on them," said Slim.

Nick held his breath. *I hope Slim knows what he's doing by bringing me into this,* he thought.

"Nick?" whispered Otis.

"He walked in on them by accident. Mr. Billings told Nick that Parker had come to inform him about a Black Stallion miner trying to get a job at the Falcon Mine by sharing information about new veins at the Black Stallion Mine. Nick was rattled, particularly by some of the comments Buck made. When I ran into Nick yesterday evening, I asked him how his day went. He told me what happened."

"Well," said Otis, "this makes the investigation look pretty suspicious. If Billings knows about the diamonds, he would have taken the information to Jenkins. He needs financial backing to save the Black Stallion Mine."

"It looks like more people know about your find than you realized, thanks to Parker. There's no telling how many people he has told," said Slim.

"That worm. I will deal with him and Buck later. Buck was probably planted here by Billings. If they are conspiring with Billings, then they must be plotting to take over the Falcon Mine. Slim, I might lose the mine," said Otis, his fear evident in his voice.

"Otis, you can get out of this situation very easily. All you have to do is register the find tomorrow morning at the Land Claims and Patent Office. Then come clean with the financial board. Once the board knows, Jenkins won't be able to use the investigation to blackmail you, which was probably his intent. And you'll be ensuring that the mine stays in your control," explained Slim.

The room was silent for some time. Nick waited anxiously for Otis's response. Eventually, Otis spoke. "You're right, Slim. I am so sorry that I didn't confide in you. I just let the thought of all of those diamonds affect my judgment."

"Greed gets to a lot of people, Otis. You're only human," said Slim.

Otis groaned. "Slim, it's worse than you know."

"What is, Otis?"

"I thought you were going to discover the diamonds and ruin everything, so I gave Parker permission to deal with you. He was going to plan an accident for you," whispered Otis.

"Parker couldn't plan himself out a crate," laughed Slim.

"But, Slim, if he's working with Billings, there might be other people involved already," said Otis.

"Hmm, good point, Otis." The room was silent again for some time, then Slim spoke up. "Well, being aware of the order and keeping my eyes open will hopefully keep me out of trouble. We should think about ways of trapping them into confessing their plan."

"Well, your name is still on the deed for the mine as my beneficiary. Unless you're named in the investigation, if I were to lose the mine, it would automatically fall to you. That would certainly slow them down a bit. It would be difficult to get to you without drawing too much attention," said Otis.

"Well, we both have some thinking to do, Otis. I give you my word that I will do everything I can to help get you out from under this. First thing tomorrow, we can work on calculating the value of the diamonds. Then we'll file all of the necessary paperwork and start contacting those who need to know," said Slim.

"Sounds like a good plan," said Otis. Nick heard the scraping of chairs. "Why don't you meet me here at sunrise, Slim?"

"Sure, Otis. I'll be here first thing in the morning," said Slim. "Don't worry, we'll get this whole thing worked out."

Nick heard footsteps and raced quietly down the stairs and around the corner of the building. He heard the door open, and then Otis said, "Thanks, Slim, for giving me a chance, and helping me get out of a mess that I got myself into."

"Otis, we all make mistakes. I will always be your friend first. So, I'll see you tomorrow then. After we get done at the claims office, let's go to lunch."

"Thanks, Slim. That would be nice," replied Otis.

There was silence after the door closed. Nick was not sure what to think. He stood in the dark for a few minutes, pondering what he had heard. Eventually, he crept out of the shadows to the path and stomped up the stairs to announce his presence to Otis. He tapped on the door and Otis called out, "Nick, is that you?"

"Yes, sir," replied Nick, opening the door and walking in. "I saw Slim leave, so I figured you were done meeting."

"Yes, we're done for now. Listen Nick, Slim told me that you saw Parker, Mr. Billings, and a miner named Buck at the Black Stallion Mine office yesterday. Is that true?"

"Yes, sir," said Nick.

"I'm sure Buck is a plant from the Black Stallion Mine. This is just getting more and more complicated," sighed Otis. He stared absently at the map on his desk, forgetting that Nick was in his office. A loud knock on the door made his head jerk up. "Who is it?" he called.

"It's Parker. I need to talk to you, Otis. Something has come up."

"Parker," whispered Otis. "Nick, quick, we've got to hide you. It just occurred to me that you could be in real danger. If Parker saw Slim leave, and then found you here, that could be very bad." Otis whipped his gaze around the room, looking for a hiding place. He jumped out of his chair and crossed the room. "Here, get into this cabinet. There's just enough room. Parker will never know you're here."

Nick moved quickly to the cabinet and crawled in. Otis shut the door to the cabinet before opening the office door to let Parker in.

"Parker, I thought I told you that we'd do the payroll first thing in the morning," said Otis.

"I'm sorry, Otis, but Mr. Jenkins and Mr. Billings are here, and they are asking to see you."

"So the vultures are circling already, eh? Ready to blackmail me, huh? Oh and Parker, don't think for one moment that I don't know exactly what you've been up to. One of the men saw you and Buck over at the Black Stallion Mine office. That can only mean one thing. How long have you been conspiring with Pernell? Or with Jenkins? Never mind, I don't need to know. You're fired, Parker. Get out, now. And if you step one foot back onto Falcon Mine property, I will have you arrested," growled Otis.

"Otis, what about the pit? I'll tell the whole world about your treasured secret," retorted Parker.

"Go ahead, you weasel. Tomorrow morning I will officially notify the claims office and contact the board. I'm going to come clean and process this find the right way, instead of trying to hide it."

"Otis!" shouted Parker.

"Get out!" screamed Otis. "You can tell Jenkins and Billings that I won't see either one of them tonight. I have nothing to say to them. This is still my property and I want them both off, or I will have all of you removed by force. Do I make myself clear?"

"Yes, Otis, perfectly clear!" Parker yelled back. Nick heard some rustling and then a metallic clatter as something was thrown onto the floor. The sounds of stomping footsteps and the slamming door told Nick that Parker had left.

Otis took a deep breath and blew it out. "You can come out, Nick. I believe it's safe."

★   ★   ★

Meanwhile, deep in the mine, the real Michael, Keenan, and Christopher had discovered the pit in the floor of a cavern and were exploring it.

"Guys, you will not believe what it's like down here," yelled the real Keenan.

"Keenan!" called Michael, "Can you get some samples from the wall, or do we need to lower you deeper?"

"I think I'll be able to get some samples from here. No need to send me any deeper," echoed Keenan's voice.

"How are we doing on time?" Michael asked Christopher, who was standing next to the pit with the rope wrapped around his waist.

"We've only been here about an hour. I think we're alright on time. But the question is, how is Slim doing with Otis?" replied Christopher.

"I don't know, but I will feel a lot better when he gets here," said Michael.

"Well, feel better then," called out the real Slim as he rounded the corner.

"Hey, Slim, how did it go? Were the guards still out cold?" asked Christopher.

"Not to worry, boys. The pills I put in the coffee that Jesse took to them should keep them out for a couple of hours," said Slim as he walked up to the edge of the pit. "And I poured some alcohol on them so that if anybody checks up on them, they'll smell like they've been drinking."

"Yeah, they smelled like they had been drinking before we got here anyway. It only took a couple of sips of the coffee to knock them out completely," grinned Christopher. "They'll probably wake up with headaches, but we can hope that they'll think they drank too much."

"Good. Now, how are we doing with this pit?" asked Slim.

"Keenan is just about done; we'll be pulling him up in a minute," said Michael. "How did it go with Otis?"

"After he finally calmed down enough to listen, I made him realize that Parker is probably conspiring with Billings and that he is in danger of losing the mine. I'm going to meet him here early in the morning, and we're going to go down to the claims office and file the correct paperwork. Then we'll talk to the board so that everything will be out in the open," explained Slim.

"Pull me up. I'm ready," echoed Keenan's voice.

"Do you think we have time for me to go down and take a quick peek?" asked Slim.

"I think we would be pushing it," warned Michael. "By the way, have you seen Nick today?"

"Yeah. He was actually in Otis's office when I arrived. He delivered the first half of the explosives order. It looked like Otis had been giving him a tour of the mine because they were looking at maps. He took a walk while I talked with Otis. Although Nick is just as curious as I am, so he was probably listening at the door," said Slim with a chuckle. "He wasn't around when I left, but I'm assuming Otis was planning on taking him back to town."

"Here are your samples," said Keenan as he climbed back onto the log over the pit. He threw a pouch to Slim. "It's really beautiful down there."

A small group of men—Angus Jenkins, Pernell Billings, Parker Owen, Jeb Larkey, and Buck—stood at the edge of the forest near Otis Walkins's office talking quietly. Several feet away stood four invisible spirits—Slim, Keenan, Christopher, and Michael—who were watching the group intensely.

"Are you sure Nick is here?" whispered the invisible Slim.

"Yes. The last time I checked on him, Otis was giving him a tour of the mines," said Christopher.

"And when I checked on him a few minutes ago, I transmigrated to the path to Otis's office. You don't think he could still be in there with Otis, do you?" asked Keenan.

"Unfortunately, Otis's tour probably included a study of every map of the mine, information on local geological issues, and story after story about the history of the mine. My guess is that Nick is still in the office," said Slim.

"This is not good. We are forbidden to enter that office tonight, and we don't have much time. How are we going to get Nick out of there without the killer seeing him?" whispered Michael.

"Well, according to what we just heard Parker say, he obviously didn't know that Nick was in there. Maybe Otis hid him," said Slim.

"I have an idea about how we can get him out of there, but I'm not quite sure how to pull it off," whispered Keenan.

"What's your idea?" asked Slim.

"The real Slim and the guys are currently exploring the pit and collecting samples. They put the guards to sleep. I checked on them before arriving here. If we were somehow able to get word to them that Nick needed help and was in Otis's office, maybe they would be able to get Nick out safely," said Keenan.

"You might have something there, Keenan. It's risky, but for Nick's sake, we've got to try something," said Slim.

"Hey, Slim," whispered Christopher. "Something is going on. Jeb and Buck are heading toward Otis's office. Mr. Jenkins and Mr. Billings are taking off."

"This could be it," whispered Michael.

"Let's hurry! We don't have much time. You guys head into the mine and find a way to get the guys to realize that Nick is in trouble and needs help. You're going to have to split up. You'll need to plant a message somewhere where they'll find it, keep an eye on the cavern to make sure your real selves don't leave without noticing your message, and watch out for the next round of guards. They might be showing up soon. I'm going to stay here and try to keep an eye on things," whispered Slim.

★ ★ ★

Nick stepped out of the cabinet and stretched. He walked around for a few minutes until he could feel the blood flowing freely back into his legs.

Otis was a little shaken by his confrontation with Parker. He walked back to his desk and poured himself a glass of brandy.

"Are you okay, Mr. Walkins?" asked Nick.

"I will be in just a few minutes," he said throwing back his head to gulp his drink. "Nick, I'm going to trust you not to repeat what you just heard. Can I do that?"

"Absolutely, sir," Nick replied with a firm nod of his head.

"That was the toughest thing I ever did. You know what, Nick, it's been quite a day. Let me just put some things away and we'll call it a night, shall we?"

"Sounds good to me," said Nick, thinking they just might get out in time after all.

It took a few minutes for Otis to clear his desk and lock up some things in his safe. He had a few more maps to put away, and when he picked them up, he found some papers he had forgotten. He asked Nick to put them in one of the cabinets for him.

Nick retrieved the papers from Otis's desk and walked over to the row of cabinets. He opened one of the smaller drawers and placed the papers inside. Just as he turned back to Otis, the office door burst open and two large men wearing kerchiefs over their mouths leapt into the office. Nick's heart almost stopped as he realized that Otis's time was up. He was going to witness the murder and probably be killed himself if he did not do something, and quickly.

The bank of cabinets was in shadow and the men were totally focused on Otis, so they did not notice Nick. Nick eased the door of the cabinet he had occupied earlier open and folded himself inside as quietly as possible. Otis saw Nick out of the corner of his eye and tried to distract the two men.

The ruckus that followed began with Otis grabbing bottles and throwing them at the two men, who were approaching him with menacing glares. The sounds of glass shattering resounded in the room. "Get out of here!" yelled Otis.

"You need to be taught a lesson, old man," growled one of the men.

Nick could tell a fight had begun. He heard the sound of wood splitting and glass breaking. Obscenities were being screamed as Otis fought back. Then Nick heard a thud and Otis groaned. It sounded like Otis had caught a blow.

The fight continued. Nick tried to push open the cabinet door and found it blocked. Trapped, he could only cover his ears and pray that the fight would be over soon.

Finally, one of the men said, "Enough! I think we've made our point."

"We need to make it look like a robbery. Can you crack open that safe?"

"Yeah, I think so. I have some gunpowder."

"I'll check his pockets and his desk."

Nick waited.

A few minutes later, there was a small explosion and the room filled with smoke. A little seeped through the cracks of the cabinet door and swelled inside Nick's throat. He was able to hold back the cough that was trying to force its way up from his lungs. The jingling of coins told Nick that the two men were in the safe.

Nick knew that he needed to try to identify who the men were. He thought he recognized at least one voice, but he couldn't place it. It was too muffled by the kerchief. Placing his shoulder against the cabinet door, Nick pushed cautiously until it opened just enough for him to peer out with one eye. He could only see part of the room, but the part he saw was in total shambles. Furniture had been broken into pieces and the desk had been tipped over. Nick saw the dark shadows of imps as they danced around the room in obvious delight. Nick could see the two men pulling out the payroll and placing it into a bag on the floor. The smoke had cleared, and thinking they were alone, they removed their kerchiefs, exposing their faces—it was Jeb Larkey and Buck.

Satisfied that he could identify the men, Nick slowly and quietly pulled the cabinet door closed and hoped that they would leave soon.

Chapter Thirty-One

MURDER

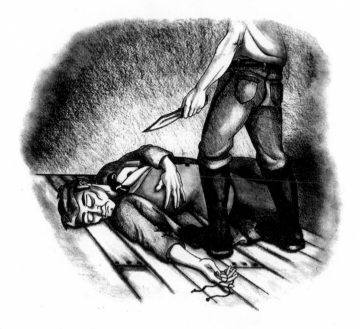

In the mine, the real Slim and the guys had finished putting back all of the equipment they had used and were riding up in the lift. They stopped to check on the guards, who were sleeping soundly. When Keenan bent to check on one guard, he found a note that had been tucked between the buttons of the man's shirt. Puzzled, he handed it to Slim.

Slim opened it and quickly scanned it. "This is strange," Slim whispered. "Someone who says he is a friend of ours left this note to let us know that Nick is in trouble and is trapped in Otis's office."

"Who knows we're here? It can't be Artemus; he's in town, and he wouldn't know where to find us. And if someone knows we're here, why didn't they just come down to the cavern to tell us about Nick? Could this be some kind of trap?" asked Keenan.

"For some reason, I don't think so. If this is true, we need to check it out, for Nick's sake. We'll just have to keep our eyes open, and be extra careful.

"Let's get to Otis's office. We need to see what's going on there. If Nick is in trouble, we've got to help him," said Slim.

★ ★ ★

The office was quiet as Jeb and Buck finished packing up the payroll. "Let's get out of here. Somebody could show up," said Jeb, and Nick heard him open the door.

"Yeah, I think we did enough damage to send a pretty clear message," responded Buck as he left the office, closing the door behind him.

The office slipped into a strange quietness. Nick held his breath for several moments, waiting, just in case they returned. Finally, he couldn't wait any longer and ventured out of the cabinet to search for Otis. Nick carefully weaved his way across the floor, trying to avoid the glass and broken furniture. He found Otis lying on his left side on the floor behind the desk.

Kneeling down beside him, he gently shook Otis, not sure if he was dead or alive. To Nick's surprise, Otis was alive, but beaten severely.

"Are you okay, Otis?" asked Nick.

"Nick . . . you're still here . . . they didn't find you. Yes . . . yes, I am fine. Good fight there, but going to be pretty sore tomorrow. I used to get into scrapes all the time, but I am getting too old for this now. Do me a favor, Nick. Go and see if that bottle of brandy is still intact. It's in my desk," said Otis.

"I'll check, Otis," said Nick.

Nick got up and carefully pulled out the desk drawer. He felt for the bottle, but just as he put his hand on it, he heard the doorknob turn.

"Nick, hide!" whispered Otis urgently.

Nick ducked and slid across the floor to a small table that sat near Otis's desk. It was the only piece of furniture that hadn't been overturned. He pulled the solid back of a broken chair in front of the table to conceal himself, then held his breath. Heavy footsteps sounded as someone walked across the floor and stopped next to Otis.

"I heard that you had a change of heart, Otis," said a man in a deep voice. "I heard that you're planning to come clean with the finance board in the morning. Well, my friend, I cannot let you do that. That would destroy my plans. So let me say that I am deeply sorry to have to do this, but taking over the Falcon Mine would be much easier if you were gone."

"So you were the mastermind behind this? Do you think you can really get away with this?" asked Otis.

"I definitely expect to get away with this, especially since I have the perfect fall guy," responded the man.

The voice was low and the words were delivered slowly. Nick's mind raced as he tried to place the voice; he knew he had heard it before. Suddenly, Nick heard a thump, as if the man had hit Otis . . . then another thump and another . . . then Otis gasped and moaned.

"Again, let me say how deeply sorry I am, Otis, but you left me with no choice." Thump!

Nick heard the man walk across the office and out the door, closing it behind him.

Nick pushed the chair away and rushed to Otis's side, not caring if the man came back. He was shocked into stillness by what he found. Blood was pouring rapidly from four knife wounds in Otis's chest. Otis was still somewhat conscious and breathing heavily.

"Otis," Nick whispered. He sat next to Otis and lifted his head into his lap. "I'm going to go get help," whispered Nick.

"No," exclaimed Otis in a gasp. "It's too late, Nick. No one can help me now. This is my own fault. If I had not been so greedy and tried to keep the diamonds to myself, none of this would have happened. Just stay here with me. I don't want to be alone."

"I have to do something!" cried Nick.

"Nick, do you pray?" whispered Otis.

"Yes, sir."

"Let me pray with you," said Otis.

Nick began to recite The Lord's Prayer out loud, and Otis slowly repeated it. At the end of the prayer, Otis added a last request, "Please forgive me for everything I've done," he whispered.

Nick sensed that Otis was going quickly. Leaning over him, he asked, "Otis, who did this to you? Did you see his face? Do you know him?"

Otis briefly opened his eyes and looked at Nick. "Yes, Nick," he whispered, but then his eyes began to shut again.

"Otis!" cried out Nick. "Who was it? Who did this to you?"

"It was . . ." gasped Otis. Then he slumped into Nick's arms and died.

Nick held Otis's lifeless body. Panic overwhelmed him as memories of his mother's death flooded his mind. Fighting with everything he had not to lose control, Nick gently laid Otis's head on the floor and stood up. He stared around the room, unable to move—until his eyes fell on Slim's journal lying just a few inches from Otis's feet. Nick's mind was spinning out of control, and darkness was slowly creeping into the edges of his vision, but the sight of the journal forced him to act. He felt like he was moving through water as he stepped over Otis's body, reached down, picked up the journal, and slipped it into his pocket.

Just then, the door burst open again and more men came in. Nick just stood there, covered in Otis's blood, unable to protect himself. He was too tired and overwhelmed to move.

"Oh my . . . Nick, what happened?" called out the real Slim as he stepped into the office. He saw Otis lying on the floor with blood pooling around him, and he rushed over to check for a heartbeat.

"Oh no, this doesn't look good," moaned Keenan, who was right behind Slim.

Michael walked in next and scanned the office. As soon as he saw Nick, he rushed over to him, checking him for wounds.

"Oh, Slim, is he dead?" whispered Christopher, coming in last.

"Yes," said Slim, in a profoundly sorrowful voice. "He has been stabbed. Be careful and don't touch anything."

That was the last thing Nick heard before he gave in to the darkness and collapsed. Michael was there to catch him. "Slim, I think we'd better get Nick out of here—now. He's in shock."

Christopher rushed over to Michael. "Give him to me. I'll get him outside into the fresh air."

"You're right," said Slim. "There's nothing we can do for Otis now. We need to get the sheriff right away. Christopher and Michael, get Nick back to the ranch and make sure he's okay. Keenan and I will search for the sheriff. Keenan, go to the sheriff's office. I'll head to his house," said Slim.

After carefully making their way back across the room, they hurried out of the office. Slim, the last to leave, turned and stopped for a moment to take one last look. "Oh, Otis," he groaned, "if you had just done things the right way." He sighed deeply, then pulled the door closed and locked it.

The four cowboys made their way through the woods to their hidden horses, carrying Nick's unconscious body. Off in the distance, four ghostly forms watched with great concern.

"Don't worry, guys, he's alive. I can feel him," sighed Slim. "They're heading to the ranch now, so he's in good hands."

"Wow, what happened in there?" asked Keenan.

"I'm not sure," said Slim. "While you were leaving the note, Jeb and Buck were in Otis's office. I went and checked on Billings and Jenkins. When they hit the main road, they headed in different directions, Billings toward the Black Stallion Mine and Jenkins toward town. When I returned, Jeb and Buck were just coming out of Otis's office, so I followed them. They talked about beating Otis, but they didn't say that they had stabbed him. It seemed that they weren't the killers, so I came back here just when you three showed up and the guys were heading to Otis's office. I think we missed Otis's killer, and at this point, only Nick can tell us who it was."

"What's next for us then?" asked Christopher.

"Keenan and I will follow Nick back to the ranch," said Slim. "Christopher and Michael, you stay here and check out the office. Everybody's gone and there aren't any imps around, so it should be safe for a while. Maybe you can find some clues to work with until we get a chance to talk to Nick."

"Sounds like a plan," replied Keenan as they all started to fade away.

Nick remained unconscious throughout the bumpy ride back to town in Christopher's arms. Once they hit town, Keenan broke off from the group and rode to the sheriff's office, while Slim turned and rode toward the sheriff's house. Christopher and Michael quickly rode through town and out to the ranch.

When they arrived at the ranch, Michael took charge of the horses and led them to the stable, while Christopher dismounted with Nick. He took him into the house and laid him on the bed in the room that he had been staying in. Christopher started a fire in the fireplace to chase away the chill that had settled in the house. He returned to the bedroom, lit the lanterns, removed Nick's boots and clothes, and pulled a long nightshirt over his head.

"You need sleep right now more than anything, Nick. You've been through a terrible ordeal," whispered Christopher as he pulled the covers up to Nick's chin. "No kid should see what you saw."

Michael stepped into Nick's room and stood over him. "We have a big problem," said Michael. "How much did Nick see, and was the killer aware that he was there at the time?"

"I wish I knew the answer to that question, too," said Christopher.

"How is he?" asked Michael.

"He doesn't have any wounds, so all of the blood must have been Otis's. But he is in shock. I hope that sleep and warmth will help. But I am concerned about how rigid he is," said Christopher.

"Well, for now, all we can do is let him sleep," said Michael. "Come on, let's go make some coffee. We can check on him in a bit." Michael led Christopher from the room, quietly closing the door, then headed for the kitchen to begin preparing for the coming hours.

When the door to Nick's room closed, two ghost-like forms materialized and stood next to the bed.

"Looks like he's asleep," whispered Keenan.

"I'm not so sure," commented Slim. "He looks very stiff right now. Unfortunately, we need information right away, so let's see if he's just asleep or in a coma." Slim walked to the end of the bed, then rose in the air and floated over the bed to hover directly over Nick's unconscious form. He rotated his transparent body so that he was in the same position as Nick, then he began a slow descent, until he disappeared into Nick's body.

Keenan kept watch over Nick's form as he waited for the signal to pull Slim out. He listened carefully for footsteps coming up the hall.

Eventually, a ghostly hand rose up from where Nick's hand lay on the bed. Keenan quickly reached down and lifted Slim out of Nick, and guided him to the edge of the bed. Slim moved into a standing position and floated down to the floor. Nick slowly rolled over onto his side.

"He's going to be okay now," said Slim reassuringly. "He had slipped into a coma. What he saw collided with his memories of his mother's death and sent Nick into a dark place in his mind. I coaxed him out of that place. He's resting comfortably now in a normal, deep sleep. He will wake up in the morning feeling better."

"You were with him quite a while. What did you learn?" asked Keenan.

But just then, they heard the sound of a horse approaching the ranch.

"That's me returning," said Keenan. "I think we should leave now."

"Okay," said Slim. "Meet me at the workshop." Then they both faded and disappeared.

A few hours later, all of the spirits had returned to the workshop, and Slim was describing what had happened in Otis's office as he had seen it in Nick's memories. "Otis was alive after the beating. After Jeb and Buck left, a man entered the office. I must have just missed him. Nick heard the man stabbing Otis. He was hidden, so he didn't see the man," he told the guys. "Nick thinks he has heard the man's voice before, but he can't identify it yet. Oh, and Nick also found my journal a few inches from Otis's feet. He took it just before the real gang showed up. It's in the pocket of his jeans in the house."

"Goodness, if Nick took the journal, then Nick has single-handedly saved the real Slim from hanging," said Keenan excitedly.

"Keenan is right," said Michael. "We have completed what we set out to do."

"Well, before we start celebrating, let's get through the next few days. We are not out of the woods yet. The person who committed the murder has not been brought to justice. We can't leave and then find out that the murder was blamed on another innocent person. And I can't shake the feeling that something else is going to happen," said Slim.

"And there is still the issue of the mining accident and the lives of all those men. I don't think this assignment will be complete until we know what really happened and stop it if we can," replied Keenan.

"Christopher is right," Slim said, nodding. "We're here until we're sure that all of the innocent people involved in this mess are safe."

★ ★ ★

The sun was shining brightly, flooding the room where Nick was still sleeping. He groaned once and rolled over so that the sun was at his back, then he drifted off to sleep again. Some time later, Nick felt a hand on his shoulder gently shaking him, and somebody was calling his name. He struggled out of the dark fog that surrounded him and opened his eyes. He awoke to Keenan's grinning face.

"Hey, Nick, welcome back. Think you can rouse yourself up to eat some breakfast?"

Nick slowly sat up and rubbed his head as the memories began flooding back. "Oh, my gosh, Keenan, I was there. Otis died in my arms," Nick's voice cracked. "They beat him up, and then some guy stabbed him," sobbed Nick.

"Nick, Nick, just let it go," said Keenan in a soothing voice, sitting on the edge of the bed and holding Nick as he cried. Finally, Keenan whispered,

"Slim and the sheriff have spent the night at Otis's office. They are taking care of everything. Christopher went to the general store to let Mr. Guillot know that you would be out for a couple of days, and he's going to help Mr. Guillot while you rest. For right now, you should try not to think about it. Come eat something, and then go back to bed. Slim wants you to take it easy today and stay out of town. We have to make sure that no one knows that you were in Otis's office last night. The sheriff and Slim will be back for dinner tonight. They'll want to talk to you then. Come eat breakfast and then you can get some more sleep, okay?"

Nick nodded as he wiped tears from his eyes. Keenan got up and headed toward the door.

"Nick, who are your mother's friends? I'm going to need to contact them to let them know what happened, and that you're safe."

Nick pulled his legs up to his chest and wrapped his arms around them and buried his head,

"Nick?" questioned Keenan.

Nick stuttered as he began to speak. "My father and I had a falling out after my mother was killed. He buried himself in work and was never around, so I left. I ran away and came here to try to build a life for myself," explained Nick. "I was fortunate to get a job at the general store right away, and then I met Mrs. Corrine, Miss Terri, and several of the other townspeople. They were all so nice, and for the first time I felt like I belonged. So the truth is, I'm not really here visiting anyone. I just have a room at the hotel."

"Does anyone else know about this?" questioned Keenan.

"No, I've been careful not to let anyone know. I didn't want to be sent back to my father. If I go back, I want to go when I'm ready," said Nick.

"Hmm . . . Well, knowing Slim, I'm sure that under the circumstances he would rather you stay with us. So let me handle it," said Keenan.

"Keenan, the last thing I remember is standing in Otis's office. How did I get here?"

"We were all at the mine last night. We were exploring the new tunnel and we found a deep pit, which is where the diamond deposit is. We explored it and took some samples. When we were leaving the tunnel, we found a note on one of the guards. We had slipped something into their coffee to make them fall asleep. The note said that you were in Otis's office and that you were in trouble and needed help. We went to the office, where we found you and Otis, and we immediately brought you here," explained Keenan.

"I don't remember seeing you there. But you probably saved my life," said Nick.

"Well, now we have a habit of saving each other's lives. So, welcome to our gang, Nick. You're one of us now for sure. Now come into the kitchen and eat. I'll tell you some of our funnier stories," Keenan said with a wink, then turned and walked out of the room.

"Will you tell me what happened at the pit, too?" called Nick.

"Yeah. But only if you get in here and eat my cooking," echoed Keenan's voice.

Nick threw his legs over the side of the bed and headed to the kitchen, suddenly hungry and feeling a bit better.

★   ★   ★

Slim and the sheriff were standing in Otis's office, having spent most of the night there. The sheriff was collecting every bit of evidence he could find. He had been at it for hours. Suddenly, a miner rushed into the office before they could stop him at the door. He looked around the room in astonishment, and then he spotted Otis lying on the floor in a large pool of blood. The miner turned and stared at Slim for a moment and then rushed out of the office, running into another miner. Stammering fiercely, the miner grabbed the other man and said, "Mr. Walkins is dead. He's dead, I tell you. Someone stabbed him."

Slim stepped out of the office, grabbed the miner, and shook him hard. "Pull it together," he yelled. "The sheriff is here and he's already begun the investigation. He's going to want to talk to anybody who was here late last night. Spread the word to everybody that they need to come up to the mine entrance and wait to talk to the sheriff."

It took a few minutes for Slim's orders to sink in, but finally nodding that he understood, the miner pulled away from Slim. Turning, he ran down the path and headed to the mine entrance.

Slim sighed deeply. They just needed to keep everyone out of the office. Slim walked back into the office and stopped just inside the door. He let his eyes wander around the now bright room. The office was in total shambles. Papers and broken furniture were strewn everywhere. The safe was open and the payroll was gone. Otis's desk was on its side a few feet from the body. Footsteps behind him caught his attention. He turned around as Parker stepped up to the door.

"Morning, Slim, I see you're back," said Parker. As he looked past Slim, his grin disappeared and his face became white. "Oh no, no, no," stuttered Parker as he glanced around the room. "Otis!" he cried, and he pushed past Slim and rushed toward the body.

"Don't touch anything!" yelled the sheriff. "Get out of here, Parker."

"What happened?" cried Parker, stopping in the middle of the room.

"I don't know for sure, but what I do know is that Otis has been killed and the entire payroll has been stolen."

Parker just shook his head as he stared at Otis. When he spoke, his voice shook. "Great, just great, the men are going to need to be paid today. I guess I'll need to head to the bank and get a loan to cover their wages and file paperwork concerning the mine ownership."

"Parker, though I appreciate your interest in helping settle everything so quickly, it is my responsibility to handle any loans or paperwork concerning the Falcon Mine Company," said Slim.

Anger clouded Parker's face. "What are you talking about? You were on the outs with Otis the last time I talked to him."

"You forget, Parker—Otis and I have been friends for many years. In the event of his death, ownership of the Falcon Mine falls to me."

Total shock washed over Parker's face. He began to shake, then he stammered, "What? Do you have proof of this?"

"Yes, Parker, papers were filed more than ten years ago at the claims office in town. As soon as Otis's will is opened, you will also find it there, and if that is not enough, there are also papers filed with the federal mining offices in Washington, D.C."

Parker shuddered. "Otis never said anything about that to me."

"Parker, think about it, there was no reason for you to know about it. To you, working here has always been just a job," said Slim.

Anger sparked in Parker's eyes. "So what are you saying? I now work for you?"

"Well, Parker, not exactly. You see, I've gotten some disturbing information concerning your recent activities, which can only be described as showing conflicting loyalties. So I regret to inform you that my first order of business is to fire you."

"You can't do that!" yelled Parker.

"I can, and I just did," said Slim calmly.

"Hey, what's the problem?" asked the sheriff, who hadn't been paying attention to the conversation.

"I just fired Parker, that's all," said Slim. "He's not happy with me at the moment."

Parker turned to the sheriff. "He can't do that, can he?"

"Tough break, Parker. So sorry," said the sheriff.

"It can't be true. It just can't be," said Parker in dismay.

Becoming annoyed, the sheriff turned to Parker and placed his hands on his hips. "I hate to be the bearer of bad tidings, Parker, but it is true. If anything happens to Otis, ownership of the Falcon Mine goes to Slim. I am the witness who signed all the paperwork. I am also the witness to Otis's will. Now are there any more questions I can answer for you, or can I get back to work on this crime scene?" asked the sheriff.

Parker stood in a state of shock with his mouth open. "You'll regret this decision, Slim. You will regret it. I can promise you that," he growled as he turned and walked quickly out of the office.

The sheriff sighed, and then glanced at Slim. "My friend, you made an enemy today."

"Not really. He has always hated me, so that's nothing new," said Slim.

"Well, I'm going to send one of the miners hanging around outside to fetch the undertaker and notify my deputy, so they should be here within the hour. For your protection, I am going to take over the office and ask you to leave. Besides, you need to take charge of the men, Slim. There is nothing you can do here now."

"Yeah, you're right. I also need to go to the bank this morning and make sure that I have money to meet the payroll today, or the miners won't show up for work next week," said Slim.

"Well, do me a favor then. Place a miner that you trust outside the door. No one is to enter unless I clear them."

"Hey, will I do?" chimed a voice.

The sheriff and Slim looked over at the door and saw Michael standing there.

"You'll do just fine, Michael. Just let the undertaker and my boys in. In fact, I might need your help later, too," said the sheriff.

"Say, where is Christopher?" asked Slim.

"He went to tell Mr. Guillot that Nick was going to be out for a couple of days. He decided to cover for him at the general store so that Mr. Guillot wouldn't be shorthanded," explained Michael.

"How's Nick this morning?" asked the sheriff.

"He was still asleep when we left. Keenan is staying with him all day and keeping an eye on him. I told Keenan to make sure that Nick took it easy, and to make sure he didn't go into town," said Slim.

"That was a good idea," responded the sheriff.

"Well, I had better go. I have lots of work to do," said Slim.

"Good luck, Slim," called out the sheriff as Slim left the office.

"Yeah, I'm going to need it," he muttered under his breath as he looked out at the sea of faces in the yard waiting for some word.

"Can I have your attention please," began Slim. "Gentlemen, there has been a tragic incident. I will tell you what I know at this point, and I will tell you what we are going to do next."

Chapter Thirty-Two
THE INVESTIGATION

Nick spent the first hour of his morning listening to Keenan's tall tales. The stories helped keep his mind occupied, but the memories of the previous night were waiting just below the surface, waiting to pounce the moment he let his guard down. He finished the breakfast Keenan had prepared, and then excused himself and went back to bed, hoping that sleep would keep the memories at bay. He slept for several more hours, but his dreams were dark and frightening.

Keenan cleaned the house, fed and brushed the horses, and prepared for the long days and nights to come. He checked on Nick several times, sometimes finding him sleeping peacefully, and other times finding him moaning and tossing.

In the early afternoon, Nick stirred at the sound of the squeaky kitchen door. He sat up and looked out the window to see Keenan striding toward the barn. "How are you feeling, Nick?" asked a voice from Nick's side. He turned his head to find the ghostly image of Slim appearing next to his bed, and beside him stood an already solid Michael and Christopher.

"We thought we might stop by and check up on you. You had quite a night last night," said Michael with a troubled frown. Concern was evident on all of the spirits' faces.

Nick leaned back against his pillows. "Where were you last night?" he asked.

"Outside Otis's office. Remember, we were not permitted to go inside. When we tried to check on you, we transmigrated to the path to Otis's office, so we figured that you were probably inside," explained Slim.

"Yeah," added Christopher. "We thought that you were going to need help, so we wrote a note and left it on a guard who was knocked out near the pit where the real guys were."

"We watched them bring you out of the office," said Michael.

"It was horrible," said Nick.

"You don't have to tell us what happened, we already know," said Slim.

"How?" asked Nick.

Slim put his hand on Nick's shoulder. "When the guys found you in Otis's office, you were in shock. You passed out and slipped into a light coma, which can happen when you're in shock. Michael and Christopher brought you back here and put you to bed. That's when Keenan and I came in to check on you.

"We could tell you were in a coma by how rigid you were, but we weren't sure how severe it was. We needed to help you—fast. We also needed to know what had happened so that we could figure out how to proceed. I merged with you, and I was able to read your memories of the night. I also coaxed your subconscious out of the coma and into a normal sleep pattern."

"What do you mean, *merge*?" asked Nick.

"Well," began Michael. "Like most of the things we do, it's a little hard to explain. We are able to enter your conscious and subconscious mind, see your memories, and communicate with you on a very basic level."

"Wow," said Nick quietly. "That explains why I woke up this morning feeling like I had talked to you last night," he said to Slim.

"Yeah," said Slim, "that can happen."

"So, what about Otis?" asked Nick.

"When the guys took you back to the ranch, Slim and Keenan followed, and since everything was over, Michael and I were able to go into Otis's office," said Christopher.

"The room was in shambles," added Michael. "We found Otis's body, but we encountered something we hadn't expected."

"What was that?" asked Nick.

"Otis's spirit," said Christopher.

Nick just sat there for a moment with his mouth open. "You . . . you saw him?" he whispered.

"Yes, Nick, we did," said Michael. "I don't know how to explain this except to say that everyone has a specific time to die. When the time comes, it comes. What you believed and accomplished in your lifetime determines your future in the spiritual world. Otis's path was changed last night; he was given a second chance. Slim confronted him about the situation, and he made the decision to change the path he was on. And in death, he asked for forgiveness, with you there to witness it."

"Me?" asked Nick.

"Think of it as being in the right place at the right time," explained Michael. "Who knows—it's something the Almighty probably had planned from the beginning."

"Wow!" said Nick. "Then what happened to Otis? Did he tell you who killed him?"

"No, he was very confused, which is normal for someone who has experienced what he had just experienced. He couldn't tell us anything. So Christopher guided him to where he needed to be," said Michael.

"Which is where?" asked Nick.

Christopher grinned broadly. "The main gate of Heaven. You have to check in first."

"What would have happened if he hadn't made the decision to change and ask for forgiveness?" asked Nick.

"He would have continued down the destructive path he was on, and the imps would have taken him. We would never have seen him again," said Christopher.

"Wow!" said Nick. "There's a lot more to dying than I thought."

"A lot of people don't think about dying at all until it happens. Then one day, they have to face it and are totally surprised and confused," said Michael.

"So what's the plan now?" asked Nick.

"Well, since you picked up the journal from Otis's office, there's no evidence to point to the real Slim as his murderer," said Christopher. "Slim was the one who found the body, but this time he had three witnesses with him. And then, of course, there's you, too."

"What will happen next is anybody's guess at this point," said Slim. "We're working from a clean slate now. Our history from here on out doesn't exist as we once knew it. It's being written all over again."

"So in order to find the real murderer, we need to review the facts. Who was at the mine?" asked Michael.

Nick tried to work through the events of the night, stopping before the murder. "Besides our Slim, there was Parker, who told Otis that Mr. Billings and Mr. Jenkins wanted to talk to him. But they never came in because Otis refused to see them. Oh, and Otis fired Parker. Then Jeb and Buck came in after Parker and beat Otis, but they didn't kill him. After they left, somebody else came in, but I hid, so I couldn't see him. Did Mr. Billings and Mr. Jenkins just leave after Otis refused to see them?"

"Well, I was keeping watch on the office while Michael, Keenan, and Christopher tried to contact the real guys by leaving a note on one of the guards they had knocked out," explained Slim. "Parker left with Billings and Jenkins, and then I saw two men enter Otis's office. I knew there was nothing I could do at that point, so I slipped away for a minute to see where the others were going. Billings was heading toward the Black Stallion Mine, and Jenkins was heading toward town. But I didn't see any sign of Parker. I went back to Otis's office after that. When the two men left—I found out it was Jeb and Buck from you, Nick—I followed them, assuming that they were Otis's murderers. But I heard them talking and it was obvious they hadn't intended to kill him. I returned to the office right away, but by then it was too late. I saw the real us rush into the office to help you, but I didn't see anybody leaving."

"So, we know for a fact that Mr. Billings, Mr. Jenkins, Parker Owen, Jeb Larkey, and Buck were in or near the office. One of them, or all of them, is involved in one way or another. And even if one of them did not actually kill Otis, any of them might have sent someone in to do it. So now the plan is to watch their movements, listen to their conversations, and see if we can pick up any clues. If we find out who did it, then we need to figure out how to set that person up to be caught. The right person must be arrested and brought to justice before this is over."

"Slim, the real Keenan is coming back to the house," said Christopher.

"He'll check in on you, Nick, so we had better leave," said Slim. "We have some work to do, anyway. Will you watch the guys and the sheriff? As long as they can keep the news quiet that you were in the office at the time of the murder, then you should be able to move around freely. We'll check on you and keep you updated if we find anything out."

"He's in the house now and heading this way," whispered Christopher, as the sound of footsteps echoed up the hall.

"Bye," said Nick. The guys disappeared just as the door opened and the real Keenan came in and smiled at Nick.

Mr. Jenkins left the bank by the back entrance, unaware that Keenan—invisible—was following him. He loosened his horse from the hitching post, mounted him, and turned to head in the direction of the mines. He rode hard after he turned onto the road to the Black Stallion Mine. When he arrived, he almost jumped off his horse, tossing the reins to a nearby miner.

"I'm here for a meeting with Billings. My horse needs some water. Take care of it. I'm sure your boss will understand," growled Mr. Jenkins.

"Uh, yes, sir," replied the miner, taking the reins of the horse and walking away with a slightly confused expression.

Mr. Jenkins walked quickly up and burst through the office door.

Mr. Billings, who had been talking to Jeb, looked up with a start. "Most people knock before they enter an office," he said.

"Don't take that tone with me, Pernell," growled Mr. Jenkins as he pulled up a chair. "Nothing you have to tell your gorilla here can compare to the problem we've got on our hands."

Leaning back in his chair and placing his hands behind his head, Mr. Billings sighed deeply. "I thought we were taking care of our problems, Angus. So what is it now?"

"Otis is dead, you idiot, and the sheriff has called for a full investigation."

"Someone got to old Otis, eh? So what's the problem? No one can place us at the mine. All we have to do is stay low until everything blows over. We'll file the paperwork as soon as the mine goes up for sale," said Mr. Billings. "Everybody at the Falcon Mine who knows about the pit is now on my payroll, so nobody is going to say anything to the sheriff about the diamonds."

"Otis's death is not the problem," said Mr. Jenkins coolly. "Otis willed the mine to Slim more than ten years ago. Otis's will was filed in town, with the state, and in Washington, D.C., with the miner's association. The mine will not be going up for sale."

"What?" yelled Mr. Billings, quickly sitting upright.

"You heard me," replied Mr. Jenkins.

"That just can't be," said Mr. Billings as he slammed his fist onto his desk.

"It's true. I got a visit from Slim this morning. He filled me in on what happened to Otis. He officially filed for ownership of the mine so that the mine could continue to operate until Otis's will is read," explained Mr. Jenkins.

"Wait a minute—he can't take ownership of the mine if he's a suspect," reasoned Jeb.

"Slim was one of the first suspects cleared this morning, you idiot. He found Otis's body, which could have been suspicious, but he was with those three friends of his," growled Jenkins.

"But what about his journal? I left that by Otis's feet before we left the office," said Jeb.

"So you guys are responsible for Otis's departure, eh?" asked Mr. Jenkins, glaring at Jeb and Mr. Billings.

"No!" yelled Jeb. "I can't help it if he died. Buck and me went in and just worked him over. That's all. We took the payroll to make it look like a robbery. We left Slim's journal by Otis's feet to make people think that maybe he had something to do with the beating. A lot of people knew that he and Otis had been arguing recently."

"You left Slim's journal by Otis's feet? Are you sure about that?" asked Mr. Jenkins.

"Positive, I put it there myself," replied Jeb.

"Hmm," purred Mr. Jenkins. "I've heard plenty of rumors in town, but there's been no mention of Slim's journal. Of course, the only thing that Slim said this morning was that Otis had been stabbed to death. I haven't spoken to the sheriff yet. I was going to head over to the Falcon Mine from here."

"Well, that proves that Buck and I didn't do it. We definitely didn't stab him. We didn't even have knives on us."

"Well that's not the best defense, so you'd better not get placed at the scene of the crime. I doubt a jury would believe you," mused Mr. Jenkins.

"He's right, Jeb," agreed Mr. Billings. "No one would believe you just happened to be there to work Otis over and weren't involved in his murder. So if they found Slim's journal, we don't have as much of a problem. Even if he has an alibi from his friends, his journal being found at the scene will cast some suspicion on him. But, if they didn't find it, we have a pretty big problem. And where did it go? Did someone take it? Who, and why, and when?" asked Mr. Billings.

"Who do you have at the Falcon Mine or close to the sheriff's office who can tell us what they've found at the scene?" asked Mr. Jenkins.

"Well, Buck is working at the Falcon Mine. I can have him ask questions. You know, play the role of the curious miner," said Mr. Billings.

"Well, that's a start. The more information we can retrieve, the better. I can ask a lot of questions as head of the financial board, but I have to be very careful. We don't want them looking at me as a suspect, and they know I was beginning an investigation of the Falcon Mine. I don't think I need to remind you, Pernell, that right now we are in danger of losing everything we've worked for. I'm going to want regular reports on what you find," growled Mr. Jenkins.

"I haven't let you down yet, now have I, Angus?" drawled Mr. Billings.

"Not yet," responded Mr. Jenkins. "But this has the potential to be your first failure, and if it is, I guarantee it will be your last. Now am I making myself perfectly clear?"

"Perfectly," replied Mr. Billings through gritted teeth.

"I will leave you to your meeting, gentlemen," said Mr. Jenkins. He rose from his chair and walked out of the office, closing the door behind him.

"Confound it!" yelled Mr. Billings. He pounded his fist on his desk again. "What happened, you idiot?" he yelled at Jeb.

"I have no idea, sir. I absolutely placed Slim's journal near Otis. If they haven't found it, I have no idea what happened to it," explained Jeb.

"Get in touch with Buck and have him plant himself near that office until he hears something. We have to come up with a new plan, and this one had better work," yelled Mr. Billings.

"Yes, sir. I'm on it right now, sir," mumbled Jeb, as he jumped up and rushed out of Mr. Billings's office.

Before Nick knew it, evening was approaching. Christopher, Michael, Slim, and the sheriff arrived at the ranch, and they sat at the kitchen table. Nick took a deep breath, and then told the sheriff everything he remembered. But despite his efforts, he could not come up with a name to match the voice of Otis's killer.

"Well, Nick, you're the only witness to this crime," mused the sheriff. "But all we have to go on is a voice we can't identify yet."

"Any other leads, Artemus?" asked Keenan.

Rubbing his face with both hands, the sheriff sighed deeply before going on. "Yes. We found a watch fob in Otis's hand. He probably grabbed it off of the killer before he died."

"Watch fob," echoed Nick. "The watch fob, what was it made of?"

"Do you remember something, Nick? It looks to be solid gold with the emblem of an eagle on the end," said the sheriff, looking at Nick intensely.

Hesitating briefly, Nick tried to figure out how to tell them how he knew about the watch fob without talking about what he had found in the pool. Suddenly, he remembered something even more important. "Not about the watch fob," he began, "but Otis had a small pouch on him with a gold coin, a gold nugget, and one of the diamonds from the pit. Did you find that?"

"No," said the sheriff.

"Otis showed it to me when we were in the mine. Whoever has that pouch is your killer," said Nick.

"Well, that's two leads," said Christopher. "Did you find anything else in Otis's office?"

"Parker's keys—the chain had a small piece of wood with his name carved into it—were under Otis's body."

Nick spoke up: "I'm pretty sure I heard Parker throw his keys when Otis fired him."

"Well, that's it. There wasn't anything else out of the ordinary," replied the sheriff.

"Wait a minute," blurted Nick as the memory of the moments just before he blacked out surfaced. "I found Slim's journal by Otis's feet and I picked it up. It's in the pocket of my jeans."

"My journal? I've looked for that everywhere. I thought I must have lost it in the mine."

"How could it have gotten into Otis's office, let alone right next to the body?" questioned Michael.

"Well, maybe Otis found it and had it on his desk. The room was pretty torn up," reasoned the sheriff. "But for some reason, I've got the feeling that it was put there. The whole thing seems so planned. The murderer took advantage of the fact that Otis had just been beaten, so he must have known about that. By planting Slim's journal, there would be multiple suspects, and Slim could have become the main suspect," reasoned the sheriff.

"Since Nick picked it up, there's nothing to point to Slim. This is going to cause whoever did it quite a problem," added Christopher.

"Well, at this point I would say we're one step ahead of the killer," said the sheriff. "Now I just need to rattle everybody's nerves a bit and see who caves in and talks. I'll talk to Jeb, Billings, Jenkins, Parker, and Buck tomorrow and ask them what they were doing at Otis's office last night."

"What about Nick?" asked Slim. "Does this put him in danger?"

"Not yet. We're the only people who know that he was there. When I question our suspects, I'll have to say that a miner was leaving late and saw them in the yard. Nick, you'll need to head back to work and keep your normal schedule tomorrow. We don't want you to draw any unnecessary attention. Don't tell anybody anything, even your mother's friends."

"He will be staying with us from now on," stated Slim with a wink toward Nick. Keenan had obviously told Slim about Nick's situation.

"Well, that's even better. We can keep an eye on him," said Christopher.

"Yep, that's what I was thinking—there's safety in numbers," said Slim with a smile.

Chapter Thirty-Three
OTIS'S FUNERAL

The sun slowly spread its warm rays across Nick's sleeping form. Moments later the smell of bacon wafted through the air and slowly aroused Nick to consciousness. Sniffing the air appreciably, Nick rolled over onto his back and opened his eyes. Again, memories of Otis's death rushed to the surface, overwhelming him. He quickly rose, dressed, and headed to the kitchen, trying to shake the dark memories that plagued him.

"Morning," he called out.

"Morning, Nick," chimed Michael, Slim, and Keenan, who was still working over the stove.

"What's the plan for today?" asked Nick

"Artemus wants you to go to work," said Slim. "Michael and I are heading to the mine to try to get operations back to normal."

"Christopher and I are heading to the church to meet with Pastor Greg and make arrangements for Otis's funeral," stated Keenan as he handed Nick a plate of food.

"When is the funeral?" asked Nick.

"Tomorrow," replied Slim softly. "I'm going to give a eulogy."

Michael watched Slim's face cloud over with emotion. Turning to Nick, he said, "Both mine companies will close for the day out of respect for Otis and so that all of the miners can attend the funeral."

"Morning," said Christopher, as he walked into the kitchen. "I heard what you just said, Michael. It will be interesting to see who actually attends the funeral, particularly from the two mines. I can't help but wonder if Otis's killer will be there," he pondered.

"Would the killer really be that vain or stupid?" snapped Keenan as he plopped down into his chair.

Slim sighed deeply and frowned as he stirred his coffee. "You'd be surprised what some people will do," he whispered.

"Well, Nick," began Michael, "you could borrow a horse to get into work, but I think it would be smarter if one of us takes you in and picks you up after work until this situation is settled. So when you're finished with breakfast, I'll take you into town."

"That's fine, I'm ready," replied Nick. He rose, put his plate and mug in the sink, and headed for the door. Christopher reached across the table and pushed the sugar bowl in Nick's direction. Nick grabbed a couple of cubes for the horses. "Bye, guys. I'll see you tonight."

"Have a good day, Nick," called out Christopher and Keenan.

"I'll meet you in the stable," said Michael, heading out of the kitchen to get his boots.

Nick shut the door behind him, stepped down the two wooden steps, and shielded his eyes from the bright sun. His gaze drifted to the dark windows of the workshop. "Where are you guys?" he whispered. He didn't get a response, so he headed across the yard toward the stables.

Unseen eyes watched from the window of the workshop.

"Hey, guys," yelled Christopher's transparent form. "It looks like Nick's heading into town this morning. Michael's heading to the stables, too, so it looks like they're not letting him go alone."

"That's good," replied Slim's wispy form. "Okay, everybody, we've got lots of work to do today. That meeting between Billings and Jenkins yesterday shed a little light on the situation, but not much. So here are your assignments. Keenan, follow Nick, and when you can get him alone, find out what he knows. Christopher, head over to the Falcon Mine and see what's going on over there today. Michael, I want you at the Black Stallion Mine to watch Billings, Jeb, and Parker. It's good for us that Billings hired Parker yesterday to keep him quiet. It makes watching all of them a bit easier."

"What are you going to do?" asked Keenan.

"I'm going to check on Stanley, and then I'm going to pay Jenkins a visit to see if I can find out what he's planning to do with the transfer of ownership paperwork the real me filed yesterday. He's probably going to hide them or destroy them," reasoned Slim.

"That shouldn't make a difference, should it?" asked Michael. "You're named as beneficiary in Otis's will. Nothing's going to change that, right?"

"True, but if Jenkins destroys the paperwork I filed yesterday, it will delay the official transfer of ownership."

"Could that cause any problems?" asked Christopher.

"Not sure, but I'll try to find out. Is everyone clear on what to do today?" asked Slim.

"Yes," echoed the cowboys.

"Good, then let's get going. Come find me if there are any problems," added Slim.

Moments later, they had all disappeared into thin air, just as the real Slim, Christopher, and Keenan exited the house and headed to the stables.

Michael dropped Nick off at the general store and continued through town toward the Falcon Mine.

"Morning, Nick," called out Mr. Guillot as Nick walked through the front door. "How are you feeling?"

"Hi, Mr. Guillot. I've still got a bit of a headache, but I feel much better than I did yesterday," replied Nick.

"Well, if you start feeling worse again, just let me know. I don't want you working hard if you're sick," said Mr. Guillot.

"Thanks, I should be okay though," said Nick.

"I'm assuming you heard about Otis's murder Wednesday night?" asked Mr. Guillot, his expression becoming sad.

"Yes, I'm staying with Slim and his friends at the ranch, and they told me what happened. They were really shocked. Are there any suspects?" Nick asked.

"None that I know of. I hear the sheriff is setting up a fairly intense investigation. The whole town is buzzing with rumors, and people are concerned that the murderer may strike again. I'm expecting that business will be slower than usual until they catch him," explained Mr. Guillot with a sad shake of his head, partly for Otis and partly for the lost business.

The bell above the front door rang and two customers walked in, almost in defiance of Mr. Guillot's last statement. Mr. Guillot turned to assist them, and Nick headed to the back to prepare for the day's deliveries.

A light flick to his earlobe let Nick know that one of the spirits was nearby. "Who is it?" whispered Nick.

"It's Keenan. Would you mind grabbing me a mug of coffee and meeting me out back?" came Keenan's quiet voice.

Nodding, Nick went to the stove, poured a mug of coffee, and slipped out the back door.

Keenan was sitting on a barrel when Nick came out of the store. He gratefully took the mug of coffee from Nick, then reached up and gripped Nick's left shoulder with his free hand. "How are you feeling, Nick?"

Nick could see the deep concern in Keenan's expression. "It's easier if I keep myself busy," Nick replied. "But the moment I close my eyes, I see everything again."

Keenan nodded, released Nick's shoulder, and took a drink of his coffee. "It will get better with time, I promise you. Now what are the guys planning to do today?"

"Christopher and Keenan are planning Otis's funeral. Slim and Michael are heading to the Falcon Mine to make sure that everything is running smoothly. There has been talk of tracking Parker, but they haven't started that yet," explained Nick.

"I'm glad that you're staying with the real guys. It makes it easier for us to move around. Oh, Parker was hired by Billings, and Billings has him tucked away over at the Black Stallion Mine."

"Should I find a way to tell the guys where Parker is?" asked Nick.

"No, not yet," said Keenan. "Let's see how things play out. Besides, our Slim will need to make the decision about what you tell the real guys, and when."

"Let Slim know that the leather pouch I found in the fountain was Otis's. He showed it to me the night he died. When the sheriff searched Otis's body, he didn't find it. My guess is that the killer took it," said Nick.

"I'll pass the word on to the guys to keep an eye out for it. That could be the very thing that helps us discover who the killer is," said Keenan.

Jeb was angry. He paced restlessly in front of Mr. Billings's desk. "I knew this would happen, I sat in this office and told you that we couldn't trust Parker," he yelled. "And I knew he would ask for my job, especially after we heard Otis fire him."

"Calm down, Jeb," replied Mr. Billings, clearly irritated by Jeb's ranting. "I have to give him your job for now to keep him quiet. It doesn't mean that he's going to keep it."

"What are you going to do? Add another body to the sheriff's investigation?" fumed Jeb.

"Well, if you'd done what you were supposed to do, the focus of this investigation would be on Slim, not us! Now the sheriff is coming here to question me, and all you're worried about is your blasted job!" yelled Billings.

Suddenly there was a loud knock at the door.

"Come in!" yelled Billings.

The door opened and in walked Parker. "Reporting for work, sir," he chirped, smirking at Jeb.

Jeb glared at Parker, fury clouding his face. He started to stalk toward Parker with his fists clenched.

"Jeb! Jeb!" shouted Mr. Billings. "We're done here. I want you to go home. We'll talk later."

Taking a shaky breath, Jeb headed toward the door, whacking his shoulder into Parker as he walked by. He slammed the door on his way out, rattling the walls of the office.

"Jeb seems a bit upset this morning," mused Parker.

"Parker, don't even start," warned Billings angrily. "I want you to go check on Stanley and work with the miners over there until further notice."

"Why?"

"Sheriff Chamberlain is on his way here to question me about Otis's murder. I don't think it would be in our best interests for the sheriff to discover that you're working here now," growled Billings.

"Okay, okay. I'll see you later," mumbled Parker. He turned and left the office, mounted his horse, and headed for the other side of the mountain.

Michael had been in Mr. Billings's office for most of the morning, standing invisible in the corner. He decided to track Jeb down and follow him for a while, since Parker would be cooling his heels in the tunnel on the back side of the mountain. He transmigrated to a safe place in the woods near the Black Stallion Mine and called Keenan's name. A few moments later he could sense Keenan.

"Hey, what's up?" asked Keenan.

"I need you to take over for me with Billings. He and Jeb just had a nasty fight, and Jeb is heading into town. I want to follow him. But the sheriff will be here soon to question Billings," explained Michael.

"Okay, go. I'll take over here," said Keenan. Then both spirits were gone.

★   ★   ★

Jeb arrived in town, went straight to the saloon, and ordered a full bottle of whiskey. He sat at a table and slowly began to work his way through the bottle.

Several minutes later, Mr. Jenkins walked through the swinging doors, strode up to the bar, and asked Ike for a drink.

"I wonder what's going on today," mused Ike.

"What do you mean?" asked Mr. Jenkins, throwing back his head to gulp down his drink.

"I've never seen Jeb spend a morning drowning himself in a bottle of whiskey. And honestly, sir, I've never seen you here before noon."

"Jeb?" questioned Jenkins, disregarding Ike's comment about his own drink. He turned around and scanned the room, spotting Jeb at a table in the corner. He watched Jeb for a few minutes then walked over to the foreman's table and sat down.

Ike watched the two men talk. After several minutes, Jeb nodded, and the two men rose and left the saloon, leaving the bottle on the table. "Things are getting really interesting around here," muttered Ike.

★   ★   ★

Nick spent the day stacking boxes in the back, waiting on the handful of customers who came in, and making a few deliveries around town. At five o'clock, the real Keenan came to the general store to pick him up, and they headed back to the ranch.

It was six o'clock before all the guys arrived at the ranch for dinner. When Sheriff Chamberlain arrived, he quickly became the center of attention. He suggested they have some dinner before discussing the day's events. As everybody finished eating, the sheriff pushed his plate aside, took a swig of his coffee, rested his elbows on the table, and began.

"It was an interesting day, to say the least," said the sheriff. "I interviewed Jenkins first thing this morning. He seemed quite surprised that I would even want to question him. He assured me that he had only seen Otis Wednesday morning, when he notified him about the pending investigation with the Falcon Mine. When I told him that someone could place him outside Otis's office with Billings that evening, he became a bit unnerved and edgy. But he composed himself quickly and explained that he was only there to follow up on the investigation. He made sure that I was aware that Otis had refused to see him and Billings that night, and that Billings is witness to that fact."

"Who did you talk to next?" asked Slim.

"Billings was next, and he pretty much said the same thing. I wasn't getting anywhere with him, so I asked to speak to Jeb. But Billings said that Jeb was sick, so he had sent him home for the day. I'll have to catch up with Jeb after Otis's funeral."

"Yeah, if he shows up," said Keenan. "Did you talk to Parker?"

"Well that's an interesting situation. I can't seem to find Parker. No one seems to have seen him since Slim fired him."

"Parker's gone?" questioned Nick, startled by this news.

"Yep, no one seems to have a clue to where he is. It's almost like he fell off the face of the earth," said the sheriff.

"Is Parker your prime suspect?" asked Michael.

"Well, actually Jeb and Buck are also prime suspects. But to bring them in, I would have to reveal the fact that Nick was in the office. That would put Nick in real danger. So, finding Parker's keys at the scene and this disappearing act are enough for me to bring him in and keep him in jail awhile. Besides, who knows what interesting information he might be convinced to share," explained the sheriff.

"Don't worry, Sheriff, we'll find Parker. Right, guys?" asked Christopher.

"Right!" echoed Keenan and Michael.

"How are you going to do that?" asked Nick.

"We'll track him, just like any other animal," explained Michael.

★ ★ ★

The next morning, Slim and Keenan were already cooking breakfast when Christopher walked in through the back door and Nick walked in from the main room.

"Hey, Nick, how are you feeling?" asked Christopher.

"Still a little rattled. I can't seem to shake the bad dreams," said Nick.

"Be patient. It will take some time," said Slim. "Today is Otis's funeral, and the whole town is coming out for it. We'll need to keep our eyes and ears open."

"Oh," said Nick.

"Think you're up to it, Nick?" asked Keenan as he set a plate of food on the kitchen table.

"You don't have to go if you don't feel up to it," said Slim, studying Nick's face.

Nick sat down at the table and accepted the glass of milk Christopher handed to him. "I can do it," he said.

Michael stood in the doorway. "Don't worry, Nick, we'll all be there with you."

"What time is the funeral?" asked Nick.

"One o'clock this afternoon," replied Michael as he took a seat next to Nick.

"Michael is right, Nick, we'll all be there," said Slim. "And rest assured that no one knows that you were in the office that night except the sheriff and us. He wants to keep that fact real quiet in order to keep you safe. But he also might need you as a key witness in the trial."

"Hey, everyone, enough talk about the investigation," piped up Keenan. "Breakfast is ready, so everyone have a seat and eat up. We can worry about the other stuff later."

A few hours later, Nick and the real guys rode through town to the small white church, with Nick sitting behind Slim on his horse. There seemed to be a sea of people in black slowly making their way on foot to the church.

They dismounted, tied up the horses, and walked up the stairs to the open doors. Nick studied the people attending the funeral as he followed the cowboys into the church. He recognized several faces from both the Falcon Mine and the Black Stallion Mine companies. Toward the very back, Buck and Jeb sat with expressionless faces. He couldn't believe they had the guts to show up at the funeral of a man they had beaten just before he was killed. He tried not to glare at them. Arriving at the first pew, he turned to take a seat and found Mr. Billings and Mr. Jenkins, along with other members of the town's financial community, sitting in the second pew.

The church was packed. People stood in the back and a crowd milled about outside the open door. When the pastor of the small church stepped up to the pulpit, a hush fell over the crowded congregation. The only sound was an occasional sob.

The pastor spoke for about fifteen minutes, praising Otis for his charity and kindness. He named several people who worked closely with Otis and gave them the opportunity to share their memories and thoughts. Nick was half expecting to hear Parker's name called out. But as he gazed around the room, he realized that Parker was not in the church.

After several miners gave their eulogies, Slim finally stood and approached the pulpit. It was clear that he would be the last to speak. Nick could feel the air tighten with tension as Slim turned to face the crowd.

"I knew Otis Walkins for a very, very long time. He was truly a good, honorable, and fair man who knew how to challenge and draw the best from all who worked for him. He was a man of many hopes and dreams, not only for himself, but for this town as well. As most of you know, he invested a lot in Silverado. Some of our local businesses could not have gotten started without his help. Otis truly loved this town and its people, and his life reflected that love. I believe that all of us will deeply miss Otis's generosity, but there are many of us who will miss Otis the man—his laughter, his kindness, and his contagious excitement over new ideas.

"It is with great sadness that I stand before you today to say goodbye to our good friend. His death was unfair, untimely, and a diabolical crime, and we of the Falcon Mine Company and the town of Silverado are committed to discovering the responsible parties. We are committed to bringing his murderer to justice.

"The legacy of generosity that Otis established in this town will carry on through myself and the staff of the Falcon Mine Company. We will never forget you, Otis Walkins. We will carry on your dreams."

The church exploded in a roar of applause, most people rising to their feet. Tears filled Slim's eyes as he stepped down from the pulpit and walked back to the pew. After a few moments, six Falcon miners who were close with Otis came forward, lifted the closed coffin up onto their shoulders, and carried it out of the church. The pastor released the first pews to follow the coffin to the cemetery. Everyone was still standing, and the applause continued as Slim, Nick, and the guys walked down the aisle. Nick noticed that even though Mr. Billings was standing, he was not clapping like everyone else. As he exited the church, Nick glanced at Jeb and Buck. They remained in their seats, looking grim and uncomfortable.

It was a short walk to the cemetery. When the crowd had gathered around the open grave, Pastor Greg spoke a few words and led the mourners in prayer. The coffin was lowered into the ground. The pastor reached over to a pile of dirt beside the grave, grabbed a handful, and dropped it into the open grave on top of the coffin. One by one, the mourners did the same thing before walking away from the grave. Michael leaned over to Nick and explained that this was their way of giving tribute to Otis. So Nick reached forward, took a handful of dirt, and threw it into the open grave. "I know you're in a good place now, Otis," he whispered softly, "a good place with many new friends."

After the funeral, most of the townspeople left. The remainder stood in small groups talking, crying, or just sharing memories. Nick stood between Keenan and Christopher, half listening to their conversation, when a low, rumbling voice caught his attention. Nick's skin crawled, and the hairs on the back of his neck stood up—it was the voice of Otis's killer. The voice faded away, so he waited and listened. A few moments passed, and he heard it again. It was faint at first, but it grew louder until Nick could make out what the man was saying.

"I realize . . . Slim . . . of the mine. We'll meet this evening to discuss this further," growled the voice. "I have some things to do this afternoon, some information to collect. Then we can figure out how to proceed."

Nick slowly turned and looked for the face in the crowd that went with the voice. All he saw were townspeople milling around, and he could only distinguish the voices of those closest to him. The low, rumbling voice was gone.

"Nick, are you all right," whispered Keenan. "You look like you've just seen a ghost. You're white as can be."

Nick was shaking when he whispered, "I heard the same voice that I heard in Otis's office. The killer was just here."

Keenan popped his head up and looked around, but in the crowd, there was no way of telling who they were looking for.

"Come on," said Keenan grabbing Nick's arm. "Let's get over to Slim and the sheriff and tell them what you heard."

Keenan quickly walked Nick over to Slim and the sheriff, but they were in deep conversation with a group of people, so Nick kept quiet.

Later that evening, as they sat around the kitchen table with the sheriff, Nick told them what he had overheard.

"Well, it sounds like he may have been talking about the mine and me, but we don't know what that means," sighed Slim. "All we know for sure is that the killer hasn't left Silverado."

"So where do we stand?" asked Christopher.

"Well, one interesting point is that, as of this morning, the investigation of the Falcon Mine has been dropped," said the sheriff. "It seems like the investigation was going to be focused on Otis, and the board couldn't see any point in pursuing it now that he's gone."

"So we know that Billings and Parker were probably conspiring to take over the mine, and that Mr. Jenkins was probably involved, too," said Slim. "They may try to cut their losses and give up, or they may try to come up with another plan. If they do that, then we have a better chance of catching them," said Slim.

"You're right," mused Michael. "Any other takeover attempts will draw a lot of attention."

"So it almost sounds like all we have to do is just sit back and wait for them to make the first move," added Christopher.

"It doesn't quite work that way, Christopher, at least not for me," said the sheriff. "I have to actively follow every lead in this investigation, and Parker's keys were found at the scene. That makes him a suspect. I'm going to have to bring him in for questioning."

"Listen, we'll help any way we can," said Keenan.

"It'll be really interesting to see how uncomfortable some people get when I put Parker in jail. I wonder if he'll talk," said the sheriff with a yawn. "Well, that's all for me, guys. I need to get back to town. Tomorrow is going to be a busy day. I've got to try to find Parker." The sheriff rose from his seat as the men said goodnight, then headed out the back door of the kitchen. Slim put on a pot of coffee, and Nick went to the window and watched the sheriff ride out and disappear in a trail of dust.

Slim came up behind him and watched for a moment. "We'll get this all figured out really soon, Nick. We'll never give up until we've found justice for Otis."

Nick watched the dust settle as the sun slowly began to set in the distance.

Chapter Thirty-Four

ROBBERY AND KIDNAPPING

Sunday was the quietest day of the week. After church, Nick spent the day at the ranch doing chores for the guys. Keenan, Michael, and Christopher spent the afternoon tracking Parker, working from the last time anybody had seen him. Later that evening, they returned to the ranch and told Nick what they had found.

Parker had been seen in town the night of Otis's murder. He was seen again early the next morning on horseback heading toward the mines. But the trail ended at the Falcon Mine where Slim and the sheriff confronted him at Otis's office. Though he was seen leaving the Falcon grounds, no one saw him return to town. He had disappeared without a trace.

★ ★ ★

Nick awoke early Monday morning, quickly got dressed, and headed to the kitchen. He was hoping that he would be able to learn something while he was making his deliveries today. Maybe he would even identify the murderer.

Slim was already up and had breakfast ready. As he finished off a cup of coffee, he chatted with Nick. "I'll be taking you in this morning on my way to the mine," he said. "Christopher and the guys are still asleep, and I'm going to let them rest a bit longer. They'll catch up with me and the sheriff later."

"Do they have any leads on Parker yet?" asked Nick in between bites.

"No, not yet, but it's just a matter of time. We still have more people we need to talk to."

"Do you think they'll find him?" asked Nick.

"Probably. The sheriff reports to the mayor this afternoon, and soon the whole town will know that they're looking for Parker, so everyone will be on the lookout for him. When they catch him and he finds himself under arrest for murder, he may be pretty willing to talk.

"Say, are you ready? We need to get going. I think the transfer of owner-ship paperwork I filed on Thursday will probably be finalized this morning. That means I can register the diamond deposit as the new mine owner and call a meeting of the financial board."

"Yeah. Give me just a minute to brush my teeth, and I'll meet you out at the stable," replied Nick.

Later that morning, at the Black Stallion Mine Company, Michael, in-visible, leaned in a corner with his arms crossed, waiting patiently for any activity. Mr. Billings sat in his big, black overstuffed chair, resting his chin in his hand and staring out the window.

Suddenly, a knock on the door made both of them jump.

"Come in," Billings yelled.

"Morning, boss," said Jeb as he walked into the office.

"It's eleven o'clock, Jeb. It's good of you to finally join us," replied Billings sarcastically.

Jeb stopped in front of Billings's desk and sank into a chair.

"Well, to be honest, I wasn't sure if I wanted to, considering the Parker issue," he answered.

"And what made you change your mind?" asked Billings.

"A run-in with Mr. Jenkins this morning," replied Jeb. "He wanted me to deliver some information to you."

"Really? Well, please proceed," sneered Billings.

"Slim went in this morning to finalize the paperwork that will give him full control of the Falcon Mine. Then he produced the forms for registering the discovery of the diamond pit, complete with samples. Slim submitted the paperwork to Jenkins and asked for an official meeting with the investment board," explained Jeb.

"Confound it!" yelled Billings, slamming his fist onto his desk.

"Now, now," said Jeb with a malicious grin, relishing his employer's anxiety. "That was the bad news. If you can control your temper for a few minutes, I'll tell you the good news."

"How can there be any good news if Slim is telling everybody about the diamonds?" growled Billings.

"Well, the first piece of good news is that after Slim left the claims office, Jenkins took the forms and the samples and locked them away. He scheduled the meeting with the financial board, but not until next week. He couldn't stop the filing of the paperwork for Slim to take over the ownership of the mine because of Otis's will. But he can delay the filing for the discovery of diamonds," explained Jeb.

"So what's the second piece of good news?" asked Billings in a calmer tone.

Jeb took a deep breath. "Slim was too preoccupied with the filing of the diamond deposit; he didn't file any paperwork naming a beneficiary. He owns the Falcon Mine right now, but if something should happen to him, the Falcon Mine would be put up for sale. Jenkins told me to tell you that he's done his part; the rest is up to you."

Billings stroked his mustache thoughtfully. "Well, I'm working on a back-up plan, so it's possible that we won't need the Falcon Mine at all. But I need the explosives that Otis ordered to be sure. Slim might get rid of those explosives or use them any day now, so we need to grab them."

"What are we going to do about Slim?" asked Jeb.

"After we get the explosives, we'll kidnap Slim. I actually need his expertise for a day or two. After I'm done with him, I'll decide what to do."

"Get word to Buck. He's fairly resourceful. We can move the explosives tonight, then figure out a way to grab Slim," explained Mr. Billings.

"What about the other half of the explosives?" asked Jeb.

"I don't know if we'll need them, but we'll keep an eye out for them. Nick should be delivering them soon. We can have somebody keep watch to see if he makes a big delivery to the Falcon Mine. Then we notify Buck right away," explained Mr. Billings.

"But how is Buck supposed to grab Slim?" asked Jeb.

"Right now, with everything that's going on, Slim is constantly traveling back and forth between the mine and town. You and Buck can track his movements. Then it should be as simple as a knock on the head and a quick ride through the forest to the cave where we're holding Stanley."

"I'll tell Buck," said Jeb, rising from his chair and heading out the door.

"Jeb," called Mr. Billings.

"Yes sir?"

"You're not still sore at me for giving Parker your position, are you? I promise it will only be temporary."

"No sir, business is business," replied Jeb, with a strange glint in his eyes.

Jeb closed the door behind him, and Mr. Billings turned to stare out the window again, muttering, "This is our last chance."

★ ★ ★

Nick spent most of the day handling local deliveries, which was fine as far as he was concerned. As much as he wanted to find the murderer, he really was not ready to go to either mine. He had finished his deliveries and was putting some of the empty crates behind the store when he saw the ghostlike image of Keenan appear.

"Hey, bud. How are you?" asked Keenan's spirit.

"Good. How are you guys doing?"

"Well, so far no one has admitted to killing Otis. I've been watching Billings, but he's stayed in his office all day. He seems pretty worried," said Keenan, staring down at his boots. "We're keeping a close eye on Jenkins. He met with Jeb on Friday and promised him any job he wanted in either the Black Stallion Mine or the Falcon Mine. It sounds like they are planning to double-cross Billings. We're not sure what Jenkins is planning, though. The real Slim has no idea that Jenkins is involved in the attempt to take over the Falcon Mine."

"I know," said Nick. "I've wanted to tell him, but wasn't sure if I should. He's suspicious, but I don't think he thinks that Jenkins would do anything really illegal."

"Well, this morning Slim went to the claims office to get the finalized paperwork on his ownership claim, and he filed paperwork on the diamond deposit at the same time. He even gave Jenkins samples. After Slim left the office, Jenkins promptly locked everything up in his safe. He's supposed to telegraph Washington with the claim information, then send copies of the paperwork and the samples by courier to the national mining offices. But of course, that didn't happen. It seems like Jenkins found a loophole. Michael overheard Jeb tell Billings that Slim hasn't filed his beneficiary paperwork yet."

"What does that mean?" asked Nick. "I thought he had filed it right away, before he was arrested."

"Yes, but the time line has changed. Slim was not arrested, and now he's distracted by the pit, so we have no idea when he'll file the paperwork. Whoever killed Otis might go after the real Slim," said Keenan quietly.

"We've got to warn him!" exclaimed Nick.

"No, Nick, you've got to trust me on this. This may be our opportunity to find out who the killer is. It's risky, but it's our best lead," warned Keenan.

"Okay, okay," murmured Nick. "What about Stanley?"

"Stanley is fine. They're actually taking good care of him, but he's constantly guarded. Our Slim is working on a plan to draw the real Slim or the sheriff to the tunnel where they're holding Stanley. Slim says that in order to do that, we're going to have to let Mr. Billings get away with a few things, such as moving the explosives from the Falcon Mine to the Black Stallion Mine."

Nick noticed that Keenan kept shifting his gaze to the ground, and he seemed to be hesitating. Almost as if he realized Nick was watching him, Keenan jerked his eyes up to meet Nick's gaze and continued. "They're supposed to move them right to the shaft that Stanley and the other miners are working in. This will give us the opportunity to find out if the flood was really an accident," explained Keenan.

"Anything I can do to help?" asked Nick.

"Not yet. Everything is still in the planning stage, and we just don't have enough answers yet. We can't risk putting you in danger, particularly now that you're the only witness to Otis's murder," said Keenan.

"I'll be able to help in some way, won't I?" asked Nick.

"Yeah, sure, Nick. But, at this point, we're not even sure how this is going to play out. Whatever you do, just keep your eyes open and be smart. These men are ruthless. Remember, you're more involved than anybody knows, so let's do whatever we can to make sure that you're not hurt. So promise me—no heroics, okay?" asked Keenan, staring into Nick's eyes.

"Yes, I promise. No heroics," replied Nick, feeling a little scared by Keenan's intensity.

"Nick!" yelled Mr. Guillot.

"I've got to go," said Nick.

"Okay. One of the other guys will check in with you later," said Keenan as he faded away.

Nick hurried to the front of the store. "Yes, sir?" he called as he approached the front counter where Mr. Guillot was working.

"Hey, Nick, I just wanted you to know that I received notice that the second half of the order that Otis put in will be arriving tomorrow morning. They haven't received word about Otis's death yet, so I need to find out if Slim still wants me to fill the order," explained Mr. Guillot.

"I'll be seeing Slim tonight, Mr. Guillot—I'm staying with him," said Nick. "I can have an answer for you in the morning."

"That would be a big help. Oh, I also heard from Ben. He should be back sometime this week. His letter said that he had a great time and his sister had a baby boy, so he's now a proud uncle."

"Hmm, I wonder if he's changed him yet?" asked Nick with a smirk.

"Ben? Are you kidding me? He would have hightailed it back here faster than a jackrabbit if he had to do that," laughed Mr. Guillot. "Heaven help him if he ever gets married and has children. Well, why don't you finish straightening the back room, then come up here and cover the counter until closing so I can get some paperwork done."

"Okay," replied Nick, and he grabbed a broom and headed to the back room.

The rest of the day was uneventful. Nick listened to people gossip as they shopped. It seemed that a lot of the townspeople were happy that the sheriff had identified a suspect, but they were upset that Parker was still on the loose. The question was circling: Did Parker kill Otis, or was it someone else? Nick could tell that people were on edge and fearful. They wanted this case to be solved—and fast.

At about five o'clock, the real Christopher stopped by the general store to see if Nick needed a ride back to the ranch. He chatted with Mr. Guillot as Nick finished up.

On the way back to the ranch, Christopher filled Nick in. "Slim, Michael, and Keenan will be late tonight. They're prepping the cavern to get it ready for explosives."

"What are they going to blow first?" asked Nick.

"The wall on the other side of the pit. They have to run timbers across the mouth of the pit and put some planks down so that the men can move around safely down there," explained Christopher.

"It seems like Slim's jumping in with both feet," said Nick.

"That's Slim for you. He's very enthusiastic, but he likes to make sure that things go as smoothly as possible," said Christopher.

Back at the Falcon Mine Company, Slim, Michael, Keenan, and a few miners were hard at work pushing long timbers across the pit. It was tedious work and very dangerous, but it was necessary to enable them to reach the far wall safely. One false move could send a man tumbling to his death.

Slim was getting ready to wire the wall with explosives. He had explored the cavern thoroughly and thought that there might be another cavern on the other side of the wall. Another cavern could mean another diamond deposit.

Sighing with satisfaction, Slim wiped his forehead with the kerchief hanging around his neck.

"Goodness, Slim, this is quite a job," groaned Michael as he stretched his back.

"Yep, but just think about it. Sometime tomorrow we should be able to blow it," said Slim gleefully.

"Only you would get excited about blowing through a wall," chuckled Keenan.

"Are we done here, Slim?" asked one of the miners.

"Yes, I think we're done for tonight. Report back here tomorrow afternoon and we'll get ready to blow through. Thanks for staying late to help get this ready," said Slim. As he shook each man's hand, Slim slipped several gold coins into each palm.

"That was pretty generous of you, Slim," said Michael as he flipped a gold coin in the air and caught it.

"These guys have been through so much these last few days. And they worked hard so that the other miners will be safe. I think that deserves some appreciation, don't you?"

"Yep, I agree," said Keenan.

"Well, why don't you guys head out. I'm going to put some of this equipment away and then stop by the office and pick up some maps. I'll just be a few minutes behind you," said Slim.

"Okay," said Michael. "Let's go, Keenan, I'm starving."

"See you at the ranch, Slim," called Keenan as he headed toward the lift.

"Save me some dinner," called Slim. He examined the far wall for several minutes, planning the placement of the charges. "Tomorrow we'll see what other secrets you might hold," he said with a grin. He spent a few minutes gathering the last of the equipment and piling it neatly against the wall of the cavern. He finally grabbed the last lit lantern and headed toward the lift.

Lost in thought, Slim rode the lift as it rose slowly from level to level. Finally, the lift stopped at the main cavern. Slim stepped off and walked down the wide tunnel to the mine entrance. Suddenly, a loud crash echoed throughout the tunnel. Slim stopped in his tracks, listening intently. There were faint voices coming from one of the smaller caves. "No one should be here at this time of the night," he whispered. Changing direction he headed toward the cave to investigate. As he approached the cave entrance, the voices became clear.

"You idiot! You about crushed my foot," a man growled angrily. "You're lucky you didn't ignite it and blow us sky high."

"I'm sorry, Jeb," replied another man. "It doesn't look like it opened."

"You're lucky," replied Jeb.

Slim stepped into the cave. "What the heck do you think you're doing, Jeb!" he yelled.

Jeb and Buck stood very still, stunned by Slim's sudden appearance. Finally Jeb spoke up. "Uh . . . Otis Walkins sold these explosives to Mr. Billings before he died. We're just here to pick them up."

"Yeah, right. Let's see the bill of sale, Jeb. Billings really wants this mine bad, doesn't he? So what's he got planned for all of these—"

Thump!

Slim crumpled to the cave floor, unconscious. Buck stood over him, wielding a chunk of wood. "There's your bill of sale," he sneered.

Jeb bent to check on Slim. "Well, he's alive. I guess now we don't have to come up with a plan to nab him, do we?

"And Mr. Billings should be happy. We're actually ahead of schedule," mused Buck.

"Well, let's get going before somebody comes looking for him," said Jeb. "Tie him up and gag him. We'll load him up with the crates. You know, this really couldn't have turned out much better."

Out at the ranch, while wolfing down their dinners, Michael and Keenan described the work they had done in the cavern. On their way back to the ranch, they had stopped to check in with the sheriff. Sheriff Chamberlain was frustrated; he had not been able to discover any new information about the watch fob or any other lead. As Nick had suspected, based on the townspeople's gossip, the sheriff was feeling the heat to find the killer. If not Parker, then someone—and soon.

After Michael and Keenan had finished eating, the gang relaxed around the fireplace and tried to unwind. The warmth of the fire slowly took its toll on the weary men, and they began to nod off to sleep. It was getting late, and Slim had not arrived yet. Nick realized that he, too, was tired and finally slipped away to his room to escape the snoring. He just hoped he'd get a chance to see Slim in the morning to ask him about the second half of the order, and maybe casually ask if he had named a beneficiary for the mine.

Michael and Keenan—the spirits—slowly appeared in the workshop. Christopher sat by the potbellied stove, and Slim came around the makeshift wall from the washroom. "Hey guys," he said. "What have Jeb and Buck been up to? Did they get the explosives?"

"The real Slim has just been kidnapped," replied Keenan, watching Slim intently.

"Jeb and Buck are taking him to the Black Stallion Mine. They're probably going to keep him with Stanley," reasoned Michael.

"Well, we knew they were planning it," said Slim. "I just didn't think it would happen so fast . . . All right, it's going to be a long night. You guys work out a rotation and get back over to the Black Stallion Mine to keep an eye on the real me and all of our suspects. Jeb won't stay in that tunnel because he's going to have to report what happened to Jenkins. I'll follow him. We've got to figure out what they're planning. Things are happening fast, guys, so we need to stay on top of it," replied Slim.

"What do you want to tell Nick?" questioned Keenan.

"Nothing right now. He's been through a lot with Otis's death, and there's nothing he can do tonight anyway. We'll try to catch up with him tomorrow," reasoned Slim.

Chapter Thirty-Five
THE SEARCH FOR SLIM

The next morning, as Nick walked into the kitchen, Michael and Christopher were talking about Parker.

"We need to help the sheriff out. Parker is still on the loose, and to be honest, I think by now he's probably heard that he's a prime suspect. He may already be far away. And I'm worried that the townspeople are getting anxious; if a posse finds him, they might hang him, guilty or not, just to ease their minds," said Christopher.

"What do you want to do?" asked Michael.

"Let's talk to some of the men at the Falcon Mine and find out who Parker usually hangs around with," said Christopher.

"I think we all agree that Parker was probably not the murderer," said Michael. "Nick had heard his voice just a little while before the murder, so he probably would have recognized it. We just need to find him and convince him to come in quietly, for his own safety if nothing else. We can convince him that talking to the sheriff will help keep him out of the noose. This disappearing act of his only makes him seem more suspicious. If he doesn't cooperate, he'll be hung for a crime he didn't commit."

"I'll go in this morning and talk to the sheriff and let him know what we're planning," said Christopher.

"Good idea," said Michael. Nick cleared his throat and Michael and Christopher looked up to find him standing in the doorway. "Hey, come in, Nick. What do you have going on today?" asked Michael.

"Where's Slim this morning? I've got a question for him," said Nick.

"I didn't hear him come in last night. He's probably still in bed. What did you need to ask him? Maybe I can help," replied Michael.

"Mr. Guillot told me yesterday that the second half of Otis's explosives order would be coming in this morning. Should I go ahead and deliver it or tell Mr. Guillot to send it back?"

"Hmm, I don't believe that Otis actually needed all of the explosives he ordered," pondered Michael. "But then again, I could be wrong. I don't think we'll know for sure until Slim starts working on the wall. Since it's already on its way, tell Mr. Guillot to send it up. If we don't end up needing it, Slim can always sell it to another mine. I'll ask Slim as soon as he gets up. If anything changes, I'll come to the store and let you know."

Nick sat down at the table, wondering if he should bring up his other question. *I promised not to mention it to Slim, but it's got to be okay to ask a question,* thought Nick. "Uh . . . do you guys know if Slim named a beneficiary for the Falcon Mine yet?"

"That's a good question, Nick. I don't think he has; he's been so busy with the pit. He probably hasn't given it much thought. I'll mention it when I see him," said Christopher. "Are you ready for work? I'll be taking you in this morning. You'd better eat up or you'll be late."

"Okay," said Nick, and he dug into his breakfast.

Keenan shuffled in, yawning and stretching. "Wow, which one of you cooked this morning? I thought for sure you'd be waiting on me to do it."

"I decided to give you a break this morning, Keenan," replied Michael, chuckling.

"Well, thanks. I just hope you didn't burn the coffee. Say, where is our boy, Slim? He's usually up before the rest of us," said Keenan as he sat down next to Nick.

"He's probably sleeping in a little this morning," said Christopher. "He still wasn't home when we finally made it to bed, so he must have gotten in really late."

"Something tells me he's going to be spending quite a few late nights at that mine, at least until he finds a new foreman," said Michael.

"That could take awhile. I'm not sure he's going to be able to trust anyone, except us," said Keenan.

"Well, here's your chance to get out of the cattle game," said Christopher. "You should take the position of foreman, Keenan."

"And miss out on all those cattle drives? No way, bud. Besides, you have the build for a miner, not me," said Keenan.

"I prefer cows to rock any day. At least cows have personality," replied Christopher with a chuckle. He rose and turned to Nick. "We should get going, Nick. Are you ready?"

"Yep," said Nick as he stood and put his dishes in the sink.

"Well, you guys have a good day. I'm going to wake up Slim," said Michael, and he walked out of the kitchen.

"Tell Slim I'll see him this afternoon," called Nick as he walked out the door and headed to the stables with Christopher.

Keenan got up from the table and walked over to the kitchen window to watch Christopher and Nick climb onto Christopher's horse and take off down the road.

"Keenan!" yelled Michael.

Keenan whirled around as Michael burst into the kitchen. "Slim isn't in his room and his bed doesn't look slept in. I don't think he came home last night."

"What?" exclaimed Keenan. "Okay, okay, let's not panic. He may have met up with the sheriff, or he may have fallen asleep in the office. Let's head into town and find the sheriff, then head out to the mine."

"Let's get going. We aren't going to get any answers by standing here," said Michael.

"Michael, I don't like this. Not with everything that's happened," said Keenan as they walked out the door.

"I know, I know, but let's not jump to conclusions. We need to catch up with Christopher at the general store."

"What about Nick?"

"Let's not say anything until we know what's going on," said Michael as they mounted their horses and headed into town.

★　★　★

The air was chilly and smelled old, damp, and musty. Slim was stirring, slowly returning to consciousness. He moved slightly, and could tell that he was lying on something cold and hard. He tried to lift his head, but a dull throbbing in his temple forced him to give up. He groaned as he rolled over onto his side. Moving very slowly, he maneuvered himself, inch by inch, into a sitting position. He opened his eyes into a squint and looked around.

Slim discovered that he was in a small cavern. The cavern seemed to be empty except for two torches attached to the far wall that were burning brightly. A tunnel opening in the wall between the two torches appeared to be the only way in or out. He was sitting on a rough blanket. He thought about getting up and trying to make it to the opening to get out, but common sense told him that he had been brought here by force and that there was probably a guard outside the cave. And he wasn't even sure he could make it to the tunnel without passing out.

Slim leaned back against the cold, hard cave wall and closed his eyes. Just then, someone called his name.

"Slim!" cried Stanley as he came through the cave entrance. He ran over to where Slim sat. "Slim, are you all right?" he asked, gently touching a large bruise that had developed on Slim's face.

"Yes, Stanley. I'm a little sore and my head really hurts, but I think I'm all right. What about you?" asked Slim. "And where are we?"

"Gosh, it's so good to see you, Slim," exclaimed Stanley. "I'm okay, but I'm not thrilled to be here. They're taking good care of me, giving me plenty of blankets and food. But we're working long hours, and I have no idea where I am or why I was brought here. I was just told that it would be in my best interest not to ask any questions."

"Have you seen Mr. Billings in here yet?" asked Slim.

"No. I've only seen Parker and Jeb, and a few other miners who I've been working with. Parker and Jeb were talking to the foreman a few days ago," answered Stanley.

"How long have I been here?" asked Slim, rubbing his head as he glanced up at Stanley.

"They brought you in last night, but you've been out cold. I'm glad to see you awake. I was getting pretty worried," said Stanley.

"What exactly do they have you working on here, Stanley?" asked Slim.

"A tunnel," replied Stanley. "But it doesn't make sense, Slim. I haven't seen a single sign of gold or silver deposits."

"I'm afraid the plans for my current project are not available for viewing." Mr. Billings's voice echoed in the small cavern.

Slim slowly turned his head and raised his eyes to meet Mr. Billings's cold hard stare. Jeb emerged from the tunnel and stood beside Mr. Billings.

"I'm assuming that since we're being graced by your presence, Billings, we are somewhere in the Black Stallion Mine," said Slim through gritted teeth.

"I see your ability to reason is unimpaired, even though you're not in the best form at the moment. So sorry about that. I think Buck was a little too heavy-handed with you yesterday," chuckled Mr. Billings. "But you are correct. You are in the Black Stallion Mine. I have to be honest—it's so good to have you here, Slim. I find that I'm in need of your expertise."

"Pernell, I didn't volunteer for this, so I don't think I'll be helping you with whatever plan you've cooked up now," said Slim, glaring at Mr. Billings.

"Tsk, tsk. Jeb, my boy, I think that Slim needs to be persuaded," sneered Mr. Billings.

"You don't scare me, Pernell. Beating me won't get you anywhere."

"Jeb, Slim seems to think he has the upper hand in this situation. Please convince him otherwise," said Mr. Billings.

Jeb's mouth curled into a sinister smile as he leisurely strolled over to Slim and Stanley. Instead of grabbing Slim, though, Jeb grabbed Stanley, jerked him to his feet, and punched him hard in the gut. Grabbing Stanley's slumped form, he threw him against the wall of the cave. Stanley groaned pitifully as he collapsed to the floor in a heap. Slim tried to get up to protect Stanley, but a sharp pain in his head dropped him back to the floor.

Mr. Billings moved to stand over Slim. "That was very noble of you, Slim, trying to protect Stanley, but you're not in the best health right now, so I think you should stay right where you are. I doubt that you'll be any help to us today. It doesn't seem that Stanley will be able to dig today either. I'm going to be generous and let you both have the day off to recuperate. But tomorrow morning, Slim, I expect you to cooperate fully, or you can watch Stanley being beaten until he begs for death, which we can easily grant."

Slim lowered his head and said nothing.

"I believe we have made our point, Jeb. I will leave you to consider your position, Slim," said Mr. Billings.

"What about Stanley, Pernell? He could really be hurt," whispered Slim.

"I will send in our doctor to check your injuries and make sure they are not serious. I should warn you before I go that you should not try to escape. I have guards everywhere, and they have been ordered to shoot to kill. There are no second chances, understand?" asked Mr. Billings.

Slim nodded slightly.

"Good. Ah, here is your breakfast. Eat up—you need to build your strength. And get some sleep. It will help you heal faster. Here are some extra blankets to warm things up a bit. Try to make yourself and Stanley as comfortable as you can. Tomorrow I will show you what I need you to do for me," said Mr. Billings.

Mr. Billings turned on his heel and left with Jeb. Two men came in with plates of food and coffee. One of the men helped move Stanley next to Slim.

"I'm so sorry, Stanley. I thought Jeb was coming for me," said Slim.

"It's okay, Slim. Who knew what Billings was thinking? I'll be all right. I'm just a little sore, that's all. Now go ahead and eat before your food gets cold."

"The doctor will be here in a while," said one of the miners as they were leaving.

Slim and Stanley slowly started to eat. Eventually, Stanley pushed his plate and mug aside, lay down on a blanket, and drew several more blankets over him.

"I think I'm going to sleep now," Stanley murmured.

"Are you sure you're okay, Stanley?" asked Slim.

"Yes, Slim, I'm okay," whispered Stanley as he drifted into sleep.

Slim knew that he should get some sleep too, but he couldn't stop worrying long enough to relax. He spent some time staring at the wall, trying to figure out what to do next. About an hour later, a doctor came in and checked on both of them. Aside from some major bruising, both men were all right. After the doctor left, Slim lay back down and finally drifted off to sleep.

Christopher dropped Nick off in front of the general store and then headed to the sheriff's office to see if there was any new information. Nick went in and checked the schedule in the back, picked up the broom, and returned to the front of the store to sweep around the front door. He had just finished when Mr. Guillot came down the stairs with his mug of coffee.

"Morning, Nick. How are you?"

"Good, sir. Is the schedule still on for the other half of the order for the Falcon Mine?"

"Yes, it is. It should be here in about two hours. I think we'll be able to get it all in our wagon, so we'll load it up and you can take it to the mine after lunch. That is, of course, if Slim said it was okay to send it. After all, it was Otis's order," replied Mr. Guillot.

"I got the go-ahead this morning," said Nick.

"Good. I don't like to store explosives here. They're too dangerous."

At that moment, the front door burst open and Michael rushed in, out of breath. "Hey, Nick, is Christopher still here?" he asked.

"No. He went down to the sheriff's office. Is something wrong?" asked Nick.

"Uh, no, I don't think so. I'll have to fill you in later. I've gotta run now," said Michael, and he rushed back outside to his horse.

Nick walked up to the big picture window and watched Michael take the reins for his horse from Keenan and climb into the saddle. They turned and took off toward the sheriff's office. Nick watched as their dust trail faded. He could not shake the uneasy feeling that something very bad had happened.

"I wonder what that was all about?" asked Mr. Guillot.

"I'm not too sure. Everything was fine at the ranch this morning," said Nick.

"If you're concerned Nick, go on down to the sheriff's office and see if you can find out what's going on," suggested Mr. Guillot.

"Thanks, Mr. Guillot. I'll be right back," said Nick.

Nick stepped outside and ran toward the sheriff's office. He was almost there when he saw Michael, Keenan, Christopher, and the sheriff rush out of the office and climb onto horses tied to the hitching post. They turned quickly, and then rode full gallop through town toward the mines. Nick watched them as they passed, his nervousness increasing, then retraced his steps back to the general store.

Nick surmised that something had happened at one of the mines, but he had no idea what it was. There was nothing he could do except make the delivery to the Falcon Mine and see what he could find out. If nothing had happened there, Nick was willing to take the chance and ride up to the Black Stallion Mine to snoop around.

Nick kept as busy as he could in the morning with the few deliveries he had in town. When the supply wagon arrived, he helped the driver unload it and checked everything in. He and Mr. Guillot finished loading the general store wagon around lunchtime, and Nick still hadn't seen the sheriff or the guys. He was ready to drive up to the mine, but had to wait while Mr. Guillot finished preparing the invoices.

Nick went to the saloon to have lunch and visit Ike. Ike had seen the guys rush through town, but he hadn't heard that anything serious had happened at either mine. "But I might not find out until later when the miners come in for drinks before going home," said Ike.

Nick finished his lunch, said goodbye to Ike, and then rushed to the general store. Mr. Guillot had the invoices ready. He handed them to Nick and said, "Do be careful driving, Nick. I know that you are anxious to find out what's going on, but remember that you're carrying explosives. I would hate to see a big black plume of smoke coming from the road to the mines."

"I'll be careful, I promise," said Nick as he took the paperwork and turned to go.

As soon as Nick was outside of town, his first instinct was to drive faster. But he checked himself, remembering what Mr. Guillot had said. Safety was more important, so he paced the horse.

As he was pondering what might have the guys so excited, Nick heard the familiar sound of the creaking seat beside him, and Christopher's voice suddenly came out of the air.

"Hey, Nick, how are you?" asked Christopher.

"Boy, am I glad to hear you. What's going on?" asked Nick.

"Oh, you don't know yet? I thought for sure one of us—the real us— would have told you by now," said Christopher.

"They haven't had a chance yet. They rushed straight out of town," said Nick. "Now what happened?"

"Nick, the real Slim was kidnapped last night at the Falcon Mine by Jeb and Buck," said Christopher.

"Oh, no! Is he okay?" asked Nick.

"Yes. He's a bit sore, but otherwise okay. Jeb and Buck took him over to where they're holding Stanley at the Black Stallion Mine. They've got him pretty well guarded. It seems that Mr. Billings needs him for whatever this project is that he's working on. Unfortunately, we haven't figured out what it is yet," said Christopher.

"Do you guys have a plan for getting him and Stanley out of there?" asked Nick.

"Our Slim is working on it, but I haven't been briefed yet. Right now, Michael and Keenan are taking turns keeping an eye on Slim and Stanley. Slim and I are following Parker, Jeb, and Buck."

"What can I do?"

"Nothing right now. We're still collecting information and trying to figure out what Mr. Billings is actually up to."

Exasperated, Nick threw his hands in the air. "There's got to be something I can do."

"I'm sure there will be, but not yet," said Christopher. "Right now the best thing you can do is just go about your day as usual. Are you making a delivery now?" asked Christopher.

"Yes, I'm delivering the other half of Otis's order to the Falcon Mine."

"Hmm, with Slim out of the way, Jeb and Buck will be back over at the Falcon Mine tonight to steal these explosives. I have to get back to our Slim and let him know. We might have you help by making sure the real guys are there when Jeb and Buck show up," said Christopher, thinking out loud.

"I can do that!"

"Nick, I think we may have just hatched a good plan. Let me get back to Slim and see if we can sort this out. You go ahead, and we'll hook up with you later and let you know what the plan is," said Christopher.

"Okay."

"I'll see you later."

"See you later, Christopher," said Nick as the seat creaked again, indicating that Christopher had left.

Nick was excited as he continued to guide the wagon on the steep, winding road. At least now he knew what had happened, and he knew that Slim was okay. He was going to help nab Jeb and Buck, and that felt good. By the time he reached the Falcon Mine, he was almost happy.

Chapter Thirty-Six

WRONG PLACE, WRONG TIME

Nick parked the wagon outside of the main office as usual. Looking around, he did not see the real Michael, Keenan, Christopher, or the sheriff. *That's strange*, he thought. *And if Slim's not around, then who's running the office today?*

Nick bounded up the stairs to the office, stopping in front of the closed office door and glancing around the yard. Men were working as usual, so they clearly didn't know that Slim had been taken. Nick knocked hard on the office door. "Maybe the guys' horses are tied up somewhere else," murmured Nick as he knocked a second time.

Nick waited, but there was no answer. He tried the door handle, which turned easily in his hand. He pushed the door open and peeked in. Looking around the office, Nick was stunned by the memories of that night as they came flooding back. He had to take a deep breath before finally walking in.

The office looked nothing like it had that fateful night—it had been put back in order as if nothing had ever happened.

Nick took a few more steps into the room. Deep in thought, he didn't notice the door shut soundly behind him. He examined the office a bit more for signs of the murder, then finally decided he had better go find somebody to sign his paperwork. He turned and took a step toward the door when he heard a familiar voice.

"Well, well, if it isn't my favorite delivery boy," snarled Buck.

Nick's head jerked up quickly, and his eyes met Buck's. Nick was stunned. "What in the heck are you doing in this office?" asked Nick.

"I think the better question is, what are you doing here? The door was closed, and there was no answer to your knock, but you decided to come in anyway and snoop around," growled Buck.

"For your information, I have a right to be here. I'm looking for Slim. He needs to sign an invoice," said Nick.

"Well, Slim is not here at the moment, and I'm working in the office. I'll sign it for you," replied Buck.

"You can't sign it. It has to be the owner of the mine or his assistant. Slim's assistant is Michael right now, so where is he?" demanded Nick.

"Well, aren't you well-informed. Michael isn't here either. He's down in the mine," snapped Buck.

"Then I'll wait," said Nick. "I can't leave here until I unload my cargo anyway."

The two of them glared at each other until a loud knock made them both jump. Buck jerked the door open and, to Nick's surprise, in walked Jeb. He quickly shut the door behind him when he saw Nick.

"Problem, Buck?" asked Jeb.

"That depends on your way of thinking. I think our boy Nick just brought the other half of Otis's explosives. Seems like he needs a signature to finish the delivery," sneered Buck.

"Hmm, may I see the paperwork, Nick?" asked Jeb, trying to look friendly.

"Jeb, why in the world would I give you the paperwork? You don't even work here," said Nick.

Jeb rushed toward Nick before Nick had a chance to move. He clamped his hand quickly over Nick's mouth. Nick squirmed violently in his grasp. "Grab that rope over there and give me your kerchief. We're going to have to take him with us. Go out and drive his wagon around to the back of the office. I'll bring him out in a minute. Oh, what happened with Michael?"

"He shouldn't be a problem. He and his friends and the sheriff are searching the mine for Slim. Michael was down by the pit, and the others had spread out to other tunnels. Michael caught me following him, and there was a scuffle. When I left him, he was taking a nap, so to speak. But it will only be a matter of time before he wakes up or somebody finds him, so we need to get moving.

"Did you find the paperwork that Mr. Billings wanted?" asked Jeb. Buck twisted his hands anxiously. "I searched everywhere. It's not here."

"Are you sure?" asked Jeb.

"Yeah, I'm sure."

"All right then, get the wagon around back. We need to get out of here before someone comes in and starts asking questions, or Michael shows up," growled Jeb.

Buck slipped out of the office. Jeb quickly tied and gagged Nick. In a moment, Buck was back with a burlap sack. The two men pushed Nick into the sack and tied it shut. Jeb hefted Nick's wrapped form over his shoulder, slipped out of the office, and crept around to the back, with Buck following close behind. Jeb laid Nick in the wagon between some of the crates. Within a few moments, the wagon began to sway beneath him, and Nick knew they were heading to the Black Stallion Mine.

Suddenly, a very quiet voice whispered in Nick's ear. "Are you all right, Nick?" asked Keenan.

Then Christopher spoke. "We'll have you out of this mess in a jiffy." said Christopher. But Nick shook his head. Keenan reached a ghostly hand through the burlap and removed Nick's gag so that he could talk.

"No," Nick whispered as quietly as he could. "This is where I can be the biggest help now. They're taking me to the Black Stallion Mine, probably to where they're holding Slim and Stanley. If you guys come up with a plan to get us out, I'll be able to communicate the plan to them."

"I don't like this," whispered Keenan.

"But you know, he does have a point," said Christopher.

"Okay, I'll tell you what, we'll let this play out, but Christopher will stay with you the entire time, and the moment you are in too much danger, he'll port you out of there, no matter what. I'll go talk to our Slim and find out what he wants us to do," said Keenan.

"Okay," said Nick.

"Oh, I hate to see you this way," whispered Keenan, patting Nick's arm. "Okay, Christopher, whatever you do, don't let Nick out of your sight."

"I promise, I won't," said Christopher.

"I'll catch up with you later. Good luck, Nick," said Keenan, and then he was gone.

"I'll be right here, Nick. I'll put the gag back when we get closer to the mine," said Christopher, and then he was quiet.

Nick was very uncomfortable as they traveled. The sack was unbearably hot in the afternoon sun, and Nick was soon soaked in sweat. It seemed like hours had passed by the time Nick finally heard the crunch of the wheels on gravel and the squeaking of the wagon brakes. A moment later, he felt strong arms lift him out of the wagon. He was carried up a few stairs, and then he heard a door creak open. He was lowered onto the floor, and then unceremoniously pulled out of the bag.

Nick lay there for several moments letting his eyes adjust to the light. He lifted his head slightly and looked around, immediately realizing that he was in Mr. Billings's office. Jeb and Buck were standing to one side of the room talking quietly. He lowered his head just as the door burst open and Mr. Billings came striding in, reading some papers. Glancing up, he noticed Jeb and Buck.

"What'cha got for me, boys?" he asked, as he walked toward his desk. He looked down just in time to avoid tripping over Nick. "What the—" he yelled as he struggled to get his balance. "Nick! What in the world are you doing here?" He turned to glare angrily at Jeb and Buck. "Buck, I told you to leave the kid alone!"

"We had to snatch him, Mr. Billings. He walked in on Buck and me in the Falcon Mine office," replied Jeb.

"Not only that, he had the second half of Otis's explosives order with him. He wasn't going to leave the office without Slim's or Michael's signature," added Buck quickly.

"The other half?" asked Mr. Billings. He raised his left eyebrow as he gazed at Jeb. "I thought you told me that the order wasn't scheduled to be delivered until tomorrow."

"I'm sorry, Mr. Billings. I must have gotten wrong information, sir," he answered.

"For Pete's sake, untie the boy and give him something to drink," snapped Mr. Billings as he walked around Nick and returned to his desk. Jeb untied Nick and poured him a glass of water from a pitcher on Mr. Billings's desk. Nick sat up and gulped the water down.

Mr. Billings leaned back in his chair and tapped his fingers on his desk. After several long moments, he finally spoke. "Buck, did you get the paperwork I asked for?"

"I looked everywhere. I didn't find it."

"Blast!" exclaimed Mr. Billings. He glared at Buck for a moment, then seemed to calm himself. "Well, it's possible he hasn't filled out the paperwork yet. I just thought Slim was smarter than that." He stared out the window for a few moments, then turned to Jeb.

"Jeb, go see Mr. Jenkins tomorrow morning. Make sure that Slim didn't file beneficiary paperwork yesterday afternoon, and tell Jenkins to give you the forms and samples that Slim brought to him yesterday. Then bring those to me right away."

"But what if Mr. Jenkins doesn't want to give it to me?" asked Jeb.

"If that should happen, let Mr. Jenkins know that I have enough information on his illegal activities to cause some serious problems for him," sneered Mr. Billings.

"What should we do about Nick?" asked Jeb.

"Oh, yes. Nick, my boy, I'm afraid you just happened to be at the wrong place at the wrong time. You're going to have to stay here for a little while until I can figure out what to do with you. In the meantime, I think you being here is actually a good thing. You're the perfect incentive to keep Slim cooperating with us," mused Mr. Billings.

"Jeb, take Nick to the cabin and get him cleaned up a bit. He's drenched in sweat, and he'll get sick if we put him in the cavern in wet clothes. Then take him down to the cavern. I'm sure Slim and Stanley will take good care of him."

"Where do you want us to put the other half of Otis's order?" asked Jeb. "The back cabin is full. Nothing else is going to fit in there."

"Park the wagon over behind the cabin and put guards around it until I get a report from Slim tomorrow. If I get the report I'm hoping to get, then we'll have the men move it into that tunnel," answered Mr. Billings.

"Okay," said Jeb. He grabbed the glass from Nick and put it on Mr. Billings's desk. He pulled Nick to his feet and pushed him toward the door.

"Oh, and by the way, Nick," said Mr. Billings, "I should warn you not to get any ideas about trying to escape. My men have been instructed to shoot to kill no matter what. Do you understand?" Nick said nothing, but nodded his head. Jeb guided Nick out of Mr. Billings's office to a cabin several yards away. He gave Nick a few moments to clean up, and then he gave him clean clothes to wear, although they were very large. When he was finished dressing, Jeb handed him a heavy jacket, several blankets, and a pillow. Jeb then put him on a horse, blindfolded him, tied his hands to the saddle, and climbed up behind him.

They rode for some time. Nick could tell they were riding over some rough terrain and occasionally through parts of the forest, but that was it. Eventually, Jeb pulled on the reins and stopped the horse. He climbed down, untied Nick, and then pulled him off the horse. It was very quiet where they were, so Nick knew they weren't near the main part of the mine. Jeb put the blankets in Nick's arms and then turned Nick and guided him along the rough ground. Soon, Nick could tell that they had entered a cave. The cool, clammy, musty air was the first clue. He was grateful he had put on the jacket that Jeb had given him because he had the feeling they were probably going deep into the tunnel.

Nick lost track of time as they walked. He listened to their echoing footfalls on the hard rock cave floor. Eventually, they came to a stop. Jeb reached up and released Nick's blindfold. As Nick's eyes adjusted to the dim light, he looked up to see a tunnel entrance in the cave wall. On either side stood a guard with a rifle.

"This is where you're going to be staying, Nick. This is the only entrance and exit, so if you're thinking about trying something, you might want to remember what's right outside," reminded Jeb. "Well, you'd best be getting in there now. You have everything you need. Someone will be bringing you food later," said Jeb as he gave Nick a little shove in the back to propel him forward.

Nick walked into the tunnel and followed the narrow passage around a corner where it opened up into a small cavern. Two oil lanterns attached to the wall shed some light in the stony room.

Nick could see the outline of someone sleeping against one wall and another person sitting next to the sleeping form. It was Slim.

"Slim!" Slim looked up just in time to catch Nick as he rushed across the cave floor and threw himself into Slim's arms.

"Nick!" cried Slim. "What are you doing here?"

"Slim, I'm so glad to see you," murmured Nick.

"Where are the guys? Are you here to rescue us?" asked Slim.

Nick sat back. "Not exactly."

"Okay, you'd better tell me how you got here. What happened, and where are the guys?" asked Slim.

★　★　★

Michael slowly came to, moaning and reaching around to feel the knot on the back of his head. He levered himself off the hard rock floor and struggled to his feet. He leaned against the tunnel wall to gather his wits and tried to remember what had happened.

He vaguely remembered that he had just finished talking with the guards who were posted in the tunnel to the pit cavern near the lift. They told him that Slim had been there in the morning the previous day, but had left. Michael had gone down to the pit to see if he could find anything. He explored the cavern and the pit as carefully as he could, but didn't find any clues as to where Slim might be. He finally gave up and decided to go find the rest of the crew. He took the lift up to the next level and was heading down the dimly lit tunnel when he saw a man standing in the shadows. As soon as they made eye contact, the man dove for Michael. They struggled on the ground for a few moments, then Michael felt a sharp pain in the back of his head—and that was the last thing he remembered.

Michael realized that he needed to get back to the office immediately to find out what was going on. "I need to find the guys," he whispered, and then he rushed for the lift. Arriving at the main tunnel, Michael stepped off the lift and almost collided with Keenan, Christopher, and the sheriff.

"No luck, Michael. No one has seen Slim since yesterday, or last night when we were working on the pit," said Keenan.

"Are you all right?" asked the sheriff. "You look pale."

"I'm all right now, but I was attacked in the tunnel above the pit. I've never seen the guy before, so it could have been someone from the Black Stallion Mine or the Falcon Mine."

"Do you think you would recognize him again, if you saw him?" asked the sheriff.

"I'm pretty sure I would be able to pick him out of a crowd."

"Well, we need to head over to the Black Stallion Mine anyway," mused Christopher. "It's possible that somebody over there has seen Slim."

★ ★ ★

A little later, Slim's spirit transmigrated outside of the ranch's kitchen window. Slim watched through the window as the real guys and the sheriff talked and planned.

A few minutes later, Slim sensed Keenan's presence in the yard. He walked away from the house to talk to him. "Keenan?"

"Over here." Keenan's voice drifted across the yard from the stable. "How's it going?"

"I just got here. I'm getting ready to go in," whispered Slim.

"I wish I could go with you," replied Keenan.

"By the way, how's Nick doing?" asked Slim.

"Christopher was watching him, so I stopped by to let him know we all needed to meet. Nick was chattering away to the real Slim. Probably bringing him up to date is my guess," said Keenan.

"I still don't like him being there," sighed Slim.

"Well, to tell you the truth, I don't either. But I have to agree that this may be the break we've needed. Nick's in a position to share enough information with our real selves to get everyone out of there safely, and maybe blow the lid off this whole situation," said Keenan.

"Yeah, but we haven't figured out a plan yet. Where are Christopher and Michael now?" asked Slim.

"Michael is checking on Mr. Billings, and Christopher was going to stop in and check on Jeb. After that, they're going to head over to the workshop for more instructions," replied Keenan.

"Well, why don't you head back to the workshop and make a pot of coffee. I'll be there soon. Right now, I'm going in to find out what these guys are planning to do. It's going to be another long night," said Slim as he turned and disappeared.

"That's for sure," sighed Keenan as he walked across the yard to the workshop.

Later, as the night wore on, the spirits gathered, one by one, back at the workshop. There was much to talk about. When dawn came, everyone was still pacing the floor.

Keenan's ghost gazed out the workshop window toward the ranch, watching the real Michael, Christopher, Keenan, and the sheriff get up from the kitchen table and head out to the stable.

"They're moving, guys," said Slim as his wispy form appeared in the workshop. "They know that Nick was taken last night. They spoke to a miner who thought he saw the general store wagon heading toward the Black Stallion Mine, and of course, Nick never returned to the store yesterday after his delivery to the Falcon Mine. They're trying to keep everything quiet to avoid a full-blown panic in town. It's taking every bit of control they have not to storm the Black Stallion Mine, but they don't know where Slim, Stanley, and Nick are. So they're going to investigate quietly, and we are going to help. So, Michael, get to Nick right away. You'll have to get him into the tunnel that leads from the cavern to the main cave in order to talk to him. Tell him that he needs to ask for paper and ink.

"Christopher, watch the opening where the guards are stationed and make sure that they can't hear Nick and Michael talking. Warn Michael immediately if Billings or anyone else decides to visit the cave this early. When Michael finishes with Nick, follow Mr. Billings. Maybe you'll get some information we can use. Michael, you need to memorize the layout of the tunnel that leads to the cavern. I want to know the fastest way in and out. Nick has good drawing skills, so you'll help Nick draw a map. Also, take a good look at the tunnel they've been digging. We have to find out what's so special about it. And I need you to locate where they have stored the explosives."

"What are you going to be doing, Slim?" asked Keenan.

"I'm going to find Mr. Jenkins and listen in on his conversation with Jeb," said Slim.

"We're really flying by the seat of our pants on this one," said Michael.

"You're right. I didn't anticipate any of this. But, if we keep our wits about us, we should be able to get everyone out safely without exposing ourselves," said Slim.

"Okay, you all know what to do. Let's touch base in about two hours at the Black Stallion Mine," said Slim, and he began to fade away.

Chapter Thirty-Seven

THE BLACK STALLION SECRET CAVERN

Nick was dreaming when he felt a solid nudge against his shoulder. Half awake, he raised his head and peered around the dimly lit cave. He didn't see anybody, so he dropped his head onto his pillow to try to fall back asleep. Another nudge, harder this time, made him jolt upright.

Stanley and Slim were still sound asleep, if their snoring was any indication. Only one lantern was lit and it cast weird shadows on the cave walls. Out of the corner of his eye, Nick saw Michael materializing near the cavern entrance. Michael waved Nick toward him. As quietly as possible, Nick got up and crept over to Michael. Putting a finger to his lips, Michael turned and headed into the tunnel, stopping a few yards in, far from where the guards stood.

Michael reached out and grabbed Nick's shoulder gently. "Are you all right?" he whispered. "We're pretty worried about you."

"I know. At least I'm really doing something to help, though. It may be the only way to get Slim and Stanley out of here alive," whispered Nick.

"Well, Slim thinks you may be right. So here's what we need you to do. Mr. Billings is going to take Stanley and Slim down into the tunnel they've been working on. We don't think they'll take you. Like he said in his office, you're his insurance against Slim rebelling. Billings wants to make sure you're kept safe. So when they come in here for Slim and Stanley, ask for paper and ink so that you can draw to keep yourself busy," said Michael.

"Draw?" asked Nick.

"The plan is for you to draw a map of this place. I'm going to learn the layout of the cave in the side of the mountain and this tunnel, and then I'll work with you while Slim and Stanley are gone. We'll make an exact map of how to find this place, and then we'll plant it where the sheriff and the real guys will find it. Then they'll know where to find you, Stanley, and Slim."

"Hey, that's a great idea," said Nick, feeling relieved that they'd thought of a plan.

Suddenly Christopher materialized beside Michael. "Hey, Nick. It's good to see you. I hate to break this up, but Mr. Billings and his crew are heading this way. We've got to scoot and fast."

"Go back and lie down, Nick. I'll get back with you a little later," said Michael as he and Christopher disappeared.

Nick turned and hurried back to his blankets. He barely got settled before footsteps echoed down the tunnel.

"Wake up, wake up! It's time to get to work," bellowed Mr. Billings. Moaning, Stanley rolled over and slowly sat up. Slim rubbed his hands over his face and then pushed himself upright. Nick tried to make it seem that he had been sound asleep, rolling over in his blankets with his eyes wide open, but not sitting up.

"Good morning, gentlemen. It's time for Stanley and Slim to do some work for me. Nick, you are welcome to go back to sleep. You'll be staying here today," explained Mr. Billings.

"Gentlemen, if you will follow me, we have breakfast waiting for you with plenty of coffee. Nick, someone will be bringing your breakfast later," said Mr. Billings.

"So what will we be doing today, Pernell?" asked Slim as he stood up and stretched.

"I'll let you know what I need from you when we are away from prying ears," said Mr. Billings. "Let's get going."

"Mr. Billings, sir," said Nick.

"Yes, Nick?"

"Since I'm going to be alone here all day, could I have some paper and ink so that I can draw?" asked Nick.

"Draw?" asked Mr. Billings.

"Yeah, just to pass the time," said Nick.

"Well, I don't see a problem with it. I'll have Jeb bring you some things when he brings your breakfast," said Mr. Billings, then he turned and led Slim and Stanley out of the cave.

★ ★ ★

After Slim and Stanley finished their breakfast, Stanley followed the fore-man deep into the tunnel and Slim remained with Mr. Billings.

"All right, Slim, I'm going to explain why I brought you here and why I need your assistance," said Mr. Billings.

"I'm all ears," replied Slim.

"I am aware of the diamond discovery at the Falcon Mine and Otis's plan to hide that discovery from the financial board. Rest assured, despite what you may think of me, I did not kill Otis. I had a hand in creating the inves-tigation of the Falcon Mine in order to force Otis out, but Otis wouldn't see me the night he was killed," said Mr. Billings.

"You'll have to forgive me if I have a hard time believing you, especially under my present circumstances," said Slim.

"What you believe at this point is of no concern to me," continued Mr. Billings. "When I saw the pit, I started thinking. This mountain butts up against your mountain. There is a good chance that there are similar diamond deposits in this mountain. I realized that the pit you found was very deep in the mountain, so I had a few trusted miners move to the back of this mountain, where the caves run deep, and begin digging. I need your expertise to determine if there are similar rock formations to those that were found near the pit in the Falcon Mine."

"Pernell, you could have just asked me, you didn't have to kidnap me," Slim said with a sigh.

"Yes, I'm sure you would have been more than happy to take time away from your own mine to help me develop the Black Stallion," sneered Billings.

Slim had nothing to say. He knew Billings was right.

"All right, you have me now. Release Nick and I'll help you," said Slim.

"I can't do that. Nick is a great kid, but he knows too much. I can't have him running to the sheriff. But I give you my word that if you cooperate, I won't hurt him," replied Billings.

"What happens after everything is said and done, Pernell? What are you going to do with Stanley, Nick, and me?" asked Slim.

"To be honest with you, I haven't thought that far ahead. But if you're on your best behavior, I'll be more inclined to let you go. Well, Slim, as much as I have enjoyed our little talk, I need to get back to the office. I'll take you to where Stanley and the men are currently working and have the foreman guide you around the area," said Billings.

Billings led Slim further into the cave and down the tunnel the miners had dug. They were deep inside the mountain. Slim studied the tunnel walls as they walked deeper and deeper. *This doesn't feel right,* he thought. Slim sensed a change in the atmosphere. It was getting warmer, and the air was moist and musty. The sound of picks and hammers in the distance grew louder as they approached the end of the tunnel. They passed a man standing guard with a whip and a rifle, and approached a group of men who looked up briefly, but then dropped their gazes and went back to work. One man moved away from the group.

"Slim, this is Max; he's the foreman. He'll get you started and get you any-thing you need. Take good care of him, Max," said Mr. Billings as he turned and walked back up the tunnel.

"Have a good look around and let me know what you need or where you need to go. You saw the guard, I'm sure. His instructions are to shoot you if you try to pass without me," warned Max.

Slim spent some time studying the tunnel walls. He caught one of the rock fragments that fell from a miner's pick, examined it, then placed it in his pocket. "Okay, first I need to take a good look at that wall the guys are working on right now. Can they take a coffee break or something for a few minutes? I can't work while they're digging."

"I think that can be arranged," replied Max.

Nick was tired after having woken up so early and decided to try to get more sleep. A couple of hours later, the echo of footsteps reverberating off the walls of the narrow tunnel woke Nick. He sat up just as Jeb and another miner entered the cave. "Here's your breakfast, Nick," said Jeb. He walked over to Nick and handed him a plate and a glass of milk. "Billings said you asked for paper and ink, so here it is," added Jeb as the other man handed Nick a large leather pouch.

"Thank you," said Nick as he took the pouch and laid it down beside him.

Jeb brought in a few more lanterns to add light to the cavern, and the other man traded out the chamber pot for an empty one. "Someone will be back around lunchtime to get these dishes and bring you something to eat. Until then, just keep yourself busy," chuckled Jeb, and then both men walked out of the cavern, leaving Nick alone.

After he finished his breakfast, Nick opened the leather pouch to find a stack of paper, ink, and charcoal. He spent the next hour drawing carica-tures of Jeb, Parker, and Mr. Billings. He had just started doing Slim, when Michael began to appear in a dark corner of the cave.

"Hey, Nick. Good, I see that you got the paper. I have the layout of this place pretty well memorized. Are you ready to draw a map?" asked Michael.

"Yep. Let's get started," said Nick.

Nick and Michael had almost finished the map when they heard the sound of footsteps echoing down the tunnel. Michael took what they had worked on and disappeared. He reappeared after the guard who delivered Nick's lunch had left.

"The guys won't have any trouble getting in here, but they're going to need a note from you telling them about the guards. They need to know what to expect," said Michael.

"Sure," said Nick.

Christopher suddenly appeared, startling both of them. "Sorry, guys. I just wanted to stop by and find out how it's going."

"We're just about done here. What's going on with Billings?" asked Michael.

"Well, he got another visit from the sheriff this morning, this time about Slim's disappearance. Needless to say, Billings is not happy about all of the attention from the sheriff. The sheriff asked for the mine manifest, so I think he might be trying to figure out who Buck is," said Christopher. "Billings has Buck back over at the Falcon Mine snooping around. But the real Michael has placed guards around the office. No one is allowed in without his permission. So Buck won't be getting in there again.

"The real guys suspect that Buck is a Black Stallion plant. The real Keenan spotted him earlier and has been tracking him. The real Christopher is currently snooping around the Black Stallion Mine, mostly keeping to the woods, but watching all the mine entrances. It looks like he's trying to get a handle on the layout of the office and the mine entrance," said Christopher.

"What's the sheriff up to now?" asked Nick.

"After Artemus finished with Billings, he went back to town to the Land Claims office. He's pulled all of the registered maps of the Black Stallion Mine and has taken them back to his office, where he's been studying them ever since. It looks like they may be preparing to storm the place," said Christopher.

"Well, this map that Nick and I just drew will help them storm the right place—unnoticed and safely," said Michael.

"Here's the note to go with the map," said Nick as he handed Michael another piece of paper.

Michael took the note and read it, then folded it up with the map and put them in his pocket. "Well, I need to take off now and get this to Slim. He's going to plant it in the sheriff's office. Christopher will stay with you for a while and I'll send Keenan in a little bit. We'll rotate so that we can keep you company until Stanley and Slim get back," said Michael.

"That will be good. It's pretty lonely," said Nick.

"Okay, I'm off to check on the real Slim and Stanley, then I'll get with our Keenan and Slim and show them what we drew up. I'll touch base with you later." Michael slowly faded and disappeared.

Mr. Billings had Jeb running around all morning, so he did not get to town to hunt down Mr. Jenkins until after lunch. Jeb found him in his office going over some paperwork.

"Good afternoon, sir. Mr. Billings sent me. He wanted me to make sure that Slim did not file beneficiary paperwork. He also wants me to return with the diamond discovery paperwork and the sample," said Jeb.

"And if I choose not to comply with his wishes?" questioned Jenkins with a hint of amusement in his voice.

"He'll personally come down to your office and rip it out of your hand. He wants to make sure he has all the paperwork concerning the discovery. My guess is he wants to make sure that it is destroyed. His way of tying up loose ends," reasoned Jeb.

"I've come to the conclusion, Jeb, that Mr. Billings is not capable of tying up loose ends. That's probably why his mine has so many problems," said Mr. Jenkins. "As of this moment, Slim has not filed any beneficiary paperwork.

In the event something happened to him, the Falcon Mine Company would be placed up for sale. I do have the diamond deposit paperwork, but I think it's about time for Mr. Billings's luck to change. Tell him that I'll bring the paperwork to him myself in a day or two. If you and I still have a deal, I think the time has come. Notify Buck and see if he's interested in our little arrangement. If he is, then you can decide between yourselves which mine you want to run when this is all said and done. I will let you know when it's time for us to meet. I have a few things to tie up. Then I think it will be time for me and Pernell to square off for the last time," said Mr. Jenkins.

"We still have a deal," replied Jeb. "I'll keep you updated if anything changes. I'll wait for word from you about our next meeting." Jeb turned to leave.

"Good," said Mr. Jenkins. "Till then."

Slim and Stanley got back late, according to Nick's watch. They looked exhausted. The foreman had let them stop somewhere and wash their faces and hands, but their clothes were covered in dirt. The two men sank wearily onto their blankets just as two miners came in with plates of food, pitchers of water, and mugs of coffee. Slim and Stanley both just stared at their plates of food, too tired to eat.

After drinking half a pitcher of water, Slim finally picked up his fork and started to pick at his food. Not able to wait any longer, Nick asked, "What happened today?"

"I dug a lot, as usual," answered Stanley. "But Slim got to move around. From the looks of him, I think he had to crawl in places I wouldn't have wanted to go."

"Yeah, you're right, Stanley. I crawled through some spaces today that would have unnerved most guys I know. Billings shared some of his plan with me, but I don't want to disclose anything just yet. I don't want him to think that either of you knows too much." Turning toward Nick, Slim asked, "So what did you do today to keep yourself busy? Did Jeb bring you some paper?"

"Yep, I've been doodling all day," said Nick.

"Well, let's see what you drew," said Stanley.

For the next hour, Slim, Nick, and Stanley laughed and joked about the characters that Nick had drawn. Then Slim and Stanley took turns posing for Nick so that he could sharpen his skills. But after a bit, Slim and Stanley had to call it a night. Nick stayed up a while longer writing all the names of the people involved and their relationships with each other. "One of these guys is a killer, but which one?" he whispered as he finally lay down and drifted off to sleep.

★   ★   ★

The next day was pretty much the same as the day before. Mr. Billings's crew came and got Slim and Stanley early, and Nick was left behind.

Keenan stopped by after lunch. He figured that Nick could use a break and ported him back to the workshop to stretch his legs. Slim slowly appeared a few minutes later and gave Nick a huge hug.

"Glad you could join us. I want to fill you in on what we're going to do. I didn't think talking about it in the cave would be a wise idea," said Slim.

"So what's going on?" asked Nick.

"We've managed to keep a close eye on the guys and their plans. We're hoping that if we give you enough information, you should be able to help," said Keenan.

"The sheriff and the guys think that Slim, Stanley, and you are being held in the mine. So they're working on a plan to get into the mine to search for you," said Slim. "I'm going to take your map and note to the sheriff's office later this afternoon. Then everything should move quickly."

"They haven't worked out all of the details yet, but we'll let you know what you'll need to do as soon as we learn more."

"Sounds good to me," said Nick.

Nick had been out of the cave for some time, so Slim took him back to his damp and dark prison.

Nick kept himself busy doodling in the late afternoon. In the evening, Slim and Stanley were brought back from another day in the tunnels. Both men were bone tired and ate dinner in silence. Later, while Stanley rested, Slim began pacing the floor.

"What's wrong, Slim?" asked Nick.

"The tunnel that Billings has been digging is unstable. Using any more explosives will either cause a cave-in or break through to an underground river about four hundred feet right below it. The river will flood the mineshaft, and will probably flood all the lower tunnels in the main mine as well," said Slim.

"Slim, can Mr. Billings get ahold of the Falcon Mine Company?" asked Nick.

"Possibly, if something happens to me. I haven't filed my beneficiary paperwork yet. But to be honest, I don't believe Billings would risk another murder. It would look too suspicious and draw too much attention. There would be another investigation, probably including the financial board and Land Claims office. Billings would have a hard time getting his hands on the mine," explained Slim.

A few moments later, the sound of footsteps echoed through the cavern. Slim looked up toward the cave entrance. "It sounds like Billings got my request for a meeting," said Slim.

A few minutes later, Mr. Billings and Jeb walked into the cave. "I heard you have a report for me," said Mr. Billings.

Slim stood up and gave Mr. Billings a hard look. "My report is not good. The rock formations here are not the same as those in the Falcon Mine. I'm sorry, Pernell, but I see no evidence of any volcanic activity, pressure fissures, or kimberlite rock. There are no diamond deposits."

"But five hundred feet below you is an underground river. The tunnel you're digging is only going to be about four hundred feet above it. If you use any explosives, you run the risk of flooding that tunnel. If you're not careful, you could also flood the upper tunnels in the mine. Billings, you need to stop what you're doing or you could be responsible for a lot of deaths this time." Slim's tone was almost pleading.

Mr. Billings said nothing, but glared at Slim thoughtfully. Nick could see the anger slowly rising in Mr. Billings face and how he fought to control his temper.

"Well, I see what you're trying to do, Slim. You think that if you can convince me to abandon this tunnel and my search for diamonds then I'll let you all go," said Mr. Billings through gritted teeth.

"It's not a lie!" cried Slim. "You're putting a lot of people in danger, Billings. If you don't believe me, then have someone else check it out before you do anything."

Billings glared at Slim. Then he turned and walked toward the tunnel with Jeb on his heel.

"Billings!" yelled Slim. "Billings!"

There was no response. Several moments later, the sound of footsteps was gone. Sighing deeply, Slim turned and sat down beside Nick. Groaning, he lowered his head into his hands. "I shouldn't have lost my head like that. But I know Billings. He's not going to listen to me, or anyone else for that matter. He will do what he wants to do. Safety has never been important to him. As far as he's concerned, miners are replaceable," groaned Slim.

Mr. Billings was silent as he walked out of the cave to his horse. He mounted and rode to his office. He stomped up the stairs to his office, jerked open the door, and slumped into his chair. Jeb walked in a few minutes later.

"What do you want me to do?" asked Jeb.

Mr. Billings tapped his fingers on the top of his desk. "Did Jenkins give you the paperwork and diamond samples yet?"

"I told you, he's bringing it here himself tomorrow morning. He wants to talk to you," replied Jeb.

"Hmm, we need to tie up a lot of loose ends," muttered Mr. Billings.

"Yeah. When Mr. Jenkins brings the paperwork, that's the end of any paper trail concerning the new discovery at the Falcon Mine," replied Jeb.

"Possibly, but not the people trail," said Mr. Billings.

"People trail?"

"Yes, Jeb. There are a lot of people who know about the diamonds at the Falcon Mine. If Slim is right, and I haven't known him to be wrong, one well-placed explosion could successfully eliminate all of our problems— Slim, Jenkins, Parker, Stanley, Nick, and Slim's meddling friends. It would look like another unfortunate accident. Then I could volunteer to take over the operation of the Falcon Mine, keep it running, keep the men employed while cleanup was being done over here. Mining out all of those diamonds would give me the capital to buy the Falcon Mine Company. Then I could operate both mines free and clear," explained Billings.

"Mr. Billings, you're talking about killing eight or more people, not to mention those miners who are scheduled to work that day," stuttered Jeb.

"Do you have a better idea? If you do, I'd like to hear it," sneered Mr. Billings. "We are out of options!"

"I see your point," whispered Jeb.

"Good! Tell the men to come in late tomorrow. Those who don't take advantage of my generosity will just have to be sacrificed. Now, I need you to make sure Mr. Jenkins is down here for the meeting first thing tomorrow morning, let's say eight o'clock. Also, deliver an anonymous note to Slim's friends, letting them know where Slim is and that he'll be unguarded early tomorrow morning. We'll have a reunion before the fireworks show," chuckled Billings.

"Yes, sir," replied Jeb.

"Don't look so glum, Jeb. You are in this up to your eyeballs, but at least you'll end up a rich man. Now, go hook up with Buck. I want him to start setting up the explosives. The detonator should be a safe distance from the mountain itself, just in case Slim is right," said Mr. Billings.

"I'll have it set up by this evening, Mr. Billings," replied Jeb as he turned to leave.

"Good," replied Mr. Billings. He reached for a stack of papers on his desk. "At least we are finally making some progress."

Chapter Thirty-Eight
THE TRUTH

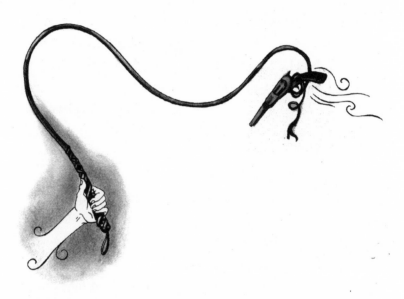

"Guys! We finally got the break we needed!" yelled the sheriff as he rushed into the Falcon Mine office.

"What do you mean?" asked Christopher.

"It's a note from Nick," said Keenan, looking over the sheriff's shoulder. The sheriff held out the map for them to examine. "If this is for real, and it seems to be, then we know exactly where Slim, Stanley, and Nick are being held."

"Where did you get this?" asked Michael.

"On my chair in my office," said the sheriff. "I'm guessing one of the miners must have befriended Nick and developed a conscience. He must have snuck it out for him."

"Well, we also got a note this afternoon. Somebody slid it under the office door," said Michael, holding out a scrap of paper.

"What does it say?" asked the sheriff.

"If we ever want to see Nick, Slim, and Stanley again, we should show up tomorrow morning at the Black Stallion Mine office. It also says that we are being watched, and that we had better not notify any authorities," replied Michael.

"Well," began Christopher "I believe we have the upper hand in this. They may be watching us, but we are also watching them."

"That's right! Has Keenan checked in yet?" asked the sheriff.

"No, he's still tracking the guy who's been following us," replied Michael. "He's going to meet us at the ranch tonight. I'm hoping he might have been able to gather more information for us."

★ ★ ★

In the woods outside the Black Stallion Mine, the three ghostly forms of Keenan, Christopher, and Michael slowly appeared. Moments later, Slim appeared next to them.

"Okay, what have we got?" asked Slim.

"Billings is planning to blow the tunnel and flood the mine shaft. Everybody who knows about the diamonds will be killed. He thinks it will look like an accident," whispered Keenan.

"Jeb is heading into town to talk to Jenkins right now," said Christopher.

"Buck is watching the real Michael and Christopher. He doesn't know that Keenan is tracking him," reported Michael.

"Okay, the sheriff got the note and map from Nick, but it seems like the guys also received a note in the mine office. It said that if they want to see the real Slim, Stanley, and Nick, they are to report to the Black Stallion Mine office tomorrow at eight o'clock," said Slim.

"What do you want to do?" asked Christopher.

"We need to get to Nick and brief him on what's happening. I want him to know that we're going to let the situation play out a bit longer," said Slim. "We have to make sure he's safe, guys, so let's gather as much information as we can."

Moments later, the four wispy figures had disappeared.

The real Keenan returned to the ranch house later that evening with his report. He briefed the sheriff, Michael, and Christopher about what he saw when he tracked Buck to the back of the Black Stallion mountain. In turn, they told Keenan about the notes they had received. The four of them stayed up all night developing a plan, but they knew that in the end everything would depend on what Mr. Billings was planning. So in the wee hours of the morning, they left for the back of the Black Stallion Mine mountain to survey the cave and tunnel and try to discover Mr. Billings's plan.

When they arrived at the mountain, dawn was several hours away. They were surprised to see miners working around the cave, carrying torches to light their way. They spotted Jeb working some distance from the cave behind an outcropping of rock.

"There seems to be a lot of movement considering it's the middle of the night. Makes you think they might be up to something," whispered Keenan.

Michael chuckled quietly. "Yeah, but my question is what is Billings even doing on this side of the mountain?"

"I have no idea," replied the sheriff. "None of the registered maps from the Land Claims Office show any activity on this side."

"Well, clearly something's going on. And I'm guessing with all the movement this morning and the note from Billings, it's something big," said Keenan.

"Hey, it looks like some of the men are leaving," whispered Michael.

"That's good. The fewer men we have to handle when we make our move, the better," said Keenan.

"Do you have the map, Artemus?" asked Michael.

"Yes, right here. I'm thinking we just need to wait for most of the men to leave, keep an eye on Jeb, and then make our move."

"Well, it won't be too long," whispered Keenan. "Looks like all the men are leaving. There's another group coming out of the cave right now."

"It could be that Billings had a night shift working," said Michael. "No men are arriving, so we should make our move soon."

Nick was in a deep sleep when somebody shook his shoulder and whispered in his ear. Rousing himself, he opened his eyes slightly and peered in the darkness. A soft light shone from the entrance of the cavern. Nick rose and slowly made his way over to the tunnel.

When he peered around the corner, he saw the glowing form of Keenan waiting for him. "Sorry, Nick, for having to wake you. Slim wanted me to brief you. You have to be ready for anything this morning. Billings is clearing the workers from this side of the mine, and he's planning to blow the tunnel they've been working in. Jeb used more explosives than necessary, so there's no telling what the result might be. Billings is hoping to get rid of all of his problems—at least the people—in one big explosion. Your map was delivered as planned, and the sheriff and the real gang are outside waiting for the miners to leave before they make their way in here."

"What do you want me to do?" asked Nick.

"Just be alert. We aren't sure at this point how this is going to play out, so we will be keeping a close eye on everything. The most important thing for you to remember is that we are here. Even though we have some restrictions, we will do everything we can to help. The moment we think you're in real danger, we'll get you out of here, no matter what," said Keenan.

"Okay," replied Nick, as fear and excitement battled to control him.

"Now, try to relax. We'll see you in a little while," said Keenan.

As the night sky began to lighten, the last group of miners got on their horses and rode away. The rescue party was ready to enter the cave when they heard the pounding of horse hooves heading toward them. They quickly took cover.

Jeb and Parker emerged from the cave and watched Mr. Billings dismount.

"Is everything ready?" asked Mr. Billings.

"Yes, sir. Everything is set up just as you asked," said Jeb.

"Where's Buck?" asked Mr. Billings.

"He's around here somewhere," said Jeb.

"Fine time for him to be roaming around," growled Mr. Billings. "Let's just go and get this over with then."

"Yes, sir," said Jeb.

The three men climbed the rocky path that led to the cave and then disappeared inside.

The sheriff turned to Michael, Keenan, and Christopher with a serious look. "I believe it's showtime. Let's go, boys." They scrambled out from behind the bushes and climbed up to the cave.

Nick was still awake and his heart was beating fast when he heard the resounding footsteps echoing through the rock corridor. *It's time,* he thought. He glanced toward the still-sleeping forms of Slim and Stanley.

Shortly, the light from a torch illuminated the tunnel that led to their cavern. Nick reached over and shook Slim's leg, then sat up just as Mr. Billings, Parker, and Jeb entered the cavern.

"Good morning, gentlemen," said Mr. Billings, a malicious grin twisting his mouth.

Slim sat up and stretched as Stanley opened his eyes and yawned.

"I have good and bad news for you," said Mr. Billings.

Slim rubbed his chin and glanced up. "Billings, it's early. What are you talking about?"

"The good news is that I'm not going to make you or Stanley work today. You could say that I'm giving you the day off."

"What's the bad news, Mr. Billings?" asked Stanley.

"I'm afraid that I have no more use for your services," answered Mr. Billings.

A few moments passed before the meaning behind Mr. Billings's words dawned on the men. Slim and Stanley leapt to their feet. Feeling threatened, Billings and Jeb pulled out their six-shooters.

Slim became still, staring at Mr. Billings.

"So that's your plan? You're just going to shoot us? I suppose you think that with me gone you'll be free to grab the Falcon Mine and the diamonds, is that it?" asked Slim.

"Now, Slim, I know this news is quite upsetting, but you're just too clever for your own good. You did make one mistake, though; you never filed beneficiary paperwork. Once you're gone, the mine will go up for sale. I'll get the diamonds out of there and use them to buy the mine. It's fairly ingenious when you think about it."

"But what about Nick?" asked Slim. "He's just a boy. You just can't snuff out his life like this. Let him go. I'm sure he won't tell anyone if he promises not to," said Slim.

"Ah, Nick, my dear boy," said Mr. Billings as turned his gaze to Nick. "I am so sorry that you got caught up in this. Please believe me, it's nothing personal. It's just circumstances."

"Don't do this," pleaded Slim.

"Well, I am not going to shoot you, if that's what you're thinking. Jeb has wired the tunnel wall with explosives, and we're going to blow it this morning. Since we aren't sure of the outcome, we thought it would be best to leave you all here. If you're right, then I will have buried all my loose ends with a big bang and a flood. If you're wrong, then we'll have to reevaluate our plans."

"Billings, you're crazy. What about your men on the other side of the mountain?" asked Slim.

"Well, thanks to you, we decided to do it early and told the miners to come in late today. I think that was very considerate. Only a handful of miners will have arrived, so few will be lost."

"Billings!" Into the cavern walked the sheriff, Keenan, Michael, and Christopher. They all held rifles leveled at Billings and Jeb. "You won't be blowing up anything today, my friend. You and your sidekick here are under arrest, so put your guns on the ground and your hands in the air," growled the sheriff.

Nick rose from where he was sitting and walked over to stand beside Slim, who put his arm protectively around Nick's shoulders.

"Boy, am I glad to see you guys," said Slim.

"After hearing what Billings just said, I don't doubt it," said Michael. Keenan stepped forward to retrieve Mr. Billings's and Jeb's guns.

"I think I've heard and seen enough to put Billings, Parker, and Jeb away for a long time. I might even get a conviction against you for Otis Walkins's murder," said the sheriff.

"Oh, don't be so stupid, Artemus. I had nothing to do with Otis's death. I needed him alive to blackmail him. Which, in the long run, would have made this whole situation unnecessary," retorted Mr. Billings.

"A likely story," said Keenan.

"Ah, yes, a likely story indeed. But unfortunately he's telling you the truth."

Whirling around, they all were shocked to see Mr. Jenkins and Buck standing in the entrance to the cavern holding rifles.

"Now, isn't this interesting," growled Mr. Jenkins.

Suddenly Nick felt cold, the hair on the back of his neck stood up, and he began to shake. Stammering, he said, "I know that voice. It was you . . . you killed Otis."

"Jeb, please relieve the sheriff and his friends of their guns and bring them here. Now, Nick, the only way that you would have known that small detail is if you were in the office that night," sighed Mr. Jenkins as he pulled his watch out of his pocket to check the time.

"I see you're missing your watch fob, Jenkins. It was your watch chain that Otis had in his hand, wasn't it?" asked the sheriff.

"My, my, what a smart group! Nick, it's a terrible shame you witnessed Otis's murder. You leave me with no choice. I will have to kill you, too. I can't have you walking around knowing the truth, now can I?" asked Mr. Jenkins.

Mr. Billings took a step forward, and Mr. Jenkins stopped him.

"Now, Pernell, where do you think you're going?" asked Mr. Jenkins.

"I was going to stand by Jeb. After all, we've been partners from the beginning," said Mr. Billings.

"That is true, but I would thank you if you returned to your spot. I'm terminating our partnership. I've been told that I was supposed to be another victim in this flood you're planning. I'm fed up with your bungling. You're nothing but an egotistical moron, and to be honest, I am glad to finally be rid of you," said Mr. Jenkins.

"Jeb? Buck?" Mr. Billings's voice carried a note of desperation.

"Billings, Jeb and Buck work for me now. Jeb has been keeping me informed of your plans since you gave his job to Parker. So, with his help, I am taking over. I promised that I would reward them greatly and give them ownership shares in both mines," replied Mr. Jenkins.

Mr. Jenkins turned away from Mr. Billings and said to Buck, "Go ahead and get going. We'll be there in a few minutes."

Nodding, Buck took off out of the cavern.

"Now, Nick, I want you to come stand by me," said Mr. Jenkins. Nick hesitated for several seconds. As he scanned the cavern, looking for anything that might help them out of this situation, he saw imps creeping out of the shadows. Nick breathed in deeply, trying to bury the fear that threatened to overwhelm him. He did not want to draw the imps' attention.

"Now, Nick, or I will be forced to put a bullet in Slim."

Quickly, Nick left his position beside Slim and walked up to Jenkins. Jenkins placed his free arm around Nick's neck and pulled him close.

"Now, gentlemen, please be seated. Any sudden moves or heroics, and I will shoot you and then Nick. Jeb, tie them up."

Jeb lay down his rifle and moved around the group of men, tying everyone up with rope. Once he was done, he returned to his place by Mr. Jenkins and Nick and picked up his rifle.

"What are you going to do with Nick?" asked Slim.

"The boy is going to go with me. He's my insurance policy to make sure that we get out of here safely. Don't worry! Once all of you experience the big bang, I'll take care of Nick. Besides, Buck's been asking for him, so I will probably let him deal with him," explained Mr. Jenkins in a cold voice.

"Oh, and by the way, Slim, I didn't file your new discovery papers, and I didn't send the samples to Washington. And because you failed to file your beneficiary paperwork, I am now in a perfect position to buy the Falcon Mine Company when it finally becomes available. We're taking care of anybody who knows about the pit," chuckled Mr. Jenkins. "Well, I'm afraid it's time for us to go, we do have someone waiting for us." He slowly turned Nick around and walked toward the tunnel.

Meanwhile, at the other end of the tunnel stood the invisible forms of Slim, Michael, Keenan, and Christopher. They had watched as Buck and Mr. Jenkins had entered the cavern, discussing their plans. It had become obvious that Mr. Jenkins was Otis's killer. Buck had just emerged from the tunnel and headed for the cave exit, so they knew they didn't have much time.

"What do we do now?" asked Keenan.

"Frankly, I'm tired of this guy," replied Michael.

"Me too," said Christopher.

"Then we're all in agreement. Let's settle this for the last time. The old fashioned way, shall we?" said Slim, with an almost cheerful lift in his voice.

"Boy, I was hoping you would say that," said Christopher.

Just then, Nick emerged from the tunnel, followed by Mr. Jenkins and Jeb. The imps danced and leapt all around them, and a few were balancing on Mr. Jenkins's and Jeb's shoulders. They were obviously delighted with the current turn of events.

Nick was doing his best to remain calm. As he stepped out of the tunnel from the cavern, he saw the two guards who had been guarding the entrance sprawled out on the ground. "Be prepared for anything," he muttered under his breath, remembering Keenan's advice. He peered about the dimly lit cave, searching for a clue to what was going to happen next.

"What the—!" exclaimed Mr. Jenkins when he spotted the guards on the floor. Before he could move toward the closest guard, the gun he had pressed in Nick's back was suddenly snatched away and was flying through the air, seemingly of its own accord.

Mr. Jenkins stood still, his mouth hanging open in shock. Jeb stepped around him to see what was going on and tripped. The rifle he was carrying slid across the ground.

"What's going on here?" Mr. Jenkins yelled. He spotted his gun where it had landed against a rock wall. He took a few steps toward it, and it slid along the ground, moving away from him. He kept reaching for it, and it kept sliding away.

Nick noticed that the imps were wandering about, looking baffled. They were clearly unsure of what was going on.

Jeb picked himself up from the ground and headed toward his rifle, muttering, "It's nothing. I just tripped, that's all." As he bent down to pick up the rifle, he sprawled onto his stomach again.

"Jeb, I'm telling you, something's going on here. I can't get my hands on my gun. It keeps moving away from me," growled Mr. Jenkins. Frustrated, he lunged for the gun and crashed to the hard stone floor.

Jeb got up again, this time holding his ribs. "Okay, so what's happening?" he asked as he reached for his rifle one more time. Before he could lay a hand on it, Christopher materialized right before him. "What did you just do? How did you get out?" sputtered Jeb.

Christopher smiled lazily. "I'm just one of those special people that you'll never forget. Now, I've had just about enough of you, Jeb." He threw his fist into Jeb's jaw. Jeb crumbled to the floor, unconscious. "Goodnight!" whispered Christopher before disappearing.

"What did you say?" asked Mr. Jenkins as he turned around, only to discover Jeb lying on the ground. He caught a glimpse of Christopher's fading figure. He shook his head, then whirled around and glared at Nick. "What's going on here?! Are you responsible for this, boy?" yelled Mr. Jenkins.

"He isn't. I am," said Slim as he materialized right behind Mr. Jenkins.

Mr. Jenkins whirled around and came face to face with the wispy figure of Slim, who was slowly materializing. Then Michael, Keenan, and Christopher began to appear beside him.

"What the . . . how? This isn't possible," stammered Mr. Jenkins.

"It's a long story, Jenkins, and where you're going, you'll have plenty of time to try to figure it out. But right now all you need to know is that this is for Otis," Slim said. He slammed a fist into Mr. Jenkins's soft belly and then another into his chin, flipping him backwards onto the hard, cold floor of the cave. Mr. Jenkins lay there unconscious.

"Are you okay, Nick?" asked Slim.

"Wow, I am now," chuckled Nick. "That was great!"

"Yeah, that was pretty good, Slim," said Christopher.

"Hey, Nick, how did you like my fancy bullwhip trick?" asked Keenan with a huge grin.

"That was awesome. I was wondering how the guns were moving on their own," said Nick. "Hey, what about Buck? He's probably by the detonator, waiting for Jenkins and Jeb to come out."

"We had better let the real guys out first. Then they can deal with him. I think we've taken enough risks for today," said Slim.

"What happened to the imps? They just disappeared into thin air when they saw you guys," said Nick.

"I was afraid of that. Nevertheless, that was a risk we had to take. I don't think they can do much more damage since we've solved the mystery and exposed Mr. Jenkins as Otis's killer," explained Slim. "But right now, let's concentrate on getting everybody out of here. Nick, go back in there and untie everyone. We'll keep an eye on these guys until you can get someone out here to tie them up."

"Okay," said Nick, turning to head back into the tunnel. Then he stopped, turned back to his friends, and ran into Slim's arms. One by one, he hugged the others. "Thanks, you guys," he whispered.

The men were surprised to see Nick run back into the cavern. Nick dashed to the sheriff and untied him first. Then they worked to free everyone but Mr. Billings and Parker.

Nick quickly explained that some miners had come to his aid and knocked out Jeb and Mr. Jenkins, which was true. He just didn't mention that the miners were spirits. Grabbing the loose pieces of rope, the real Michael, Keenan, and Christopher ran through the tunnel to the main cave and quickly tied up Mr. Jenkins, Jeb, and the two guards. The sheriff ran out of the cave to round up Buck while the others dragged Mr. Jenkins and his gang to the entrance of the cave. Mr. Billings and Parker walked ahead of the gang with their hands tied tightly behind their backs. Stanley kept a rifle trained on them as they walked.

Nick had to cover his eyes for several moments when he emerged from the mouth of the cave to let his eyes adjust to the bright morning sunlight. It was good to be out of the damp, gloomy darkness. He took a deep breath of the fresh air.

"Nick, why don't you come with me to get a wagon. We need to transport all of this trash into town," said Keenan.

"Sure," replied Nick, happy to have an excuse to get away from the scene of so much violence and anger.

As Nick and Keenan left to retrieve a wagon, the real Slim and Michael went to find the sheriff, heading for the outcropping of rock where Jeb had been working earlier. Christopher and Stanley stayed behind to guard the prisoners. And on a not-too-distant hill, the four spirits watched over their real selves.

Slim and Michael slowly made their way over ledges and around the boulders. But when they finally climbed over the last ledge, they found the sheriff sprawled out on the dirt unconscious. Slim rushed to his side and carefully turned him over.

"Is he okay?" asked Michael, as he squatted down next to Slim.

"Yeah," answered Slim, relief clear in his voice. "He's coming around."

"Look at the knot on the side of his head. He's going to have quite a head-ache," said Michael.

"What happened, Artemus?" asked Slim as the sheriff opened his eyes.

"Buck must have seen me exiting the cave and realized that something had gone wrong. When I got here, he was gone. I detached all the wiring and removed the firing pin from the charge unit. I stood up, and then felt an incredible pain behind my ear. That's all I remember; I must have blacked out."

"Well, Buck's gone now. We'll have to look for him later. We need to get you back to town and have the doc take a look at you," said Slim. "Think you can walk?"

"Yeah, I think so," answered the sheriff, wincing as Michael helped him up.

"Stay close to him, Michael. He may get dizzy or pass out again," said Slim.

The three of them slowly worked their way back to where Christopher was waiting with the prisoners. A bit later, Keenan and Nick came up the path in a wagon, with horses in tow, to transport everyone back to town.

When they returned to Silverado, the group went directly to the jail and deposited Mr. Billings, Mr. Jenkins, Jeb, and Parker into separate cells. They had dropped Stanley off at his house, watching as his family had surrounded him, crying with happiness and relief. The sheriff took off to tell the mayor about the arrest, and Nick and Slim headed for the Grand Hotel to get cleaned up. Michael, Keenan, and Christopher took care of the wagon and horses. That evening everyone met at the hotel restaurant for a celebratory dinner. Otis's murder had been solved.

Chapter Thirty-Nine

LEAVING THE PAST

Nick did not get to see his ghostly friends at all during the next week, but he sensed that they were close by, watching over him. The week was a blur of activity as a posse hunted Buck and the trial began for Mr. Billings, Mr. Jenkins, Jeb, and Parker. Nick was called to testify for the prosecution, and when he was not on the stand, he was allowed to watch from the gallery.

It only took about a week to convict Mr. Jenkins of Otis Walkins's murder. He was to be hanged the following week. Mr. Billings was convicted on charges of racketeering, kidnapping, and the intent to commit murder. He was sentenced to life in prison. Jeb was convicted of conspiracy, aggravated assault, and kidnapping. Parker was convicted of conspiracy and kidnapping. Parker and Jeb also received life sentences. Mr. Billings, Parker, and Jeb were scheduled to be transported to the closest prison after Mr. Jenkins's hanging.

The evening before the final verdict was read in court, Nick found a note on his bed from the spirits.

Nick,

It's finally time to go back to your time zone. We will be leaving in three days, which should give you time to say goodbye to everyone. Let the real guys know that on Tuesday you need to be waiting for the coach in front of the general store at one o'clock. When the coach arrives, get in. We'll take it from there.

See you soon.

Your friends

Nick crumpled the piece of paper up into a ball and sighed. He had known this time would eventually come. All he wanted was to stay. Throwing the crumpled ball into the fire, Nick watched as it burned and then disintegrated into ashes.

That night, Nick told the real gang that his father had sent him a letter asking him to return home. He would be leaving in three days. By the looks on their faces, Nick could tell they were disappointed, but they tried hard not to show it.

The next day Nick returned to work, and was surprised to find Ben in the back room. As Ben told Nick about his trip, Nick could not help but smile. Timing was everything, and this seemed to be a sign that it really was time for him to go. That morning, he told Mr. Guillot that he would be leaving on Tuesday.

Nick's last three days in Silverado went quickly, as he tried to find time to say goodbye to all of the people he had met. On Tuesday, the real Slim and the guys brought him to the general store at noon. They had had lunch one last time at the hotel. In the distance, they could see the platform being built around the tree where they were going to hang Mr. Jenkins the next day. Nick was glad that he would not be around to see it.

A small crowd began to gather outside the general store to see Nick off. First, the only people were Mr. Guillot and Ben. Miss Corrine, the sheriff, and Stanley came over from the saloon. Then more people came from all directions, including Miss Terri.

Michael was standing beside Nick when he caught his first glimpse of Miss Terri. She glided over to Nick to give him a hug. Nick glanced up at Michael and could tell by the flush in his cheeks and the slightly glazed look in his eye that he was overwhelmed by the beautiful woman.

"I happen to know that she is unattached," whispered Nick as Miss Terri walked away.

"Really, now," mused Michael. "Sure she's not your gal, Nick?"

"She's too old for me! I think you should take the time to get to know her," replied Nick.

"Hmm . . . we're going to be staying with Slim for a while anyway, helping him get the Falcon Mine running smoothly. Maybe I'll stay at the ranch a bit longer than I was planning," said Michael, with a wink.

For Nick, his last thirty minutes were some of the hardest, as he talked to everyone and received lots of hugs from the ladies and strong handshakes from the guys. When the coach finally pulled up, the real Slim, Keenan, Michael, and Christopher stepped to the front of the crowd.

Christopher loaded Nick's burlap sack onto the coach. Nick had crept out to the workshop to retrieve his backpack the night before and had stuffed it into the burlap sack this morning. Turning to the guys, Nick found himself at a loss for words as tears welled up in his eyes.

Keenan was the first to speak, breaking the awkward silence. "We talked about this, and we don't know when we might see you again, so we each wanted to give you something that you could remember us by. This is for you, Nick, from me. Learn to use it safely and wisely." Keenan handed Nick his bullwhip.

Before Nick could utter a word, Michael stepped up, pulled out his beautiful pocket watch, and handed it to Nick. "All our names are engraved in the lid. Every time you look at this watch, know that we are thinking about you and looking forward to the time when we will see you again."

Christopher stepped up immediately after Michael. "This is from me. Use this safely, wisely, and only when you absolutely need it. It is not a toy, so be careful," he said as he handed Nick his big bowie knife and sheath.

Slim was the last to come forward. "I hope that you will accept all of these things from us, Nick. If you had not been here, I am not sure what would have happened. So this is just our way of saying thank you. You were our best asset, and we loved working with you. If you ever need a place to live, know that you will always have a home with us wherever we are. We consider you family." Then, reaching up, Slim removed the medallion from around his neck and placed it around Nick's neck.

Tears slipped quietly down Nick's face. He did not say anything but threw himself into Slim's arms. Then he hugged each of the guys, whispering his thanks. Finally, the coach driver coughed loudly, letting Nick know that it was time to go. When Nick was done saying his goodbyes, he turned and climbed into the coach. Slim shut the door behind him and reached up and wiped a tear that was sliding down Nick's face. As the coach pulled out, Nick hung out of the window and waved, yelling, "I promise I'll never forget you!" Nick kept waving as the coach rolled through town. He could see the guys wiping tears from their eyes. But they kept smiling, waving, and yelling until the wagon was finally out of sight.

As the coach rumbled along, Nick slid back inside and finally let go of the tears that he had been trying to hold back. He examined each gift the guys had given him. He felt so sad to be leaving, especially since he was uncertain what he would have to face upon his return home.

Nick pulled his backpack out of the burlap sack. He removed his jeans, T-shirt, and sneakers and carefully placed his friends' gifts inside. He changed his clothes and placed his cowboy clothes on the coach seat. Zipping up the backpack, he rested it beside him, and then reached up and touched the medallion that the real Slim had given him.

"It looks good on you," said a voice beside him.

Startled, Nick looked up. "Okay, where are you guys?" asked Nick.

"Well, right here, of course," said Keenan as he began to materialize opposite him.

"Are you okay?" asked Christopher appearing next to Keenan.

"Change is hard for everyone, Nick," replied Slim as he materialized right beside Nick.

"I'm okay, but honestly, I'd rather stay here than go home," said Nick.

"Your father needs you, Nick," said Slim quietly.

"My father just needs his work and his students. That's all he cares about," said Nick.

"Things change, Nick. People change. Especially when they lose something they didn't realize they could lose," replied Slim quietly.

"Slim's right, Nick. People do change, but sometimes only when they are forced to," added Christopher.

"Well, not my father," said Nick as he stared out the window.

"Say, where is Michael?" asked Nick, suddenly noticing that Michael was absent.

"He's up in the driver's seat with Otis," chuckled Keenan. "Michael wasn't so sure of Otis's driving ability."

"Otis is here!" exclaimed Nick.

"Yes. We thought you might like to see him. You wouldn't have recognized him when we were in town. Pretty good disguise, don't you think?" asked Slim with a wink.

The four of them continued to talk as the wagon bumped along. By the time it arrived at its destination, the guys had Nick chatting and laughing.

The carriage came to a stop, and a moment later, Michael popped his head in the window of the carriage door. "Hey, Nick! We're here. We'd best get going. We're on a schedule."

Everyone exited the carriage. Nick could see that they were back at Eagle Cliff Mountain. Turning around, he saw Otis climb down from the carriage seat.

"How are you, Nick?" asked Otis as he walked up to Nick and shook his hand.

"I'm fine, sir. But how are you?" asked Nick.

"Still learning the ropes, but I'm really happy," Otis said with a grin. "Nick, I just wanted to have the opportunity to thank you for not leaving me that night. Having you there made me think back to my childhood and the things my mother had taught me. She told me that there was someone who was always watching over me, trying to keep me on the right path. When you are facing death and the unknown, that starts to make a lot of sense. So at least I got a few moments to settle the things I had messed up, thanks to you."

"I'm just glad we found out who committed the crime," said Nick.

"And we're glad that you figured out that the mine accident wasn't really an accident," said Keenan.

"Yeah, we went on and lived normal lives," added Christopher.

"I'm grateful, too," said Michael. "I ended up marrying Miss Terri, and we had three kids. Two boys and a girl."

"Wow!" exclaimed Nick. "I never thought that all of your histories would be affected by us solving this mystery."

"You did great, Nick," said Slim as he patted him on the back. "You did more than what any of us thought you were capable of."

"Say, we'd better get going," said Keenan.

"Are you guys coming back to my time with me?" asked Nick.

"We are," said Keenan. "But Christopher needs to take Otis back, and then he'll meet us at the waterfall."

"Well, I guess I had better go," said Otis. "Thanks again, Nick, for being a smart kid, and for being a determined and responsible young man."

Nick walked up and gave Otis a hug. "You take care of these guys," he whispered.

"I will, Nick. Although I think they'll be taking care of me for a while," chuckled Otis.

Christopher and Otis slowly disappeared as Nick, Slim, Keenan, and Michael turned to climb up the mountain toward the cave, which they could see only a few hundred yards above them. They reached the cave quickly, and after a half hour of walking through its winding tunnels, Nick could suddenly hear the roaring of the waterfall. When they rounded the corner, the waterfall was already glowing brightly, and Christopher was waiting for them near the pool.

Slim looked at Nick. "Are you ready?"

"I know this is silly, but I have to ask. Isn't there some way I can stay here with you guys?"

"Nick, if I had my way, I would let you stay. But the Almighty says you have to return. You are needed there," said Slim.

Sighing deeply, Nick turned toward the waterfall. "I guess I'm ready then."

"Okay, let's go, guys," said Slim as he stepped onto the clear surface of the pool. Nick followed, holding Slim's hand, and Keenan, Michael, and Christopher brought up the rear. Several moments later, the group disappeared into the waterfall.

They didn't notice the shadow slipping from bolder to bolder, listening intently to their conversation. Imps moved aside as a solid man stepped from behind a bolder and approached the brilliant sparkling waterfall, staring at it suspiciously. He paused for a few moments, then took a deep breath, stepped onto the surface of the water, and then hesitantly walked into the waterfall, several imps leading the way.

The journey back through the waterfall was as beautiful as the first time through. Nick stretched his hand out to let the twinkling fall of light cascade over his hand. He dreaded going back to his time zone, but the fact that all the guys were with him somehow made it easier.

They reached the other side of the waterfall and began negotiating the maze of tunnels. To Nick, the journey seemed to take much less time than when he and Slim had traveled to the waterfall so long ago. The guys teased each other and told stories as they walked. Eventually they came to the end of a tunnel and stopped. Just beyond the wall of rock they could hear the pounding of hammers and the roar of machinery.

"What's going on out there?" asked Nick.

"That's the search party that has been looking for you the past two weeks. They couldn't get through the actual cave-in because it was too unstable. So they checked the old maps of the mine and figured this was the safest way to get into the main network of tunnels," said Slim.

"Two weeks? I've been gone at least a month," said Nick.

"I guess you could say our time zone moves at a faster pace than yours," explained Christopher.

"Nick, your father has been camped outside this cave this entire time. Thinking he might have lost you has changed him significantly," said Michael quietly.

Stunned, Nick just stared at Michael. "Wow," he whispered. "I never thought he even cared about me. I thought all he cared about were all those bones and his students."

"People do have the capacity to change, particularly when they are forced to see things in a different light, Nick," Slim said, putting a hand on Nick's shoulder. "Otis did, and so did your father."

"So what now?" asked Nick.

"Well, if it's okay with you, we're going to check out what's going on out there. From the sounds of it, there are a lot of people looking for you. So, give us a few minutes, and we'll return with a full report. Then at least we'll know about how long it will be before they're going to punch through the wall."

"Okay," said Nick as the guys quickly spread out and disappeared.

Nick sighed and began to pace the rock floor, trying to think of what he would say to his father, and how would he explain what had happened to him. Suddenly, he heard a small rock bounce and clatter, the sound echoing throughout the tunnel.

He stopped and looked around. "Who's there? Slim?"

"No," growled a voice. "I bet you didn't think you'd be seeing me again, now, did you, boy?" sneered Buck as he stepped forward into the light of the lantern. "You and your friends ruined everything. We had it all tied up. We were going to be rich. I was never going to have to grovel for anything again. My family was going to have a better life. But you had to step in and ruin it for all of us." Buck took a step toward Nick. "Well, now's my chance to at least get my revenge. You've taken everything of ours, so now I'm going to take everything of yours, starting with your life," growled Buck as he lunged for Nick and wrapped his hands around his neck.

Nick lost his balance and was pushed backwards by Buck's weight. He gasped for air as he clawed at Buck's hands.

"I'm going to have the last laugh now," chuckled Buck.

Moments passed, but they seemed like hours to Nick. He could see imps dancing around them. Nick began to feel darkness closing in on him, and he struggled to stay conscious. He heard his name being called by someone far away. Keenan slowly began to materialize a few feet from them. "Hey, Nick, you won't believe . . . Oh, no!" yelled Keenan. "Christopher!" Stunned by Keenan's sudden appearance, Buck loosened his grip on Nick's neck. Nick began to cough. A moment later Christopher, Michael, and Slim suddenly appeared. Buck, shocked, released Nick, who fell backward and struck his head on a rock, slipping into unconsciousness.

Slim took two long steps toward Buck, grabbed his arms, and whipped him around. "If you have done anything to that boy, by the time we get done with you, you will wish you had never been born."

"But . . . but . . . but," stammered Buck. "You're not even real!"

Slim pushed Buck toward Christopher. "Take him back to where he belongs. Tie him up outside the jail. I know the sheriff will be glad to see him."

Before Christopher had a chance to grab him, Buck took off like a shot down the tunnel. Christopher, Keenan, and Michael went after him. They tackled him and restrained him as Slim cared for Nick. As they hauled the struggling Buck back to where Slim sat cradling Nick, the sounds of the equipment breaking through the rock became much louder.

"Is he going to be okay?" asked Michael.

"Yeah, I think so, but I think this time it's going to take some time. His breathing is shallow, and he has a concussion," answered Slim.

"Well, they're about to break through, and I'm sure they have a doctor out there. So what do you want to do now?" asked Keenan.

"You guys go ahead and take our uninvited guest back to Silverado. I'll stay with Nick," answered Slim.

"Guys, they just broke through," yelled Christopher over the roar of machinery.

"Quick, get going before someone sees you," yelled Slim, becoming invisible.

Keenan, Michael, and Christopher began to disappear, hanging on to a screaming Buck who was still trying to escape.

Bright light was streaming in through the new hole. A man's face appeared in the opening, and then disappeared, replaced by a foot, and then a whole leg. Moments later, a man climbed through the hole, using a rope to lower himself to the ground. The beam from his flashlight landed on Nick's crumpled form.

"Guys, get a doctor in here now, and send in a stretcher! He's here!" yelled the climber.

"Is he alive?" yelled another voice.

Unhooking himself from the rope, the climber quickly walked over to Nick and felt for a pulse in his neck. Sighing in relief, he turned and yelled back, "Yes, tell his dad he's alive!"

It took an hour to get Nick onto a stretcher and out of the cave. Slim stood invisible and silent by Nick the whole time, even as they traveled in the ambulance to the hospital.

Chapter Forty

BACK HOME

Nick woke up with a throbbing headache in the back of his head. He ran his hand over the surface beneath him and realized that he was lying on a mattress. So he was no longer in the cave. He gingerly opened his eyes and slowly scanned the room. He recognized the bright white walls of a hospital room. The curtains were wide open and the sunshine flooded in. Nick groaned, closing his eyes and rubbing his head.

Someone pushed open the door.

"Good morning, Nick. I see you're finally awake," the nurse said cheerfully. "Here, take these." She put two pills in his palm and held out a glass of water. "They'll help get rid of the headache that you probably have."

"How long have I been here?" asked Nick.

"Three days," she answered, picking up his chart and flipping through the top sheets.

"Three days?" asked Nick. "That can't be right."

"Yep, three days. I'm not too sure how long the doctor wants to keep you here, though," chattered the Nurse. "He'll be glad to hear that you're conscious. You were in that cave for about two weeks before being rescued. The first rescuer said he thought he heard screaming. When you were brought into the emergency room, we found bruising around your neck. I don't know what happened to you in there, but I think you were pretty lucky to get out alive. Do you remember anything?" she asked.

"Bits and pieces. But I do remember the cave," said Nick.

Nick was only half listening to the nurse chatter when the mention of screaming jogged his memory. *Buck . . . It couldn't have been just a dream,* he thought. *It was so real.* Sitting up, he took the pills and then looked around the room for his backpack. It was sitting on a chair in a far corner. After the nurse left, he waited a few moments and then carefully dropped his legs over the edge of the bed. He eased himself off the bed, slowly putting his weight onto his legs. He had to grab the bed as a wave of dizziness washed over him, but, determined, he slowly worked his way over to his backpack. He grabbed the shoulder strap, and then slowly made his way back to his bed, dragging the pack behind him.

After climbing back into the bed and resting for a moment, he unzipped the pack and dug deep inside several pockets. They were empty. Discouraged, he unzipped the last large pocket and reached inside. Immediately, his hand closed around something. It was the coiled whip that Keenan had given him. His memories began to flood back. Turning the whip over in his hands, he ran his fingers over the initials scratched on the handle. Now excited, he reached in again and pulled out Michael's watch, then Christopher's knife. He dug deeper and came up with what felt like a handful of loose gravel. When he opened his fist he realized he was holding the rough diamonds he had brought back from the pit. He was happy to see the diamonds, but there was something missing. No matter how many times he looked, he could not find the medallion that Slim had given him. Disappointed, Nick carefully placed everything back in the backpack and set it on the floor right next to his bed.

"Are you looking for this?" said a familiar voice.

"Slim?" whispered Nick, looking around with a hopeful expression.

"Yep, but not just me," responded Slim as he, Keenan, Michael, and Christopher slowly appeared around Nick's bed.

"I think this belongs to you," said Slim, handing him the medallion.

"Last time I saw this, it was around my neck," said Nick.

"Buck had it in his hand when we tackled him. It must have come off when he was trying to strangle you," replied Christopher, with a look that could have frozen fire.

"What happened to Buck?" asked Nick.

"Well, after he tried to kill you, he tried to run. If it hadn't been for Keenan and Christopher, he might have succeeded. Now he's back in his time and has been sentenced to life in prison. Of course, he's also crazy now, babbling on and on about ghosts. Seeing us did not sit well with him," explained Michael, with an almost satisfied expression.

"What happened to the imps?" asked Nick. "I saw them before I blacked out."

"They're still around, Nick," said Slim. "They always have been and they always will be. Time means nothing to them. You have them in your time. But now that you are back where and when you belong, you can't see them. But remember to watch your temper, and don't let fear control you. If the imps can get their hooks in you, even for a second, you'll start believing their lies. And then they'll be able to control you."

"There's something that was bothering me before we came back here, to this time. I forgot to ask you about it when we were in the cave. Why did I find Otis's pouch in the pool by the waterfall?" asked Nick.

"Buck must have taken it from Otis after he and Jeb beat him up," explained Slim. "Do you remember when you took the tour of Silverado, during the class trip? The tour guide said that they had found a body in a cave, and they thought the murder was related to Otis's. Of course, we know that that was Stanley, but we changed his timeline, too."

"Right," answered Nick with a smile.

"We think Buck probably killed Stanley in the original timeline sometime after he broke into the bank for Jenkins to steal the watch fob. Buck probably drowned him in the pool, and the pouch fell out of Buck's pocket during the struggle. Thanks to you, Stanley is safe. He lived a normal life, and continued to design beautiful jewelry using stones he found in the mine."

"Say, guys, someone is coming," whispered Christopher.

"Don't go away, please," pleaded Nick.

"We'll be right here," Slim reassured him, and then they all disappeared.

Nick's father walked into the room. Discovering that Nick was awake, he rushed over to him and folded him into a gentle, but strong, hug.

"I thought I lost you, Nick," his father sobbed. "Things are going to be different from now on. I'm going to be a better father. I promise."

Nick held his dad as tears slid down his own face. "It's okay, Dad," he whispered several times.

The door opened again and in walked the police officer who had questioned Nick about the stolen journal before Nick had disappeared. "Sorry to disturb you, but I understand from the nurse that Nick is awake. I need to talk to him," said the officer.

"Of course," replied Lee, stepping away from the hospital bed.

"Nick, I have good news for you. I know you've had a tough couple of weeks and I thought you could use some good news. The boys who accused you of stealing the journal from the display case finally confessed that they did it. They were paid to do it by Mr. Bud Barkley. He's the owner of the casino in Silverado. He's being charged with theft and contributing to the delinquency of minors."

"What was his interest in an old journal?" asked Lee.

"Well, when we pressured the boys, they finally told us the truth. They even told us that a security guard who worked at the museum and the casino turned off the security system in that room for them. They still had the money Mr. Barley had given them, and we were able to trace it back to the casino. After we put the pressure on, especially about involving minors in his crime, he started to crack. The town of Silverado is going up for sale soon, and Mr. Barkley wants to buy it. There's a story that's been passed down in his family that started with a crazy old ancestor, something about a waterfall to the future and the ghost of Slim Marano. Barkley was hoping to find some information in the journal that would help him discover what his crazy ancestor was talking about. He thought he might be able to find something in the surrounding mountains that would help draw more upper-class clientele to the town and make him rich when he bought the town."

"They're selling Silverado? And to somebody who's going to turn it into a big casino town?" asked Nick.

"Yep, that's the plan," said the officer. "It's owned by a man who's a direct descendant of Slim Marano, who became the owner of the town back in the 1800s. But there aren't any other living descendants, and the current owner is elderly, so he's selling it."

"Wait a minute," said Nick's father, suddenly very pale. "What's the last name again?"

"Marano," said the sheriff.

Nick's father reached for a nearby chair and sat down quickly.

The sheriff looked at Nick questioningly. "Your last name is Lewis, isn't it?" he asked.

"Yes," answered Nick.

Lee stared at Nick for a moment. "Nick, your mother's family name, her maiden name, was Marano. And she was from Colorado."

"How come I never knew that?" asked Nick, feeling a tingling in the pit of his stomach.

"Well, her father and I didn't get along, and he forbade us to marry. We married anyway, and your grandfather basically cut your mother off from the family."

"Hold on," said the sheriff, looking confused. "Are you saying that Nick is a descendant of the Marano line here in Colorado?"

"Yes," said Lee.

"Well, that changes everything."

"Why?" asked Nick.

"Because the deed to the town specifies that as long as there is a living descendant of Slim Marano, the ownership of the town must stay in the family," explained the sheriff.

"Dad, aren't any of Mom's relatives still alive?" asked Nick.

"I don't think so, Nick. Her parents died before you were born, and there was a great-uncle who she didn't really know, but that was about it."

The sheriff scratched his chin. "It's possible that the current owner of the town, Marty Marano, is your wife's great-uncle. Does that name ring a bell?"

"Actually, I think it does," replied Lee. "I know I still have her old family photo albums, and some papers about the family's genealogy. I can check them."

"Well, Mr. Lewis, this is going to take some time to sort out, but I know the board of trustees for the town will help you check into it," reassured the sheriff. "Nobody was very happy about selling the town. If you come outside with me, I can give you all of the information you need to contact the board."

"Sure. I'll be right back, Nick," said his father, and he got up and left with the sheriff.

Nick sat in silence, trying to understand this new revelation. He finally asked, "Are you guys still here?"

The four spirits slowly materialized. "Did you know?" asked Nick.

"Yes. Your mom told me," answered Slim. "But she felt that it would be best if you didn't know until the assignment was over. She didn't want you to become too attached to the real me, just in case something happened."

"Someone is coming again," whispered Christopher.

"Probably that nurse again," mused Keenan with a twinkle in his eye.

"Seems like you have a lot to handle, Nick. We are going to give you some time to think. We need some time to tie up our loose ends. We'll catch up with you later," said Slim.

"We'll be back," promised Michael. Then the guys slowly disappeared right before the nurse walked back into the room.

The sun slowly crept over the distant horizon, spilling its bright yellow rays over the town. The Silverado Ghost Town was preparing for another busy day. The town itself had changed quite a bit in the last six months. The casino and its sleazy clientele were gone. The buildings had been refurbished and painted. The museum was being expanded to include a wing of Native American artifacts. Everything had a new shine to it.

Nick came out from an alleyway, stepped onto the street, and looked around. It hadn't been that long since he had been rescued from the cave, but a lot had changed. Finding out that he was a Marano opened a whole lot of doors for Nick.

It had taken a month to sort out everything and prove that Nick was in fact a direct descendant of Slim Marano's. But in the end, they were able to prove it. Laura's great-uncle signed the papers handing ownership of the Falcon Mine Company, Silverado Ghost Town, and Slim Marano's ranch over to Nick. It was a bit overwhelming for Nick. He was now a Marano, and he had a sizable trust fund, thanks to the contents of the pit. Because they had changed the timeline, Slim had been able to mine the contents of the pit and set up trust funds for his family and the town.

Nick's father was surprised to find that his son was suddenly less interested in video games and was now interested in restoring the town of Silverado. He assumed it was a reaction to being trapped in a cave for two weeks. They didn't talk much about what had happened, partially because Nick told his father he didn't remember much.

Nick surveyed the shops along the street. He was proud of what he and his dad had been able to accomplish in the town. It looked exactly like the town that he remembered. All that was missing were the people he had grown to love. Nick felt that he owed it to the town and the people who had built it to make sure that it lasted. They had taught him so much, it was the least he could do.

"You've done a great job, Nick," said a voice behind him.

"Thanks," said Nick. "I only hope that Slim and the others would have been pleased."

"Believe me, I am very pleased," replied the familiar voice.

Nick turned to find Slim materializing behind him. "Slim!" he cried, throwing himself into Slim's arms. "It's so good to see you. Where are the guys?"

"We're right here," said Keenan, as he and Michael and Christopher appeared.

Nick stepped back and looked at them all with a big smile. "Let's take a walk. I want you to see some things. I want to know what you really think."

"Don't worry, Nick, we've been keeping an eye on you. We all think you've done a tremendous job. Making the town of Silverado a living museum was a great idea," said Michael.

"We have people working in the shops in period costumes. We also have lots of shows that give people a good idea of what life was really like back then," explained Nick.

"You really have done a great job, Nick," said Christopher.

"The revenue that we generate from ticket sales or merchandise sales goes to support the research facility and the museum. We also support the community and provide college scholarships," said Nick.

"Wow, Nick, this is impressive. What does your father think of all this?" asked Slim.

"Dad and I are doing much better. I think he's surprised by my interest in Silverado and its restoration. I don't think he understands how it is I know so much about how the town should look," Nick said with a mischievous grin. "But I can't take all the credit. Most of the staff are descendants of people who built Silverado," explained Nick.

"Well, you've done a great job, and you're helping a lot of people, too. I can't begin to tell you how proud your mom is," said Slim, putting his hand on Nick's shoulder.

"Thanks for telling me that. Let her know that I am proud of her and everything she has done for me. And tell her I promise to take care of Dad," said Nick.

"What happened to Slim's ranch?" asked Christopher.

"Oh, I had Slim's ranch totally restored, too. Dad and I are going to move into it next week. The workshop that we stayed in is now a huge workroom for Dad with all of his equipment. He's real happy. He's going to use one of the barns as a working classroom for some of his students. I also bought a horse," said Nick, trying to contain a big grin. "So what's next for you guys?"

"We don't know yet, but there's always someone in need of help, so I'm sure we'll be given another assignment," responded Michael.

"Do you think the Almighty would let me help you out again?" asked Nick.

"Possibly. I know He is very pleased with all the things you've done. You've proven yourself to be courageous, kind, and smart. I wouldn't be surprised if He let you go with us again. We'll just have to see what He says," said Slim.

The pager on Nick's belt began beeping. "Oh, I've got to go now. I might be the owner of an old ghost town, but I still have to go to school," Nick said with a grin. "When will I see you all again?"

"Hopefully soon, Nick," answered Slim as he bent down and gave him a hug.

"You take care of yourself," said Keenan as he hugged Nick.

Christopher hugged him next. "Hey, you should hook up with Chris, Mike, and Kip. They're in your class. I'm sure you'll get along with them just fine," Christopher said with a chuckle.

Nick stepped back and looked at Christopher. "Wait, are you telling me that they are your descendants?" he asked.

Michael grabbed Nick and gave him a bear hug. "Yep, that's what Christopher is trying to tell you. We all had children, and those three boys are our descendants."

Nick released Michael and started to laugh. "If they are anything like you guys, I know we'll get along just fine," said Nick.

"Believe me, they are true to their families' natures," laughed Slim. "Now you better get going, or you'll be late, bucko."

"Okay, okay," stammered Nick as he began to walk away. "I love you guys," he said, and then he turned and walked toward a horse that was tied up in front of the general store.

"We love you, too," answered the cowboys.

The four friends watched Nick as he climbed on his horse and rode out of town.

"He's turned into a very respectable young man," said Michael. "You should be proud, Slim."

"I am," said Slim.

"I would love to work with him again," said Keenan.

"Me, too," said Christopher.

"Well, let's go ask, shall we?" said Slim as they turned and started walking down the street.

"Say, I'm hungry," said Christopher. "Think we could stop for something to eat first?" he asked.

"How about Mexican?" suggested Michael.

"Hmm, that sounds good," said Keenan.

"Great, let's go eat. Then we'll head home, see what our next assignment is, and find out if we can take Nick with us again. How's that sound?" asked Slim.

"Great!" replied Keenan.

"Super!" said Christopher.

"Sounds like a plan," said Michael. The four cowboys laughed and teased as they walked down the dusty street of the town of Silverado. Then they slowly disappeared into thin air.

IN APPRECIATION

This has been a very long journey—building a life, discovering the artist within me, and overcoming obstacles. I could not have made it this far or finished this project without the help of some wonderful people who surrounded me with their love, support, time, encouragement, and prayers.

I am deeply indebted to these great people for becoming part of the Nick & Slim team and bringing their passion, commitment, experience, and expertise to this project: Bryan and Linda Guillot (managers), Tim Van Dyke (copyright attorney), Charlie Crammer (White Wolf Studio attorney), Peter Chamberlain (finance manager), Colin Mariano (writing coach), Linda Ziglar (manuscript reader), Tawanda Mills (manuscript reader), Lari Bishop (manuscript editor), Tom Lange (freelance artist), Simon Cox (freelance artist), Jim Keller (counselor), Joanne Tzuanos (best friend), Rusty Smith (presentation set-up), Tomomi Shimizu (presentation set-up), Tony Annen (presentation set-up & horses).

To my family: Carl (dad), Faye (mom), Randy (bro), Kris (sister-in-law), Peter and Brent (nephews), Leann (niece). Also, thanks to the Sand Lake Starbucks staff who kept me caffeinated through the long hours of writing.

To the Colorado Kaper Gang: Judy Helman, Terri Treadway, Carol Anderson, Jonathan Stine, Neil Rickard, Jennifer Shenkerberg, Matt Mossman, Brett Thomas, Freas W. Hontz III, Sandi Zumbro, Colin Mariano, and Steve Ferrier. This journey began in Colorado during the Kaper Single Conference. Your friendships, laughter, love, and personalities, along with the surrounding mountains, fueled my imagination. You breathed life into me after a difficult time, as well as into my imagination and my characters. You made our Kaper's moments together full of fun and unforgettable.

I love you all!

P.L.V. Henn